CRUELLY DIVINE

Book Two of the Divine Providence Series

M.N. Lash

Cruelly DIVINE

Book Two of the Divine Providence Series

M.N. LASH

TABLE OF CONTENTS

Copyrights — VII

Content Warnings — IX

Dedication — XI

The End of The Beginning — XIII

1. Chapter 1 — 1

2. Chapter 2 — 23

3. Chapter 3 — 42

4. Chapter 4 — 51

5. Chapter 5 — 69

6. Chapter 6 — 84

7. Chapter 7 — 101

8. Chapter 8 — 118

9. Chapter 9 — 132

10. Chapter 10 — 144

11. Chapter 11 — 153

12. Chapter 12 — 166

13. Chapter 13 — 191

14. Chapter 14 — 205

15. Chapter 15 — 217

16. Chapter 16 — 231

17. Chapter 17 — 252

18. Chapter 18 — 265

19. Chapter 19 — 279

20. Chapter 20 — 298

21. Chapter 21 — 304

22. Chapter 22 — 322

23. Chapter 23 — 337

24. Chapter 24 — 356

25. Chapter 25 — 363

26. Epilogue — 375

27. A New Life — 386

Acknowledgements — 389

About the author — 391

Also by — 393

CONTENT WARNINGS

Hi there! So, listen, this page is important. If anything on this list may be triggering to you, please do not read! Your mental health is important! I have listed all of the warnings I know of, but don't read this book if you have any doubts.

-Graphic/explicit violence and death

-Mental/emotional/physical abuse

-Mentions of death of a parent

-Animal experimentation mentioned (no specifics, just what these animals look like)

-Sexual activities

-Self-harm/Suicidal thoughts/actions

-Discrimination

For the Undivine like me who want to be part of the change in this world and every other.

THE END OF THE BEGINNING

"**I**'m sorry. I'm so sorry." I whisper in despair. This is all my fault. My fault, my fault, my fault. I close my eyes as the wagon rattles along, holding my sister's hand tightly.

When I open them again, I have decided who I will become for her. What has to be done. I will do whatever it takes to ensure she is safe and gets the happy life she deserves, even if it means playing a part in a game I don't understand.

"I'm ready for a drought," I say.

"Me too."

"Alright, then. Here you go. To death." I clink my vial against hers and swallow in one gulp.

And so I die.

The darkness is comforting. I like the warm embrace, like an old friend or a lost lover come to claim me at last. It is better than any feeling I have ever had. Calms me like nothing else ever will.

I think I want to stay in this dark place as long as I can.

Because as long as I am here I don't have to acknowledge what I am about to become: a cruel Divine seeking refuge in an even crueler Court.

CHAPTER 1
Celeste of the Solar Court

Celeste

I used to love apples, but now...now, after fleeing what should have been *my* kingdom and killing a prince, I've grown to despise them. The thought of apples sickens me, the mere mention of their sweetness leaving an ache in my heart. I don't deserve anything *sweet* in my life. Yet, for some reason, the wagon I boarded—escaped on, if I'm being candid—at the Lunar Court is full of them. Darius, our driver and an old friend, was kind enough to allow my sister and me passage on his way to the Solar Court to drop off said apples. According to him, there is a shortage. That's not unbelievable, since their Court has a shortage of *everything*.

I should feel goddess-blessed to be on a wagon with no shortage of food, even if that food includes an excessive amount of a singular fruit, but I know the truth, so how I *should* feel doesn't matter. *I am goddess-damned*, and there's no hiding from my sins in this vast barren land surrounding us.

Our horse neighs in the distance and I briefly glance toward it and the full wagon attached to the reins. This journey has already been tedious and harrowing since we have had no shelter against the elements. Heat, rain, wind—Irissa, Darius, and I have been exposed to it all. The thin sheets we were provided with do nothing to protect us, and even Darius has begun to gripe about things from his small bench at the front of the wagon. Overall, I would describe this whole horrid experience as *miserable*. Times like these are the only enjoyable moments because I can stretch my legs and shake off the tingling in my limbs.

"How much longer?" I turn to Darius, raising an eyebrow at my old acquaintance. He grunts, staring down at me wearily.

"Probably another one or two weeks at most, if I keep this pace." He squats down and dips his hand down into the stream of water before us, rubbing cold water over his arms.

"At most? You are certain?" We have been traveling for four weeks already and the weariness had set in long ago. I've never traveled this large of a distance before, and so far the sights have been terrible. Dead trees, dead grass, and dead animals are all our side of the continent has to offer.

"Positive," he snaps impatiently. "Who's the driver here, girl?"

"Shut your filthy mouth, Undivine," I spit back, stiffening at his harsh tone. "You have forgotten who you speak to." I set my harsh glare on him, refusing to bend my spine.

"Ah, yes. I'm sorry. I forgot that I am speaking to a disgraced High Divine who was forced to run from her own Court after murdering her fiancé's brother. My apologies, miss." His gaze never wavers, and I am the first to break. My lips slide up, uncontrollable laughter bubbling up and out. He finally breaks, too, letting out a chuckle and a tiny smile he saves just for me.

"You are great for bitchy princess practice, Darius. Truly. Irissa just can't be mean enough to me. You, on the other hand...well, you aren't a ray of sunshine, that's for sure."

He clicks his tongue, scooping a few handfuls of water into his mouth. "Hmm. I seem to remember you telling me otherwise—several times. Besides, you barely talk to Irissa. I usually just hear you back there crying."

"Darius!" I scowl, throwing a rock toward his head. He dodges easily, coming to a standing position with a glare.

"He isn't lying." Irissa laughs lightly in her deep, rough voice as she emerges from the trees. She had taken a few steps into them to relieve herself, not that they offered much privacy. Only a few trees have leaves and even those are dying.

"What else do I have to do? Your company bores me to tears," I grumble, slouching in defeat. I don't particularly want to talk about how often I sit in this wagon and cry. All I can do out here is *think* and I'm tired of my brain. I don't want to think about Kyelin or his beautiful green eyes, I don't want to think about the flames that were missing from said eyes in those last moments, and I don't want to think about the look Prince Zaeden sent my way as his hands raked through his brother's ashes. But out here...the only things I *can* do are think and worry and cry.

"Alright, enough chatter. We need to go." Darius clears his throat, glancing toward my sister with a knowing expression as though sensing where my thoughts have gone. "I want to gain as much time as possible before she..."

"I know. I do too," I agree while Irissa stays silent. Her eyes are cast downward in shame, arms wrapping around her body. I run a hand down one lovingly, doing my best to comfort her.

Although we just celebrated her twentieth birthday last week, my sister is unable to appreciate this new age. Not when nothing about her situation has changed, not when her curse still runs rampant in her mind and body. When I was an Undivine and I had plans in place, I was able to take care of her and make sure she was safe. Out here in the open, she can't be contained, and we have all experienced that truth firsthand.

"Hop in, girls." Darius holds out a hand for each of us, and I allow Irissa to rise first. I follow close behind, snuggling up next to my sister. We haven't bothered hiding under sheets for weeks because, after being a few days out of the Lunar Court, we considered ourselves safe. Hardly any merchants travel this far out of the Courts, and most who do travel between Courts don't have strong ties to any particular one since they are never in one place for long. Hopefully, that means news of my escape and Prince Kyelin's murder are as slow to reach the Solar Court as we are.

I keep telling myself that this is a good thing. Not the murders, obviously, or the power snatching. Just...the new start. This Court means a new beginning, means new people. I can guard myself better and can become someone new. I don't have to be an Undivine maid or be preyed upon by the Divine anymore. I am a High Divine now, and that comes with a lot of perks that I am eager to explore. Even if it means living in the City of Rot, as Ryleigh once called Solar City.

"I'm sorry." The whisper is quiet and defeated beside me.

"Don't be. This isn't your fault, Iris. We will handle it. We always do."

"I'm going to be a nightmare. You should just tie me down and get it over with."

"I'm not tying you down," I spit out, turning toward her with a glare.

"You don't get to make decisions for me, Celeste. I'm tired of constantly arguing with you over *my* choices."

"I'm your—"

"My *sister*. Not my mother. Not *me*."

I fall silent, unsure what to say. She is right: I'm not her mother, even though I was the one who raised her after we ran away from our abusive mother five years ago. Despite my motherly instincts, she still isn't *mine*. Sometimes, it is hard for me to remember that she isn't the child she so often becomes. That she is not a child at her core and that it is just something that happens to her. I can't hold her curse against her, or treat her the same way I do in those moments when she *is* a small child. The two sides of her are just...hard for me to separate inside my brain.

Tonight is the full moon, the first full moon since we have begun our travels, and we all worry about the effect it is going to have on Irissa. My sister has a very...unique power and an even more unique curse. Mentally, she has no idea that she isn't herself or that her body is aging. She's just...her. But a toddler is not easy to take care of on the road, especially ones with uncontrollable Shifter powers that cause a *lot* of pain. It's horrible to watch and even more horrible to hear. She attacks you without realizing it, she harms you with no ill intent. The transformation hurts her so badly that she has no way to stop herself from *doing* bad things.

Each month on the full moon is when the Lunar Court citizens are at their strongest and when the Royals, their rulers, renew their powers. The Lunar Court is where we were born and lived our whole lives. So, when the full moon comes around, everything is heightened. Everyone else gets to party and celebrate, to feel this amazing rush of power that is better than any drug—a feeling I was close to experiencing during the last full moon. I think that may have had more to do with the full moon ritual I performed with Kyelin that night, though. We hadn't been able to keep our hands off each other, and the high that started during the weird ritual never stopped. I don't want to think about that night because then I have to think about how he picked Silvi over me, how he admitted to using powers of persuasion to make me like him, and how he tried to make me his *side bitch* right before I killed him. Well, to be more accurate, when I sucked the powers right out of his body and deposited them into mine until he turned into a pile of ashes on the ground. Yeah, I *really* don't want to think about that for the thousandth time today.

If I go down that road, then I have to think about how it's my fault that we are in this position right now. It's my fault that we are on the road and not safely in our home, which would have provided Irissa with a comfortable and familiar place to transition, and my fault for doing something so horrible that it can never be forgiven by our Court. I was the one who forced us into the choice of flee or die, all because my ex-boyfriend was brutally murdered. The issue is...I was the one who killed him. And the worst, most horrifying part of this whole nightmarish ordeal? I killed Prince Kyelin, heir to the Lunar Court throne: *my fiancé's brother.*

Prince Edge and Princess Valaine of the Solar Court found me in those terrifying moments that followed, moments in which I was on fire and burning from the inside out. Valaine helped me put out the flames and then the two siblings offered me something I could not turn down—safety for me and my sister in another Court. I accepted their offer, which is how we ended up traveling to their Court and trying not to raise suspicions by flying through these roads. Besides the inherent danger of *appearing* to be fleeing, the horses would never be able to make such a grueling trip. We stop and rest for hours at a time, moving at an infuriatingly sluggish pace. But that's my fault, too. If I wasn't a highly sought-after criminal, we could speed things along and not have to worry about running into someone who is looking for me. Divine goddesses, my life is a mess.

"Decide soon, girls. There are much more violent things than Irissa in these woods at night." Darius mentions this often despite our lack of trouble on these roads. He says the monstrous beasts come out at night but refuses to speak of his experience with them. I'm sure he has had a run-in with them by the haunted look that enters his eyes when he speaks of them. It makes me wonder if they are the reason he finally decided to exclusively travel in the Lunar Court years ago. What is out here that terrifies him so?

Darius has reassured us that if we stick to the path, or stay close to it, nothing bad will happen. This is our territory, and beyond the path is the beasts'. It's almost like...like they are trained. The territorial lines are why the path cuts so close to some of the streams—travelers like us have to get fresh water somewhere. As long as we don't toe the line, we don't need to worry. Irissa has been bravely—or stupidly, depending on how you look at it—testing that theory with her trips behind the trees to relieve herself. She either hasn't gone far enough, or they smell the predator in her, too.

"Tell her to tie me up, Darius. I'll be fine and we all know it. I won't even remember it."

"I'm sorry, Celeste, but I agree. If she gets as hostile as you claim...well, I don't want to be on the receiving end of her tantrum."

"I do," Irissa confirms solemnly. "I'm horrible. I will hurt you and I won't *stop*. I am uncontrollable."

"Irissa!" I hate hearing her talk about herself like she is some monster when that's not who she is. She is so much *more* than this violent version of herself. And that may be hypocritical for me to say when I've been calling myself a monster for weeks for a power I can't control, but I know things are different with her. I know she would never *want* to kill, she would never like it. Not like I did. Not like I *do*.

"You need to stop coddling me, Celeste. I know what I am and what I am capable of. I don't know Darius at night, something you have both noticed. I'm violent and angry with him, upset with the strange man in the strange environment. I have yelled, I have hit, I have thrown apples and some of our other precious and feeble stores. I won't let him rest, refusing to let him sleep when he needs to, and it has only gotten worse. What do you think is going to happen tonight, Celeste? That I'm going to be *better*? Because news flash, I won't be.

"My talons can slice through his skin and rip out his intestines before he *blinks;* I've done it to many animals before. My wings could take me into the woods and out of your sight in seconds, and I could wake up covered in my sister's blood surrounded by monsters. And what then? What good does that do anybody? You won't be able to stop me unless you are prepared to hurt me, which I know you won't do. You won't be able to look for me because my wings could take me farther than you could ever travel. If I don't accidentally kill you, you will have to leave without me and will always wonder what happened to me. You will never know if I died or if I just can't find my way back to you. We aren't *risking* this, Celeste. Tie me up when it gets dark. It's not up for debate." Irissa's eyes are dark and sharp, her arms crossed over her chest. I want to argue some more, but how can I? How can I say she is wrong when she isn't? How can I convince her we will find another way when we won't? We have limited resources, limited time, and limited options. Nightfall is approaching too rapidly.

"I coddle you because I love you. Because I am your big sister and I am supposed to take care of you," I say, eyes trained on the trees far down the road.

Out of the corner of my eye, I see Irissa's features scrunch together as though she is in pain, eyes shut tightly as she forces out quiet words. "I know, Les, I know. But I'm twenty years old now, and you are almost twenty-three. We are past the point of treating each other like children, don't you agree?"

Reluctantly, I whisper, "Yes."

We fall into a comfortable silence as Darius yanks on the reins, forcing the horses into motion. The sounds of horses trotting and wheels spinning are comforting, but there are no other signs of life to accompany them. No chirping birds or noisy critters, no subtle breeze or pattering of rain: only the sounds we create and the silence we hate.

"Do it." Irissa is the first to speak as darkness invades the sky, and I turn to see a rope dangling from her shaky hands. She won't look me in the eyes, choosing to look toward the sky instead.

"Iris…"

"Do it," she repeats, voice quivering.

"Turn around." The words barely leave my lips, stuck in my throat like glue. I manage to take the rope from her as she turns her back toward me, her long, straight blonde hair dancing with the movement. I do my best to pull it all over her shoulder in an attempt to be gentle, but she still winces as I accidentally tug on it.

Irissa helps by pulling it over gracefully before asking, "Do you miss your long hair, Les?" It's an obvious attempt to get our minds off the inevitable, but I happily accept it.

"Every day," I whisper as I pull her hands behind her back, hooking the rope around her wrists over and over and over. My wild, blonde curls used to be the same length as hers, hitting my waist in an unruly mess. Now it's cut bluntly at my shoulders, much shorter than the average Divine woman keeps it. Not only is my thin body different from those of the voluptuously beautiful Divine, but now my hair is, too.

"Then why did you cut it?"

I laugh darkly, tensing at the memory of what really happened emerging in my mind. Fear, adrenaline, panic. I put a hand over my heart, forcing it to slow before I speak. "I didn't. Prince Edge Zorander of the Solar Court did, and he didn't give me a choice, either."

"You never told me that." She whips around the second I am done, her icy blue eyes meeting my fiery gaze. Thinking about Prince Edge brings that fire to the surface, bringing a burning hatred to a boil deep in my gut.

"No, I didn't," is what I settle on saying, trying to force my flames back inside me. They love to come up and caress me at the thought of the dark prince, which is much too often for my liking. It's a strange feeling, having powers, and I am not sure I will ever get over it. For most of my life, I didn't possess a drop of power—not until Silvi Merkelly unwittingly invited them out to play. Even then, I believed I only possessed the power of creating shields. Prince Edge informed me upon my departure that I am an Absorbid, an ability that allows me to sap the power of any other Divine upon contact. Without that power, a Divine will crumble into nothing. *I'm a soul-eater.*

"Why not? What even happened? I thought he was good. He saved you. He saved *us.*"

"Oh did he?" I can't help but scoff, flames rolling once more.

"Um, yeah? You don't remember him helping you escape from a castle crawling with guards? What about when he put you and me both in a carriage and gave you a super hot, intense look? Because I do."

"He only did that because he wants to use my powers, Iris. Not because he cares about me, or you, or our well-being.

He may have helped me escape imprisonment at the Lunar Court, but he's putting me in a different kind of cage at the Solar Court."

"Why are you talking about him like that? He is bringing you to his own Court at risk of waging a *war*, Celeste. He helped you even though you literally killed another prince. You could easily kill him, you know? I'm sure he knows that, too. Yet here you are, on your way to a cushy castle away from all the danger. With your sister, who any other person might have left behind, might I add? He chose to save you instead of letting you die, Celeste. I don't understand how—"

"He tried to kill me, Irissa! We fought in that castle he stole me away from, and we both took souvenirs when we were done. He took my hair and I took his finger. *That's* how I can talk about him like that. We are *enemies*, Irissa. We always will be. I *hate* him."

"That sounds like an even trade," she says with a sniff and plops down, glaring at me like I didn't just tell her the Solar Prince had tried to *kill* me. "And now things are uneven again because he has saved your life and you have done nothing in return. Except be an ungrateful, whiny bitch. That's what it sounds like to me, anyway."

"That's what it sounds like to you because you are a child who is infatuated with her hero prince. Being pretty does not make you a good person—Silvi is proof of that. I don't think he is even a *decent* person, Iris. So go ahead. Call me a whiny little bitch all you want. That doesn't change the facts *or* my mind."

"You sliced his finger off and he didn't have you killed immediately. He could have, you know? It would have been easy, I'm sure. He wouldn't even have to prove it was you, I bet. It's within his rights as a prince to demand anyone who harms him to die. That's the Royal way, after all. The Divine way."

"And how would he have explained that, huh? 'I'm not sure why Celeste chopped my finger off after I pulled her into a room and tried to murder her. I guess she was just having her monthlies!' Yeah, *that* would have gone over well. He didn't turn me in because he wanted to save his own ass, Irissa. The only reason he saved me is because he wants to use me for his own sick needs. Obviously, you haven't heard about what he does when he is at home." I clamp my mouth shut, regretting the words as soon as they leave my lips. I don't want her to know where we are really going; I don't want her to know about the evils lurking in plain sight at the Solar Court, or why Solar City is known as the City of Rot.

"What are you talking about?" Her tone is harsh and hushed, her blue eyes turning black in the darkness. They often change to black when she has these mood shifts, and they give her this horrifying ability to make your stance waver.

"Nothing. I'm sorry, I'm taking things too far. Forgive me." I reach out to touch her hand lovingly, releasing a sigh of relief when she squeezes it reassuringly.

"I always forgive you, Les. Even when you murder your fiancé's brother."

"I know." I inhale sharply, rolling my eyes. "And I am forever grateful for it."

It wasn't hard to tell when midnight hit. Irissa's eyes lightened, her gaze far in the distance as she dissociated and fled from her own mind. When she turned back to me, her expression was kind, soft, and young. I know it isn't my real sister looking back at me—real being a relative term in this situation. She makes a motion as if to reach out, but her arms don't move. Her eyes quickly flick to black, like an eclipse snatching away the light. Her expression hardens as she realizes the horrible thing I have done. I suck in a sharp breath, wincing at the scared cry that escapes her.

"What did you do to me?" Her childish voice hits my ears as her wings thrash behind her, but they can't move because they are pinned underneath the arms tied behind her back. A single, fearful tear slips down her cheek, those black eyes boring into my brown ones.

"It's for your safety, Irissa. Please, settle down before you hurt yourself." She shrieks as her talons break through her skin, whimpering for a few minutes before replying.

"Les, let me go. I'm a good girl! Let me go!"

"You are such a good girl," I choke out, stroking her hair lovingly. "But I have to protect you. That's my job as your big sister, and today I have to protect you from yourself, even if it is in a way you don't agree with." She cries and screams as her wings disappear, only to painfully rip through her shoulder blades and into the same trapped position once more. Then she begins thrashing around again, screaming angrily and trying to reach me. I shut my eyes tightly, hands shaking. I hate this.

I hate it, I hate it, I hate it.

"Good girl."

She whimpers again, screeching as the talons retract. They burst through her skin in a horrifyingly rapid moment, tearing through muscle and causing blood to begin to soak through the rope. She pulls herself up into a standing position, wobbling without the use of her arms. Her wings stretch out slightly in an attempt at balancing herself, her body twisting with the weight. I don't have time to dodge the tip of the fluffy white wing, wincing as it slams into me. Her wings are strong, the ends just as thick and muscular as the rest. I stumbled a little when the large wing hit, but, when I crouched to catch my balance, her eyes found Darius.

"Irissa, please, let's just settle—" Her eyes practically turn to slits, her body stiffening. *Here we go again.*

"Who are you?" she hisses out, wings feebly spinning out again as she turns to look at him. I take a step forward at the same time she does, an action I immediately regret. Her wing hits me even harder this time, the momentum sending me flying back. I move to cover my face as she turns once more, crying out as she hits me *again*. Her wings are powerful and heavy, and the first hit was enough to send me to the edge of the open wagon, my balance already severely hindered by the movement as we roll along the path. The second and third ones? Those toss me out of it altogether.

I hit the ground hard, my body rolling with the force of the impact. My back hits first, pain radiating through my spine upon impact. My head hits a rock, warm blood trickling down from the wound immediately. I groan, attempting to stop myself from rolling by pushing my hands down into the dirt path. But I'm no longer on the dirt path—I'm on the edge of a patch of grass, perched at the top of a steep hill. My heart races with fear as I take in my surroundings, trees in every direction I look. How far away did I land? Before I can even process *that* thought, my feeble balance wavers and I'm tumbling over the edge.

This fall is worse than the first one, the pain from before stabbing into me each time my back hits the ground. Not to mention the throbbing in my head, or the rocks that keep slicing different patches of skin. As I hit the bottom of the hill, a tree in my path stops my momentum. I hear a crack, and I can't help but scream at the intense pain in my side. Was that a rib? I can barely breathe as I slowly pull myself into a sitting position, clutching onto my side with a whimper. I reach up to touch the gash on my head, feeling the slick blood immediately. *Shit.*

I have this sense that I should be panicked, that I don't belong in the space I am occupying. Actually, it's more than a sense. I know, deep in the back of my mind, that something is wrong. I just…can't seem to acknowledge the fear fighting its way to the surface. I can't acknowledge the fact that death could be lingering nearby.

"I'm fine. Just fucking dandy, actually," I mutter groggily to my audience in the wagon, my vision swimming. Spots of black appear and disappear, and I can't focus on anything. How far away am I? There's no way I've stayed on our side of the property line if I managed to touch the grass and find this many trees. I have to go. *Now.*

"Celeste, hurry! Hurry! It's behind you! Get up, Celeste! Get up!" Darius is screaming at the top of his lungs from…somewhere. The panic lacing every word heightens my senses, my head spinning as I turn to look behind me.

"What? What's behind me?" My vision tilts with the sharp turn, my head still foggy.

"For fucks sake, Celeste, just get up!"

"Wha—" I blink and see red eyes only inches from my own. The…*thing* has its lips curled back into a snarl, spit smacking me in the face as it lets out a growl. Its teeth are huge and sharp, definitely strong enough to split me in half in only one bite. Its body is the size of a panther, its glistening dark hair hinting at the creature it may have once been. Its breath smells *disgusting,* a mix of sulfur and iron penetrating the air. I shake as I think of the creatures

Kyelin kept as pets, remembering how eerily similar their appearances were. But those creatures were docile for the most part—this one is definitely not.

I notice a drop of blood staining one of those sharp teeth, and then I see the rabbit's head lying carelessly next to it. I watch the veins throbbing underneath its skin, drawing haphazard patterns down its body. I swallow hard, the fear of death finally encasing me. "*Shit.*"

The answering roar rips through the trees, shaking the dead branches above us. I can barely breathe as I put my hand against the tree next to me, using it to slowly pull myself into a standing position. I grit my teeth through the pain, attempting to see through the spinning darkness. I don't let my eyes leave those glaring red ones, and I do my best not to make sudden movements. I try not to panic even as my heart races, reaching for the powers inside of me because I would do anything to get back up that hill and back onto the path. *Please listen* I beg the thing inside me that is not my own *Please help me survive.* I almost cry in relief at the flames that hit my fingertips, at the warmth swarming my body.

"Leave," I whisper, voice shaking as I try to force even an ounce of courage to come out. "I don't want to hurt you."

The noise it makes mimics laughter, the sound echoing through my bones. Fear races through me, the flames at my fingertips flaring out. I don't mean to let them escape, but my poor control punishes me once more and the beast takes it as an invitation to attack. I hardly see it as it leaps toward me, its speed beyond that of any normal animal or

Divine's abilities. I try to dodge, but one of its clawed paws slams into my left wrist. I scream as it tears through to the bone, crying for the first time since I fell.

Am I going to bleed out before I can make it back to my sister? I can hear her and Darius screaming at the top of the hill, but I don't dare look up to see if I can spot them. I whimper as a green goo rises from the fresh wounds, my blood visibly boiling. I don't let myself think about what it could be, about what poison may have just entered my body, about the unimaginable pain as my nerve endings are boiled away. I throw out a wall of flame before the beast can attack again, barely controlling the fire that escapes me.

"Celeste!" I hear Irissa in the distance, the fear in her voice causing my heart to stop. I don't turn toward her, though, and I don't answer. Instead, I take a deep breath and let that awful power rise inside of me. It engulfs my body, lighting up the forest around us. My hair whips back into the crackling flames, but not a strand is singed. I have just enough control to do this, despite the pain that is bringing forceful tears to my eyes.

"I warned you," I whisper after releasing a painful scream and closing my eyes. I don't want to watch the horrific things I am about to do to this poor, mutated animal. It makes that hideous laughing noise again, stepping forward as if it has no concept of fear.

I thrust my uninjured hand forward, fingers tilting in its direction. The flames rush forward at my command for the first time, leaving my body to engulf the beast. It screeches out in agony as it is overtaken, the smell of burnt flesh hitting my nostrils in seconds. I gag at the smell, doing my best to hold in the vomit rising in my throat. I wait until those hideous noises stop and I can't hear movement any longer. Then I open my eyes and fall to my knees, vomiting into the dead patches of grass beside me.

I glance over at the dead beast, my stomach tumbling once more at the sight of its burnt and bloody body. Hastily, I force myself to my feet. There are bound to be more of those things hiding around here. I need to run as fast as I can from this space, but I can barely walk. I struggle to make my way up the hill, falling to my knees and crawling several times. Just as the dirt path comes into view I hear the cries of other beasts, hear the thundering footsteps as they race to their fallen friend. I force myself to go faster as I beg my body to go numb, listening to Darius and Irissa screaming.

It hurts, it hurts, it hurts.

I scream in relief and fury as I focus on the dirt path, dragging myself toward it at an infuriatingly slow pace. I'm not fast enough. One of the beast's friends catches up to me, surprising me as its claws strike the back of my right ankle. I scream as I tumble forward, hitting the edge of the path. I throw a flame haphazardly behind me, pulling myself over the invisible territory line. The beast cries out, and I hear it tumble back down the hill.

Darius is by me in seconds, dragging me up and into the wagon. I cry and scream the whole way, blood dripping behind my limp body. I look toward the trees as he pulls me up, a dozen pairs of red eyes staring back. My strength is fading fast, my vision is even worse than before, and I know I have to be near the point of blacking out. But I also know I have to do *something*. So, I use the last of my strength to throw out a roaring inferno, forming a wall down the territory line. I hear satisfying cries of fury, and a few howls of pain follow as they ram into the unexpected fiery barrier. Their pounding footsteps echo around us as they race alongside it, looking for a break in my wall. They won't find one. I put every last bit of my energy into that wall and it *will* keep us safe until we are far, far away from this spot. These are the flames of a Royal, and that power is stronger than any of these creatures could ever hope to be.

I smile up at Darius and Irissa, my eyes blinking rapidly. I don't hear Darius screaming or Irissa crying. All I hear is sweet nothingness as I fade into a deep sleep.

CHAPTER 2

Celeste

The light above me is so, so bright. It invades the peaceful darkness behind my lids, attacking with a viciousness only the sun could possess. I don't want to open my eyes—*I can't*. Not only is the light too bright, but I'm also not sure I can muster up the energy to do something as simple as move those fluttering muscles. I can tell I am still traveling and can hear the eerie silence that envelops these roads. The horses trot along, their clacking soft and familiar. And...and is that sobbing? I can barely hear it over hooves clacking, but it's there. It has to be Irissa. What time is it? She has to be so worried.

"Can't you go faster? Come on! I know Darius has been spoiling you with a slow pace, but I need you guys to do this. Celeste needs help! Do you two have no sense of danger?" I hear Irissa screaming at, presumably, the horses. She sounds normal, so it must be past noon. I try to say something, anything, but my lips are sewn shut while my body is tight and unmoving.

My body screams in pain as I try to move, a sudden sensation that overwhelms me enough to force out a gurgling gasp. I hear movement as I whimper and try harder to move my eyelids. My lips are the first to open, though, chapped and aching as I pry them apart.

"Celeste! Are you awake?" I feel Irissa's presence as she comes next to me, as well as the abrupt pause of movement underneath me, and I whimper as she smooths my hair off my cheeks. Even that slight movement hurts, pain shooting down and across my face. For Divine's sake, how badly am I injured?

"Y—y—y—"

"It's okay," she soothes me, jerking her hand away. I feel cool liquid on my lips, water rushing into my mouth in a sudden gush. I almost groan at the relief it provides, choking a bit as I greedily swallow every drop. "You are going to be in a lot of pain, Celeste—you're very badly injured. Don't move, okay? I don't—I don't know what to do. I don't have any clean bandages, any salves, any tonics. I have *nothing*. I know Divine are supposed to heal faster but I don't think you are healing fast enough. I—I thought you were going to bleed out before the first night was through." The last sentence is a hesitant whisper, her voice cracking. First night? How many nights have there been?

I try to answer again, but only muffled noises escape once more. I concentrate, attempting to force the flames inside me to flood my body. The process is slow, but they obey. The warmth is soothing, the use of my powers healing. I practically moan at the rush that fills me, my eyes finally opening. I blink rapidly as they adjust to the harsh sunlight, Irissa's features focusing in my line of sight. No more blurriness or spinning, thank the goddesses.

"Awake," is all I can manage.

"Thank the goddesses for that," she whispers, tears hitting her cheeks. I blink up at her a few more times before glancing down at myself, wincing at the blood coating my body. I am wrapped in torn pieces of fabric, most of my skin covered. My left wrist and arm throb the hardest, my right ankle competing with them. My dress is torn to shreds, the loose fabric exposing red and scratched skin.

"How long?" I barely get the words out, still struggling to move my lips.

"You've been asleep for two days. Your wall of flames is making it a little hard for the horses to walk, so we haven't made much progress."

"I didn't mean—"

"You were trying to help. It's okay. It doesn't hurt them, they are just spooked. I'm handling it."

"Why are you—?"

"Are you in pain?" She ignores my question, scanning my body as if looking for new injuries.

"A lot of it," I groan out, moving my head slightly to the right. I see an arm poking out from underneath a few apples, and I blink rapidly to make sure I am not imagining it. But no, it's real. Is...is Darius hiding under a pile of apples?

"Irissa...is that Darius? Why—why is he there?" Words are getting easier, but they still hurt. And looking at a random arm poking out from a bunch of apples makes me think I'm not as lucid as I believed myself to be.

"No. It isn't Darius."

"Then who? Why is there an arm?" Her eyes shut tightly, her bottom lip poking out as she shakes.

"It's Darius's arm. I...I didn't know what to do with it."

"Where is he?" I whisper, horrified. What happened in those two days?

"The first night was okay. We helped each other. I didn't cause too much trouble because I saw him help you, I guess. We had a tentative truce. But then the second night, when I saw him...I don't know what happened. I just...woke up and found it. Darius was gone. I must have done something, must have gotten angry and attacked him. I mean, that's the only logical conclusion. None of those beasts could have gotten through your wall and he wouldn't have chopped off his *own* arm. I don't know if he willingly left or if I made him. I don't even know if he is alive." She cries as she explains it to me, clearly unable to understand what happened or why.

"It's not your fault," I say plainly, glancing away from the arm. Okay, time to list the things I know: I'm badly injured, Darius is gone or maybe dead, we don't know where we are going, these horses are moving at a slug's pace, and I could be dead soon.

To be frank, our situation is looking pretty shitty.

"Well, there isn't anything I can do about it right now. Other than feeling guilty and praying he isn't dead. I've been trying to make a plan, and I think I have one. You have to get to a healer quickly, quicker than it will take for us to get there in this wagon. You've lost a lot of blood and there's nothing on this blasted thing that can help you. At this rate, the horses could take another fucking month for all I know. They keep stopping and freaking out about the fire."

"So negative," I murmur playfully in an attempt to lighten the mood.

"Well, you know me. I'm no ray of sunshine." Irissa smiles tentatively as she repeats the familiar phrase the three of us have teased each with these weeks, taking a deep breath before speaking again. "Since this route of travel is no longer useful, I have thought of an alternative. One that you aren't going to like."

"I never like your ideas."

"Yeah, that's because you are allergic to good ideas."

"Whatever. Just tell me your horrible plan already." I brace myself, knowing what she is about to say.

"I'm going to fly us to the Solar Court."

"No!" I practically scream the word, pain rushing through me as I try to sit up.

"It is the only way, Celeste. I can get us there in two days if I can keep up a fast pace. And I *am* fast. When it hits midnight, you will just have to talk me through it and encourage me to stay on course. I can do it, Celeste. I know I can. *Let me do this for you.*"

"This isn't a good idea, Irissa."

"I'm not sitting around and watching my only sister die. And I don't need your permission, Celeste. What are you going to do, huh? You can't even move right now."

"I can—"

"You can be mad all you want at the Solar Court, but you can't be mad at me. I'm strong. *I can do this.*"

My nod is slight, but Irissa cries out in joy. She hops out of the wagon, and I can hear her fiddling around with the horse's reigns. Then she tells them to run, patting them lightly to encourage them. The pounding of hooves echoes around us, the horses whining as they gallop away. At least they have a chance to survive—they are smart creatures who will make their way home.

"Alright!" Irissa is next to me again, gazing down at me with her hands on her hips. "This is going to hurt," she warns me quietly as she leans down over my frail body. She lifts me as gently as possible into her arms, grunting and groaning as she pulls me up with her. Every inch of my skin cries out, screaming in agony. I release a blood-curdling scream, hating myself for letting it loose. I don't want Irissa to feel bad: She did the best she could.

"I'm okay." I pat her cheek weakly, nodding at her in thanks.

"Divine goddesses, what have they been feeding you in that castle?" she jokes, allowing her wings to slip free.

"Large servings of ego and a heap of arrogance." She laughs at me, shaking her head as she bends her legs and jumps. We are airborne in one swift movement, along with a quick flap of her large wings. I cling to my sister tightly, my stomach clenching as we climb higher and higher.

Irissa is fast. Each beat of her wings sends us propelling farther, her eyes tracking the path far, far below. We soar through clouds and beams of light, her smile large and radiant. I thought it would be more terrifying to be so high and to fly so fast, but the adrenaline rush was just what I needed. It gives me something to focus on that isn't pain, something to cling to that isn't Irissa's arms.

I thought I would be heavy and she would weaken eventually, but she showed no signs of discomfort. We don't speak over the heavy wind, our ears clogged with the air surrounding us. The wind does burn against my open wounds, only a stinging sensation hitting my covered ones. Overall, it isn't as bad as I imagined it would be. It may even be better than if I had stayed in the wagon and jostled with each rock hit and each hole we ran over.

I am the first to speak after hours of comfortable silence. "You move faster than I thought possible."

"I tried to tell you. I can span miles in minutes, Celeste. I used to practice while you were gone at work. I know I shouldn't have, but I did. I would fly to the sea, dip down, and touch the water with my wings. It was exhilarating." I fall quiet at her admission, debating yelling at her. But can

I blame her? My own powers are addictive and uncontrollable, but I have to admit I get a rush from using them. I like the heat at my palms, the shields I wield. And even though I don't like the way it feels to suck someone's powers up, it's still like drinking caffeine straight from a straw: energizing, addicting, *delicious.*

"I am choosing not to yell at you, Iris. You are unharmed and never got caught. So..."

"Exactly. Nothing to yell at me about," she chirps happily. I cringe as I laugh, pain radiating from the small movement. I still try to enjoy this moment between us, to enjoy her opening up to me about something she has kept secret for what could be years. I like not yelling at each other all the time.

"Well, you are relatively safe now, so no harm done, right?"

"We are safer up here than we were down there," she says gravely, glancing down again.

"Those creatures...I've seen similar ones. But none that size. None so violent." I shiver as I think about those red eyes and the howl that will echo in my dreams.

"What are they?"

"They used to be normal animals. Still predators, but not so...crazy and malformed. They've been modified and tested on. Kyelin was keeping mostly small animals that had been tested on as pets in the castle. Normal, cute animals that were turned into something unrecognizable. But they weren't violent, from what I saw. They got a little snippy with each other, but never with Kyelin. He told me the Lunar Court was using the animals for experiments and that he planned on ending those experiments. I'm not sure what's going to happen now that Za—Prince Zaeden is inheriting the throne." I can't bring myself to just call him *Zaeden* anymore. Like he's a friend. Now, he is Prince Zaeden and he always will be to me.

"Our Court made those?" The question is quiet and hesitant as though she is unsure if she should be asking something so treacherous.

"I think so," I admit. "It seems extremely likely at this point. I just don't understand why they would make these things just to set them free in the woods. Unless—unless—"

"Unless what?" Irissa's voice shakes as she asks.

"Unless they created these things *to* roam the woods. To keep us in and other Courts out," I breathe, heart pounding. There have always been rumors about these horrible beasts, and it discourages so many from traveling. Were they purposely isolating us?

"Why would they do that? I don't understand. Don't we want to encourage trade? Don't we want our people to experience the world?"

"No. *They* don't want that, Irissa. They don't want us to be happy. They don't want us to go and see what other Courts have to offer, to see how much better it can be elsewhere. They want one thing and one thing only: *control*." The divide between Divine and Undivine doesn't matter in this regard, not when a Royal gets to make all the decisions either way.

"Fuck."

"Yeah, fuck."

We fall silent once more, lost in our thoughts about the Court we were born into. I never held the Lunar Court in high regard, but it still stings to know the people who rule over us are even crueler than I had ever imagined. Creating creatures to kill and maim anyone trying to get in and out of our Court? All so they can maintain the control they were never at risk of losing? Those beasts almost killed me for goddess's sake! What could they do to a traveling Undivine merchant? No wonder our Court suffers so much. Our Royals were so stupid and egotistic that they were leading us straight to death without realizing they, too, were getting caught in the trap.

I close my eyes and rest against Irissa's shoulder, not wanting to watch the moon and the stars that twinkle in the night sky. I don't want to watch the light leave my sister's eyes, don't want to think about what may happen in just a few minutes. I can feel her heart slowing, her arms twitching underneath me. When I open my eyes again, I can see the softer features of a child and the innocence in her eyes. Her wings stop for a brief moment and we plummet a good ten feet before she picks them back up.

"Irissa!" I scream, my heart racing. "Don't do that! You scared me!"

"Weeeeeee!" She giggles in response, bringing us higher.

"This is fun, isn't it?" I speak softly, watching her wearily. Now I will need to convince her to keep going. I hope her *wanting* to keep the wings out will keep them from going in and out like usual, but that's only a theory. Hopefully, the talons don't do any more damage to my body than what has already been done.

"So much fun! I never fly! You never let me!" She laughs again, dipping low once more. I swallow the bile that rises, clenching my eyes shut.

"I know. Today is a special treat. You have been such a good girl lately, Iris. So good. I thought you would like this."

"Oh, I do. Thank you, Les!" Her arms tighten around me and I hiss in pain.

"You're welcome," I breathe out, trying not to shout at her.

"You're hurt. Why?" A deep frown fills her features, her eyes worried and scared.

"Irissa, listen to me very carefully, okay? You see that path down there? The dirt one way below us?" I wait until she nods her head before continuing. "There are some very bad things down there, okay? We can't go to the ground. Do you understand? We can't. Those bad things hurt me very badly, so now we have to fly. Just follow the path, Iris, and we will be okay. We are on our way to a healer, so that's why we are flying there. The healer is very far away, Iris, but they are very special and can heal me very quickly."

"Is she nice?"

"I didn't say it was a she." I lift a corner of my lips in amusement. "But I am sure they are nice. I've never met them."

"Okay. I can do it!"

"Such a sweet girl, and so very smart. You deserve more than this world could ever give you." I smile up at her, relieved that she isn't upset about me being hurt or meeting a stranger.

"You say that all the time," she says with an annoyed sigh, spinning us in circles as we go.

"And it is never less true." Irissa squeezes me painfully once more, and this time it *is* too much.

I black out.

I wake up to find that Irissa is back to normal, the sun low in the sky. I can't help but cry in relief, proud of her for never faltering. She has been awake for over twenty-four hours now, so I know she must be exhausted—the bags forming under her eyes hint at such.

"How long was I out?" Irissa jerks at the sound of my voice, glancing down at me in surprise.

"I don't know. When I came to, you were out. It's been a while, though. I think it is going to be dark in an hour or two."

"I'm so sorry, Irissa. You squeezed me last night and the pain—"

"It's okay, Celeste. Really. It's not your fault. I need to pee, though. Can I land real quick? I think I see some water down there."

"Yeah, of course. I'm surprised I haven't peed on myself by now. I usually can't hold it for that long," I laugh, but I don't feel like I have a bursting bladder. I think all of the other painful sensations are drowning it out, honestly.

Irissa floats us down to the ground with ease and grace, and we hurriedly take care of business. I can barely stand upright, much less crouch, but I manage by holding on to a tree trunk. My flame wall didn't make it out this far, and Irissa says she stopped seeing it a little after she came to. Somehow, it stretched that far. I hurriedly sip water from the stream alongside the trail, splashing some onto my arms and legs to wash a little of the blood and grime off. It stings, but it makes me feel cleaner and gives my wounds less chance of getting infected. By the time we are done, Irissa is pulling apples and dried meat out of her pockets.

"I'll try to eat it." I only eat half of mine, but Irissa happily devours hers and my leftovers. Apples aren't necessarily fulfilling, but it's better than nothing at this point. She needs her strength and so do I.

"Alright. Enough lounging around. Let's get back into the air, yeah? The sun is almost completely down and I don't feel safe down here anymore."

"I couldn't agree more, sister." I crawl into her arms again, wincing at every touch.

"Sorry, hold on, Celeste. I need to—" Irissa moves me slightly and I scream, but it's cut off abruptly.

Everything is dark again.

"Wake up, Celeste. Oh, goddess, please wake up. Fuck, what am I going to do if you don't wake up?" I groan as my eyes flicker open, greeted by the night sky.

"What are you going on about?"

"Thank the goddesses!" Irissa cries out, actual tears pooling in her eyes.

"What's wrong?" My heart leaps as I assess our surroundings, but I see no danger. Only endless sky.

"It's time."

"Oh. Oh, okay. I understand now; I definitely shouldn't be blacked out when that happens."

She can only nod, her arms slackening underneath me. We stay silent, waiting for the change. We don't have to wait more than five minutes before young Irissa is present again.

"Les! We are flying!" She giggles, letting us fall before flapping her wings again. I don't scream this time, expecting the fall.

"Yes, we are. Do you remember me telling you about the special healer we are going to see?"

"No!" Her answer is cheery, if slightly confused.

I go into details about our destination again, reminding her of my injuries. I finish by saying, "We are still going there, okay? So I need you to keep flying."

"My wings hurt," she pouts, stretching them contemplatively. "And I'm sleepy. Everything else hurts, too." Obviously, this trip is wearing more on Irissa's body than she let on.

"I know, Iris. I know. But we have to keep going, okay? We have to make it there so they can fix me."

Irissa only nods, flapping her wings and doing tricks happily. But that doesn't last long. Within the hour, I notice our pace slowing. Every once in a while she dips low and her talons shoot out. Her hands are placed to where she won't cut me, but I can tell the lack of control means she is growing weary. At night she is usually screaming and in constant pain because of the wings and talons. But my theory, thank the goddesses, proved to be correct and her *wanting* to keep those things out kept them from being so uncontrollable. She isn't scared of them right now and isn't trying to force them away. They just *are*. It's something to consider in the future. For now, though, I need to focus on getting her to continue flying.

"Irissa," I say, tapping on her shoulder. She barely blinks, dipping low, low, lower. I scream as we plummet, shaking her violently. But she won't wake up. We fall at full speed now, plummeting towards the ground. I scream and scream, begging her to wake up and catch us. But she doesn't. The ground is approaching fast, and I can only do one thing: throw a shield down.

We slam into the shield together, my aching body scream-ing as it shatters beneath us. The impact lightens our fall and we hit the ground much more gently, but the pain is too much again.

Not again I think just before I black out.

This time, I don't think I was out long. The reason why? Irissa is curled up next to me on the path, the night sky still looming above us. And the thing that woke me? A series of howls that echo in the silent night.

"Divine goddesses," I groan, forcing myself into a sitting position as I curse the blasted women *again* on this tireless trip. I am met with a pair of red eyes just off the path, watching me with a predatory gaze. I send a flame its way, scaring it away momentarily. *We need to move.* I no longer trust that these paths are safe, not when the beasts are all desperate for revenge against the Divine that killed their friends.

"Irissa, wake up. Irissa! Come on. Please, Irissa. Wake up!" I shake her violently, but her eyes don't even flicker. The exhaustion is too much—the trip has taken too much out of her. "Oh, great. What do I do? *What do I do?*"

It's time to think about my options. I can barely walk, I've opened some of my wounds and am bleeding anew, and I don't think our horses will find us. So what can I do? What options *do* I have? I want to ball up and cry, want to scream and curse the goddesses some more. But I can't do that. I have to *think*. I have to do something. And the only thing I can think to do is so revolting I might puke, but I have to. *I have to.*

"I'm so sorry, Irissa. I'm so sorry. I won't kill you. I won't," I reassure myself and her, my tears falling hard and fast. *I have to take some of her powers.* With other Divine, I have slowly chipped away at their powers without even knowing. One simple touch and I was absorbing their very essence and I had no idea. But I've never done that with Irissa. I don't know why I don't have a single drop of her inside of me. Maybe my powers can sense the strangeness in hers? Maybe they can tell she is cursed.

I tentatively reach out my hand, shaking as I rest it on hers. I've never purposely used this power before, so I don't know how to call it to me. I close my eyes and reach deep inside, pushing away the flames and the shields and looking for that something that is *me*. When I find it I cling to it, forcing it to obey. I pull and tug it free, bringing it up to the surface above the others. Then I tell it to feed.

It is slow at first, a coldness that seeps into my very being. And then it is racing through me, filling me in a way I have only remembered feeling once before. I groan at the pleasure of it all, trying to keep my sanity. I can't kill my sister. I can't. I barely manage to yank my hand away, tumbling backward painfully. I hit my back hard, crying more as the pain radiates through me and ignites my other injuries. But the pleasure lingers, and it numbs the pain just enough to help me sit again.

"Okay, Irissa. Let's try these wings out."

I reach inside of me for the new power and I find it easily. It's much more willing to come out and play, and it feels so different from the others. It's calm and free and so, so easy. I scream as the wings rip out from my back, finding myself glad to already be sitting down. The skin is sore and tender, and I can't help but whimper as I try and lift the heavy muscles on my back. It takes five tries for me to lift them, and even more attempts to figure out how to flap them. I manage to lift myself into the air after at least an hour of trying, and I decide that that is going to have to be good enough. I can see more red eyes in the distance and can hear more cries filling the night: We are running out of time.

"This is going to hurt." I reach down and pull Irissa into my arms, screaming out in agony as the motion rips at my open wounds. Blood is seeping through my bandages already, but I don't stop and I will myself not to black out again. With a singular flap I am in the air, but it isn't smooth sailing. We slip and tumble several times, wobbling uneasily as I adjust to all the new sensations that a pair of wings brings. Not to mention the pain that keeps shooting through me with every movement. I don't stop, though. I'm not allowed to give up right now.

Eventually, I get us back into the sky at the same elevation as before. I swiftly figure out how to speed us along, all while gritting my teeth through the pain. My whole body hurts and I'm still bleeding, albeit slower. And these *wings*. Every movement is like moving a sore limb, like massaging sore muscles that you worked too hard. I keep going through the night, pushing through into the day. I don't give up. By the time noon hits, I can finally see the castle. It is large and looming even from here, but I still cry in relief. I have to cry now while I still can.

CHAPTER 3

Celeste

I rissa woke up just before we entered the Solar Court, her small cry of surprise startling me into dipping us a little too close to the top of a tall, pristine building. I hear screams from below, and I watch wearily as fingers point up at us. I can only grit my teeth and ignore them, looking at my sister instead.

"We're here," she states, laughing in disbelief while gazing around in awe. Truly, the Solar Court is a sight to behold. We are only flying over a village now, but even it seems grand compared to the Lunar Court. The Undivines have decent housing, all of which look updated and clean. I can see wagons traveling below and hear laughing children who seem to be chasing each other around. I have never seen children be so...*joyful.*

As we fly into Solar City, I notice the same things in each village: clean, up-kept buildings and happy citizens. There is no fighting, no blood and gore littering the streets like Ryleigh said there would be. I guess everything she told me *had* been a lie. Why were those rumors circulating? Was it the Solar Court themselves spreading them, or was the Lunar Court using the lies as another attempt to keep its citizens as willing prisoners?

The white stone buildings shine at us, and yellow and orange hues on windowsills, doors, and flags cast reflections everywhere. The people wear flowing clothes that dance in the breeze, beautiful shirts, dresses, and jewelry dancing in the light of the sun. I don't see fear or hesitance in those nearest to the castle, and they don't try to stay as far away as possible. It's like...like they *want* to be close to their Royals. I can see it in the faraway gazes, in the way their bodies seem to gravitate toward the one place they should stay far away from.

The castle itself is enormous, so much bigger than the one in Lunar City. Its structure is one of marble, though, and prettier than I could have ever imagined a castle to be. Its windows display stained glass that tells stories of the Divine, their beauty impressive and awe-inspiring. Some show displays of power, while others picture the goddesses as they blessed our ancestors. Further down I see the giant and imposing main door, the size enough to take at least two people to open it. My gaze falls to the tall, stone wall surrounding it, but I'm not sure they even need it with the lack of discord in their streets.

The Solar Court seems oddly peaceful—the complete opposite of what I was expecting it to be.

"How did you end up carrying me?" Irissa asks in my arms, her eyes catching on something moving in the distance. I follow her line of sight, noticing the many guards littering the castle grounds.

"You were too exhausted and we fell. Which hurt a lot, by the way. I had to steal some of your power—I hope you don't mind."

"Of course not. You can borrow my power anytime." *That's* why I was able to so easily use hers—she wanted me to have it, despite her being unconscious at the time of passing it on. I want to cry from the sentiment, from the simple truth that she trusts me entirely.

"Good, because I may need it again if they don't want to help me."

"They will help you," she says confidently as the guards slowly become more than little waving flags below us.

"They will help me," I repeat with as much confidence as I can muster. "Alright, prepare yourself: I'm going to swoop low and fast." Despite my words, nothing can prepare me for such a thrilling drop. My heart leaps, my stomach drops, and I grin in satisfaction. *I can get used to flying.* I aim directly for that large door, hoping I can manage to land on my first attempt with minimal harm. I swoop around a few bulky buildings and straight over the castle walls, grinning at the cries that erupt from the streets. Guards scream from below, pointing weapons up at us; I can only hope they don't use them.

Our landing is not as graceful as I had hoped it would be. Quite the opposite, actually. We practically crash into the ground, my feet hitting too hard as I stumble forward. I drop Irissa and she rolls, but I manage to face-plant. I shake it off, though, standing as if nothing happened. As if every inch of me isn't screaming out in agony, as if I didn't fight off another blackout. Only my will is keeping me awake now, and I force the edges of black creeping into my vision away with pure stubbornness.

"You good?" I question my sister, watching her stand and dust herself off. "Sorry about the rough landing. I didn't have time to practice that part."

"Yeah, I'm—"

A booming voice interrupts her, guards approaching us steadily. "Hands up! State your name and business!" We do as we are told, arms reaching up high. Well, as high as I can manage to raise them through the agony that motion creates. I glance around at their guns, swallowing hard. These look much deadlier than the ones our guards carry at home.

"I am Irissa of the Lunar Court, sent here by Prince Edge and Princess Valaine of the Solar Court for refuge. This is my sister, Cerina Celeste of the Lunar Court, who was previously engaged to Prince Zaeden of the Lunar Court." I try to stand tall at my sister's words, hoping I don't look weak and intimidated. I watch the flashes of recognition across the soldiers' faces, watch as fear creeps in behind it.

"You're early." The one who yelled at us is the first to speak, motioning for us to put our arms down. We do so gratefully, and I try not to wince with the movement.

"I know. We were attacked on the way here. Our driver is most likely dead and our horses were spooked off. I was injured in the fight, and I need to see a healer." I use my newly developed sneering Royal tone, not daring to blink at the soldier. I don't tell him how urgent it is, or how I'm probably nearing death by exhaustion at this point.

"Let her in," an unfamiliar voice shouts from behind the door, dripping with authority. The guards do so without question, pulling it open with great effort. Irissa smirks playfully, smugly, and strides gracefully past them. She pops her wings out, letting one brush up against a soldier on her way by. She giggles when he jumps away, practically falling over himself to get away from her.

"It was a pleasure, boys," I purr, striding behind her. Every step hurts, pain shooting so fast and violently I can't tell where it originates. My vision swims, too, but I follow dutifully behind my sister like nothing is wrong.

"Quickly, girls, quickly." The voice ushers us, its source directly ahead. An older woman stands before us and I take in her dark skin, dark hair, and dark eyes. Even without seeing the golden crown with gleaming peaks across her brow, I would know who this woman was: Her children have inherited too much of her.

"Thank you...um...miss...?" Irissa doesn't know what to call her, but I do.

"Queen Alvina Zorander of the Solar Court at your service," she remarks playfully, her voice light. "And I don't need to ask who you are." She doesn't seem upset that we have literally crashed at her front door. Quite the opposite, actually. Clearly, she was expecting us.

"Is my reputation that bad?" I can't help but wince as we follow her down the long hall, my breathing getting heavier and heavier. At least when I was flying I didn't have to use my legs.

"My son sent word of your arrival, though you are earlier than expected. Don't let the idea of fame get into your head."

"I wouldn't dream of it, Your Majesty."

"Please, call me Alvina. I'm sure we will be seeing each other much too often to go by such formalities."

"Oh? You think?"

"Oh, I *know*." She turns and sends a wink over her shoulder, motioning to her guards. "We need to get to the healer. Now."

"Please," I can't help but grind out, blinking away the blurry specks in my eyes.

"Why aren't you healing?"

"I don't know. I've never had healing properties. Though, I've not always had powers, either. Nor the beauty and strength that comes with said powers."

"But you have them now. You should have all of those things and more." It's barely a whisper, her worried eyes haunting me. Within seconds of those words leaving her lips, the hissing whispers hit my ears.

The first growls, "Divine Slayer."

A second follows with, "Royal killer."

"*Divine Slayer.* I quite like that. Do you want to see how I did it? Do you want to see what your friend looks like as a pile of ashes after I rip the power from his weak body?" I meet the eyes of each Low, curling my lips into a snarl. I'm not going to be a cowering, sniveling, *stupid* girl here. *I am going to be feared.*

I step forward when the guards step back, attempting to threaten them with my closeness. My body has other plans, though. My last step is one too many and I collapse, hitting the ground hard and fast. I blink in and out of consciousness, vaguely aware of someone lifting me into their arms.

"Gentle, boys," Alvina commands as I cry out in pain. "I don't want my husband to know of the Lunars' presence yet. Though, I suspect their dramatic entrance may not do us any favors."

"Can't you hurry things along? My sister needs help!" Irissa is screaming at someone, but I can barely maintain my vision at this point. Pain is still shooting throughout me, and I cry out again as I am jostled once more.

The queen grinds out, "I told you to take her to the healers *quickly.*" Even I would be scared of her if I *could* be scared right now. Her direct order seems to snap the man holding me out of his daze, our pace suddenly increasing. It makes me sick, and I am close to vomiting all over this guard.

I hear footsteps chasing along after us, long strides that match our pace.

I wish I was observant enough right now to remember the corridors, to remember the twists and turns that flicker in and out of focus. I don't know how long it takes to reach the healer. It could have been mere minutes or it could have been much, much longer. The cold seeping in around us hints at being underground, but I can't be certain. We did go down a set or two of stairs, but all the movement kept knocking me in and out of consciousness.

I am carted into a room even colder than its hall, white walls gleaming under bright lights. Cots line up against those walls, the only comfort the beds offer being white sheets and flat pillows. There is a door to the left, storage or a bathroom, maybe? Before I can take in more of my scenery, I am being dropped harshly onto the first cot we approach. My back hits the rough material after a three-foot drop and I can't help but scream out, a single tear escaping as I shake from the pain.

"You could have been gentler!" Irissa cries out, and I can see the blurry shape of her wings as they stretch out threateningly.

"Of course. My apologies." His tone isn't very apologetic.

"What have we here?" A new voice now, one coming from the direction of the door on the left. I can barely turn my head to look at the healer dressed in white robes, meeting gentle and genuine eyes.

"A Divine Slayer." I attempt to grin. "Or so they claim."

"Ah. Celeste of the Lunar Court, I presume. The whole castle has whispered about you."

"All good things I assume?" He shakes his head, a matching smile plastered to his face.

"Was it the beasts?" Down to business now, I guess. He approaches with no caution, snapping on a pair of rubber gloves.

"Yes. I feel like I'm dying." I don't know how I am still talking, how I am still awake. Every move hurts, every word excruciating. Every inch of my skin stings, I'm still bleeding, and my energy is severely depleted. I know I have a couple of broken bones, probably some bruised organs. My clothes are dripping with blood, and my face is covered in dirt and dried tears. Maybe I *do* have some of those Divine healing abilities because, surely, I shouldn't be alive right now. Willpower and stubbornness can only carry me so far with injuries like these.

"That's because you are."

CHAPTER 4
The Missing Princess

Silvi

Zaeden paces around the dark war room, tugging and pulling at his hair angrily. I feel that anger radiating off his body, the intensity hot and torturous. A similar feeling is emitting from most of the Divine surrounding us. It's hard to ignore, hard to not reach out and tug on the strands of emotions that entangle the room. I know how fun it would be to change their anger to happiness or their resentment to relief, but there is no time for fun and games anymore. Besides, there is no situation where such recklessness wouldn't get me killed.

"How did she get away?" I am one of the few who don't flinch when Zaeden slams his fists down on the table suddenly. His father, King Alexis Mourner, is seated at the head of the table with his wife, Queen Lyra Mourner, by his side. Zaeden is supposed to be seated across from her and to my left, but he won't sit for more than a few precious seconds.

It's utterly exhausting.

Three other men sit at the black metal table, one of which is the advisor to the Lunar king. I believe the one across from me is the coins master and the one across from Valaine manages the villages, as far as I understand. A map of the Lunar Court is laid across the table, marked with several figures to show where they have searched for Celeste. I tilt my eyes up, ignoring the shining chandelier made of gilded antlers above us. This room was created with a man's view if the sleazy posters of Divine women on the wall were any indication.

"You are the one who let her walk right out of your room," Prince Edge snorts from my right, picking at his fingernails absentmindedly. "Don't point fingers at the rest of us when *you* didn't stop her, either." I purse my lips, effectively hiding my amusement. Edge always has such good points, despite his other, and quite numerous, flaws.

"You will not speak to my son in such a manner. Not while you are considered guests in my Court, Zorander. Remember where you are and who is graciously hosting you." King Mourner's voice is coated with a thick venom, his sharp gray eyes turning toward the Solar prince. Edge doesn't outwardly react, and I don't sense any rising fear or any budding worry. Though, I have always struggled to read him. He's too good under pressure and too Royal for my abilities.

"Spoiled brat." It's barely a whisper but Valaine hears the words from his other side, elbowing him deeply in the ribs in response.

"We checked every exit, every corridor," a man says from the door, stepping forward to speak directly to the Royals. He is dressed in a different color than the other soldiers, the shining silver of his jacket a stark difference from the plain navy of the others. He runs a hand through his buzzed brown hair, his hazel eyes full of delicious fear.

"Check them again!" Zaeden bellows, discolored poison dancing around him as he paces back toward me. Despite the color of his poison fading into a revolting shade of gray, it still inspires fear in the captain of the guard. "I want you to bring every Undivine *and* every Divine in this castle to me! I want to interview every single one myself! I *will* find out who was behind this and I *will* kill anyone who helped that Divine climbing bitch escape!" I shift from beside him, breathing deeply. Celeste is anything *but* a Divine climber. A bitch, however...*that* she can be.

"Let me have the honor of interrogating your subjects, my love. As your future wife, I want nothing more than to help you find the Divine Slayer." My words slide off my tongue with ease as I tilt my head back down, a small smile grazing my lips. I reach out to run a hand along his arm, drawing his attention to my touch as I release lustful endorphins into his skin. Then I tilt my head, waiting for his response.

"Don't call her that, Silvi." His voice is low and heavy, annoyance bouncing off his words. His sullied gray eyes meet mine only briefly, but it's all I need. It's enough to show compassion and determination through subtle changes in my face, enough to prove my worthiness with only a tiny push into his devastated mind. "Fine. I will allow you to be the interrogator, as your abilities have proven to be much more useful than mine. As my future queen, it only makes sense that we work together on this." This time Zaeden looks toward his father, waiting for the nod of approval. One he barely gets.

"Of course, my love," I purr, bowing my head in a sign of respect. I can feel the vague hints of satisfaction from Edge and Valaine, though their faces don't show it. Like most of us at this table, we have become accustomed to hiding what we feel from others. Zaeden still needs practice in that area—he's all too easy to read.

"And if you don't find anyone?" Valaine is the next to speak, staring into the dark eyes of my Lunar prince. I trace a pattern across his arm, distracting him if only slightly.

"We will. She has to be *somewhere* in this damn Court!" Once again that poison rises, his anger all too evident. It's obvious to everyone here that he is out of control, that his emotions are leading him around on a leash. Soon, I will be holding a leash, too.

"And what if she has escaped? What then, Zae?" Valaine only uses the casual nickname to piss him off.

"Then I expect every Court to willingly hand her over upon her arrival." His voice is hard, his face tense. He's honest, at least. He *is* expecting that. Too bad things are never what we expect them to be.

"And if I don't want to?" Edge has moved on to twirling a coin around, tossing it in the air, catching it. The corner of his mouth is pulled up into a smirk, and I can't help but admire the balls he has to act this way in such a serious conversation.

"Then you can expect a war, Zorander. And we all want to avoid that, don't we?" Zaeden tenses as he awaits Edge's reply. Poor boy. He *really* isn't prepared for this crown.

"Of course." Edge is calm, collected, unruffled. The threat of war is nothing new, nothing unexpected.

"Is there anything you want to say, Solar Prince? Anything you want to admit to?" Suspicion rolls off King Mourner, flickering in and out. I can barely feel the emotion, but its strength is what hits me. The Divine around us are shocked, as they should be. Because who would dare question a Royal about his loyalties to his own?

"Little ol' me? Do you *think* I have something to admit to? Something to be guilty of? That's a hard accusation to be throwing toward my Court right now, Mourner." Edge sits up, snarling at the Lunar king. Valaine tenses, hands cupping over one another as she struggles to maintain her composure. Because, yes, there are many things Edge is guilty of. One of them being the very thing this meeting is about—harboring a fugitive. Too bad they won't know until it's too late.

Run, Celeste, run.

"Of course not. We mean no harm. We are only distraught at the loss of our beloved prince, our heir, our son. You understand, don't you?" Queen Mourner is a mediator, calming the tension in the room with her gentle pleading. Her kind, light green eyes search for a softness that doesn't exist within her husband, midnight hair glistening in the lights.

Valaine speaks before Edge can, shooting him a pointed look. "Yes, Your Majesty. We understand completely."

"This instance is the only one that will be forgiven. Accuse me, or any member of my Court, again and the alliance you seek will not hold." Edge has turned cruel, crueler than I've ever known him to be. Even *I* feel threatened by his words. His body radiates power and dominance, and the other Royals can sense it hiding within every move he makes.

"Oh, Edge," I sigh, rolling my eyes in an attempt to ease the air. "You never could play nice. We don't need a show of power right now, do we, boys?"

"I have to admit, I am curious about your powers, Zorander." Zaeden stalks toward him, a false smile on his lips as he opens his hands placatingly. "I haven't seen you use your powers since you arrived, but I sense them. I'm sure we all do. A show of power may be called for, after all. If only to demonstrate your Court still has the strength you claim it does, of course."

"You don't want me to use my powers on you, asshole. If you challenge me to a fight right now, all you will see is death. All you will *know* is death." Edge stands to face Zaeden, crossing his arms and staring into those poisonous eyes.

"Ah, so *you* are Death now?" Zaeden teases, waving his hand dismissively. I know Zaeden himself has been described as death incarnated by several people, mostly the Undivine who fear him; it's why he is attempting to dismiss Edge's threat so blatantly.

"And if I am?" Edge's grin leaves a shiver down the other prince's spine, a cold chill sweeping over the room. Unlike Zaeden, Edge isn't joking.

"Enough," King Mourner interrupts as he runs a hand through thinning gray hair, but the action isn't enough to break the tension between the two princes. "I'm tired of this. Why aren't your men out looking for the girl, captain? She is a traitor to the crown and she must pay for what she has done. Silvi, be prepared to conduct interviews all day. No one leaves until they are cleared!" I bow my head to the king, acknowledging his words.

"Are you going to kill her?" Edge drawls out, eyes finally leaving Zaeden's.

"If we so wish."

"So you know what she is, then?"

"Of course we do. She is a High Divine that was raised as Undivine, brought here to kill our son. She planned to kill him all along. Those ungrateful Undivine put that idea in her head and trained her for this moment. They are the reason he is dead. She and all the others are going to *pay*."

Celeste is a lot of things: beautiful, smart, powerful, cunning, brave. But one thing she isn't? Cold-hearted. That's one of the things that attracted me to her so quickly, that brought me to my knees at the thought of her. She is kind and gorgeous and caring, and she probably would have loved me eventually if only I had been honest. But she can't and she doesn't, and I ruined everything, anyway.

I'm too selfish to deserve someone like her.

"Ah, but that's not true, is it?" Edge chuckles, flexing his fingers and stretching his arms behind his head as he tilts back in his chair.

"I was there. I know what is true and what isn't," Zaeden snaps back next to him.

"I know exactly who was there and what happened. *And* I know what she really is. So, I will repeat my question: do you?"

"I don't know what you mean." I'm not the only one who sniffs out King Mourner's lie.

"Don't worry. I haven't told anyone about your little secret," Edge lies, not sparing a glance at me. "I know what she can mean for our Courts and the weapon we may soon possess if we find her." I know he is doing this to protect Celeste and to keep her alive if she does get captured, which is the only reason I can stay so calm. Fuck, I still want her alive, too. Even if my heart would hurt less without her in it.

"What are you suggesting?"

"I'm not suggesting anything, Your Majesty."

The king stays silent, watching the Solar prince intently. The room stays silent with him, pleading to be released from this awkward torture. Finally, he breaks the silence with a low sigh. "Help us find the girl, Edge, and we may speak on the subject more."

It is as good a dismissal as any.

Edge

Weeks have passed with no sign of Celeste in the Lunar Court or any possibilities as to where she may have gone. It doesn't take more than a full month to receive word from my Court about her arrival, despite it being much too soon. I've sent a few telepathic messages out to my mother, as she is the only one who can respond, but it's hard to ensure those messages are delivered when there is such a large distance between her and me. So, when I finally get a response, I know I have to leave this fucking Court. Fast. The message is brief and concise:

She is here. Near death. Come home quickly.

My mother's powers are not as strong as mine. She can hardly form sentences when we communicate in this way, so it would have been a struggle to send such a large amount of words. She told me what she could as quickly as she could, and now it is up to me to do the rest. It's not her fault; the power we share isn't really hers. She only holds a hint of what I do because it is not the power she was born with. During her pregnancy with me, she gained the telepathic abilities she is now clinging to. It happens sometimes in pregnancies with very powerful babies, albeit very rare. Bits of power are left within the mother, powers that typically fade over time. It won't be long before this particular ability of hers is gone—it shouldn't have lasted as long as it has.

I barge into my sister's room, dismissing the servant attending to her hair. "Val, we have to go."

"Oh?" She turns, relief flooding her features. Honestly, I feel relieved, too. This Court is a fucking coffin, and if we stay any longer I'm not sure we won't be buried alive inside of it.

"She is hurt. Near death." I relay the message I received without giving names or titles—she knows who I am speaking of.

"So soon? We weren't supposed to leave for another week. How did she—?"

"I don't have all the information, but...yeah. It was quick travel. Quicker than any wagon could have taken her," I say softly, slowly. We both know that the only other option would have been her winged sister. How they pulled that off, though, I can't be sure.

"Much quicker," she agrees, standing. "Was it the beasts?"

"Most likely." Those demonic creatures plague our lands like a disease, hunting and killing at their pleasure. They aren't gentle beings, and I worried something like this might happen if the sisters didn't heed warnings.

"Then we must go," she breathes, bobbing her head in excitement.

"Have the maids gather your things. We must go speak to King Mourner"

We try to keep our pace casual, our minds racing with possibilities and relief. I don't wish for Celeste or her sister to be hurt, but I am glad they found their way to the castle ahead of schedule. At least now we won't have to travel the long way there as we have an excuse to teleport. I hate the Lunar Court, its lies, and its treatment of its people. I'm glad to be rid of it and even gladder to know that we now hold the Absorbid in our Court. Now that she is in our territory, there is nothing the Lunar Royals can do to harm her. Not unless they want a war, that is. And if they do start a war, then *I* will be the one to finish it.

"Your Highness's." A soldier bows as we approach the throne room. "Have you come to see King Mourner?"

"Yes, it is very important, friend," Valaine says softly, sending him a shy and flirtatious smile.

"Well, usually you need an appointment—"

"Ah, *we* don't, do we? I mean, we are *Royals* after all." She brushes her hand against his arm, pressing her body closer and invading his personal space.

A blush fills his cheeks, his mouth opening and closing like a gurgling fish. "O–Of course," he stutters, swallowing hard before stepping aside. "Of course, you may enter."

"Goddesses bless you," she purrs with another soft touch to his shoulder. He shudders underneath her fingertips, eyes following us as we stride into the opening double doors.

"Goddesses bless you," I mock her, snorting afterward. Men and women alike fall apart at my sister's fingertips, which is a very useful skill. Even if it is incredibly painful and infuriating to watch her flirt with anything that fuck-ing breathes.

"Shut up, Edge. I'll—" Her whispered hiss is interrupted by the angry voice of a pompous king.

"Zoranders. What are you two doing here? You can't just barge in whenever you feel like it. I don't know how things are run in *your* Court, but things are more civilized *here*."

"King Mourner," I smile wickedly, giving him a dramatic bow. "What a pleasure to see you again."

"What are you doing here?" King Mourner grits his teeth as he repeats himself. He lounges on a large silver throne, a dark blue cushion squished underneath his Royal ass. His wife is notably absent from her smaller seat beside him, his advisor standing at the bottom of the steps leading up to the thrones.

"I am sorrowful to announce that we must head back to our own Court today. I have received an urgent message from home and we must make haste in our return." No details, no reasons, no questions.

"Is it really that important, Zorander, or are you just desperate to leave?" he questions and snorts dismissively.

"Can't it be both?" I ignore the bony elbow that jabs into my rib.

"We still haven't found the girl. This important matter at home wouldn't involve her, would it?" I see the nervous tapping of his fingers on the throne and the faraway look in his eyes as he considers all possibilities.

"You insult me and my Court once more," I spit, taking a single step forward. "What use would I have of the girl?" There are actually *many* uses I can think of for her, but I clamp them all down. *He* doesn't need to know what I think about the tiny little blonde with an ever-growing attitude.

"What use would you have of a beautiful, dangerous weapon who hates my Court? Hmm. Yes, what use indeed." His fingers still as he leans forward, flames dancing in his eyes. A very useful power, one that was just as strong as his son's, I'm sure. Too bad mine is stronger.

"So you admit it, do you? You admit what she is?" *I knew they were lying.* I have to make sure they won't kill her, that if she is captured she still has a chance. Because without her...there may not be a chance for anyone else.

"I admit nothing. Is there something weighing on your chest, Zorander? A secret you need to let out?" Those flames are scorching the surface of his skin, dancing across the throne in a barely controlled threat. A few nearby soldiers jump away, fear in their eyes as they watch their own king.

"You have insulted me enough for one day, Your Majesty. My sister and I will be taking our leave now," I snarl, letting my abilities rise to the surface. The darkness is cold and familiar, dripping out of my skin upon my command. It's thicker than smoke but still gas-like. It feels like a worm wiggling out of my skin, like ice bursting from my veins. It doesn't hurt, doesn't overwhelm, doesn't overcome. It circles me and my sister, shielding us in utter darkness. I can hear King Mourner cry out in surprise, quickly composing himself enough to shout at his useless guards. After another elbow, I let out a humorless laugh and let the darkness seep back inside.

I hate doing that, but I love making a scene even more.

My power is much more terrifying than Zaeden's—it's not some silly little slime that can kill you upon impact. No, mine is a power born from the deepest, most powerful, and oldest fear the world has ever known: the darkness. And everyone is terrified of what can hide in the dark.

"What was that?" His voice is shakier than it should be, his anger hidden beneath fear.

"Zaeden asked me before if am truly Death," I grin, twisting my fingers and playing with a strand of shadow. "And I just might be."

"I want you out of my Court."

"Oh? You don't want to play anymore? What a shame, Mourner. I was just starting to have fun," I pout, turning to grab my sister's hand. "Come, sister. Let's go home. It's obvious we are no longer welcome here."

"Of course, brother. Thank you, King Mourner, for the hospitality you have shown us," Valaine purrs, sending him her own terrifying grin. The king hardly hides his surprise at the expression. She has been so docile, so kind, so helpless. I hope he is beginning to realize he doesn't know who, or *what*, he has allowed into his Court.

"See them out!" He bellows to the poor fellow at the doors, fury and fear overtaking him. "And make sure that carriage leaves our Court!"

And they do.

Three soldiers follow our steady-paced carriage, escorting us out of the Lunar Court efficiently. They follow us into neutral territory until our carriage disappears into the woods—not that it matters. Two Lows and an Undivine wouldn't have been able to stop me if I decided to turn around and kill their king. The only thing that *is* stopping me is my mother, and even she holds a short leash when it comes to my control or lack thereof.

"What the fuck did you two do?" the driver hisses, her hood dropping as she spins to glare at us through the window. We can hear her quite clearly, though. Valaine can't help but flinch, hesitantly opening it to reveal one of our closest allies and best spies.

Valaine purses her lips as she watches the Undivine who should have been working in this castle still gathering information, but has unfortunately been placed under too much suspicion since Celeste's disappearance. If I were Mourner, I would be keeping close tabs on her, too. She was

Celeste's boss and best friend, after all. "Now, Ryleigh, don't be angry, but—"

"What the fuck did you two do?" she repeats, only slower. Even I swallow now.

"Nothing serious," I shrug, sending her a lazy smirk. "Just showing off, that's all."

"We need them on our side, Edge Zorander," she spits, her finger wagging in my face. "You know what your mother is going to say if you two ruined our chances at an alliance? It's in the plan, you fucking idiot. You were supposed to follow the *plan*."

"It's not my fault. Besides, Celeste strayed from the plan first. Maybe you should yell at her instead."

"Oh, I will. She'll wish a beast had eaten her by the time I'm through with her," she fumes, distracted. I wink at Valaine playfully, but she only shakes her head and scoffs.

"We don't know what happened. It may not be her fault," Valaine tries to defend her, glaring at me.

"All of this is her fault," I say, and it's true. Even if she didn't mean to cause such a big mess.

"Quit talking about her." Ryleigh's demand is final, and neither of us questions it. "Now, are we doing this or what?"

"Stop the carriage," I huff, pushing past my sister roughly. I ignore her shouts and kicks as she topples over, leaping out of the carriage before the horses have fully stopped.

"Show off," Ryleigh mutters as the darkness pools beneath my skin, my power tingling at my fingertips.

"Do you have any useful powers?" I snap back, ignoring her hearty laugh.

"The world knew it could not handle a version of me with powers." The bad thing is, I believe her. A Ryleigh with powers *would* have had a devastating effect on the world.

"Let him concentrate, Ryleigh," Valaine shushes her, light laughter following. I grunt my agreement as my hands begin to move, dark shadows slinking up into the sky.

My hands perform a familiar dance, twirling and twisting as I push and push and push. My arms strain from the effort, veins bulging with the pressure of the shadows within me. But I keep calling them, allowing more and more to enter my body and escape. One by one, I begin removing my rings. Each one falls to the ground silently, spinning around and around. Finally, the darkness begins to take shape, forming a gigantic sphere. That sphere lifts above the ground, directly in front of the horses. It hovers a few inches as it grows and grows, more and more shadows joining. I hear Valaine grabbing my rings before she pulls me with her back into the carriage.

"Go, Ryleigh. Go now!" I barely get the words out, my strength waning as I struggle to keep the portal intact. There is no answer, but the carriage jolts to a start. The horses race without fear, leaping into the pitch-black sphere with no hesitation. They are the first to be swallowed, their steady gallops sucked into oblivion. Ryleigh's stunned laughter echoes and disappears as we, too, are enveloped in darkness.

"Maybe I should have warned her to hold on tighter," Valaine laughs as she grips the edges of her seat.

"What's the fun in that?" I grunt, not daring to blink. We are engulfed by my power for only seconds, swallowed and spat out before we can think to panic. The light is a welcome sight, the carriage bouncing as we hit the ground. This is one of the hardest parts of my power to control, and I am thankful that I didn't get us lost in that dark hole. That, this time, I was able to keep it contained. I can hear Ryleigh yelling, struggling to control us with all the jostling that running through a portal creates. Abruptly everything falls still, and I feel the shadows reaching out to find me once more. I collapse against my seat in exhaustion, a smug grin overcoming me as I try and ignore the overwhelming presence of those shadows.

"Welcome back to the Solar Court."

CHAPTER 5

Celeste

My screams of agony echo around the room, bouncing in and out of my ringing ears. My back arches as I writhe on the cot, sweat pouring from every pore. The healer above me grunts an apology as I fall back down, tears falling down my cheeks like a waterfall racing off a cliff. I can't hold back the tears, can't hold in the screams, can't accept the apologies. My vision wavers but I blink through it, forcing myself to stay focused. I can't pass out, I can't fade away.

I deserve this, I deserve this, I deserve this.

The healing tonic I had been given an hour ago didn't help the pain, it didn't soothe the burning fire that was searing through my veins. Upon the first snicker of a soldier at my screams, Irissa kicked them all out. Now, they stand laughing outside the room, listening joyfully instead. Due to her, it's just me, Irissa, the healer, and Alvina. The latter stands by my side, hand encasing my own. It's a foreign touch and feeling, but I cling to it and the unfamiliarity that anchors me to this moment. I have heard horrible things about this Court and its rulers yet their queen is comforting me, holding my hand and whispering that it will all be over soon.

"You have to stop," I manage out, pleading with the little strength I have left. I can't do this anymore; I can't keep telling myself I deserve the pain. I can't stay awake much longer. "Please. You have to stop."

"You are going to die," the healer says through gritted teeth, hands working on a particularly sore spot. "I can't stop." I know he must be tired. His powers are being pushed to the max, not to mention the mental tax that the threat of someone who can suck him dry has. He probably wishes for this to end, too.

"What is that gunk in her blood?" Irissa whispers, a horrified expression crossing her face. I look away, not wanting to know what, exactly, she sees.

"It's the venom from the beasts. Few make it to our Court in time to be saved," Alvina replies, kind eyes following the healer's careful hands. Her hair is cut short, just below her ears, and it bobs with every movement. As I stare at her I notice a few gray streaks that I hadn't seen before, her dark eyes flashing to my sister and back only briefly. I *must* be in bad shape.

"Lucky me," I breathe out, half delirious. I suck in a breath as the pain hits once more, and my exhale is a long, high-pitched scream.

"Why is it hurting her so much? You gave her a tonic!" Irissa is angry and demanding. I would be, too, if it were her on this table bleeding out and screaming in agony.

"I thought it would help, but..." The healer glances up at his queen, swallowing hard. "I was wrong."

I am coated in a sticky substance, most likely a mix of blood and poison. Its warmth coats my skin, fighting against the coldness of the cot. How can being coated in blood feel *good?*

"It's okay, Romanus. You are doing your best," Alvina reassures her subject.

"It's *not* okay. You need to fucking fix her!" Irissa shrieks from next to me, temper flaring. I watch her wings lift, talons extending as she steps forward.

"Calm down, child," Alvina demands, authority dripping from her tongue. The healer pauses to wipe his forehead with a damp rag, ignoring the exchange entirely. The queen isn't harsh, but the authority she exudes makes Irissa remember where she is and who she is with. Silently, her powers retreat.

"Your powers control you, Shape-Shifter." Romanus spares her a glance, eyes running over her in assessment. "Why haven't you sought out a healer?"

"We were poor," I answer for her, glaring. "And who would have helped a cursed Undivine?"

"She has never been Undivine and neither have you," Alvina sighs, shaking her head. I watch her hair bounce, focusing on that instead of the shaking of my body as the healer reaches out to touch me again. "Your Court has done you wrong."

Irissa shrugs. "Their loss. Besides, it's like Celeste said: I'm cursed. No healer can fix that. Why is it hurting her so much?" She hadn't forgotten the original question that started this conversation.

"I'm having to pull the venom from her body. It's like...like a rope in her veins that I'm slowly tugging out. It burns and pulls and jerks. It's uncomfortable. It's fire, it's ice. She's burning and she's freezing at the same time. Her body can't figure out what to focus on, so she feels both in succession. It's brief seconds of fire, brief seconds of ice. The rope is leaving a rash, the emptiness it leaves behind soothing it. And all this venom is pooling up in certain areas, concentrating on spots that will kill her faster. So, yeah, it hurts."

"Less talking and more healing," I snap, my body flying up off the cot with the force of my scream as he does just that. I scream and I cry and I black out briefly, shaking when I come back down.

I manage to growl a series of profanities through the aftershocks of pain, one of which may have been, "Fuck you, you fucking shithead Divine."

"What a dirty mouth," a drawling voice purrs, a tall figure strutting through the door. I try to hiss at the Solar prince, to direct my dirty mouth at him, but Romanus is striking at the venom before I can even move my head. I scream again, my surroundings fading in and out. The flickering light above me is what I focus on now, and I watch it with utmost concentration as I try not to die.

"You got my message." Alvina releases my hand, leaving my side and swallowing her son in her arms. Valaine is next in line, head tucking into her mother's shoulder lovingly. I look away, panting. I don't want to see a mother doting on her children at a time like this.

"What a happy reunion. I'm so glad I'm here to witness it," I grind out, eyes fluttering shut as I consider letting myself fade into this fuzzy feeling trying to overtake me.

"Stop talking," the healer demands from above me. "I'm about to start removing the venom from your heart."

I breathe out more expletives, wincing as his hands hover above the sensitive organ. My eyes are wide open now, blinking up pleadingly at the evil healer.

"How fun is this?" Edge is grinning; I can hear it in his voice. Irissa is on him in seconds, wings raised high above her head. Her face turns to stone, her body stiffening in a protective stance.

"You aren't welcome here," she says plainly. I know it's hard for her to stand in front of him like this, to speak to him so callously. She raved for so long about how heroic he was, how handsome, and then I had to ruin it. Because of me, she's now speaking to him in a manner that could get her killed.

"Are you going to make me leave?" His voice turns cold, the playfulness gone.

"If I have to," she shrugs, giving him a once over. "I don't care how pretty you are—you aren't getting near my sister right now."

"Do you know what your sister did to me? Has she told you about that little monster inside of her that likes to hurt people? Likes to hurt *me*?" I know he enjoys the pain that flashes across her face, the hesitation.

"I don't like it," I interject, still shaking.

"I don't like liars," he says simply.

"Get—" I'm not allowed to finish my sentence, not allowed to even begin threatening him. The healer had used our argument against me, using the distraction to begin the tugging on my heart. He pulls that rope and everything inside of me hurts. The pain is unbearable, that fire and ice leaving an impact on every cell. My heart feels like it's about to be ripped straight from my chest, the blood in my veins thumping as its source screams out in mercy. I scream until I'm deaf, scream until I'm no longer sure it's *me* making the hideous noise. Every inch of me screams, all the way down to the molecules that make up my very being. They weep and weep and *weep* through the pain.

"I can help." I hear his gentle voice faintly, hardly registering him pushing past a stunned Irissa. He approaches me with caution, hand coming to rest over my heart right next to the healers.

"Don't touch me." I can barely form the words, can barely argue about unwanted touches. I don't want him to touch me, I don't want him to look at me, and I certainly don't want him to know how weak I truly am right now.

"Celeste, I can help."

"Don't touch me," I repeat.

Irissa is the one to speak now, saying, "Do it. She's not in the right state of mind. She can't permit you right now, but I can. So do it."

I don't have time to argue or to become angry. *As if I even have the energy to be angry.* I feel his power push into me, feel the cool darkness soothing me inside and out. Suddenly, I'm able to breathe, able to relax down into the stiff cot. I take several shuddering breaths, blinking down at the shadows that cover my entire chest. Then, I turn my gaze toward the Cruel Prince.

"You're a Bender." I can't help but be amazed; there are no Benders in the Lunar Court that I know of.

"A bender of shadows," he agrees, his singular steel blue eye flickering up to meet my brown ones. I focus on his wide forehead, glaring at the cropped black hair on his head and the little lines on the sides to avoid that stare.

"What is a Bender?" Irissa asks quietly, watching us with apprehension as she chews on her bottom lip. Edge shrugs his shoulders, gaze not leaving my own as he begins to explain. My point of focus drifts lower to his eye patch, to the 'x' shaped scar stretching out from beneath it.

"Benders have...unique powers. There are two types: light and shadow. They can use their abilities to do many things, things that are sometimes associated with other powers, too. Shadow Benders like me do exactly as it sounds: We bend shadows. We take them from one place to another, allowing them to enter and exit our bodies when we desire them to. We are a conduit for the dark. I can use my shadows to get into your mind and see your thoughts like a Mind Reader, soothe your pain like a Healer, and move from one space to another like a Transporter. With a single thought, my shadows are inside you, listening to your heartbeat, and becoming the final factor in deciding which moment to take it away.

"I've many talents, and I'm sure there are some I have not discovered yet. Light Benders work in very similar ways. Unlike me, they use the sunlight to fuel their abilities. They can create mirages, heal, tinker with time, and some can even shift into animals. Their skill set is astronomically different from mine, and I'm not entirely sure how it all works. Their powers come with a caveat, though. Once it hits nightfall, and the sun has gone down completely, they are rendered essentially powerless. An Undivine for the night. As far as I understand things, anyway. Light doesn't touch as many places as the darkness does."

"That's how you got here, isn't it? You used your shadow-transporting powers. You weren't supposed to be here. *We* aren't even supposed to be here." I am the first to speak, somehow coherently and without wincing. Irissa is stunned into silence at the door. Her hand covers her mouth, her body shaking. I'm not quite sure which part upset her, but *something* did.

"I was told you were hurt, so I came." His tone makes it clear that that would be all he says on the matter.

"My savior," I mutter bitterly, breaking our prolonged eye contact.

"You should thank him," Irissa breaks her silence to scold me, a dreamy look overtaking her shocked features. I groan, letting my eyes roll to the back of my head as I wait for the naive words that are about to leave her mouth. "He is helping you. After everything you did, he ran as fast as he could to be here for you. *Because he heard you were hurt. It's so heroic.*"

"Should I get down on my knees and beg for your forgiveness, Your Highness?" I scoff at Edge before hissing at my sister, "Have you forgotten, Irissa, what his motives are? I'm their prized possession right now. They are helping me because they want to *use* me. Just like Kyelin, only this time I can't kill him."

"I am *nothing* like Kyelin," Edge snaps, hand beginning to clench over my chest before abruptly pausing. He moves to clutch my hand instead, our fingers entangling. "And as much as I would love watching you grovel before me, I will have to reschedule for another day. Don't worry, the begging can come later." His words remind me of something Zaeden said to me not so long ago, distracting me from the fact he had almost squeezed my breast.

"What, do you want me to get on my knees and beg? That will not happen. I will not cower like a dog beneath you. I won't kiss your ass like everyone else likes to."

"Not yet, I don't. But don't worry. We can get to the begging and ass-kissing later."

The memory sends a shiver down my spine and leaves a bad taste in my mouth. Though, that may just be a mixture of blood and venom. One can't be too sure when in a state like this.

"Don't be so rude, Celeste. He saved you." Irissa is still giving him those pathetic puppy-love eyes and I *hate* it.

"He has effectively trapped me in this Court, Irissa. Do you know how hard he tried to get me off that throne? And guess what? He succeeded. I should be married to the love of my life right now, happy and content. Instead, I am here, hiding like a coward because he deems it to be so," I spit bitterly, flaming eyes turning to the prince.

"Happy and content and *stupid,*" he hisses back, squinting his good eye at me and ignoring the silent crowd around us listening in. "Don't blame me for your failures."

"I loved him!" I shout, leaning up and snarling into his face. We are so close now, only inches apart, but I feel nothing but *anger*.

"You didn't love him. You never did. You love the *idea* of love. Kyelin was all too happy to fulfill his role in that fantasy, wasn't he?" Edge snarls back, just as harsh and pitiless as ever. His humorless chuckle slivers across the room, taking the air from my lungs for a brief moment. When my breath has returned to me, I turn away.

"I should have been killed." Even I can hear how broken I am. Maybe it's the pain that is making me feel so inebriated right now, so tired, so vulnerable. I don't have the energy to argue, to fight, to *care*. Because Edge is right. Unfortunately, he usually is.

"You want to be dead?

"I want to be punished. I deserve to be punished." I killed two people. I killed them and wish they had just killed me, instead. Because now I have to keep killing, whether I want to or not. That's why I am here right now, why they are putting so much time and attention into me.

I am going to be their shiny new assassin.

"I've told you before that guilt is punishment enough for you," says a familiar voice from the still-open door.

"Ryleigh." My heart constricts as I see her form, despite knowing I should be angry with her. Only relief floods me now, a soothing remedy to my aching heart. She lied to me, hid secrets, and used me, but...she is a familiar face in an unfamiliar Court. She is my friend. Probably my best friend.

I forgave her long before she ever betrayed me.

"Stop arguing with the Solars. Accept their kindness and move on." The absolute certainty in her voice used to scare me, but it doesn't now. It's meant to put me in my place like it always did before, but I'm not like her. Not anymore.

"I can argue with whomever I please. I don't *want* kindness from the Royals. I want to be as far away from them as possible."

"Then I won't be kind." Edge shrugs carelessly, releasing my hand dismissively. The shadows he was using to calm me flew away, their soothing coolness leaving my body and quickly replaced by a burning fire. The pain hits all too fast, my body reeling into itself upon recognition. I feel myself arching up off the bed, erupting into flames as I scream in agony. The healer jumps away at the searing heat that rises, growling under his breath until they are gone. Then he is descending upon me once more, tugging on that never-ending rope. I can't even speak to beg for his help, to beg for the darkness to return. I can't plead for my suffering to end. Luckily, I don't have to.

"Please!" Irissa leaps forward and grabs Edge's hands, bringing them to her chest as a single tear slips down her cheek. "She is stubborn and hurt in more ways than one right now. I know you two don't have the best history. I know she hasn't been kind. But I will beg for her since she will not. Help her. *Please, help her.* I can't stand to see her like this." I watch through blurry eyes, noticing his stare lingering on that single tear. With a slight growl of frustration, he pulls away in a dramatic flourish only to place his hand on my chest once more.

"You are lucky your sister possesses a kinder soul than you." I feel the shadows before I see them, the darkness sweeping my pain away in the span of a heartbeat.

"Would you mind closing some of the smaller wounds, Your Highness? I've almost worked all of the poison out, but she is losing a lot of blood," Romanus questions, looking toward Valaine as he speaks.

"I am honored to be of service." He blushes under her cool gaze, blinking hard before turning away at her approach.

"I thought you were an Elemental," I say as she, too, hovers over me. "You had water powers at the Lunar Court." I stare at the blue streaks in her short black hair, avoiding the kindness in her deep and murky blue eyes.

"Water has healing properties. Now, that's not to say I'm as good as Romanus here. Quite the contrary, in fact: I'm a pretty mediocre healer. But I have more than the average Water Elemental since I'm a Royal. Mostly I heal shallow cuts, bruises, and scrapes that draw blood. I can't stitch you up or anything, but I may be able to encourage your blood to replicate faster." Her tiny hands run over me, cold water striking my fresh cuts. I can no longer feel the pain it should leave behind.

"Most Water Elementals can hardly heal a scratch, much less blood wounds and bruises," Romanus scoffs, turning red after he realizes who he is talking to. Not that I blame him. Valaine may be extremely thin for a Divine, but she is still beautiful. Her soft features and beautiful smile entrap men and women alike, her dark skin's golden hue entrancing. I can't say I feel the same way about Edge's golden hue—his is almost threatening when paired with such dark powers.

Valaine laughs. "That's true. I am eternally grateful for the gifts I have." Each scrape and bruise begins to evaporate into thin air as she cleans and heals my bloody body.

"Beautiful and powerful. What a combo," I whisper, sending her a small, peace-making smile.

"You're one to talk," she rolls her eyes without glancing up.

"I'm not beautiful."

"You have a lot of things to learn about yourself, Cerina Celeste."

"Just Celeste."

I zone out as they finish healing me, the powers of three Divine racking over and inside me. I try not to think too deeply about it. I don't want to snap and take anything, though I'm not sure how much of a choice I have in the matter. I don't want these Royals to know how little control I actually have. As far as they know, I got too emotional and killed Kyelin. As far as they know, that wasn't the first time I've used my powers in such a blatant manner. I know that I unwittingly took some of Zaeden's powers, and I'm pretty sure I stole from Silvi, too. Who else am I stealing from right now? Who else will die by my hands because I have no control?

"I need everyone to leave," I sputter out suddenly, leaping off the cot. I rip my hand away from Edge, avoiding the pain in my sister's face. I can feel the fear rising inside of me, the heartache, the guilt. Have I already taken a bit of each of them? Have I already stolen something that doesn't belong to me? The thoughts send a shiver down my spine, my guilt radiating. I'm too close to these Divine—they need to get away.

They have to.

"You heard her," Alvina bellows, ushering everyone toward the door.

"She isn't done here," Edge argues, reaching for me. I jerk away, wrapping myself in my arms and shaking my head furiously.

"Leave!" I shout again, flames erupting from my skin. They stay relatively contained, but it's enough of a warning.

I can't calm the roaring waves, and they couldn't care less about what I want them to do.

"She doesn't have control yet! Everyone get out! Now!" Irissa is the one to confess my sins. She has seen what I am capable of on our journey here and has witnessed me losing my control before. "Don't touch her. She might kill you!"

I choke on a sob at her words, closing my eyes tightly. She is right. Why does she have to be right? A killer: that's all I am now. It's all I will ever be.

Even Edge doesn't question my sister, the meaning of her words clear. I am the Divine Slayer, and I have power over them all.

Each person rushes out of the room, my flames inching after them. I try to tug on their leash, to keep them from attacking those who were only trying to save me. When the door slams shut, I let go, and I allow the fear and the flames to swallow me whole.

CHAPTER 6

Celeste

The storm within me unleashes.

I can't do anything but ride the waves, bearing the harsh winds and tumbling tides. I don't fight the flames that take over, allowing them to consume me and the world surrounding me. Thoughts of Kyelin flash through my mind, distant memories that don't belong to me. With a start, I realize they belong to *him*.

Kyelin laughs after he kisses a girl for the first time, his nervous chuckle erupting from his chest. The pretty red-haired girl ducks her head, a blush forming across her cheeks and down her neck. I can see their youth and spot the differences between the Kyelin I knew and the one I now see. His hair is so much shorter, barely reaching past his ears. He has no beard or even a hint of stubble. He is missing a lot of muscle mass, his small frame so very different from the one I knew. How old is he here? Fourteen? Fifteen?

The scene changes.

Fire bellows from his hands, his face hard and set. Those terrifying flames are an unwelcome fight in this battle, a battle that the Lunar Court is obviously winning. I didn't know he had ever gone to battle, or heard of something like this happening, but there were hundreds of men and women on both sides with weapons drawn and powers on full display. I can barely breathe as I watch, can barely think about anything other than the beauty behind his form. The Lunar Court wears midnight blue, but the other side is dressed in all white so I can't tell who they are or why they are fighting. I jerk when I see those monstrous experiments who had attacked me emerging from the trees, growling and hissing as they prepare to attack. They don't seem to care who, exactly, they kill. They attack at random, leaping for the Divine and Undivine that are fighting. I watch as Kyelin is forced to kill the Divine's creations. Is this the real reason he harbors some of those beasts in the castle?

"I get it," I cry, unsure if I'm speaking aloud or within my head. "Please. No more. No more!"

But there *are* more. So, so many more. The flames held onto every memory, and each one was a slap more painful than the last.

Kyelin laughing as he drinks with his brother.

Kyelin stealing animals from the laboratories.

Kyelin begging for his life before me.

The last one is enough to bring me to my knees, reminding me of the horrible power that I have discovered within myself. Reminding me of the exact moment these flames realized that I was not him and that I never would be. How can sentient powers be so vicious? How can they know exactly what to show me to make me *hurt?*

My head falls into my hands, tears soaking my bloodied skin. "I don't understand how you can do this. How can you show me these things? How can you understand?"

Of course, I receive no answer. I receive nothing but the relief of the power sinking back down inside me, allowing the heat and the guilt to dissipate. Allowing the air to finally be still. Somehow, without their company, I feel suffocated. The room is too small and my body is too large. I feel like eyes are on me, hunting me, waiting for this exact moment. I need to leave. I need to get out of here.

I can't be around myself right now.

"Let me out!" I find myself barreling toward the door, pounding on the metal surface. "Please, please let me out! I need out. Please!" My pleas are weak, that suffocating feeling squeezing my throat. I was supposed to be strong here. I was supposed to act like one of them, uncaring and cruel, but how can I pretend to be cruel when it feels like this? When the world is falling on top of me and there is no possible way to escape?

"Calm down, Celeste. I'm opening the door, okay? Step back." I barely have time to register the healer's words, my feet moving accordingly. The door swings open, revealing Romanus's kind face waiting for me.

"Help me," I beg again, clawing at my skin.

"What's wrong? Are you in pain? Hey, don't do that—"

"I have to get out of this room. I have to find my sister." Irissa always makes me feel better. She can help me this time, too. I shove past Romanus harshly, hating myself over and over again. I scratch and scratch and scratch my skin, hating the fact that Kyelin's essence lives under it. Lives in me.

"Let me help you." His hand wraps around my arm tightly, sending every one of my nerves on edge.

A male Divine is touching me.

The thought rings through my head, echoing in my ears. It's all I can think, all I can understand, and my body fights back like it couldn't before.

I don't feel the shadows leaving me. I didn't know they were inside of me, lying dormant. But they are. They *were.* Now they are swallowing Romanus, spitting him up and out. I watch in horror, unable to stop, as his body flies into a wall. I hear the sickening crunch as he makes contact, watching as his body falls limply to the floor. The flames within me streak across the ground, barreling toward him at the speed of light. I hear him scream, though, so he can't be dead. He screams and screams and screams, the flames surrounding him, circling him, trapping him.

With wide eyes I take a few steps forward, intending to help. But those screams…they are so familiar. Too familiar. *The screams of Dola, the screams of Dove, the screams of me.*

My heart thuds against my chest as I realize what I did. As I began to understand exactly whose powers I had done it with. My fears had come to life. I *did* steal powers, even when I was trying so fucking hard not to. And now those powers are in me, swirling around in the giant cavern that hides inside.

I'm dangerous.

I can't be around anyone, or they will end up dead, too.

Just like Dove.

Just like Kyelin.

"Call them off, Celeste! Make it stop! You *can* control this!" I can barely hear his desperate pleas, much less digest them. I can't hear over the thumping in my ears or the roar of the flames residing in my heart.

I force my feet forward, not caring that I don't know where I am going or that I'm not sure where my feet are going to take me. Because, really, it doesn't matter as long as I get away from here. As long as no one ever comes near me again.

That's the only way anyone will be safe from me.

I dart down hallway after hallway, my breaths shallow and hard. My body is encased by those awful flames again, their instinct to protect their host. Even if that host is me, even if I did steal them from their owner. I have to live on for them to live on, too. I'm not convinced that either of us should live on, though. If Kyelin doesn't get to live, then why do I?

Those memories won't leave my head, his laughter echoing in my ears. He had laughed with me that way, had loved me the way he loved those animals. I choke up when I realize that Prince Zaeden doesn't know about them, that they may be dead because of me, too. How many deaths will I be responsible for? All because I couldn't listen. He should still be here, should still be laughing with me. He would be if I had just agreed to stay by his side always, even if it meant no one else would know. I should have never gone to that room, should have never let my anger get in the way of us. I should have done anything for him, just like I had agreed to in the very beginning. And how can I help him now? How can I help anyone? *I can't.* The only thing I can do now is accept my fate, to get everyone out of my clutches. Without me here, my sister will be safe.

I'll make sure she is safe and that she always will be.

I remember that last night with him, dancing underneath a full moon on a high I didn't want to come down from. I remember Kyelin pulling me into the depths of that shallow pool, hands roaming my body and lips going dangerously low. I remember the night I let myself go completely and allowed him to have every part of me. Parts I had refused to give anyone before him.

I ripped a life full of that pleasure away from us.

I ripped a life destined for greatness out of this world.

The flames within me sizzle, agreeing with my worst thoughts. I definitely shouldn't be here, existing without him. Why should I live when he doesn't? When Dove doesn't? My only Divine friend had been on top of me, eyes empty and gone. And *I* did that to her. She had been a sympathizer. She could have been a great ally, could have been my greatest tool in helping the other Courts see reason. And now? Now she is gone.

I fall to the ground with a sudden urgency, my legs too heavy to carry on. My body shakes in despair, ugly tears still streaming down my face.

Irissa will be safe here. Protected. She doesn't need me anymore. I did the hard part in getting us here, away from the Lunar Royals. She will be even safer without me. All I do is cause pain and suffering. I'm a Divine Slayer, and I have no way of controlling the murderer inside of me. I have no way of holding back, even with those who matter the most. There is only one way to stop myself. Only one way to make sure I never hurt anyone ever again.

I crawl forward, hiccuping as I realize where I am. I traveled down those long corridors, ran up and up and up the stairs. All of which led me to this spot on the roof, peering over the edge of the castle to look down upon the city that encompasses this place. It must be fate intervening, proving that I was right.

I have to die.

I can hardly breathe as I lean forward, hardly comprehending how far the fall truly is. Does it matter? As long as I am gone, as long as I can escape this world, everyone here will be safe from me. Irissa will never be used as leverage for anyone ever again. Another life will not be stripped from this world. I don't know how many lives are at stake, how many powers I can hold. I don't want to find out. Anyone who comes in contact with me is in danger.

I stand on surprisingly steady knees, my mind made up. My flames soar up in an attempt to calm me, caressing me with a gentleness they had never shown. But it's too late. I know what they are and what they can do. They start flashing memories again, but this time they aren't of Kyelin. Now it's memories of my precious sister, the ones they have witnessed while within me. But I don't pay any mind to their tricks. This has to happen.

I have to die.

That step over the edge is like nothing I have ever felt before. I thought it might be like flying, similar to the familiar feeling of soaring through the sky, but it isn't. It's a plummet, hard and fast and exhilarating. It's liberating knowing that I got to choose how I died and that I was able to find peace with myself before death. It is calming and relaxing, as though there is nothing and no one to hold me back. And there isn't. Because I am aiming straight for the unforgiving ground below me, and there is no convincing me to go back.

"Celeste? Where—oh shit. Shit, shit, shit!" I don't acknowledge the panic in that drawling voice, don't call out to greet it. I don't care how he found me or what led him to this moment. Maybe my flames left a little crumb trail, tiny little scorch marks that showed him exactly where I went. Maybe he guessed. Maybe he was following close behind the whole time. None of it matters; I'm already halfway down. I'm already too far gone.

I feel my body twisting in the air as a gust of wind slaps me, my back now facing the ground. I can see Edge, fear and misery hiding in his gaze. In mere seconds that hopeless expression changes. His jaw ticks, his eye hardens, and determination sets in.

I try to smile at him and convey in my calm gaze that it is okay even though it isn't. But he isn't looking at me anymore. He's staring at his hands as they begin to move, his body straining as his powers are evoked. My smile quickly fades.

"No!" I try to shout as I reach up, but I know he can't hear me over the roar of flames that are still encasing me.

Suddenly shadows are creeping up on me, sweeping me into their arms. I screech as the darkness swallows me and I fall straight through a black hole. My flames extinguish inside the portal, disappearing under the fear of the shadows taking them, too.

I was meant to be a fallen star, meant to die the same death as one. Instead, I have been placed back into the sky, never to find freedom from my constellation.

"Hello, Little Flame." I feel his arms around me before I hear his voice. I had fallen directly into his grasp, fallen straight down from the sky I had just leaped from. I don't struggle or try to fight my way out. What's the point? I have no control over my powers. There's no way I can fight him. And I'm certainly not going to rip his powers out of his body and kill him just to get away from this moment. It sickens me that I can just *do that.*

"Why?" I struggle to get the one word out, avoiding his gaze.

"You're important, Celeste. Whether you realize it or not. Important enough for me to damn near drain myself, apparently."

"I'm a killer," I choke on the words, laughing unkindly as I lie limply in his arms. "The Divine Slayer. I deserve to die; it's the only way to keep everyone safe."

"We can teach you control, Celeste." He sounds so calm, so sure.

"Control over my soul-sucking abilities?" I spit out, shaking my head in exasperation. My limp, dirty hair shakes with me, tickling my face.

"Please listen to me. We can fix this." The tone of his voice makes me pause, the fear in his singular steel eye real. But why? Why am I so important? Why was I chosen to have this horrible ability? Why did I have to be a killer? Why did I never know?

Holding back a helpless sob, I voice these questions the best way I can. "Why me?"

"I don't know, Celeste, but you can change everything." I've never heard him so serious and sincere. He always hisses out every word, tending to be sarcastic and snarly. This time, he means his words. He *really* thinks I am special.

"I don't know if I can learn," I whisper, shutting my eyes tightly and leaning into him unwittingly as I curl up. I don't want him to be disappointed, and I don't want to see his expression when he realizes I'm *not* special.

Gently, Edge drops down to his knees. He places me on the ground, allowing me to curl my knees underneath me, too. I still avoid his gaze, my head dropping as my hair curtains around my embarrassed flush.

"I didn't think I could learn, either," he admits softly, tucking my hair behind my ears. I turn my head away, unable to bear the fierceness of this moment. But Edge grips my chin with two fingers, forcing my head to turn back to his. I swallow as I stare at him, my eyes roaming down to his lips as he speaks again. "Our powers are more than most individuals can handle, but our bodies were built to hold this power. You can learn, Celeste. If I can manage to keep the darkness at bay, then you can, too."

I hiss out weakly, "I wasn't born Divine. Your body was prepared: mine never was. This power is more than I can handle. If I don't die now, I'll just end up taking in even more. Can't you see that? It's better this way."

"You have always been Divine, Celeste. You have always been meant for this."

"I don't look like the Divine. I don't act like them. I was never treated like one of them." I try to brush his words off, a chill running down my spine. I know, deep inside, that there is a reason my powers have been blocked off for so long. That it is highly plausible I *was* born Divine. I just can't think of those possibilities, about who blocked them or why. I *can't* right now.

"You, Little Star, are a completely different version of a Divine." It isn't a reassurance that I am beautiful or that I do fit in with the Divine—it's a reassurance that I am who I am, and I don't have to be like the other Divine to be beautiful or worthy of power. The words stop my heart, my lungs, and my brain as my eyes lift back up to meet his. What is he doing to me?

"No." It's the only word I can muster, the only word that comes to my mind.

"Let me take you back inside. I can explain more, but I don't want you out here any longer. Not if you are just going to try and hurt yourself again." I ignore the bitterness in his tone, the caring nature in his voice gone. But the thought of being away from the one creature in this world who may understand me, of having only myself for comfort, is displeasing.

"I won't hurt myself," I say calmly. With a shrug, he sits back on his heels and begins the process of stretching out his long limbs. I try not to lean on him for support as I shift to move beside him, but I am still weak and wobbly. He holds out his arm without question, though I choose to ignore the evil grin he sends my way as I pull myself over to his side.

"I'm sorry. I don't—I don't know why I did that." It seems silly, now, to jump off a roof without a second thought. I don't still want to be with Kyelin. I would hate myself if I was stuck in that situation right now. I don't know why I was ever doubting my decision to dump him. And Dove *did* try to kill me. I don't know what happened or how my brain slipped up so astronomically.

I almost died.

"You had a panic attack." He shrugs like it's no big deal.

"No. No, I've had those before. This was…"

"A freakout? A slip of sanity? A dip into madness? Yeah, that's a panic attack. They come in different forms, some way more intense than others. Those flames may have influenced the severity of it, though. Kyelin's essence is still in there, after all, and I'm sure he was very upset with you in those final moments."

"Oh." I frown, tapping my fingers on the ground. "Well—"

"Your father was a Divine."

"That's what you choose to start with?" I stutter out, eyes wide. He can't just interrupt me with a statement like *that.*

"We are unsure of his identity," he continues without looking at me. "But your mother confirmed it. Are you really surprised? Look at yourself. Your sister. You had to get it from somewhere. Powers that strong aren't random mutations, despite what the Lunars told you."

"You're wrong." I shake my head, refusing to believe it. "My egotistical mother would have told me."

"Would she now?" His voice is light, not a hint of questioning within it. He isn't acknowledging my denial.

I snap, "Yes."

"You grew up Undivine, yeah?"

"Obviously."

"And how was that life?"

"It could have been better." My voice turns cold at the direction this conversation is heading.

"And how do you think life as a Divine would have been?"

"Privileged." That is the first word that comes to mind, but many more follow.

"Really? What an interesting assumption." The drawling voice makes it seem like he thinks the exact opposite. I wouldn't be surprised if that was the case. Most Undivine think poorly of the Divine and vice versa—it's to be expected.

"Where is this going?"

"Have you seen Silvi's scar? My own? Have you seen the scars of the Divine in your own Court, Cerina Celeste?"

"Don't call me that. I don't go by Cerina anymore." My father picked out my name, and it's too hard to hear it most days. Celeste was my mother's choice, a safer name to go by. She refused to tell us his last name because of some bullshit lie about hiding from his debt collectors, and I refused to go by hers. Celeste is all I have left.

Reading my mind, Edge says, "Because it's associated with your father, yeah? He chose it for you. And that's why you don't have a last name, isn't it? Because your mother wouldn't give his to you?"

"I'm sure the Divine here are much worse off than those at the Lunar Court," I say, desperately trying to change the subject.

"Oh? Do you believe so?"

"Are you trying to say that my mother didn't tell me about my father because of the devious Divine in our Court? If so, that's outrageous. She wants—"

"Your mother is irrelevant when it came to that decision. She told me so when I tortured the information out of her."

He grins at the surprised look I send his way, nodding in confirmation. "Your father was the one who wanted you hidden. By the time he died, it was too late for you to emerge into the Divine world without too many questions. But you made sure the whole world would see you, didn't you? You made sure we would never turn our eyes away again." His voice turns low and raspy, that cold gaze burning a hole into me.

"I didn't know I was Divine," I breathe, head spinning. Is it true? I hardly remember my father, but I know how much my mother, Urona, loved him. I know he loved her just as equally. His death is what tore her apart and sent her on the spiraling path that turned her into the evil witch she is now.

"But you do now, don't you?"

I ignore yet another question, saying, "They were Soul Divine. She would have done anything for him, and him for her. Sometimes I think she resents us because he might have loved us more than her."

"Soul Divines are an interesting topic. Are you a believer?" He raises a single eyebrow, his eye patch shifting slightly.

"Sometimes."

"Did you believe Kyelin to be your Divine?"

"I don't know." I twist my hands uncomfortably, shaking my head roughly. "I loved him." *I think.*

"Did you?"

"Yes! And I'm sick of you telling me that I didn't!" I stand in anger, flames rising around me. Edge casually leans away, smirking.

"And you still killed him." The nonchalance angers me beyond belief. I hadn't *meant* to kill him. Why did no one understand that?

"Would you like to see how I did it?" I could have become Death incarnate at this moment, just as I accused Zaeden of being in the moment I killed his brother. In a fury, I could have taken Edge's life and every bit of power hiding inside that muscular body. The thought makes me sick, giving me pause.

I'm terrified of what I am becoming.

"You won't kill me, Celeste." He looks up at me inquisitively, as though I am an interesting puzzle he can't wait to solve.

"How do you know?"

"You just tried to throw yourself off a building because of how guilty you feel for killing other people. You won't do that to yourself again."

"I didn't mean to kill him," I say, falling back to the ground and slumping over weakly.

"But you didn't love him, either."

"I don't know. Maybe not. He did kind of suck in bed. It would have been horrible to spend a life having sex that bad," I laugh, body stiffening as soon as the words leave my mouth. A blush rises to my cheeks as I realize it's not my sister I am talking to, but a man. A prince.

"Ah, the curse of marrying an inexperienced man." He smirks, patting my thigh empathically.

"Maybe I could have trained him." I sniff, ignoring his touch successfully.

"Didn't you guys spend a whole ceremony night together? Not a single moment of that night was *good?*"

"Well, I mean, I was *really* high, in my defense. So, at the time, all of it was good. But in the morning..." I wince, shaking my head. "I realized it was all sloppy and rushed."

"I would have wanted you to kill me, too, if that's how you went around talking about *my* bedroom skills." He bursts out in laughter, body shaking with the force of it. It's the first time I've heard anything joyous leave his lips, and the noise makes my heart leap in an unfamiliar way.

"Just being honest." I blush, turning away. I definitely shouldn't have said any of that to *Edge.*

"So, just to clarify, you didn't kill him because he was bad at sex?"

"No!" I hiss, slapping his arm. "I told you, I didn't mean to kill anyone. And you're right: I'm not going to do that to myself again."

"If we are being honest with one another right now, that puts me in quite a horrible situation."

"Why? You want me to kill you?" It's my turn to raise an eyebrow now. I watch as he turns away, refusing to look into my eyes. He begins to scoop up some discarded rings I hadn't noticed before. When had he dropped them? It had to have been before he saved me. But how had he dropped *all* of them? Had he thrown them down? And if so, *why?*

"No," he chuckles humorously, meticulously sliding each ring down his thick fingers. "I want you to kill *for* me."

CHAPTER 7

Celeste

I sputter out, "Absolutely not. I don't understand—"

"Then shut up and listen." He is no longer calm and understanding, his voice switching to the cold calculation I'm accustomed to.

"How dare you talk to me that way?" I hadn't meant to say it, but it came out anyway.

"Do you believe yourself to be so entitled that you can question a prince? You are one of my subjects now. I can and *will* speak to you however I wish."

"You are such an asshole," I hiss, glaring at the annoyingly handsome man. My eyes trail over the sharp edges of his square face, past the round cheekbones, and straight to the full lips. I ignore the fluttering nerves in my stomach and rip my gaze away, grinding out, "And I am *not* your subject."

"Oh? Then who do you belong to, hmm? The Lunar Court?" He scoffs, dismissing my futile objections easily.

Flames crackle at my fingertips, little sparks that aren't meant to harm shooting out. "I don't belong to anyone."

"*You belong to me.*" His sulking shadows encircle me as he leans forward, snarling the statement so harshly that spit flies from his mouth. His face is only inches away now, his lips pressed into a thin line. Once again I think of something Prince Zaeden said, a memory surfacing from when I first discovered my powers over four months ago.

"You belong to me now, Celeste. My brother and I have claimed you and sworn to protect you. We didn't do that lightly. Your enemies are mine."

It's something I should have noticed in the beginning—his possessiveness. Maybe then I would have expected the beast inside the man. Is this the moment I discover Edge's true colors? Is this where the cruelty Ryleigh raved about shows up?

"I—what—no!" I am unsure what to say or how to escape this situation.

"You owe me, Little Flame. I am your savior. It seems I have been twice now. So, until those life favors are repaid, I own you." His words leave me shaking, rattling me down to my very core. I will not be owned, not by Kyelin, not by Prince Zaeden, and not by *him*.

"I'm tired of Divine like you trying to control me. I will *not* be controlled. Do you want a rematch of our battle to discover how loud that truth rings?" My hands erupt into curling flames, my new power obeying for the first time since obtaining it. I try not to express my surprise.

"Settle down, Little Flame. I have a proposal for you. One you won't be able to refuse." Edge taps his fingers on the ground in annoyance, hardly sparing my flames a glance. I'm sick of that nickname, *Little Flame*. It sends a bubbling anger down my throat that gives me indigestion. I much prefer the affectionate *Little Star* from earlier. That, at least, sounded kind when leaving his lips.

I bite out, "Is that so?"

"Oh, yes. Do you remember darling Zae?"

"How could I forget that evil man after everything he did to me?"

"Poor princess," he soothes mockingly. "I heard you reveled in his attention and boldly stated how you eagerly awaited that attention. I heard that they planned on sharing you like a delicious meal. Maybe Zaeden would have been better in bed than the twin you mistakenly chose instead."

"That was when I was desperate to win *and* before I fell in love. Before I realized who he really was. And I told them both I never would have let them pass me around like that! That's what got Kyelin killed. Maybe I will kill you, after all, since you seem to think it's okay to speak to me so maliciously." Edge dares to blink in surprise, but the emotion is gone in seconds. The glint in his eye returns hastily.

"And who is he?"

"More like *what* is he—a monster." I hope my hatred for Prince Zaeden wins me some points in this argument.

"Good. I'm glad we can see eye to eye." He stands and circles me like a predator on the hunt, his tall stature leaning over me. I abruptly pull myself up, too, not daring to let my guard down or extinguish the flames.

Edge saved me, but at what cost? "What do you want, Edge?"

"I want you on your knees, professing your loyalty to me." Something sinks into the pit of my stomach, my mind malfunctioning. His voice had turned sultry and dark as if trying to seduce me with his villainy.

"Oh, is that all?" I take a step back, attempting to escape his suffocating presence. But he's pressing in on me in a heartbeat, unbothered by the flames. His body pushes flush against mine as a hand hits my lower back, his head bending forward so his lips touch my ear.

"I want Zaeden dead, and I want you to be the one who kills him."

My heart doesn't just skip a few beats: it stops entirely. "As tempting as that sounds, I can't." I can't think with him breathing down my neck, can't see reason beyond his closeness. I try to shove him away, but he only pulls me into him even harder until my hands are trapped between our bodies.

"I want you to suck every bit of that power out of his body and to destroy every ounce of his being. Then I want you to work for my Court. I want to put you in his place so you can rule on my behalf."

This is madness. Complete and utter madness. "You ask too much."

"Do I?"

"I just—I tried to—"

"Yes, and?"

"And you expect to be able to flip a switch in my mind? For me to suddenly be okay with killing someone? Not just killing, might I add, but taking the very essence of their life right out of their body?" This isn't a fun little game where I can go around taking whatever powers I want. This is *murder*. The worst kind of murder. And it will have very serious consequences.

"Do you need some motivation? Have you forgotten whose Court your sister belongs to now?" he hisses, lips touching my ear once more.

My throat closes up at the threat. This man is not the same one who just comforted me, nor the same one who spoke so kindly and laughed so heartily. This was the version of him I had been told to fear. "No. You wouldn't. You went through a lot of trouble to bring us here. You wouldn't just kill her." I let my voice drop an octave, attempting to sound deadly despite my shaking and weak body betraying me.

"I went through a lot of trouble for *you*, dear. Not your sister."

"But what about Ryleigh? About her—organization." I quickly stumble over the words, not wanting to mention the Undivine Army aloud.

"Are you foolish enough to believe they don't know about this conversation right now? That they aren't fully on board with my plan? That they won't do whatever it takes to meet their goals?"

"What does killing Prince Zaeden have to do with destroying the mindsets of the Divine?" My throat is not only closing but tightening now, fear racing through my mind and body. I didn't know that they would be okay with killing innocent people like my sister. I didn't know that they would be willing to go as far as it takes. I know I agreed to be part of their schemes, but we agreed on no killing. *They know I can't do this.*

"We don't want to destroy their mindsets, Little Flame. We want to destroy their system."

I choke out, "No. That's too much chaos. Every Court would fall apart—" Ryleigh told me this wasn't going to happen; they just wanted things to change for the Undivine. She didn't say they were going to uproot the entire system. The system is unfair, sure, but it's what we rely on. Mass destruction and casualties would be what this results in. How many more lies has Ryleigh told me? How many more secrets is she still keeping? Maybe I shouldn't have been so relieved to see her, after all.

"Not if they have a good ruler." His grin sends a chill down my spine and leaves me questioning all of the things I did just because Ryleigh told me to.

"That's why you want me to be one of them."

"Yes." Somehow, he presses in even closer, every inch of me pressed into every inch of him. "We know how powerful you are and how powerful you can be. With a little guidance, you can be wonderful, Celeste. Can't you see it?"

He is a madman. Truly. "You're mad," I speak my thoughts aloud, even though I'm sure he heard them.

"Maybe so." He chuckles, tracing a finger down my cheek and marking an unknown pattern across my freckles. "But is it really that crazy to believe a world as merciless as this one can change?"

I shove at his chest, shouting angrily, "I wanted change! I was going to have it! And then it was ripped out of my hands before I could even catch a glimmer of it. I will not sit here and let you dangle that in front of me again. I will not allow you to give me *hope*!"

"I'm not dangling," he snarls, grabbing my shoulders and squeezing. "We will have it—it *will* happen. All we need to do is push, Celeste! A push and it will be ours."

I hiss, "I already gave a push. And look what it did to me."

"Then we will find another way." His breathing has become sporadic, a spark lit behind that steel-blue eye. "Please, Celeste. We need you to make this work. *I* need you."

"I'm nothing. A nobody. You don't need me. You're better off without me; everyone is."

"Even now you don't realize what you are. You would be dead if you were anything less than extraordinary."

I close my eyes so I don't have to see his admiration as I repeat, "I am nothing."

"You are *everything*. *You* are what the Courts will fight over. *You* are a weapon the Divine will seek to neutralize. *You* are a new beginning for the Undivine. *You* are the hope for a horrendous, calculated world. *You* will be the light in my dark, dark world." Edge has become nothing more than a pleading little boy, begging for all of the things he cannot have. It's enough to make me consider his proposal, enough to convince me that there *is* hope.

"I will not be someone's property," I whisper finally, opening my eyes once more. "I will not obey anyone other than myself."

"I can work with that."

"Can you? Because it sounds to me like this could be a fatal flaw in your plans."

"I was trying to scare you into agreeing," he admits after a pregnant pause. "I'm sorry."

"I won't bow to you."

"I don't expect you to."

"And I won't get on my knees."

"We can discuss that later."

"And—"

"Little Flame," he stops me with a grin. "Enough of this. What are your terms?" It's obvious that I am caving, despite the thing inside of me screaming not to. Despite the guilt gnawing at my bones.

"I won't kill anyone unless it is absolutely necessary. As in, life-or-death situations only. I don't like using my true powers and I plan on doing that as *little* as possible."

"You won't kill anyone *except* Zaeden," he says pointedly. "Term accepted with that exception. Next."

"I want you to swear on your life that you will keep my sister safe. That no harm will come to her by your Court's hands while we reside here."

"I swear it." It looks like it pains him to do so, but it doesn't matter. The words have been spoken: He is bound to them if he is superstitious in the slightest.

"I want to be in the loop on everything. I want a choice in all of the decisions. I will not be left out of any conversations."

"That will take some—"

"I don't care what it takes. Make it happen," I hiss, flames roaring around me. He tenses only slightly at the sight of them, grabbing the bridge of his nose and pinching.

"Fine. Anything else, dear?"

I look away, not wanting him to see how much his silly nicknames affect me. "I want you to help me decode my past. I want to know who my father really was. I want to know how I came to be a Divine, and why no one bothered to tell me my whole life. I want to know why my powers never emerged before."

"That's a dangerous road you are heading down," he says slowly, questioning me.

"I've already become unraveled, Edge. I'm beaten down and broken. What is a little more damage, really?"

"I agree to your terms. In exchange, you will help the Undivine Army with future missions to destroy the Divine system. You will rule over the Lunar Court once we succeed.

You will be advised by our team. And you will not betray us. We will get all of this in writing, too, of course. The punishment for breaking any of these terms without a mutual agreement is death. For either of us. For both of us."

"I agree to your terms." The words are binding. I feel them slide up my throat and over my tongue, disappearing into the air.

"Good girl." I don't want to admit how those two little words make me feel. "Now the fun begins."

I feel self-conscious as Edge sweeps me through his home, shouting instructions at the maids who pass. My old, dirty, tattered dress has hardly made it through the fight in the woods. I have been wearing it for about a month now with little to no chance of washing it on the road. It had once been beautiful, breathtaking. Now, it is something that should have never entered a castle as pristine as this one.

Edge barks, "Someone draw up a bath! And for goddess's sake, find this woman something better to wear. Make sure it is fit for this Court; I want her to look like she was born and raised here." Maids scurry off, rattled by their prince.

"And if I wanted Lunar Court attire?"

"Go back to the Lunar Court, if that's what you want."

I scoff, allowing him to lead me on. We stop on the third floor, striding down the long, luxurious hallway. Beautiful artwork adorns the taupe walls, paintings of people and buildings flashing across my vision. Each one tells a different story, describing a different life. The stone floors are a pristine white, polished, and glistening underneath the candelabras. The curtains are thick and gorgeous, with swirling patterns covering the navy fabric.

Edge disrupts my observation as he stops me at the fifth door on the right, his shadows slipping up and pushing the door open without the use of his hands. I can't help but gape in surprise; I haven't seen him use his powers so freely.

"Where—"

He interrupts, saying, "Thank the goddesses those girls listened. Get in the bath." He shoves me toward what I assume is the bathing room, staring at me pointedly.

"I'm not getting undressed in front of you," I snap, shifting uncomfortably as I glance around the room.

The walls are the same navy color as the curtains outside, the trim a blinding white. The floors in here are carpeted, the same taupe as the walls in the hall. The curtains are of similar style and shape, but white. The bed is large, sitting against the wall on the right. It has a white comforter and white pillows, matching the color theme that seems to be recurrent on this floor. There are two side tables and a vanity against the other wall, a vanity which is covered in a variety of products. I swallow as I take it all in, accustomed to this level of luxury because of my recent stay at the Lunar Court palace. But, after months on the road in the same worn dress and no access to soap, I feel so...relieved.

"Then do it behind me. I don't care. I just need to make sure you are presentable in the next hour. Do you understand?"

"No way! I am not letting you watch me take a bath! I know you think very highly of yourself, but I do not find myself wishing to be naked with you—"

"Let me, brother," a soft voice says from the doorway, replacing the snarling, velvety one I had been arguing with.

I glance over at the newly arrived Royal, saying, "Valaine, I don't want to be undressed in front of you, either."

"I understand." She smiles sweetly, reassuringly. "Don't worry about that. I will stay in this room, okay? Edge is going to go prepare for our meeting, aren't you, Edge?"

"As you wish," he grounds out, glaring at me one last time before leaving. I watch after him hopelessly, my mind reeling.

"You don't like him?" Valaine questions, tilting her head curiously.

"I don't understand him. He is just..."

"Cold one minute and hot the next?" she suggests helpfully.

"Yes. Exactly that."

"It's an exterior thing." She shrugs, gesturing for me to enter the bath.

I don't say anything in response, turning around to do as told. Truthfully, I *want* a hot bath. Desperately. I want to sit for hours in the water, long past the point of cold. I want to rest my weary limbs and allow myself a moment to comprehend the past few hours. To think without jumping into things. But as enjoyable as that would be, I can't sit and let my worries sink in the drain. I am expected to be presentable in an hour, apparently, which is a feat I'm sure the maids are not looking forward to.

I jump when a familiar woman speaks from behind Valaine. "Come, Les. Let's get you looking back to normal. I'll multitask by catching you up on the details here." I sag in relief, allowing Ryleigh to help me undress and sink into the large tub.

"Alright, out with whatever secrets you are holding now, bitch," I mutter, sending her an aggravated scowl.

"They aren't *my* secrets, for your information." She scowls back, beginning to rub my skin with harsh rags. I know she is adding extra pressure to annoy me, but I hold in my displeasure. Most of my wounds are healed, so it doesn't hurt all that much. "I know you probably don't want to trust me right now. I wouldn't trust me, either. But I did what I had to. Even if it meant hiding things from you."

"Whatever." I splash the water as I jump slightly, hissing as she scrapes against a sore spot on my leg. With a bitter tone, I add, "*Bitch.*"

"Don't disrespect me you little shit," she hisses back, slapping me on the back of the head. I only glare, rubbing at the spot irritably. "Now, do you want to be caught up or not?"

"I do," I seethe, though part of me wants to shake in laughter. This is the Ryleigh I know, the familiarity I seek. When she acts like this, I can pretend the rest didn't happen. We can chatter and curse at one another like we always did before. We can scream and yell and never be angry with one another. *I missed this.*

"Well, obviously, the Royals here are in cahoots with the Undivine Army. Well, everyone but King Mourner. As far as he knows, Edge rescued you so that you can be a weapon for him. You keep it that way, you hear me? Don't go spouting off some shit about saving the world. He knows you are here and knows you were near death, but he also knows that Edge went to great lengths to keep you due to your powers. Plus, it pisses Zaeden off. So that's the story and *you stick to it.*"

I can only nod as the sweet-smelling soap invades my nostrils, digging into my skin with each swipe of the rag. Ryleigh is very thorough, pausing her debrief to make sure not an ounce of dirt or blood is in sight. Then she begins washing my hair, fingers massaging deep into my scalp as the soap settles in. It's all over much too quickly, and I am being pushed back into the main room with nothing but a towel on.

"Your goal in this meeting is to convince the king you hate the Lunars. That you will do anything if it means they are put down because of it. That's the king's goal. Silvi is a means to an end—a false alliance. He doesn't know about her involvement. He thinks she works for him, too, and that she's going to destroy them from the inside out while providing him with all the juicy information he needs to help. Then, once time had passed, he was going to rule through her. Do you understand?" I nod, swallowing hard. Double spies and double lies.

Ryleigh shoves me down into a chair, a large mirror propped against the wall in front of me. I'm able to watch each stroke of the brush as it is guided through my hair, the shortness a reminder of who Edge really is behind this hero facade. I clench my fists as I remember the way he fought me so effortlessly, at the way he took control of the situation so quickly. I can still hear the sound of that finger falling to the floor, the discarded digit gone but not forgotten. I wince as I turn away from my reflection in silence, ashamed.

"I don't know how you are going to fix this." I gesture at my limp, wet hair. I can feel Ryleigh scrunching it, the wild curls reappearing with a vengeance.

"Leave it. It's beautiful the way it is." I scoff at Valaine's suggestion, shaking my head in disagreement.

"Please. Short hair looks good on you. It doesn't work for *me*."

"It's beautiful," she repeats sternly.

"Oh? Your brother must have an eye for such things then, hmm?" I meet her eyes through the mirror, daring her to defend him.

"Leave it," is all she says. Though I am itching for a fight, Valaine doesn't give it to me. Instead, she begins painting my face. I close my eyes once more, taking a deep breath. I don't want to look at myself because *this* is the face of a Divine. The face of a supposed-to-be-princess. Of a Divine Slayer.

Ryleigh purrs, "Perfect. You look positively deadly. Ah. Just in time. Hand me that!" I glance over as the door opens, watching a frightened maid scurry over. She passes an outfit over to Ryleigh, flinching when their hands touch. Great—even the maids *here* are scared of the witch behind me.

Ryleigh holds up the outfit, beaming. "Ta-da!" I can't help but inhale sharply at the sight of it.

It's almost the color of blood, the same color that adorns the Solar flags. Gold lace dances across the sleeves, adorned with a gorgeous, flowery pattern. The top seems short, but on someone my height, it will probably land around my belly button. The pants have a golden hem, the same lacy pattern flowing across. The fabric is light and flowing, giving off the impression of a dress. But it isn't, and I'm amazed that *I* get to wear something so bold.

"I was told you prefer pants?" Valaine questions with a satisfied smile. I nod in agreement, slipping from my chair in a rush.

"Turn around, Val." Ryleigh swats at the princess, nodding at me once her back is turned. I drop my towel, stepping into the pants she holds before me. They are a near-perfect fit. Once the top has slipped down my chest, I realize it, too, is close to perfection. Ryleigh must have sent my measurements ahead, but I've lost weight after traveling so long.

I don't turn around, even though I know I must look so different. I just can't bear to see the person waiting in the mirror, can't stand the selfish and hateful Divine I have become. I've chosen to stay, chosen to kill. Now I must live with that choice and all of the repercussions that come with it. This meeting is one of them.

"Let's go." Valaine grins, looping her arm through mine. I allow this with a shuttering breath, shaking my head to release all of the self-depreciation within my thoughts. I have to become that horrible, selfish Divine if I want to survive this place. If I want Irissa to survive. If I want to make a difference in this world.

So, I let the princess of the Solar Court lead me to her father. I let her lead me to a meeting I dread within the deepest part of my gut.

CHAPTER 8

Celeste

"A re you ready?"

"No," I scoff, straightening. Valaine laughs softly, a warm glint in her murky blue eyes.

'That's too bad."

I open my mouth to give her a not-meant-for-princess' s-ears retort, but the creaking of doors interrupts me. A soldier had flung open the set of giant, wooden doors in front of us, the large symbol of the Solar Court burned into their centers. The image of a detailed sun stares at me, a thick

'Z' wearing a crown nestled in its center. It is similar to my birth Court's symbol but also vastly different.

Valaine hooks her arm through mine and pulls me out of my thoughts, walking forward with a dignity I no longer possess. I try to appear unbothered, my eyes roaming the long table before us in a calculating sweep. There is a total of twelve chairs around the opaque oval table, and each one is tall and looming with a blood-red fabric coating the cushions. *My dress is going to blend right in* I think bitterly. My gaze briefly turns to the walls, covered in a patterned wallpaper with black lines cracking through like streaks of lightning. There isn't a single window or another door. My exit strategy if things go wrong? Run like a goddess herself has come down to smite me.

I find myself staring at the man seated at the head of the table, noting the self-righteousness shining in his eyes and displayed across his puffed-out chest. His blonde hair and light skin are a stark contrast to his wife and children's features, chestnut eyes cold and unloving. His golden crown shines under the light of the large chandelier above us, a single ruby glistening at the tallest peak.

This is Horace Zorander: the Solar Court King.

"Stepfather," Valaine gushes, gracing him with a beautiful smile as she bows deeply. I don't follow suit, not bothering to turn away from that harsh gaze.

"Bow." His voice is deep and cool, dripping with authority.

I see a soldier flinch out of the corner of my eyes, but I refuse to do so. "I answer to your stepson, not *you*."

"Men?"

All it takes is a snap of those Royal fingers.

I'm ripped away from Valaine's side, her cries of protest futile. Edge appears behind us, his drawling voice commanding the nonsense to end. Unlike me, the soldiers *do* answer to this king. Above all others, it is *he* who controls them.

I'm shoved to my knees, arms held painfully behind my back at an odd angle as my chin sags to my chest. A foot is shoved into the center of my spine, a snarl emitting from the soldier as he pushes me down. I grit my teeth, breathing harshly as my nose touches the floor.

My powers awaken, flames alighting and shadows crackling into existence. I spit out, "How charming. Do you really need *three* soldiers to hold a little woman like me down?" I can feel their grips loosen as my power continues to outrage, their fear evident in the way they try to distance themselves while still gripping me.

"A dangerous, deadly, little woman," King Zorander retorts. I hear another snap and I'm being yanked up once more, rough hands shoving me into the seat at the foot of the table.

"My reputation precedes me," I purr, heart pounding in my chest. I meet his eyes again, hatred pooling within me. I hate these soldiers, hate this king, and hate the damn Solar Court in its entirety.

"That it does." A hearty chuckle sounds from the left of King Zorander, and I turn my head slightly to take in the shining silver hair and distinct blue eyes.

"Don't speak unless spoken to, Merkelly," he mutters, waving his hand dismissively at his advisor. This is Silvi's father, the one she thinks so highly of. I look away quickly, trying not to think about his daughter. About her betrayal and what that could mean for him and his place in this Court.

"Of course, Your Majesty." His eyes are kind as he continues to watch me, the hint of a smile playing on his lips.

"You should be appreciative of my kindness, Celeste. Bowing to me is only a token of your respect."

"You should be appreciative of my powers and the things I am offering you and your Court." I don't back down from the deathly glare. Despite the thing screaming inside of me to cower, I will not do so. I told myself the whole month it took to get here that I wouldn't bow for anyone, and I won't. My resolve to be cruel faded quickly—it's just not who I am and I can't do it. But I *can* be defiant and an utter pain in their asses.

"That's enough." Edge is rubbing the bridge of his nose again, glaring at me from the right side of his stepfather. Valaine sits next to him, the remaining seats empty.

I tilt my head, quietly asking, "Is it?"

"Stepfather—" Edge starts, sensing the change of energy before me.

"What have I told you, boy? It's King Zorander to you!" His giant fists bang on the table, rattling the cups and dinnerware before us. Edge only rolls his eyes, fingers dancing in annoyance underneath the table.

"King Zorander," he amends, pursing his lips. "Celeste will be of great use to us. You will not treat her like an Undivine while she is in our employment."

"Who are *you* to tell *me* what to do—" King Zorander's face is red, teeth grinding with each word.

"Stepfather," Valaine coos, pouting. "You know Celeste will not work with us otherwise." I notice he doesn't object to *her* calling him "stepfather".

"You will not mistreat her," Edge repeats, each word laced with venom. I suck in a breath at his tone, cheeks blazing in embarrassment. And *maybe* in admiration.

King Zorander glares at his stepdaughter, grinding out, "Continue."

"You know of her abilities."

"Oh, yes. I have heard some wonderful stories." His smile is crooked, eyes glazing as he looks me over once more. I shift in my seat, uncomfortable.

"Good, because I plan on using those abilities to take down the Lunar Court once and for all."

This catches the king's attention. "Oh? Do you think you have a better plan than my own? Please, tell me more."

"I killed Prince Kyelin," I speak before Edge can, lifting my chin despite the disgust that rolls through me. "Among others."

"The Divine Slayer," he says with a light chuckle, still eyeing me appreciatively.

"Yes. A nickname well-deserved," Merkelly chimes in.

"She has agreed to be our weapon," Edge speaks again, taking the king's attention off me.

Valaine's voice is barely a whisper as she says, "And what a weapon she will be."

"A willing weapon? I would hate it if you needed a little...convincing." The way he says it sends a chill down my spine, and I'm convinced he wouldn't hate that at all.

"Willing enough," Edge grinds out, shooting me a harrowing look as he ignores my panicked eyes.

"I hope so. I've heard of your equally beautiful sister, the shape-shifter. Irissa, isn't it? I've heard of her...ailments. Maybe, without her, you would be more willing?"

"If you know so much about her then surely you've heard of her anger problems, too? I know you have heard about the things I do to those who threaten me. Why don't you ask your stepson?" I will not let him threaten my sister's life. Not after everything I've done to get us here.

"There will be no need for Irissa's life to be taken. I believe in Celeste, as should you," Valaine interferes, defending me. The king's face softens when he glances at her, those hard lines disappearing for a few moments. It's clear that favorites have been chosen between the two siblings.

Cold eyes greet mine once more. "How does it feel to kill a prince, Celeste? To kill a Royal?"

I straighten my spine, throwing my shoulders back with an equally cold grin. "Powerful." The truth slips off my tongue easily. I don't mention the pain and guilt that racks my body with every mention of Kyelin, or the heartbreak that I still suffer from because of the deceitful prince.

"Can you control your new power yet?" He relaxes in his seat cockily, already knowing the answer.

I grit my teeth, saying, "I can control it." I don't offer more details, refusing to mention that I've only managed it once.

"Ah, so you aren't having problems getting them to bow down to you?"

"Well, I—"

"Answer honestly." The low growl he emits is a warning.

I pause, pursing my lips before saying, "The flames will not bow to me."

"Of course they won't. Don't you know how they work?"

"No," I admit reluctantly, hating the satisfaction it brings across his features.

"Of course not. You were raised Undivine. They are too stupid to know of such things."

"I told you—" Edge starts, darkness pooling into his palms.

"Just a simple truth." He waves the interruption away dismissively. "Kyelin didn't give his powers to you willingly."

I pause before a single word leaves my lips, "No."

"If they were given willingly, you would have full control at all times. There would be no fighting. The power would be yours, truly and rightfully so. The owner would have accepted defeat and would have ceased to fight you. When powers are taken unwillingly...well, they remember. They remember their master fighting against you, they remember Kyelin not wanting to let them go. So, they're lashing out against you. Strange, isn't it, how they seem to have a mind of their own? Your natural powers must learn how to tame the flames.

"It's supposed to only take a few weeks to wrangle down a lower power, some only days. But the power you possess, dear, is on par with a Royal's, even though you are not one. It is an equal match against the likes of a Royal power like Kyelin's. So, it's going to take much, much longer than usual. They will battle for dominance in your body, and you will win...eventually. An Absorbid always does. But it may take months, as it depends on the person the power was attached to originally. Since Kyelin was so powerful and so unwilling to die, I would go out on a limb and say it will be a very long time indeed."

My mind flashes to my shields, memories of the quickness with which I conquered the new abilities. But who had I stolen them from? And why can't I remember? I had to have killed someone for them, and they must have given them willingly by the end. Had my powers truly been sealed away like Dove had once suggested? Is that why I never knew about them?

"You look shocked. Of course, you would be. Maybe what I say next will sound familiar. As an Absorbid, you take from others. *Constantly.* You may not know, you may feel it slightly, but the Divine you steal from probably won't be aware. It isn't a painful process, and the Divine won't miss that stolen power. It won't harm them. It only becomes harmful when you take too much and it gets to the point of embracing death. Have you ever experienced a power you did not possess?"

"Yes," I admit too quickly. I think of the poison I used to kill Dove—Prince Zaeden's poison. I think of the time I felt

Kyelin's guilt so strongly and of the time I sat in a cell and could sense the minds of those nearby—Silvi's powers. I know I've stolen from Edge, too. I try to think about who else I may have stolen from, but my mind is running too fast. Who will be next? How am I supposed to be around anyone? How can they be okay being around me?

"Those powers are limited. It just depends on how much you take, really. I'm sure you have noticed you no longer possess some of those abilities. This transfer of power happens through touch. Wonderful, is it not? Your powers must have been starved to have made you lose control so deeply. I've been told by my informants that you stated you couldn't stop when you took Kyelin's flames. Oh, yes, you must have been starved indeed to have been unable to break contact." He cackles, clapping his hands in excitement. I don't respond to his gloating, my heart plummeting.

I can never touch anyone ever again.

No one can ever touch me.

"How do you know all of this?" My question is quiet, my voice cracking.

"I did my research." He shrugs, pushing himself up into a standing position. "This was an...interesting meeting, Celeste, but I think I'll leave you to ponder these things for a while. You and my stepson can discuss the so-called plan he has. We will be in touch." He sweeps out of the room in a flourish, leaving me gaping at his empty seat like a fool. Within five minutes of his departure, a group of people begin piling into the room. With a jolt, I realize Irissa is among them. She takes her place beside me, a sad smile on her lips. The previously empty seats around the table are suddenly filled with people I do not recognize, who I am not introduced to before the arguing ensues.

"I think—"

"This was crazy—"

"We should have never—"

"You didn't think to tell her—"

"Her powers are too—"

"We need to act—"

Everyone is trying to voice their opinions at once about the subject at hand: me. My eyes dart from person to person, trying to decipher what they are saying. But I can only make out partial fragments in the sudden chaos, their voices fast and overlapping.

"That's enough!" Edge's voice booms above the others, the authority silencing us all. I see Irissa flinch, her hand reaching out to find mine.

"Thank you, Edge," Ryleigh clears her throat as she stands, hands clasping in front of her as she looks down her nose at us all. "I know you all have your own opinions about how this should go down. But our leaders want this to go as smoothly as possible. The other leaders agree on this. That means Celeste needs to be in the loop for everything, including how her powers work. This meeting was a good thing. No more keeping secrets from her. Though she has said she doesn't want to kill anyone besides Zaeden and doesn't plan on doing so, we have been instructed to begin training her as if she will."

"But—" Silvi's father is the one to speak first, eyes wide in worry.

"But what?" Edge's snarl is enough to make a High Divine cry.

"But she is woefully unprepared." His eyes fall to his lap as he continues, saying, "Did you see her? We could all see how poorly the news affected her. We could all see the guilt and shame creeping up at the mention of the dead prince." Even though I hate to admit it, he's right. I have been trying so hard to hold it together, but my wounds are fresh—there's no good way of hiding that.

"Yes. Which is why she must undergo training. For both her powers and hiding her emotions," Ryleigh insists, eyes raking over the room.

"I will train her." Edge's drawling voice seeps under my skin, shocking me at his quick offer.

"Great." Should I be pleased about Edge volunteering? Or should I be terrified? Either way, I feel nothing other than the wish that Valaine had volunteered instead.

"I will train Irissa." Damn. It seems like Valaine is unavailable, after all. I find myself relieved that she is responsible for my sister, despite wanting her for myself. My sister doesn't need a barbaric Divine like Edge training her to be just like him.

"I need constant eyes on Celeste. I don't trust her not to run away." Shame floods me at Edge's comment, especially since I know the real reason he doesn't want me left to my own devices. His gaze seems to say, "You're welcome for not telling the truth."

"I can help teach you both to control your feelings. My Silvi got her powers directly from me. I can help you both," Merkelly boasts. It's lucky and rare when powers are distributed this way, and much easier on the children. It's probably why Kyelin had so much control—his dad taught him everything he knew. It's just another reason for Zaeden to feel the need to prove himself, to want everything Kyelin had.

I huff at Merkelly in response to his offer, eyes shooting up to the ceiling. Why did I have the two worst teachers in the world? Begrudgingly, I say, "Fine. I accept the help."

"As do I," Irissa bows her head in thanks. Technically, no one was instructed to teach her. They were offering out of kindness. I would probably feel thankful if I were her, too.

"Then it's settled," Ryleigh declares with a grin, coming over to escort me away. I follow her without putting up a fight, watching as Valaine escorts Irissa away.

"Why was I born this way?" I ask once we are truly alone. The long, sweeping hallways offer no solace, no penance.

"You were born to be a savior, Celeste. It's what the goddesses wanted." It's a poor attempt at comforting me.

"I wanted to die for what I did to Kyelin. For what I did to Dove. For what I can do to those who surround me. I can't handle this pain and guilt, Ryleigh." I can't forget that I had tried to kill myself just this morning. That I am supposed to be dead right now. And yet, here I am, playing some part in a game I didn't mean to participate in.

"Dove deserved what she got. She betrayed the Solars. It was retribution."

"What do you mean?" My head snaps to Ryleigh, anger bubbling in me. Dove did *not* deserve to die in the horrific way she did. She did not deserve to meet her end at my hands.

"She was told by Edge himself not to harm you. To let you win that game. But she didn't listen to her prince—she wanted the title of *Royal* for herself. She should have never tried to kill you. You did what you had to. You did what was right." She doesn't seem to understand my shock—I can see that in her confused expression as she watches me. Was this common knowledge to the others? Another secret I had yet to be told?

"She wasn't a Solar Court citizen. She didn't have to listen to another Court's Royal." But even as I say the words, my mind flashes back to the day I met her. She introduced herself as being from the Light Court, but she never mentioned it again. And then, at that last game, the announcer said, "Dove Airess of the Solar Court." I remember it so vividly now, but I hadn't noticed it at the time. Why would I have? I was being sent to fight my friend. I wasn't worried about introductions or Courts.

"Celeste—"

"She was lying from the moment I met her."

"I'm sorry, Celeste. I'm not sure what to tell you. Dove had us all fooled." A single tear slips down my face as I register the betrayal. She had planned to kill me all along and had never really been my friend. Was the Undivine lover she mentioned even real or was she using a fake story for sympathy? Everything I told her, everything she became—did any of it matter? Everyone in that fucking castle lied to me, especially those I considered friends.

Ryleigh led me back to my room, opened the door, and tried to come in with me. I shake my head sadly, wrapping my arms around myself as I deny her entry.

"She was lying from the moment I met her," I repeat, voice cracking as the heartache sets in. "And so were you."

CHAPTER 9
Treacherous Ray

Silvi

"What do you mean she isn't in the Lunar Court?" Zaeden seethes, spinning toward a panting messenger. My whole body tenses as I listen in, eyes flicking over in barely contained interest.

"I just came from the roads, sir. They captured the man who helped them escape. He's barely alive, from what I gather, and the girls aren't with him."

"How did they get to another Court without a driver?" he demands, allowing his poison to rise just above the surface of his skin. Over the past several days it's taken on a neon green color, no longer the vibrant purple we all recognize. Kyelin's death seems to have affected his heart, his mind, *and* his power.

I would pity the man if he weren't such an asshole.

The terrified Low Divine squeaks, "I—I don't know, sir. Please! The man was hardly breathing when we found him, and now he's refusing to speak about them. I swear, this is all I know!"

"Bring him here!" The command is enough to have the terrified Divine quaking in his shoes, his head furiously bobbing in agreement. He glances at King Mourner sitting to Zaeden's right nervously, eyes flicking to me in discomfort.

"He is right behind me, Your Highness! I swear—"

"I've heard enough of this incompetence." Zaeden waves his hand, inky poison darting out for the messenger. He turns to flee, a scream freezing in the back of his throat. He doesn't make it more than two steps before he collapses, his heart stopping entirely.

"Was that necessary, my love?" I pout, shaking my head with a sigh. "That's the third messenger this week."

"He was pathetic, anyway; just another Low Divine," King Mourner mumbles in agreement.

I open my mouth to reply, but the doors are flinging open again. Three soldiers march in, a shackled man waddling between them. His feet are cuffed together and the one arm he still possesses is pinned behind his back, making it almost impossible for him to walk properly. The soldiers are shoving him between each other, snickering as he falls to his knees before us.

The tallest one is the first to speak, saying, "The traitor, Your Majesty."

"What defense do you have prepared for us?" King Mourner asks curiously, seemingly bored. Zaeden, on the other hand, is practically bursting with the fury rising within him. I want to flinch at the harsh display of emotion, the Royal's feelings so strong they break through all my barriers.

"Does it matter? You're going to kill me either way." I don't sense anger, sadness, fear, or regret—only a sense of pride. I almost sagged in relief because I wouldn't have to destroy his mind to keep Celeste and her secrets safe after all.

"Don't talk to your Royals that way," the tall one hisses, shoving his elbow down onto the man's head. What was his name again? Don? Dan? Daniel?

"What is your name?" Queen Mourner questions, her quiet voice filling the room.

"Ray." He grins as if they were sharing a secret, but I'm the only one who senses the lie. At least, I thought I was until the Royals called him out on it.

"Liar." Zaeden's cold voice is the first to respond, his father echoing the same word closely behind.

"Maybe." Ray shrugs as if it doesn't matter, nonchalant and unconcerned. His appearance, however, is *very* concerning.

He's coated in dried blood, his body littered with deep cuts and bruises. His clothes are torn all over, the deep cuts on his skin resembling claw marks. One arm is missing from the shoulder down, and the bandages wrapping the stub are seeped through with a deep red. He looks as though he has been mauled by an animal. *Maybe he was.* The healers seem to have only done what was necessary to keep him alive for a short while longer; his life is forfeit now that he has been caught. The only reason he is alive is for questioning.

"Where are the girls?" I rub a hand down Zaeden's arm reassuringly as he speaks, staring down at the prisoner with a snarl. It's become all too easy to fool the distraught prince, all too easy to use my powers on a Royal I should have never been able to touch.

"What girls?"

Another jab to the head. "Don't act like you don't know what's going on here."

"I was taking a shipment of apples to the Solar Court. I was told they were in desperate need and to make haste. Apparently, there's a shortage."

"Liar!" Poisonous tendrils rise from Zaeden's hands as he shouts, snaking their way forward.

"Don't kill him yet!" King Mourner barks at his son. "We aren't done!"

Zaeden's eyes close tightly, lips pressed hard together as he hisses out, "Fine."

"How did they make it to the Solar Court without you?" The king raises his eyebrow as he questions the prisoner, concluding that the Solar Court must have been their destination. The absolute *moron* slipped up.

"Don't know what you mean." An elbow to the ribs.

"Who are they meeting there?"

"Don't know." A punch to the gut.

"Were they planning to stay in the Solar Court?"

"Don't know." A kick in the groin.

"Are they contacting the Solar Court Royals?"

"Don't know." A foot to the ear.

"Then what *do* you know?" Zaeden bites out, fuming. His outburst earns him a glare from his father.

"I know what I was told: Bring the goods to the Solar Court. That's all." I can't help but admire his resolve—Edge chose this man well.

"You attempted to deliver two girls to the Solar Court, one of which murdered my son and the heir to the Lunar Court. Yet you still took them? Knowing what they had done?"

"I don't know what you mean. I'm just a delivery man. An Undivine. I agreed to deliver some goods for a little coin, that's all."

"A little coin? You sold out your Court for some coin?" Zaeden is oozing anger and despair as he stands, on the edge of falling off a cliff. "You Undivine are all the same. Stupid, ungrateful, and rash."

"What bold words coming from a spoiled Royal who has never had to go without that coin he disregards so easily." Ray chuckles humorlessly, meeting the prince's eyes. He gets a black eye as a reward. Honestly, I'm not sure how he is still able to speak, much less have the energy to talk back to a room of Royals.

"What did you just say to me, Divineless?"

"Oh, are we name-calling now? Why don't you learn your place, Royal Dog? Be a good pet and listen to your daddy, aye? Maybe if you sit pretty you'll get a treat."

"That's enough." King Mourner stands, pushing Zaeden back down into his chair.

I still don't speak.

"See?" Ray's grin is one of pure satisfaction.

"Who paid you to take the girls to the Solar Court? Who told you to do it?" King Mourner tries again.

"Don't know."

"It was obviously the Solars. Do you remember how quickly they left our Court, Father? They must have gotten wind that Celeste arrived and they left before we could find out." Ray's expression doesn't change at Zaeden's suggestion.

"We can't prove that. And don't repeat those words outside of this room again. If they ever hear rumors of what you just said—"

"I don't care if they know. My brother is dead! My other half—the piece of my soul that was split in the womb. We are supposed to be here *together*. We were never supposed to leave each other. Not like this—not so early. He was supposed to be our next ruler, and I was supposed to stay by his side. We would have been unbeatable. We would have ruled this whole damned world! And now I have to do it all on my own, have to shoulder all of *his* responsibilities. He was going to be a good king. How am I supposed to be good without him? *I can't be.* His death tore through me, taking pieces of me that can never be returned along the way.

"I won't stand here and let anyone get in the way of my revenge! My retribution! She took his fucking *soul* and she left with it. She has his soul in her, his very *essence.* She doesn't deserve it; she doesn't deserve *him.* She must die! Whatever it takes to make that happen, I will do it. I *will* return his soul to the goddesses." Zaeden had started his speech angry and vengeful, spitting and furious. But by the end, it's sad and regretful, his determination setting in.

"My love—"

"All I can think about is the way my brother looked in his final moments, the fear in his eyes. I remember his body growing darker and darker until all that was left of him was a giant pile of ashes and he became *nothing.* I was being honest when I said I felt Kyelin's death run clean through me. Now, I'm going to make sure Celeste feels that, too." This is a moment I should not be witnessing. I shouldn't feel guilty for Zaeden, and I definitely shouldn't be angry at Celeste for something she couldn't control. But I do and I am.

I don't love Zaeden—not by a long shot—but I do sympathize with him. I understand his motives and I understand his grief; I can feel it every second I am near him. The king and queen—no, his mother and father, are sorrowful, too. This is a son speaking to his parents. That is until the king emerges from the father, anyway.

"Nevertheless." He clears his throat, the whispered word appearing after a long pause. "We can't forget ourselves in our grief."

"Escort him to the dungeons," Zaeden commands, tearing his eyes away from his parents. I don't have to look at him to know what's there, though. I can feel the betrayal in the air, can taste it on my tongue. And, oh, how sweet the taste of distrust is.

King Mourner nods in approval, the sentencing final. We watch in silence as Ray's broken body is dragged away. "Follow him, son. You, too, Silvi. Make him sing like a canary."

Queen Mourner smiles brilliantly at her heir as he stands. Maybe she thinks this will be what fixes his broken heart, or will at least be a step in the right direction. Truthfully, there is no such cure. A heart can take cracks and it can take beatings, but it can't take being split in half. There is no recovery from such an event.

"Oh, I will make him sing. I can't wait to see his body torn to pieces, his mind distraught. I'm going to send my poison into each digit, into each limb until one by one they fail him. Until he is nothing more than a pile of mush who craves death. And even then I won't let him out of his misery. I will let him rot until I think he earns the relief of being thrown to the hounds in the woods." The grin that lights up Zaeden's face is colder than ice, shaking even the nerves of the closest guards. This is a prince they do not recognize, a prince they will never understand. They swallow their fear as they prepare to lead us after the traitor.

I follow dutifully behind my fiancé as we begin to descend farther and farther below the surface of our world. I have been down here too many times already this week alone, and have broken far too many minds. I brace myself for that possibility once more. I didn't think it was true once upon a time, but sometimes it *is* a mercy to kill someone outright. Even if it isn't merciful for me.

Zaeden cackles under his breath, and I can only imagine the unnerving thoughts within that wicked mind. I'm sure he can't wait to stomp out every bit of the traitor's dignity, to steal the pieces of his soul in honor of what his brother endured. I watch wearily as his head snaps to the side, interrupting my corrupt thoughts.

I don't recognize the three men in a cell at the opposite end of the room, but he does. They shuffle their feet, cowering underneath his glare. We round a corner, the men no longer within eyesight. Curiosity gets the best of me as I ask, "Who are they?"

"Giant pains in my ass. I've had the thought to kill them already, but the weight of a deal holds me back. Celeste's deal. Whenever I get her back, that's the first manner of business I am taking care of. I told her she could decide their fate. So, now, I'm unable to fucking touch them without fearing the goddesses' wrath. She will uphold her end of the deal, and then I will begin killing her slowly."

"Do tell me more," I purr, slinking up next to him and batting my long lashes. Zaeden pauses for a moment, hands roaming over my body appreciatively. He begins a trail of kisses down my neck, whispering bitter threats onto my skin.

"I plan on killing her with her own guilt. I saw how she reacted to Dove and watched the expression on her face after she killed Kyelin. She hates herself. I plan on using that by forcing her to suck the souls from any Divine I wish her to until she is nothing more than a shell. Until she begs me for the sweet release that death may offer. But I won't kill her then. Not until she is no longer useful, not until her powers are too weak to take advantage of. As long as no other Divine has her, I don't care. She will be mine like she was always meant to be."

Zaeden can be so charming at times, charming enough to make me forget what lies underneath his skin. This isn't one of those times.

"How romantic," Ray snorts from nearby, coughing abruptly. Zaeden tears himself away from me, stalking up to the Undivine.

"I would shut the fuck up if you knew what was best for you."

"Do your worst," he spits back, grinning up at the Royal to hide his fear.

"Silvi, darling, would you like to have the honor?"

I nod, approaching with a teasing smile. Ray's eyes light up in recognition, fear rescinding.

"Silvi, with the silver hair." His whisper is barely audible, a mumble for only my ears to receive.

"Why don't you come back in an hour or two, my love? It's hard for me to focus around you." I lay on a sultry voice, batting my lashes as I look him up and down. Zaeden's arrogant smirk is such a turn-off.

"Be a good girl while I'm gone, Silvi. If you get what I need, I'll reward you beautifully." His kiss is wet and sloppy, his lips moving too fast for me to keep up. Nevertheless, I pretend to be left breathless. I pretend to want more. And tonight, when he knocks on my door to deliver his gift, I will be dressed for the occasion. I will close my eyes and pretend it is anyone else. Because, unlike my lovely and pure Celeste, I am willing to do *anything* it takes.

"Of course, my love." I wait until his footsteps are far, far gone and his soldiers gone with them.

"They told me about you."

"I'm sure they did." I look him up and down before saying, "Is she okay?"

"I'm sure she is. We got into a tangle with some beasts, and I got into a tangle with the sister. But they flew off toward the Solar Court, so I'm sure they made it in time. Celeste is strong."

"Her sister?" I raise my eyebrow, amused.

"Oh, yes. A little beast, that one is. Very strong, just like her sister."

I stay silent for a minute before saying, "You know what has to be done?"

"I've known since the moment I left this Court. Since Edge asked me to do the job."

"Okay. That usually makes this part a little easier."

"What will you tell them?"

"Bits of truth. A few white lies." I shrug, kicking my foot on the ground. "I'll say Irissa attacked you and took off with her sister. That you thought you were supposed to go to the Solar Court, but they went in a different direction. That you never saw the man who hired you because he wore a hood and stayed in the darkness of an alley. That his height indicated a Divine. That you never revealed your real name and you broke too easily."

"I chose Ray because she told me once that I was a ray of sunshine in her bleak and dreary life, and it became this little joke between us. I've never forgotten." He smiles sadly.

I choose that moment to attack. A moment of happiness to distract him from the pain he must endure. One quick swipe to his neck, one deep cut for the blood to spill. He barely feels it and is dead within seconds. I ignore his last, gurgling breath as I begin to add small cuts and other wounds that align with torture—it's best to do it after death. I don't truly enjoy this part like I'm meant to. Like I pretend to.

I sink against the wall as far away from his body as possible, burying my head down into my knees. After a long moment, I look up and offer him a sad smile and a few parting words.

"And what a treacherous little ray you turned out to be."

CHAPTER 10

Reality

Edge

It's not the blood that catches my attention, or the hint of ivory bone visible on the man's back. No—it's the glimmer of blonde hair in the distance, the reflection of the sun off of an abundance of curls that I'm sure I must be imagining. Fuck, am I imagining this? Is it really her out there in the crowd, so close to the secrets I wanted to keep away from her?

I pause my methodical movements, gaze trailing off into the distance to follow the stream of blonde. I squint in desperation which is unbecoming of my stature as I try to see if the blonde belongs to the one person I don't need to see right now. But, no, it isn't her. It's someone else, someone plain, someone ordinary. It's my unordinary behavior that provokes my stepfather into action, my unordinary hesitation that catches *his* attention.

"Another," my stepfather hisses, pleasantly malicious smile tilted toward the crowd. I raise the whip over my shoulder for what must be the thirtieth time, its bloody tail curling around my ankle like a lover's caress. I don't allow myself to hesitate a second time, don't allow myself the moment of composure I desperately need. I only fling my wrist back down, hating every flinch and outcry from the crowd when leather-on-flesh echoes in the chilly air. I hate the man's screams even more. Most of all, I hate myself for raising the whip again without any further prompting.

"That's enough!" The shout comes from someone in the crowd, weeping ensuing. Voices jumble together in agreement, their rage and sadness all-consuming.

"It's enough when I say it's enough," King Zorander snarls, snapping his fingers at me. I give him the briefest of nods in acknowledgment, flicking my wrist again. I avoid the bloody, meaty mess on the man's back, avoid the faces in the crowd as I tell myself not to search for blonde again. Nothing good would come of Cerina Celeste being here today.

I adjust only slightly, aiming for the small sliver of skin on his side that has gone unmarred. I can feel the Royal beside me raging, can feel his displeasure, at the small act of kindness I showed to the poor Undivine before us who is on the brink of unconsciousness. But these little rebellions are all I have, these small issues that he can't make bigger because what proof does he have that these acts are nothing more than coincidences? This is the only way I can fight back, the only way that I can repent for the sins that I am actively committing.

"Do you want me to kill him, King Zorander?" I question, drawling and impatient as usual. As if this whole ordeal is boring, inconvenient, or both.

The Cruel King stares down at the mangled body in front of us, shaking his head with a scoff as he kicks him in the ribs in one final act of tyranny. The man lets out a gurgle, clutching himself as blood dribbles down his chin. "No. No, I think not. Guards!" More snaps, more obedience, more punishment.

I watch with little empathy in my eye as the guards pick the man up and deposit him off the side of the stage we occupy, allowing him to collapse into a heap in the dusty, dirt-covered area the onlookers crowd in. I let my shadows trail after him in a lightning-fast streak, hiding them from my stepfather as I force them to make the man numb. I can tell it works when he looks up at me with clear eyes, mouth agape in shock or gratefulness—I can't be sure. I quickly turn my body away from him before anyone can question the "thank you" that isn't aimed at the bystanders who are helping him, but me, the man who tortured him.

As I turn I see another glint of gold, over by the—

"Your little performance today didn't go unnoticed."

I raise an eyebrow, ignoring the usual twinge of pain in my scar as my lips pull up into a sly smirk. "Performance?"

"You missed on purpose," he hisses down at me, grabbing me by the wrist. At one point in time, I would have flinched at the small touch, at the burning pain that made its way up my arm.

"You're beginning to sound paranoid, Stepfather. My arm was tired," I say with a sigh, flicking some invisible dust off the shoulder of his jacket. "And I was bored."

"You think I believe that?"

"Should I care if you do?" This is my favorite game to play and the most dangerous. Truthfully, I think the prize is worth it.

"Don't test me. You won't like the outcome," he snarls, nose wrinkling in distaste as he looks down at me. My shorter stature has put me in a position to be seen as a subordinate, and it irks me to no end. Despite being six feet tall, my stepfather is still at least half a foot taller. Marrying my mother and becoming a Royal gave him those extra inches but, unfortunately, I will be granted no such luck in my lifetime.

"I'm sure," I say, pulling away from his touch subtly and not giving him the satisfaction of looking up to meet his vicious gaze. "If you will excuse me, I have some important business to attend to."

I stride away from the Cruel King, from the stage of horrors, from the angry mass of citizens. I stride away from my role as the Cruel Prince, from the indifference of an obedient Royal child, and toward the glimmering golden strands I caught a second glimpse of and shouldn't be bothering to investigate.

I fade in and out of existence, disappearing into a portal and reappearing near the sight I thought I had glimpsed her. The first blonde curls in the crowd hadn't been her—the girl was close enough for me to tell immediately. But this girl, these curls, were wilder and so much more dazzling. There—entering one of the many clothing stores in the city, her sister striding behind her. My stomach churns at the sight of Celeste, guilt pestering my insides. She was so close to seeing, so close to finding out—she would hate what I have done.

Celeste isn't like everyone else here. She isn't a blood-thirsty, cut-throat villain goddess bent on getting her way. No, she's full of the same, pestering guilt and unease that I carry around. Full of the same strength that she hates to use. I think it's the innocence, the naivety, that draws me to her. Maybe it's even the fact that I know she has experienced some of this world's most heinous acts, and yet she still manages to cling to that innocence and self-righteousness. It's inspiring and nauseating all at once.

I've never met a Divine as conflicting as her. She hates me, but she still speaks to me as though I have a heart. She despises the Divine, but she still chooses to live among us. She wants to be guilty, but she also wants to be set free. It's infuriating—but I'm drawn to it like a moth to the flame. I'm drawn to *her*.

I've never been one to chase after what I want—it usually comes to me. I've never fought for affection because what is there to fight for? I'm a prince, powerful and handsome despite my many flaws. Despite my evil, despite my vile deeds, I've never had to prove myself worthy because no one has cared before if I am. The times I've felt the urge to have a woman, there was an abundance to choose from. And the urges I feel for *this* woman...they are utterly unholy.

From the moment I laid eyes on Celeste something clicked and I knew there was so much more to her than the weak little Undivine she was pretending to be. I knew I needed to find out more. And, oh, did I. That stupid, incessant naivety was so dazzlingly obvious from the very first glare she sent me way. I was sure that there was no more to the childish little woman desperate to be loved. Every interaction I had with her proved my theory to be true, proved her to be weak and a waste of time. *But I couldn't stop wanting her.* I read her mind a very few amount of times, but when I did her thoughts were so intriguing. So conflicting and hateful, so...different and new. Watching her flounder among the Highs, watching her fight so hard for a life she didn't even want—it wrapped me tighter around her finger than I will ever be able to admit to myself.

What kind of man am I, watching her shop like a creep after brutally torturing someone only a mile away? After living up to the reputation I had grown but didn't want her to know about? What kind of man am I to want her while still doing my best to make her tolerance of me vanish with the winds? I suppose I must be the crazy kind.

Her smile radiates as she turns her head over her shoulder, and I can practically hear her laughter as she speaks with her sister about something only they are privy to. It makes my heart clench and I swear at it inwardly, refusing to acknowledge how happy she seems in my Court, how well she fits in, and how quickly she is recovering. Celeste deserves more than me, more than a tortured, blackened heart who can't worship her the way she deserves.

I take a step back, refusing to look at her any longer. She's so beautiful it fucking hurts, so perfect I can't stand to watch her any longer than necessary.

"Aren't they so cute?" I cringe at the sound of my sister's voice, rubbing my cheek as I try to think of a decent excuse as for why I'm out here stalking Celeste.

"You think everyone is cute," I deflect with an eye roll, watching the brown and blue strands of her hair shift in the breeze so I don't have to look at locks of gold.

"Yes, but this time you agree. You think *she* is cute." She jerks her head in Celeste's direction, beaming.

"She's Divine. Of course she's cute," I scoff, hands balling into fists at my sides.

"Ah, don't lie to me, Edge. You never could do it right; you have a tell."

"No, I don't," I murmur, feeling my eye twitch.

"Liar," she says with a giggle, rapt attention on the winged sister. I've noticed their constant flirtations—it's hard not to when they are so obnoxious and public about it. Irissa seems just as flirty as Valaine, just as outgoing and friendly.

Personally, I think they are more suited as friends, but I may be biased.

"You like Irissa," I say, but it isn't a question.

"She's fun. A breath of fresh air. A distraction."

"And what happens when she isn't anymore? When reality crashes down and you two have to face it?"

"Reality is what we make it, Edge. It's not my fault you want your reality to be a sad little cesspool where you aren't allowed to be happy."

"That's not what my reality is."

"Oh? Care to elaborate?"

"No." My reality is this: I'll never get to escape the prison that is my body, the prison that is my power. I'll never be able to escape from the darkness that everyone shies away from or the hideous acts I have committed for the sake of making their realities a better place to live. I'll never get to chase the things I want or be the things I want to be. I'll never get to define my own reality because, as Valaine so eloquently put it, mine is a sad little cesspool that will never allow me to have anything remotely similar to happiness.

"You like her," she tries again, jabbing me in the ribs.

"Stop that," I smack her hand away, annoyed. "And no, I don't."

"Really?"

I grit my teeth, crossing my arms across my chest as I grind out, "Really."

"Then why did you come racing home to be with her? Why did you ease her pain? Why did you heal her? Why did you—"

"That's enough. You're taking everything out of context."

"Am I? What context am I missing?"

"Context that reveals me to be a selfish fuck who does things because I have ulterior motives, not because I give a shit."

"Oh, you give a shit," she murmurs with a grin, patting my arm reassuringly. "It's okay, big man. You can hide your feelings from yourself all you want, but you can't hide them from me. Now, if you'll excuse me, I was supposed to be in that store fifteen minutes ago."

I watch with utter annoyance as she strides off toward the store, waving brightly at the sisters as soon as the door pops open. They greet her, Irissa cheerfully and Celeste wearily. Watching my sister interact with her is another pang to the chest, another stab to the gut, and I turn and stride off before I can try and change my reality to fit her in it.

CHAPTER 11

Celeste

I'm unsure what to expect when Edge enters my room a week after he offered to train me. My tears have long dried and my mind is no longer stuck on the same depressing loop, but I expect Edge to notice that underneath the mask on my face I am still the same. I expect him to see through me quickly, to snarl and snap at my weakness. So, when his looming form appears in the doorway, I tense. But he says nothing as he enters the room, his steel blue eye sparkling as it lands on me. I straighten as the door shuts behind him, still not convinced I can trust him enough to be alone with him.

He scoffs, looking away to hide the hurt that flashes across his face. "Relax. I'm not going to hurt you. Can't you see past fear by now?"

"No," I admit reluctantly. "I'm not sure I ever will."

His face softens as he turns back toward me. "You will—I swear it."

"I thought we were going to train," I say after a pause, unsure where to go from here. Unsure how to navigate this new...partnership. Unsure how to look past the man who attacked me and cut off all my hair to see the man who stands in front of me now.

"You aren't in training gear."

I glance down at my shorts and thinly strapped top, shrugging sheepishly. "The gear reminds me of..." I trail off, not wanting to say what I was thinking. *It reminds me of the Games.*

"No matter." He brushes it off quickly, a small smile gracing those devious lips. I try not to watch them.

"Well?"

"Well, what?"

"Well, I thought you said—" I'm not allowed to finish my sentence. Edge dives toward me, eye flashing as he attacks. I screech and jump out of the way at the last minute, shouting louder when his arm still manages to hook around my waist and arms. Suddenly I'm spinning, my back pushed flush against his chest. My arms are pinned against him, his free hand tangling in the choppy curls at the back of my neck and pulling with just enough pressure to yank my head back.

"Gotcha," he breathes into my ear, satisfaction rumbling throughout his body.

"What in the Divine—" I sputter, eyes wide in disbelief.

"You let your guard down," he says so simply, so nonchalantly.

"You told me to! You walked in and immediately got upset that—"

"I know what I said. What I did." He chuckles, heat tickling my neck. "It's not my fault you actually believed me."

I huff out, "You tricked me. It wasn't a fair fight." I banish thoughts of the hard muscles pushing into me, of the bare skin brushing against mine. I've never felt attraction like this for Edge and I don't plan on starting now, especially when I know he can read any treacherous thoughts that slip into my mind.

"Oh? Did I?" he muses, releasing me from his grip.

I spin around viciously, arms up in a defensive maneuver. "Again."

"Again?" His answering grin sends a chill down my spine. I find myself not caring that we are in the middle of my room, fighting and shouting loud enough for the whole castle to hear. I am entirely too focused on his suffocating presence, on not letting him defeat me so easily; I quickly discovered that's a feat that will take more time.

"Ha!" I laugh as I jump from a wayward fist, proud of myself for the first successful dodge in an hour. The victory is short-lived. His leg appears behind my calves, sweeping me away. I fall to the ground with a groan, coughing as I try to remember how to breathe. He chuckles deeply as he holds his hand out for what seems to be the hundredth time, pulling me to my feet.

"You were distracted by your victory. Always be alert. You weren't focusing because you thought you had won already. Do I look unconscious or dead? No? *Then stay alert.*" I stumble a few steps back as I register his familiar words, mind flashing to the singular training session I shared with Kyelin.

"Okay, but what if they do grab me? What do I do then?" I asked after he had explained how to avoid being grabbed. Suddenly, his arms are around me, pinning mine down. He is whispering into my ear about using elbows and feet to my advantage, to use my small size to help me escape. To not forget that I am powerful and can put that power behind every hit. That I am Divine now and have the strength of one. Says that my shields should work against other Highs and that I can use them, too. So, I do as he says. I twist unexpectedly while he is whispering, ramming my elbow down into his thigh. His grip loosens and I spin out of his arms, back into a fighting position. He grabs me easily enough and I am falling. Within seconds I am on my back, growling as he pins me down.

"See? Always be alert. You did well in escaping, but you weren't staying focused. You thought you had won already. Never think that unless your competitor is incapacitated or dead." I can only nod, too worked up to speak. Kyelin sits on top of me—

"What's wrong?" Edge's voice snaps me away from the distant memory, my mind reeling at the sudden change. Will it always be like this? Will simple words always bring back painful memories?

I swallow hard, avoiding his gaze. "Nothing. We are done here." I keep my voice firm and final. I'm not going to allow the guilt to control me right now—not in front of Edge.

"We are done when I say so." He grabs my arm defiantly, practically growling at me.

"Don't forget what my touch can do to you, prince," I spit back venomously. Edge yanks his arm away as if I had burned him, surprise and unbridled fury spreading across those beautiful features.

"You do like your games, don't you, Celeste? How many times are we going to play this one? How many times are we going to circle each other like this, threaten each other to get what we want from one another?"

"As long as I have to," I hiss, teeth grinding. I hate it when he makes good points. "Leave. Now."

"No." He's leaping forward again, the muscles in his arms rippling as he strikes out. In a panic, a wall of flames spirals around me. I watch as he disappears in a cloud of shadows, reappearing right behind me. I only know he is there when he leans forward and whispers huskily, "Boo."

Edge tackles me from behind, arms twisting me around so I land on my back. He topples over me, grinning. My chest heaves underneath him, eyes boring into his.

"I hate you." I slam my fists into the ground as I writhe beneath him, attempting to escape as the flames die.

"Stop that," he murmurs, eye ablaze as he watches me in fascination.

"This is ridiculous. This is not how you're supposed to train someone. Have you ever done this before? Because you're fucking terrible at it." I still my body, rambling as I try to avoid that heavy gaze and hypnotizing touch. What's happening to me? Is he using those Royal powers of persuasion that made me fall in love with Kyelin?

"I've trained many soldiers. It's not my fault you're no good at it." He grins, pulling back suddenly into a sitting position. He cracks ring-less knuckles above me, twisting his neck to pop it, too.

"No jewelry today? How normal of you," I tease to distract myself, daring a glance up.

"Not right now, no."

"What is with those rings, anyway? Why do they always end up scattered all over the place?" I'm babbling now, avoiding the conversation to come. A conversation where I would ask him to get off me and he would make some smart remark about me liking his weight on top of me. A conversation where he will scent my lies.

"Well..." His hesitation is startling. Are they a sensitive topic? Do they mean something more than just a fashion statement?

"Sorry, is it personal? I don't mean to pry."

"They help me control the shadows." He shrugs eventually. "And you aren't prying. Most people just don't notice."

"Control? You can't control them?" Why had his stepfather lectured me on not being able to control my powers when it's something Edge struggles with, too? Maybe *that's* the reason Valaine is his favorite.

"I can," he says defensively, squinting down at me. "They are just very powerful. If I allow them to operate at full capacity at all times, they may consume me. I'll become a mad, raving lunatic. And as fun as that sounds, I'd rather not lose my sanity. Or level my entire Court in the process."

"So when you wear them you don't have access to your shadows?" Wait—no. That can't be true. I've *seen* him use his powers with those rings on.

"I have access to them, I just don't have a grip on the full spectrum of things," he admits begrudgingly.

"Like...?" I press, curiosity winning out.

"Like my portals. Especially over long distances. I could probably manage to jump around this room over a dozen times, but jumping across Courts like I did to come find you? There's no way."

"You jumped across Courts...for me?" I gape up at him, surprised. I didn't think that decision had anything to do with *me*—just my stupidity at almost dying.

He rubs his chest and winces. "Yes, and be grateful for it. It took a lot of power and didn't fare so great on my body."

"Thank you. I know I seemed ungrateful for it at the time, but...you helped ease my pain. A lot."

"I'm sorry I couldn't do more." He blinks down at me, mind somewhere else. It seems I'm not the only one who struggles to contain my guilty conscience.

"Don't be sorry, you can't heal emotional damage," I whisper back. The look I receive is intense, and I can only hope he doesn't notice my now racing pulse or goosebumps-riddled skin. I quickly throw mental shields up, preventing him from finding anything I don't want him to see.

I change the subject quickly, asking, "So, what are they made out of? The rings, I mean?"

"Obsidian. Like calls to like." His words are bitter.

"Can I see one? How do they work?" With a roll of his eye, he pulls a few rings out of his pocket. He hands one over slowly, that same hesitation still present. I wonder if he has ever let another Divine touch these precious items before.

"I haven't. But no one's ever asked before, either."

I hiss a few choice words inside of my mind before throwing a shield up over it. After a month of not needing them, I've become lax in keeping them up. And as much as I want to trust Edge, I can no longer trust anyone around me. Everyone has their own agenda when it comes to me and my abilities—Edge most of all. I can't forget that.

I pluck the ring from his hand in annoyance, examining it. Edge chuckles, holding his hands up as if to say "Not my fault!" The ring he has handed me is a simple black band, small pieces of obsidian placed around its entirety. It gives it a nice shine, almost like how a diamond or ruby would glimmer in the light.

"How do they work?" I repeat the question as I turn the ring over. Inside is a small engraving, and I squint to see what it says. All I can make out is a heart and an 'E'.

"The shadows will pass through the rings before they pass through me. The obsidian attracts them, pulls them in, and entraps them. They stay there and only come out *if* and *when* I desire them to. The obsidian has to be touching my skin for me to pull them out, though. Otherwise, it's just a hunk of rock with a shit load of untapped power. That being said, it's hard for me to pull shadows from them because they hold so much. Even that small ring can hold enough shadows to overwhelm me if I'm not careful. Sometimes, it feels like they are an endless abyss for the damn things. Though, I suppose, I am an endless abyss, too."

"An endless abyss of ego and violence," I snort playfully, dismissing the seriousness of this conversation.

"Yeah, yeah."

"What does this say?" I squint at the lettering again. I lift my eyes in surprise when I feel his body tense, my breath freezing as I recognize the murderous glint in his eye.

"Doesn't matter." He takes the ring back in a hurry. With one fluent motion, it's back inside the depths of his pocket and out of my sight. "Get up, we are going again."

"What? But—"

"Get up," he hisses, unmoving.

"Aren't you going to move?"

"Make me," he purrs sweetly, smirking down at me.

"I hate you," I repeat my earlier sentiments. How am I supposed to get him off me? He's huge!

"I am not," he pouts, looking down at himself. "Is it this shirt? Maybe I should take it—"

"No! No no. Do *not* do that," I cry out as he begins to lift his shirt by the hem. "I take it back!"

"Good. Now throw your shields back on and *get up.*"

My sore limbs burn as I am escorted down the hall, Irissa falling in line behind me. She is cheerier than usual, with an extra bounce in her steps. I huff in irritation, glancing back at her in disgust.

"Why are you so cheery?" I question as I roll my shoulders with a groan.

"I'm not," she huffs defensively, crossing her arms over her chest. "I'm just…"

"Just overly joyous for no reason?"

"No!"

"Why so defensive? Didn't you just train today? Surely Valaine didn't take it easy on you?"

"No, she most certainly did not." Irissa grins cheekily.

"Oh. *Ewww.* Don't tell me you have a crush on her," I groan, rolling my eyes. Valaine is gorgeous, there is no denying that, but I can't imagine my sister with a Royal. I know it's hypocritical, but I've learned my lesson already. I don't want her going through something similar.

"Oh, I'm going to make sure it becomes more than a crush. Have you seen her, Les?" Her wide eyes and lopsided grin make me laugh.

"She's too old for you," I argue weakly.

"She just turned twenty-two a few months ago. And my twentieth birthday was not that long ago! It's not that big of a difference. Also, *I'm an adult.*"

"Oh, yes, I forgot. That means it's already nearing winter." Irissa's birthday occurs a month or two before the winter hits, depending on the year, and the Lunar Court always gets so unbearably cold. Her birthday used to mark the end of summer and the beginning of our worst months of the year. This year, we got to celebrate it on the journey here; not that there was much celebrating to do.

"Yep. It's exciting, right? I wonder if they get snow here?"

"I hope not. I hate snow."

"We won't be spending this winter in a freezing house," she reminds me.

"But other Undivine will." My voice is soft, but it pierces through her anyway.

"Why do you always do that?"

"Do what?" I startle at her angry tone.

"Make everything so *sad.* Make yourself feel guilty over things you have no control over. You're pessimistic."

"I have reason to be," I say defensively. "And so do you!"

"Yeah? Do you realize how lucky we are right now? To be in a castle, getting catered to by a prince and princess? To be warm and fed and healthy despite all of the things we did to get here? Our situation is what we make of it. You can never be happy if you don't forgive yourself for the things you did when you weren't."

"Is that something your girlfriend told you?" I snap back, irritated.

"She isn't my girlfriend...*yet*."

We giggle together, anger dissolving. Forgiven and forgotten, as sisters tend to do.

Our progress has led us to a classroom where wooden desks are lined up in five neat rows. A larger desk sits in the front of the room, Silvi's father standing before it. There are no books, no colorful decorations, no writing utensils. There is nothing other than white walls and empty black chairs. Merkelly smiles at us, gesturing for us to enter. Soldiers file in behind us, standing watch by the door.

Merkelly claps and announces, "Welcome! What a wonderful day to teach."

"Um, yeah. I guess so." My voice cracks and I clear my throat awkwardly, glancing over at my sister. She rolls her eyes and sweeps in like she owns the place, sitting at a desk in the front row.

"Should we call you Mr. Merkelly?" she questions, seemingly not frightened by the man. Of course she isn't; she has never met his daughter.

"You may call me Ark. Please, sit, sit. Right up front girls, right up front."

I stalk forward, plopping down grumpily in the desk next to Irissa's. I watch her put on a dazzling smile, purring out, "Okay, Ark."

"Control your emotions, girls. They are quite distracting." We bristle at the sudden jab, cheeks flushing in embarrassment.

"Isn't that what you are here for?" Irissa grinds out, cheeriness gone.

"That I am! Now, let us begin. Irissa, I could already sense so much when you walked in. I didn't even need my powers, honestly. Giddiness, cockiness, annoyance. It was written all over your face and in every single step you took. Celeste, I can see fear and anger within the wrinkles of your forehead. So, today, that will be our first lesson: physical language. We use a lot of nonverbal communication in our everyday lives. The wrinkles in our forehead, the crinkles by our eyes, even in the way we hold our bodies. Every move you make shows me something about you, even when you don't want it to."

"How do I hide wrinkles?" I shake my head and scoff.

"You don't. You control them." His grin annoys me, his confidence overbearing. I put my forehead wrinkles down on the table with a groan, eyes fluttering shut.

This is going to be a long lesson.

CHAPTER 12

"This place is so dusty," Irissa grumbles, wiping said dust off a full shelf of books.

"I've never been in a library before, so I'm not sure if this is the usual or not."

"I don't think this is the usual anywhere," she replies, fingers dancing down a row of spines.

She and I had decided it would be a good day to visit the Solar Court library, but it turned out to be much larger than anticipated. When we walked in, a kind man had sat at the desk. He introduced himself as Domiel, a red-haired, brown-eyed hunk. Irissa ogled at him the whole conversation, her smile devious. I had to practically yank her away from him, thanking him for his kindness. He had pointed us toward the third floor, saying there were lots of good origin books up here. Ignoring the fact that there are three more floors above this one, we didn't quite anticipate how large *this* floor would be. There are rows upon rows of books, and they span a distance greater than two of our old cabins combined.

Each floor so far has been lavishly decorated, with golden columns and beautiful suns present on each one. This floor in particular has beautiful red walls, accompanied by stunning artwork everywhere we turn. There is a life-like painting of the castle, a sculpture of a giant woman's head, and a glass box hiding a miniature version of the city. It takes a lot of willpower not to stop each time we stumble upon something new, to not gawk at such beauty and regality. And the whole *Court* has access to this place? It's amazing! I could hardly believe it when Valaine first told me a few weeks ago, only a few days after we had begun our lessons, and today is the first break we have had in those lessons to come to visit. It was a conversation that made me realize the Solar Court might not be so bad after all, and that maybe the Lunar Court was encouraging the horrific rumors about the Solars to keep us from finding out the truth: Things are so much better here.

"What do you mean 'public library'*?" I question, brows twisting downward.*

"You don't have one at the Lunar Court?" she asks, clearly amused. "The whole Court can waltz right in if they wanted to! Knowledge should be shared, not kept hidden away on a shelf for only Royal eyes to bear witness to. We want our Court to have access to the secrets of the world. We don't want anyone feeling lesser than us when it comes to the power of knowledge. Of course, my stepfather believes otherwise. My mother has to constantly provide perfectly logical reasons as to why it shouldn't be banned."

"Well, thank the goddesses for her. A library can prove to be extremely helpful for us right now. Though, I'm not a very good reader. I taught myself and Irissa long ago, so our reading level is low. We don't have any schooling at the Lunar Court, but I did what I could. I learned a lot from working in the castle."

"No schooling? What do you mean no schooling?"

"The Divines get it, sure. But it's a privilege Undivines don't deserve. We are lesser, unimportant. Who cares if we are uneducated? We are born to serve and then we die. That's all there is to it."

She looks mortified and outraged. "That's outlandish. I'm sorry that your people face such prejudice."

"Are they my people?" I question quietly, shaking my head in dismissal. "Anyway, where is this library?"

"What about this one?" Irissa shakes a book in front of me, snapping me out of my memories. She holds a book titled *All About Shifting,* the cover a beaten green hue. I nod excitedly, gesturing for her to add it to the cart we had been pulling around on our little excursion.

"Yes! That looks promising. That's three for you. Where are *my* books?" I huff, exasperated. I have found a few on Benders, but nothing about Absorbids. I struggled just to find those few, but I struggled more with finding books on my own powers. I had added the books on Benders to our piles, despite the giggles from Irissa, because something about those abilities intrigues me. Despite my very loud protests about this to Irissa, I know it's because of Edge. He had explained his abilities so well, but I am still unsure when it comes to the amount of power he holds. As far as the Divines go, he is the most powerful one I have ever met.

He is the only one with a bottomless pit like mine.

"Aha!" I glance up at the exclamation, watching a girl who stands in the same aisle. She wears a deep yellow tunic, its bright color standing out among the dreary books. Many people roam around the library in a similar outfit, though none have dared come so close. I concluded several hours ago that they work here since they seem to be around every corner. Most of them have watched us with little interest, but a few have followed discreetly. This girl was one of them. She wears dark glasses so I can't see her eyes, but I can see her short, white hair. It barely grazes her ears, voluminous waves crashing above. Her tan skin lacks the glow of a Divine, so I know she must be Undivine.

"Hello." Her head snaps toward us as she greets us, short legs pushing her forward in a quick approach. I glance at Irissa in a panic as we simultaneously take a step back. "Are you believers?"

"Are you a Follower?" I groan with the sudden realization, shaking my head in disbelief. She nods enthusiastically, a wide grin on her face. I notice a small gap between her front two teeth, but they lack the yellow tinge of a typical Undivine.

"Yes," she agrees pleasantly, noticing my shocked face at her sweet tone. "What's wrong?"

"The Followers at the Lunar Court aren't so cheerful. Especially not around the Divine." She only laughs, holding out the book in her hand. I hesitantly take it, watching in disbelief as she turns and leaves. Glancing down at the cover, I read the simple title *So You Think You're An Absorbid* that stares back at me. Had she been following us to...help us? And she didn't even bother to lecture us about the goddesses in the process?

"Aren't they so mysterious?" Irissa and I both shout out in surprise, spinning around to find Valaine. "Are you two very busy, or do you think you could spare a moment?"

"Divine goddesses, Valaine! What was that about?" I sputter out in disbelief.

"The Followers are harmless, they just—"

"Not them! I'm talking about you sneaking up on us and giving us heart attacks! If you want us dead, there are much easier and less public ways to do so!" Irissa smacks my arm in an attempt to make me quiet, head ducking down with a blush. Valaine only laughs, however, staring at my sister with a twinkle in her eyes.

"Well? Are you two busy?" I glance from our pile of books back to her, suspicious.

"Why?"

"There are a couple of people I would like you both to meet. If you are available, that is."

"We are," Irissa agrees breathlessly, not allowing me a say in the matter. I scowl at her, not wanting to rush off with Valaine. I know she has a crush on her, but I prefer distance from other Divine. Especially Royal ones. I've already been spending most of the past few weeks with Edge for training, and Ark, too. I don't want to start *casually* hanging out with them!

"Excellent!" Valaine smiles brightly, gesturing to our books. "I'll have these delivered to your rooms!" She snaps her fingers and a soldier appears obediently. She waves her hand at the books, nodding at him in confirmation. He doesn't need more than that before taking the armful of books and disappearing.

"Um, okay, that was weird. Where are we going?" She turns abruptly, ignoring my question. I stumble after her, Irissa already glued to her side. They fall into perfect sync with one another, their steps soundless. How had Irissa already learned to do that? I still sound like a large beast tromping through a forest!

Neither woman pays me much attention as we sweep down the long aisles, heading straight for the stairway. We bound down the three sets of steps, veering off toward the exit. Domiel sends a bright smile our way as we pass the front desk. Irissa sends him an apologetic wave, watching Valaine as she does so. Valaine seems to not notice the wink he shoots toward Irissa or the "come see me again" as we exit the building. It's when we start down a dark alleyway next to the library that I become nervous.

"Where are we going, Valaine?" I demand, stopping abruptly behind them. She tilts her head over her shoulder, smiling softly in reassurance.

"Don't worry. We are just going to a secure location for this meeting. We don't want anyone to overhear us or to find out that you are here."

"Speaking of, do not leave the castle without guards again."

Irissa screams, curling into Valaine for comfort. Her arms wrap around my sister reassuringly, a scowl appearing on my face as I realize who had spoken. Great. Now *two* Royals are here.

Valaine tries to scold her brother, saying, "Edge! You gave the poor girls heart attacks."

Edge only shrugs, watching me as he replies, "They should always be alert."

"I'm so sorry, Val." Irissa fans herself dramatically, relishing the touch of the princess. "He just gave me such a fright!"

"That's my brother for you. An evil, overbearing, frightening creature." Edge sends his sister a glare, only to result in a middle finger from Irissa. I laugh, copying the gesture when he turns that glare on me. I watch in surprise as Valaine lifts her own hand in defiance. Then the three of us laugh together, Edge growing increasingly frustrated and outnumbered.

"Pathetic. Come on, let's get this over with. I'm going to transport you three to the location. Don't freak out, got it?" Irissa barely manages to nod before he pulls her into his arms, stepping into the shadows wordlessly. I squint at Valaine, still weary.

"Who, exactly, are we meeting?"

"Some friends." She shrugs nonchalantly, turning to face her brother as he reappears. He sends me a wink and a smirk before whisking away. I tap my foot impatiently, annoyed that he intentionally chose to take me last.

"Saved the best for last, hmm?" I question snarkily as his arms wrap around my body. I suck in a breath as he presses me to his chest, his warmth surrounding me. I try not to focus on the spots where his skin meets mine, on the hand brushing against a spot on my hip where my shirt rode up. We are quickly diving into the shadows, and he makes it all seem so *effortless*. But I can see the exhaustion in small little signs: a bead of sweat forming on his head, arms shaking lightly, and jaw clenching faintly. He told me before that transporting long distances takes a lot of power, so how far out did he take us?

We emerge in the corner of a small townhouse, appearing in a bedroom. I spin on him with a raised eyebrow, a scowl set on my face. What is *this*?

He scowls back, panting lightly. "Relax. I'm a little worn out. I was supposed to take us to the sitting room. My aim was a little off. The three of you are fucking shadow suckers." He stomps off, slipping his hand down into his pocket. I'm quick to follow, watching him subtly slide rings onto his fingers one by one.

"For a Royal, you are such a whiny b—" I stop speaking, noticing the two very large men waiting for us in the sitting room.

"Please continue," the black-haired one purrs, grinning widely.

"Yes, we would love to hear you chew out our dear Edge; I fear it is long overdue." Edge shoots the blond a scorching look, sliding onto the couch next to them. They each reach over to ruffle his hair and pat his back, chuckling at his expense.

"This is Eleazer Nethersole. They are the captain of my army and a large pain in my ass," Edge introduces the one with shaggy black hair, nodding in their direction. Like most Divine, they are unbelievable to look at. I assume they are a High Divine, considering they lead an army. Their tan skin indicates long days in the sun, a subtle white hue glistening underneath. I look into gorgeous green-brown eyes, noting the dimples and high cheekbones before looking away.

"Um, okay?"

"And this is Amon Ainsworth. He is Eleazer's lieutenant."

I glance over at the blond with a buzz cut, noting he, too, is a High Divine. A navy hue dances underneath his light skin that is covered in puckering burns. His soft hazel eyes dance in amusement, a light smile gracing his angular face.

Freckles are splattered across his forehead and cheeks, racing down his neck and out of sight.

"Got it."

"And you are Cerina Celeste." Eleazer is the first to address the awkward silence that follows.

"I told you to stop telling people my real name," I hiss as I spin back toward Edge, eyes narrowing as I try to control the flames threatening to escape my skin.

"Calm down." Amon laughs, patting his captain on the back. "Leave her alone, El. They're just messing with you, sweetheart." I notice the gentle stroke of his hand afterward, almost like a lover's caress. I watch the movement, wondering if Edge placed himself between them so he didn't have to deal with watching those subtle touches.

"Amon has the strength of fifty Divine. Don't you, A?" Valaine grins, waggling her fingers at him. Strength is a good thing to have in a lieutenant. With that amount of power, he can take on multiple enemies all at once. But strength only goes so far with the Divine—most powers can easily block a physical attack.

"Eleazer can take away powers for a short period," Edge answers, smirking when a glare graces my features.

"Stay out of my mind," I snap at him, growling out, "Maybe Eleazer should take your powers away for a little bit. A time-out, if you will." Everyone but Edge laughs, his glare meeting my own.

"I've tried, but alas. No luck so far." They frown over at Edge in mock disappointment.

"Let's get this over with. I have places to be that don't involve any of you," Edge grumbles, eye still trained on me. I reluctantly take a seat in a kitchen chair that had been dragged into the room, plopping down next to my sister. She doesn't notice me next to her, gaze busy following the new eye candy. I should have let her out of the house more—all she's done since arriving here is flirt with every Divine she meets.

"Got a hot date, huh?" Amon prods, elbowing Edge in the ribs.

"It's none of your business, asshole," Edge hisses back, gaze flickering to me once more. I ignore the jab of jealousy that hits me, ignore the sinking feeling in my gut. I don't care about Edge or whoever he dates. I *don't.*

"Then let's begin." Amon grins, standing and stretching. "How are we going to sneak her in to kill him?" Great. That's what this is about?

"The easiest way would be to transport her," Eleazer mutters as they stand, beginning to pace. "But we would have to be very precise about where she landed. Can Edge even get her there and back? And what if things go wrong? None of us will be able to be there. That's just too much power, even for him."

Amon joins in, musing, "If you don't want to absorb him then a knife to the heart will work but, really, sucking the Royalness right out of him is best. But then what if he alerts someone before she gets to finish? She'd need to be alone with him without anyone near and that is going to be—"

"I don't want to absorb Prince Zaeden," I say firmly, watching their pacing increase, hands rubbing chins in frustration. I crinkle my brows as I watch the lieutenant and his captain move in sync.

"Why would you not absorb him?" Amon throws his hands up in exasperation, quick to anger.

"This has already been discussed. I understand that I have the best chance of getting him truly alone. I understand that I can probably lure him off on his own because he will want to apprehend me himself. I understand that I'm the best person for the job. *I understand.* But I don't want to absorb him. That feels horrible. The rush, the exhilaration, the new powers...that's great. Until it isn't. Until you've got a pile of ashes in front of you that used to be a person. Until the guilt eats you alive and refuses to spit you back out. I've already had a taste of his poison; I don't want to digest anymore." I can feel the anger rising from the Divine in the room and can see the fear in Irissa's eyes as she watches the scene unfold. Even Valaine seems uneasy, her fingers tapping against her thighs in angst. I turn just in time to watch Eleazer reach over to brush their hand across Amon's, a gentle, soothing motion meant to calm him down. And the way they stare at each other...I feel like I'm interrupting something intimate. Edge, however, seems oblivious to this intensity in the air or the intimacy between his friends.

"That's why we are training her—she's fucking delusional," Edge spits out from his spot on the couch.

"That's ridiculous." Amon spins on me again, forcing me to stand to meet his heated gaze. Yes, definitely quick to anger, then. "You won't do this for your Court? For the Undivines who need you?"

"They turned their backs on me. Is it even considered my Court anymore?"

"Then do it for *our* Court!" He throws his hands up again, leaning forward to hiss in my face. "Do it for all of the Undivine getting whipped in the streets, for all the Divine who are too scared to argue for a change."

"I did a lot of things for the Undivine already, and where has that gotten me? I'll tell you where—on the top of a fucking castle, leaping toward my death, that's where!" I ignore Irissa's gasp from beside me.

"*Then do it for you.* For what he did to you. He's a sadist who tried to force you to marry him, to sleep with him while you were in love with his fucking brother. Don't you want revenge? Don't you want him to pay?" I ignore the sting of the truth, embarrassed. Had Edge told him these things? Spilled my secrets to this angry, unfamiliar man?

"Prince Zaeden deserves a fate worse than death, but that fate won't be dealt by my hands. I agreed to kill him., I didn't say *how* I would do it. Like I said before, trying to help everyone else did nothing to help *me*."

"It got you one step closer to sorting out the problem. You took one down, you only have one more to go!" Amon stares at me as though I'm delusional, as though I'm a child who refuses to see reason.

"I took one down?" My voice falls down an octave, a deadly calm taking over. Is that how these people view the worst day of my life? As a small step toward a greater goal?

"That Royal was just as bad as his poisonous brother," Amon spits out. It pulls Irissa to her feet, her wings unfurling in a fury.

"Don't talk about him like that in front of her. He was good to *her*." Her voice rises above Amon's, her eyes turning a deep shade of black. Shit. I need to interfere before things really start going downhill. Irissa may be in control of herself right now, but her emotions always startle her powers into action. It's better to stop things before they get intense.

"He was different. He was going to be better." My rebuttal sounds weak even to me.

"Oh, were you going to change him?" Amon mocks with a roll of his eyes. "Let me give you a good life lesson, sweetheart: Guys like that don't change. They're rotten to the core and no amount of sex will change that."

"Excuse me?" I sputter out just as Irissa leaps forward. He easily steps away from her swiping talons, gripping her wrists tightly. She twists and lashes out with a wing, smacking him hard in the head. He groans and stumbles back, furious eyes racing up to meet her own.

"Enough," Edge commands, causing both Divine to halt. "Amon, watch your mouth. Celeste, get a grip."

"I loved him," I hiss out, shaking my head furiously as I try to settle the flames that are fighting to be let out. "I didn't mean to kill him."

"But you did," Edge says, repeating the familiar words. "And now we all must suffer the consequences."

"That I can agree with." I swallow hard, my body shaking with the effort to hold in the flames I stole. "But I just...I don't know if I can do it. When the time comes, I'm not sure I can handle the pressure or the knowledge that a life is being absorbed into my body. I can't even tell you I disliked it. I was shocked, confused, and scared. But it felt good. I haven't wanted to admit that out loud, but it's true. And I'm scared of the person I will become if I absorb more. I'm scared of what a power like Prince Zaeden's will do to me."

"Why do you call him that? Not Zaeden or Zae, but Prince Zaeden?" Edge's gaze softens as he comes to stand before me, his voice gentle as if speaking to a scared animal who's ready to flee. And maybe that's exactly what I am. My heart flutters knowing this is something he picked up on, a small discrepancy in my speech that no one but him noticed.

"I can't call him Zaeden or Zae anymore." I shake my head, wrapping my arms around myself as I crack open in front of him. I focus only on him, forgetting that anyone else is here. It's just me and him, and I can't stop myself from letting out all of the thoughts that have haunted me since coming here. I can't stop myself from opening up to the one person I *know* will understand. With a shaky inhale, I stare into steel blue.

"Not since he showed me what lies inside him and the true evil he hides behind that beautiful face. Zae is the guy who helped heal me in a dark and dirty cell. Zae is the guy who was my friend, who was sweet and kind when no one else was. Zae is the guy who fought to get me and my sister raised to a Divine status. Zae is the guy who looked at me and saw more than an Undivine, who wanted me despite that. And then he turned into Prince Zaeden. A guy who covets control and power. A guy who was going to force me to sleep with him if I ever slept with his brother, who wanted to make sure he never went without anything his brother had. That guy is *not* Zae. I *know* they're the same person. In my mind, I know that. But my heart is still holding onto this memory of him. I don't want to separate the two. I want to hold onto Zae just a little longer. So I can kill Prince Zaeden and not see my friend staring back at me. So it won't hurt so badly this time when I kill a prince." I can barely breathe as Edge grabs me, pulling me into his chest. As the tears spill down onto his shoulders. As his lips touch my ear so he can whisper words only I can hear.

"It's time to let go of Zae, Celeste. It's time that those two people became one. You're strong. So much stronger than he ever gave you credit for. You *can* kill him. You are a warrior: It's time to act like one." I nod my head as I shake in his arms, whimpering at the shadows that slink around me in their own version of a hug.

"What now?" Valaine questions, her quiet voice piercing the silence. I flinch, realizing it *wasn't* just me and Edge in this room. That I just flayed myself open for all to watch. They've all been silently watching me curl into the arms of the man who is supposed to be my enemy, listening to every word that left my lips.

"We can't go to him," Edge says finally, pulling away from me and taking a single step back. "I don't have enough strength to make that many large transports. And we can't be linked to his death in such an obvious way. If anyone finds out we were in Lunar Court territory, we won't be able to recover from it. They already want to start a war over Celeste."

"A war? What do you mean?" I gape, shaking my head in bewilderment.

"They want you back. *Badly.* They issued a statement following your escape. A statement that says any Court who knowingly hides you will be cut off from them. That if you aren't returned to stand trial then the consequences will be violent. If they find out we have you, and we don't return you, they will attack."

"Then why are you bothering to keep me here?" His people are in a lot of danger because of *me.*

"Because you are worth it." He grabs my chin and tugs it up, forcing me to lean my head back and meet his intense gaze. I should be embarrassed to be so close, so intimate, in front of this many people, but I can't bring myself to jerk away. This moment is too serious, too achingly real. "Can't you see that? You hold an insane amount of power as is, Celeste. You can have an even larger amount. Don't you see what kind of weapon you are? A single touch from you is all it takes to make someone's entire existence destitute. The amount of fear a power like that sparks is worth it. You are equal to *at least* two Royals right now, plus whatever level your shields are. Imagine what more you could hold. You could take out whole armies in no time at all. They missed out, Celeste, and they don't want anyone else knowing it." Those lips fall to my ear once more. "Not to mention your beauty, your light, your laughter. So many things about you are worth it. I may want you as my weapon, but I want you here for so much more, too."

I can't even manage to glare at him. I know my powers are far beyond the average Divine's skill level, but are they really equivalent to that? Do I have the power of a Royal?

"You think I have Royal blood," I muster out after a few long breaths, unsure if I am understanding correctly.

"I know you do. And I have suspicions about who it came from." I open my mouth to beg for more, but Amon interrupts us.

"We can't go there," he says mischievously. "But what if we bring them here?"

"Bring them here?" Valaine muses, biting on her lower lip. "Whenever they come, we will have to be careful about when and if we reveal Celeste. Revealing her would catch him off guard, especially if we did so publicly. It *might* earn us the chance to catch him alone. But how could we do that? How would we ever get him here for something like that?"

"We need something a little crazy. Something they won't be able to refuse," Eleazer chimes in, contemplating.

"Like the Games, you mean?" Irissa questions with a tilt of her head. Her wings slowly drop down her back, sinking back into her skin. The fabric of her dress dangles limply in their wake, and I know from experience the large rips left behind will be unable to be fixed. It's barely being held up by her thin straps, but she doesn't seem to notice.

"Yes!" Valaine squeals, a smug grin pulling up the corners of her lips. "Or an engagement."

"You are not going to marry my sister to get the Lunars here," I snarl, pissed. Irissa and Valaine have been together constantly, touching each other in the slightest of ways and whispering conspiratorially all the time. I knew they were attracted to one another, but this? This is too far, too fast.

"Oh, no. I'm not talking about your sister and me."

"What—" I sputter at the same time Edge speaks.

"Absolutely not."

"No, I think she is right." Amon grins, pleased with whatever this new idea is. His anger seems to have deflated, likely because of my emotional rant that put a dim on the room. "It'll grant Celeste immunity."

"No way," Edge hisses again, backing away from me abruptly as he turns to his friends.

"What will grant me immunity?" I question wearily, glancing between all of the smirking faces.

"Marriage." Irissa giggles, glancing at Valaine shyly. "I can't marry Valaine. She's only second-in-line, it wouldn't make sense for them to show up to a second-in-line wedding. But if the heir was to be wed…"

"As if I would allow you to marry my sister, Shape-Shifter," Edge huffs angrily.

"Watch it." I narrow my eyes, processing Irissa's words. Do they want me to marry *Edge*? I can admit to finding him attractive and finding comfort in his presence, but *marriage?*

His tone is flat and final as he says, "I will not marry her."

"Good, because I would rather be swallowed by one of those mutated beasts in the woods than marry *you.*"

"I can have that arranged," he hisses back, shadows dancing around his feet. My flames roar to life with the challenge.

"See this finger right here." I hold up my hand, pointing to where his missing finger is located—the one I chopped off months ago when he savagely attacked me. "Yeah, where's yours?"

"You insolent little shit—"

"Enough!" Irissa jumps between us, failing to fight off her laughter. "No one said anything about actually getting married."

"You *just* said—" I attempt to argue.

"Engagement, Les. Just pretend. They show up for a wedding, we kill Zaeden before we make it to that part. Just say you are married afterward. That you did a private ceremony or something due to the unusual circumstances if anyone questions things."

"I can't get engaged! Don't you all remember what happened last time? I can't hold a wedding to kill that said fiancé. Though, now that I think about it, maybe we *should* do this, Edge. I can murder two fiancé's in one go." I send a glare toward him once more, not caring if I sound like a child.

"This way will mostly guarantee your safety," Valaine plows on, eyes wide and giddy. "Your presence is already going to be seen as a reason for war. But if you two are 'wed', there isn't anything anyone can do. You will be Edge's. You will be bound to him and our Court. The Lunars wouldn't dare go to war with that kind of protection on your back because then other Courts would need to get involved, and they don't have the power for a war on that scale. Besides, the two of you make a powerful match. No one will be able to deny that. And with the rumors that circulate about our Court, well, everyone will believe us capable of something like this."

"This is ridiculous." I slam into my chair, slumping back and shaking my head weakly. "How do you plan on killing him without it being suspicious? And didn't you want me to rule in his stead? What will you do about the current king and queen?"

"Well, it definitely rules out any option of you absorbing his powers. That's too obvious. We must continue with the plans to get him alone somehow, as well as his parents. Amon and I can work on forming a plan. We know the castle layout better than anyone. We can find a way to kill him discreetly and to kill his parents afterward. As far as you ruling...well, that possibility isn't entirely gone." Eleazer sounds much more confident than I feel.

"This is wrong," I whisper, defeated.

"You really feel that way?" Edge raises one eyebrow, a sharpness to his voice. "After what he said to you? After what he forced you to do?" I bristle, turning away. I remember that night when I was sure Edge read my mind and knew *exactly* what had happened between Zaeden and me.

"What did he do?" Irissa questions quietly. "I thought he just threatened—"

"It doesn't matter now," I interrupt, fidgeting uncomfortably in my seat.

"He deserves more than death for forcing himself on you like that," Edge growls, and I shudder as I remember Zaeden's harsh kiss.

So where did this Zaeden come from? Is it just the jealousy talking or something more? Either way, something major has changed within him. He is not the man I know. This man has lost control and is desperate to get it back. Was everything between us fake? All because he wanted to own me?

I try to speak slowly and deliberately. Try not to shake in fear. "Forget what those evil men said. They lie and we both know it. Again, I just don't have romantic feelings for you. There is attraction, of course. But I like you as my friend. Nothing more. We have a great friendship. I just don't want to take it further. Kyelin and I...well, I think we can be good together. You understand, right?" *I am starting to reconsider anything I have ever felt for this Divine. Does Kyelin know about this side of his brother? Maybe there is a reason he was born with poison inside of him.*

Zaeden doesn't respond with words. Instead, his hands snake up to the back of my head and tangle into my hair. He pulls me to his lips, forcing them upon mine. He doesn't wait for permission as Kyelin did. I try to pull away, but he is strong. The kiss is forceful and harsh, but not in a good way. I know it will leave bruised and swollen lips on both of us. It's nothing like kissing Silvi. Definitely not like kissing Kyelin. A hand slides down, moving to cup my breast. That's the final straw for—

"I would gladly kill him for you."

Something plummets down into the pits of my stomach as I'm awoken from the memory, my gaze snapping back to his. I can see the truth in his eye: *He means it.* I swallow hard, that hideous truth making me feel too many confusing things at once.

"Fine," I agree reluctantly, the strange feeling influencing my willingness to participate in this insane plan. "We can *pretend* to be engaged and *pretend* to wed."

"Yay!" Valaine squeals, Irissa whooping along with her.

"*If* you do something for me in return." My eyes are still on Edge.

"That sounds sexual. Please don't make this sexual. We don't want to hear about any kinky shit you two are into." Amon shakes his head playfully.

"You have to find out who my father is before the wedding takes place. I won't do it unless I have all of the information I need." I ignore Amon completely. Edge has already agreed to help me on this subject before, but I want this process sped up. If he needs this as badly as he says, then he's going to give me something I need, too.

"That's impossible. I only have a hunch, I don't have proof. It's impossible to find out that fast."

"Is it?" I raise an eyebrow, picking at some dirt underneath my nails. "Then I guess I can't help you."

"*You* are impossible," he hisses back.

"Just because we have an inkling—" Valaine tries.

"Do you know how fast this part is going to take place?" Eleazer interrupts.

"That is a really big request," Amon follows up.

"Fine," Edge agrees before more arguments commence. "I'll do it." Everyone freezes, surprise lighting up the room.

I smirk in satisfaction, standing and stalking toward him. "Then we have a deal," I purr, sticking out my hand. He takes it quickly, giving me a firm shake. We linger in that position for longer than necessary, neither of us pulling away.

"Promise?" he questions with a tug of his lips.

"Only if you do." With those words, we seal our fates, the power of the agreement settling in our bones. Edge seems unaffected, but I know he feels it, too.

"Eleazer, Amon. Retrieve her mother. Bring her here. You know which house she is at." With a wave of his hand, the two Divine are out of the door and disappearing into the streets.

"My mother is here?" I grit my teeth, yanking my hand away from his. "And you didn't think to tell me before now?"

"She's in a safe house with a new name and a new life posing as a Low Divine." He shrugs casually. "And I didn't think you wanted to see her."

"Of course I don't want to see her! But I should have been informed that she was in this Court! What if I had bumped into her?"

"Does it really matter? You know now and you haven't bumped into her yet, have you? No? Alright then, piss off." I gape up at him, flames sparking out of my hair. He ignores them, turning to his sister instead. "What timeline are you thinking?"

"Two months," she says after a brief silence. "The other Courts will have to travel to get here, so…that's the quickest we can do this. We will send invitations in the next few days. We will just say you are foregoing the Games because you found a love match."

"I get two months," he groans, running a hand over his face. "Great."

"And if your side of the bargain isn't fulfilled, then you can kiss this little engagement goodbye," I hiss, annoyed.□□"I will do what I can and nothing more." His cold gaze falls back to me. "In the meantime, you have to work harder on your training. You need to be perfectly in control by the time everyone arrives. We won't leave room for any mistakes. There can be no snags in our plans."

"I will do what I can and nothing more."

CHAPTER 13

Celeste

Edge and I sit silently, refusing to look at one another, while Irissa chats vehemently with Valaine about our *wedding*. I try to pay attention, I do, but it's all too much. Marriage, my mother, my *father*. Knowing my mother can be here any moment, that she has been in this Court for weeks...it's a hard pill to swallow.

Irissa and I ran away from home when I was eighteen and Irissa was fifteen, and for good reason. After my father passed away, she became unrecognizable. She had always viewed us as competition for his love, a sick and twisted part of her mind convinced that we would be her ruin. For years we endured her abuse, until one day when I finally decided I had had enough. I took Irissa and fled to another village, far enough away that she didn't find out where we went until over a year later—not that she cared enough to come after us.

I didn't want Irissa to feel the pain and unworthiness I had, so I built a better life for her. At least, I thought that's what I was doing. Now everything seems construed, and I wonder how much my biases, my protectiveness, got in the way of Irissa's happiness. I just wanted to be a good sister, caretaker, and protector. Had I been any of those things? Had she been any better off with me, considering the situation I've put her in? I feel Edge's hand come to rest over mine, shadows dancing over my arm comfortingly. I curse myself for my loud thoughts, slamming up a shield and turning even farther away.

"Just get in!" Eleazer's low growl leaves a chill down my spine. Their voice makes me sit up straighter and suddenly I understand why they were chosen as the captain of the Solar Court army.

"Quit manhandling me!" I hear Urona shriek back just as the door flies open. I watch with wide eyes as she is dragged into the room, held by each arm.

"Then quit fighting us," Amon snaps back, grunting with the effort it takes to drag her in.

"How dare you treat me like this? I am under the protection of your prince! I didn't do anything wrong! I can't be held here against my will! Let me go!" With one final push, she is released from their grasp. The door slams shut behind them, Irissa and I watching silently as the scene unfolds.

"Welcome." I stifle my laugh at her surprise, Edge's sly smile is a comforting sight. He stands, shadows trailing behind his feet. "How wonderful it is to see you again, Urona."

Her mouth snaps open, close, open, close. After a few seconds, she regains her composure and allows a smile to grace her lips. She curtsies deeply, blond hair falling forward to form a curtain. "My apologies, Your Highness. I didn't realize—"

"Obviously," Eleazer snaps, pushing past her to stand by the Royal's side.

"Hello, Urona," I say, eyes bouncing between her and Irissa. Irissa only nods in greeting, eyes falling to the floor.

"Daughters," she breathes, panic filling her eyes as she searches the room. "What is this? Why am I here?" I see Edge smirk out of the corner of my eye as he takes a step forward, a move that only startles her further.

"Why don't you take a seat, Urona?" Edge strides forward to grab another chair, placing it in the middle of the room for all to see. He holds out a hand, allowing her to use him for balance as she sits. I roll my eyes at his faux kindness, recognizing it for what it is: an act.

Uncoordinated bitch.

I startle at the drawling words inside my mind, a confirmation of my suspicions. I turn my wide eyes to Edge only to find him already watching me, a grin plastered on his face.

I cover my mouth quickly, coughing to cover my amusement. Is this because I have some of his power in me?

He's never been able to speak in my mind like this before. However, this isn't the first time in the past few weeks I've noticed I've been stealing from Edge. I've brought it up during several of our training sessions, but he doesn't seem to care. He doesn't look at me any differently, doesn't flee with fear in his eyes. He isn't even angry, like most Divine would be if even a smidgen of their power had been stolen. It's...refreshing.

"What do you want?" Urona takes her seat, graceful and quiet. I notice the slight tremor in her hands, the singular twitch of an eyebrow. *She's scared.*

"I need you to answer some questions, Urona." Edge stalks behind her, shadows brushing against her shoulders teasingly.

"About?"

"Your husband."

"My...my husband?" It's not the answer she was expecting. Her body stiffens in surprise, eyes darting around the room as if looking for a way to escape. Unfortunately for her, it's not a feasible option.

"Celeste's life is dependent on these answers." Edge tries to play on her love for me, on my importance in her life. After a heavy and revealing silence, it's clear that threatening me isn't what will make her tick. So, he adds, "Irissa's, too."

"Go on." Her reply is quick and brisk as she glances toward my sister.

"What Court did he originate from?"

"Lunar," she says far too quickly.

"Ooh. A lie. This is going to be fun." Amon grins, startling her even further. Her gaze bounces from person to person, eyeing up the threats in the room. Upon realizing there are six Divine in the room, she slumps even farther down into the chair.

"What does that mean?" I question, squinting in suspicion.

"Edge is really good at getting information out of people. Urona's experienced that before, haven't you, sweetheart?" Her wide eyes spin between the two men as she pushes herself to the edge of the chair, prepared to flee despite the risk.

"You actually tortured her?" I gape at Edge, my mind flashing back to when he had told me that was how he got information on me. I didn't realize he had been truthful!

"What was his Divine status?" Edge drawls, ignoring me and continuing to question my mother.

"Undivine." Her answer is too quick once more.

"Quit lying, Urona," Eleazer scolds now. "Tell us the truth." Edge lets his shadows rise in front of her, the thick shadows dancing across her body in a subtle move. She screeches, almost flipping her chair backward from how hard she jumps back.

"Please! Please, I can't!"

"You must." Edge squats down in front of her, leaning forward to snarl in her face. He reaches out, placing his hand over hers and allowing the shadows to swallow it. She screams out as if she was being stabbed, thrashing around in her chair. Amon leaps forward and pushes down on her shoulders, keeping her in place. Irissa lets out a noise of dismay, covering her mouth with her hands. Valaine holds her down, too, preventing her from jumping toward our mother.

"I promised! I promised!" she cries, tears falling hard and fast.

"What did you promise?"

"I promised I wouldn't tell anyone where he came from or who he is. Who his parents were. That I would never speak of his Divinity. Not unless—" Her words stop abruptly, her face panic-ridden.

"Unless what?" Edge grinds out, shadows wavering in front of her threateningly. Urona shakes her head furiously, sobbing now.

"Unless the girls asked," she whimpers, finally meeting my eyes.

"What Court did he originate from?" I ask quietly, watching her retreat into herself as I approach. She puts her head into her hands, tears slipping down into her lap.

"The Shadow Court." The words are a slap to the face. We were born and raised in the Lunar Court. We only knew the Lunar Court, and only had each other there. Do we have family on the other side of the continent? Grandparents? Aunts or uncles?

"How did you meet him?" Irissa reaches up to grasp Valaine's hands as she asks the question.

After a long pause, she says, "I was working for his family; I mostly did gardening for them. I used to have a liking for plants, but now I can hardly look at flowers without thinking of him. I haven't had a garden since he passed." It's the most heartbroken I've ever seen her. She's never talked about our father, refused to give us his name, even. It was frustrating and embarrassing growing up without a father, and I hardly have any memories of him despite being seven when he passed. I can remember his kindness, his love, his warmth. It's all I've ever needed from him.

"What were his powers?" I am breathless, leaning forward as I await more information on this man I barely knew.

"He was a Shield."

The words are a shot to the chest.

Her hatred-filled eyes don't hurt me. Neither do Irissa's pity-filled ones. What hurts me is the knowing gaze in Edge's eye, the truth that has finally been confirmed. *He'd suspected this all along.*

I stumble back, knocking into my chair in the process. I tumble over, tripping and slamming into the wall as I fall. The shock rolls through me in waves, controlling my mind enough to drown out Edge's cussing in my mind. He approaches swiftly, swooping down next to me in a flourish. He doesn't touch me, doesn't wrap me in his arms, but I don't want him to. High emotional states such as this one are what trigger the monster within me, are what causes me to lash out. I wouldn't be able to live with myself if I killed him, too.

"I killed him." My whisper pierces the air, five sets of eyes and a singular steel blue one drawn to my despair. I don't need the confirmation to know the statement is true.

"Yes. Yes, you fucking killed him! And he let you. He fucking let you! He just smiled and said he loved you and Irissa, that you two were the best things to ever happen to him. And then *poof!* A pile of ashes on the floor. He didn't say bye to me. He didn't have time to: you made sure of that." My mother pierces through my haze, her words clear and hurtful. This is why she treated us so poorly, why she always chose Irissa; she blames me for his death. Rightfully so, I suppose. And she is *jealous*. Jealous that he loved us enough to get out one final goodbye, jealous that he didn't give her that closure, too.

I watch as Valaine takes Irissa into her arms, pulling her from the chair so she can cry freely. Those cries rock through me, pulling me underneath a fierce wave of guilt. How could I have done that? Why don't I remember doing it?

"Leave," Edge turns and growls out, jutting his head toward the door. "We will come to you when we need you again."

"Les," Irissa whispers after Urona scuttles away, taking a step toward me.

"Stay away! Don't come near me!" I push myself as hard as I can against the wall, shaking. If only I could make myself disappear, or shrink to a size no one will ever be able to see. Then I would be free from these sorrowful gazes.

"I don't understand," she whispers, the despair in that one sentence ripping me in half.

"I'll kill you! If you touch me, I might start taking your powers. And I won't be able to stop, Iris. Please. *Please*," I sob, head dropping down into my hands. Valaine pulls her back into her arms upon hearing my pleas, glancing toward her brother and sharing a knowing glance. No words are spoken, only a discreet nod of his head before she pulls my sister out into the streets. Eleazer and Amon are not far behind.

I'm a monster.

The thought hits me hard, my chest heaving. It's true. I *am* a monster. I need to be put down, just like the Lunars want. I should have died already. I've killed two people—no, *three*—and I must ask myself once more: *How many more deaths will there be? Who's next?*

No, you're not a monster.

My wet eyes drift up toward Edge, realizing he didn't follow the others. I shake my head furiously, sniffing pitifully. Did I accidentally send a message his way?

He tries to joke, saying, *Your thoughts are loud. Turn down the volume.*

Piss off. I let my head droop down again. He needs to leave before I kill him, too. Wouldn't that be great? Two Royal deaths by *my* hands? Possibly three, if he was right about my father.

Edge grabs my shoulders suddenly, pulling me up on wobbly knees. I try to jerk away but he clutches on tightly, leading me toward the old, smelly couch. Only when we reach it do I succeed in pulling away, my eyes wide as I sit down.

I'll kill you. I attempt to push the thought into his mind, attempt to sear it into his head. Did he not understand what just happened? He can die just as easily as anyone else. I've killed a Royal or two before, and I could certainly do it again. Does he have no self-preservation?

"You won't kill me," he says simply as he takes the spot next to me. He is close enough for our thighs to touch, close enough for his sweet and smoky smell to overtake the mildew scent of the couch.

"How do you know?"

"I've seen the memory, Celeste. I saw it when we were on the roof. You wanted to hurt Kyelin for what he did—you just didn't realize what that would mean. That isn't your fault. No one explained things to you, no one trained you. You were left to figure out things on your own, left to believe there was nothing special inside of you. It's not your fault." Everyone tells me it isn't my fault but *it is*. It was my hands, my powers. All of the repercussions must fall on me.

"I'm a monster," I repeat, body shaking as I try to slow the tears.

"You aren't." Then, after a brief pause, "I didn't mean for this to happen. I'm sorry you had to find out this way." His hands slip over my waist and down my back, arms encompassing my body. I don't bat him away, don't fight him as I feel a tug on my body and am pulled into his lap. I allow my head to fall onto his shoulder, allowing the tears to fall freely. Edge stays silent, allowing me time to grieve.

I killed my father.

I thought I was over it already, that I was past the point of grief when it came to his loss. But this? This has brought up new waves of grief, new heights of sadness, and new pounds of guilt. I've known I was a killer for months now, but this is entirely different. I was a *child.* A child capable of something so horrific, capable of murdering someone she loved, should not have been allowed to make the same mistake again. My mother should have locked me up. Is that why I kept Irissa so contained? Did some hidden part of me fear that she would become the monster I already was? I shudder in Edge's arms, hyper-aware of his presence.

I don't know why I'm doing this. Why I am letting him hold me, letting him comfort me? This man is a monster, too. He has done awful, despicable things to the people of his Court. According to Ryleigh, anyway. I can't be sure anymore if anything she has ever told me is true. She was the one who told me how horrible this place was, how terrible the Royals were. Then she admitted she had been friends with them all along. So what is the truth? Who is Edge, really?

Are you a monster like me?

"We can be monsters together." His voice is soft as his hands tangle into my hair effortlessly, pulling me closer. My stomach lurches at the touch, my heart racing.

I need this.

I need someone to embrace the darkness with, someone to tell me that it's okay not to be okay.

"I don't remember my father at all," I admit into the silence, the guilty thoughts finally unleashing themselves. "I thought he died in an accident because I had been told the wagon he was riding in crashed while he was crossing into Lunar City. I guess that was a fairy tale Urona created to hide the truth. But how can I not remember? That was my father! My own father." My voice cracks at the end as I wipe frantically at the fallen tears.

"My father died when I was three years old. I don't remember him, either." His warm breath tickles my ear, his voice quiet and reassuring. "I know he was a good Divine. A good king. He was kind to my mother, the love of her life. When they met at the Games, he knew immediately she was the one and he told her so. It was enough encouragement to convince her to fight hard, to earn her place in this Court. She was born and raised in Solar City, so there weren't any political motivations. He just loved her. It was a perfect match. Then he got sick—the kind of sick even a healer can't fix. Within a year, she was forced to remarry. The Cruel King, they call him. Things have been out of control, the Undivines are starting to rebel, and his solution? Kill them if they step a toe out of line.

"Some of the things you have heard about me are true. I *do* torture and murder the people of my Court. I do whatever I have to to make sure he doesn't suspect me of turning against him, and that he doesn't believe me to be a threat to his reign. I've had to watch my Court crumble underneath his rule, had to watch my mother wilt underneath his thumb. I won't do it any longer. Not now that I have you."

His words seem pointed, a double meaning hidden there I just can't accept. *Now that I have you.* What am I to him, anyway? A weapon, a friend...or more?

"Are you really going to change things? So many people have promised *change* and no one has yet to deliver."

"I will," he vows solemnly. "No matter what. And I plan on aiming higher than before. Before, I just wanted my people to be safe. But now? You've inspired me. You've shown me the courage and bravery that Divines have tried to beat out of you time and time again. And yet it's still there. You've shown me a resilience that I did not know existed. You've shown me that *Divinity doesn't matter.*"

"You seem so awful most of the time, but then you go and say such sweet things."

He snorts, his chuckles vibrating against me. "Don't go around telling people that. I'll never be taken seriously again."

"Yeah, yeah. I know the drill."

"But you've been pretending, too, haven't you?" I don't answer his prying question, making the split decision to change the subject.

I choose to state the obvious, saying, "I've been taking your powers."

"I don't mind sharing the burden that is this darkness," he whispers, hand drifting across my back and toward my neck. He grips my chin lightly, pulling my head up enough to be face-to-face. My hands snake around his neck as our chests brush against each other, breaths mingling in the air. I can feel our powers sizzling around us, embracing one another like old friends. I've never felt anything like it before. They seem to dance with each other, combining and swirling as they drift into my skin. This isn't a tug and pull, it isn't a selfish moment where I take and take but never give. That's because, this time, I'm *not* taking anything from him.

He's giving something to me.

CHAPTER 14

Celeste

"Are you fucking insane? Actually, medically insane? Do you have some residual trauma still doing damage to your teeny, tiny mind? Because I can book you an appointment with a healer, we can get some tonics to fix that."

I turn my head in surprise at Ryleigh's angry voice, eyes wide as I stare at the open door and looming woman. I back up a few steps, scratching the back of my head as I try to figure out what she is going on about.

"What are you talking about?" I question, plastering on a pleasant smile. It doesn't work.

"The dumb blond act isn't really working for you, Celeste. Fess up!" I chuckle humorlessly as I shake my head, looking anywhere but her eyes. That's always the first mistake: *looking at her.*

"I don't know, Ryleigh. What do you think I did? I've been misbehaving a lot lately. That's how I ended up in this Court, remember?"

"Yeah, and is that how you ended up engaged to their prince?" Oh. That's what this is about. Edge and I have been "engaged" for days now, but I guess word has finally reached her ears. Since I have been avoiding her, she isn't privy to all the juicy gossip about my life.

"Um. Yeah, I suppose so," I say slowly, twisting my hands around nervously. "But I'm not *really* going to marry him, so there's no reason to be angry. It's just pretend." The thought of marrying Edge doesn't enrage me as much as it should. I know it sounds a little insane to an outsider—especially from Ryleigh's perspective, considering he and I do nothing but argue. In public, in private, in front of our friends; the arguments happen everywhere, all the time. I should hate him, and maybe once I thought I did. Now, I'm not so sure. And the thought of not hating him floods me with unwanted feelings. Feelings that are too terrifying to even think about.

"Oh, you aren't, are you? You really believe that?"

"I know it!" I defend lamely.

"Yeah? Do you know what kind of danger you're going to be in by putting on this little show? Do you?"

"Does it matter anymore, Ryleigh? Do you even care?"

"Does it matter?" She scoffs in disbelief, her face morphing into one of earnest desperation. "I would rather die in your place, Celeste. Do you realize that? If we were under attack I would jump in front of a bullet to make sure you survived. How dare you go behind my back and do this?"

"How dare I go behind your back?" I shout in disbelief. "Are you serious? And to answer your question, *no, I didn't realize that.* I'm not sure I do now. How am I supposed to believe anything you say, Ryleigh? Do I need to bring up the multiple, lengthy lies you have been feeding me? The years of secrets? I'm a grown woman. A Divine at that! You don't dictate my actions. You aren't my boss anymore, and I'm not even sure you were my *friend.*" I'm panting by the end, my anger endless as I release the doubts that I've been pushing off for far too long.

"I *am* your friend. And as such, I would have thought you would have consulted me. You've always done so! I gave you a job, I took you under my wing, I helped you when you found out you were Divine, and most importantly, I helped you when you went off and became a serial killer! I have put my neck on the line for you time and time again, and this is the thanks I get? You rushing to shackle yourself to *another* Royal? Maybe you *are* the Divine climber they claim you to be." Her words strike true, hitting their only target: my heart.

"If you were so great then where were you? Where were you when three soldiers cornered me in an empty corridor? When they dragged me into an empty room to punish me?

To push me to the brink of death? Where were you as I lay on the ground, screaming and begging for my life, Ryleigh? By the time you showed up, it was too late. The damage was already done. I will forever be grateful for your kindness, but I don't owe you anything. Especially not my choices." I have ensnared us with flames, the heat barely tolerable, but she doesn't seem to notice. She's too busy watching me, a single tear slipping down her face. But that could be sweat, too.

"I didn't—I didn't realize. I just thought—well, I don't know—I just...you should have told me." She winced as she said it as if knowing it was the wrong thing to say.

I turn my back to her, wrapping my arms around myself. "How was I supposed to tell anyone? I was embarrassed. Ashamed. And I thought you knew; I couldn't have been the first. But what could we have done? Who would have cared? We were lowly Undivine. I was born to be abused by the Divine system. Those men would have never been punished. No harm would have ever come to them. And I could have been fired; I couldn't afford to lose my cushy job at the castle."

"What if I was able to stop them? I could have had them thrown in the cells to rot! I have contacts! I would have made sure—"

"How was I supposed to know about all of that, Ryleigh?" I scoff bitterly, shaking my head. "Not that it matters now. Someone's already beat you to it."

"What?" Her voice cracks a little, surprising me enough to spin myself around.

"Zaeden was the first person I ever told, Ryleigh. I thought—I thought I could trust him. He made me feel like he was my only option. Made me believe that he actually *cared*. I mean, it all seemed so genuine. He saved me from one of them the day I was arrested. The guy had jumped in my cell spouting a whole lot of shit, and I couldn't do a damn thing to protect myself. But Zaeden could. *He did.* He saved me. So I rewarded him with a very personal story. One he used against me later.

"Zaeden locked those guys up and told me that I could be the one to decide their fates. He lured me in with the taste of revenge. And, oh, how I reveled in it, Ryleigh. I wanted to make them suffer. But now? Now I want Zaeden to suffer. And if I do this, *he will*."

Her shoulders sag as she says, "How do you plan on pulling it off?"

"They are going to announce our arrival after all of the guests arrive for the celebrations, presumably at a party being thrown in honor of our engagement. I will walk out on Edge's arm, a shiny new display for all Divine to see, and he will *rage*. At some point, we are going to convince him to slip, or maybe guide him, out. Then, someone will take care of him." That's as far as the plans ever made it, but we should have something more concrete soon. It's what I prefer to call a *later problem*.

"You are going to let someone else do the dirty work for you? That's cowardly," she whispers in disgust, shaking her head with a disappointed scowl. Hadn't she just berated me for becoming a "serial killer"? Now she *wants* me to kill?

"I don't care. I don't *want* to be a killer. I don't *want* to use my powers."

"If you want him to die so badly, if you want to exact revenge, then it should be by *your* hands!"

"I won't continue to be a murderer!" I hiss, turning my flames loose. They race toward her, their terrifying beauty pulling a scream from Ryleigh's throat. I pull on their leash at the last second, trying to control my breathing as they dissipate. My chest rises and falls sporadically as I try to lower my heart rate, but I can't focus well enough to do so.

"You are a damn fool, Celeste." I can see the rage in her own eyes, a rage that we have always shared.

"Maybe so."

"And you care for Edge, don't you?"

"If by care you mean *tolerate*, then sure, I care for him." At the mere mention of him, shadows leak from my skin, sliding down my body and across the floor toward her.

"You think that this task he has entrusted you with isn't meaningful? For some reason, he trusts you beyond all doubt, and you don't believe that to be a sign? Don't believe that sharing the burden of each other's powers hasn't created something else? That this...this *wickedness* you two hold won't lead you to one another despite your reservations? You are on a slippery slope, Celeste, and I'm not sure you can stop yourself from sliding to the bottom of the hill." The shadows slink back inside me, snapping back like a rubber band. I don't want to think about how wicked I am, about how evil I can be. I don't want to think about Edge and this upcoming faux wedding. I want to believe I can be good, that

I *am* good. I want to believe that the choices I'm making right now are the right ones.

"I don't want to talk about him." It's all I can manage out in my defeated state.

"A damn fool, Celeste. Both of you are."

"Maybe so," I repeat my answer from before. I don't want images of him holding me in my mind, don't want to re-member that breathless feeling his touch gave me, don't want to think about the way it felt when our skin brushed and our eyes met. How can I? The last man I fell in love with I murdered, and it feels like a betrayal to even think of having someone else.

Even if that love had been built on a pile of lies and deceit.

Even if I don't think it was love at all.

"What are you two going to do about the Games? He can't just forfeit them, can he?"

"Valaine seems to think he can. They're talking to King Zorander about it now." I shift uncomfortably, wishing she would just *leave*. "I'm not sure how that talk will go. I know the Games are made to unite Courts and find a powerful queen, but this alliance would do just that."

Ryleigh sighs after a long pause, eyes rolling to the ceiling as she begins to pace. "The King will probably go for it so that he can ensure he has full control of your powers."

"Yes. Edge said that, too."

"Edge is smart. He knows how to play with the Royals."

"There's a very likely chance that this will work, accord-ing to him," I whisper, holding myself tighter. Shadows are beginning to encase me, comforting me with their cool touch and soothing my heated skin.

"I can't believe you are doing this again," she breathes back, pausing.

"You encouraged me last time," I remind her, stiffening when she wraps me in her arms.

"I know I did. I'm sorry for the role I played at the Lunar Court, Celeste. I should never have betrayed your trust like that, even if I thought it was for the greater good. There have been things I wanted to say but couldn't, things I should have done and didn't. I let myself be blindsided and allowed myself to act selfishly. You are such a great friend, my best friend, and I acted so shamefully. What I did was horrible, unforgivable. But I hope you can. Forgive me, I mean. And I'm sorry if you were hurt by anything I've said today. Because you're right. You are a grown woman, and I am only your friend. I can give you advice but you don't have to take it. I'm so sorry. I will spend my life trying to make this up to you."

I whimper back, "Now it's my turn to do what I think is for the greater good. I don't need apologies, though I do appreciate them. I understand what huge decisions you had to make and what toll they probably took with them. Especially the ones that entailed protecting the people closest to you. I've made a few mistakes in that area, too."

"Thank you, Celeste. You don't deserve any of this. I'm sorry it had to be you." The snap in her voice breaks me, and I shudder as I try to hold back the tears that are threatening to fall. It seems that all this Court does is bring tears and misery. Or maybe I just bring that wherever I go.

"Enough of this." I suck in sharply, pulling away abruptly. "I have a few questions about my husband-to-be."

"You mean your fake husband-to-be?" She snorts with a shake of her head. "I know a lot about him. I grew up in this castle and worked here for years as I watched him grow. We got to know each other through those years. So, please, ask away."

"What you said to me before about him…is any of it true?"

"Not all of it," she admits guiltily. "I had to lie about that, too."

"Why?" How does she keep up with all of the lies she tells?

"Edge is forced to obey his stepfather, Celeste. I'm sure he's told you that. If King Zorander tells him to kill, he kills. Among other…unpleasant things. And if he doesn't listen, the crown would never be offered to him. They will find a way to pass it on to his sister instead. Or, even worse, they will send Edge away. Marry him off to another Court. He has to play a part if he wants to be in a position of power, to create the change we need. The Undivine don't know that, though. They see a heartless Bender who wants the end of their race. A Royal following in his stepfather's shoes.

"King Zorander is the one who likes to punish, the one who likes to kill. The cells down below are full, Celeste, and it isn't because of Edge. He tries to convince his stepfather of innocence, of lesser punishments when it's not suspicious to do so. And it has cost him quite a lot. He and the king don't get along as wonderfully as they used to because of his occasional defiance, but he still holds favor for the crown. For now. If I had told you that he was good, that he isn't as fearsome as he seems, and the truth got out? Well, it wouldn't have ended well for him or the people he is fighting for.

"I suspect your engagement will win him a lot of brownie points. If he makes it seem like he wants to marry you to make sure you don't leave the Court, to give him power over you, allowing King Zorander power over you both? Well, the Cruel King won't be able to resist. Edge is not a bad man, Celeste. Whatever he may lead you to believe."

Edge had admitted similar things to me only days before and had whispered about his monstrous deeds. So, that isn't much of a surprise. It *is* a surprise to learn he has a heart beneath that muscled chest of his, however.

"I didn't know," I say finally, flabbergasted and unsure of myself. "I convinced myself I hated him at first. I thought I knew who he was, but I didn't know anything at all."

"He doesn't *want* people to know. It's why he didn't kill you whenever he attacked you. I don't know what his motivations were, or his reasons, but...it was never intended to hurt you. He believes he has to wear this mask all the time. That he has to be someone else. Honestly, I think he enjoys it sometimes. He likes people thinking he is the bad guy."

"Why?"

"Because then no one can expect more from him."

I widen my eyes, shaking my head in disbelief. "I think he truly believes he is a bad guy." I think back to when he dragged me into his lap and allowed me to curl into him as we shared the darkest parts of ourselves, as we let the darkness out in a moment of utter vulnerability.

"That, too. How do you know—"

"He let me in," I interrupt, swallowing hard. "He let me take some of those shadows away. And in that brief moment of connection, I saw the deep well of sorrow that resides in the core of his very being. It's what has made me so..so unsure of my initial judgment of him."

"Maybe you can fix that, Celeste."

"I can't fix it, Ryleigh. I can treat it, but never fix it."

"Maybe you should try."

I stay silent, mind spinning. This changes so many things. I have been treating him so unfairly, so callously. But he has treated me the same, for the most part. Until I arrived at this Court. Until he seemed to morph into a new creature right in front of my eyes.

"And he's part of the Undivine Army, right?" This has mostly been confirmed, but I want to hear the words aloud.

"Yes. He joined years ago in hopes of creating a small rebellion against the Cruel King."

"It wasn't small for long."

"Why don't you attend the meeting with me in three days? Edge said you wanted to be included in decisions."

"Yes! I mean—yes, I would love to." I clear my throat awkwardly.

"Then it's settled. I'm tired of all this seriousness. We need to save our energy for arguing at the meeting, yeah?"

"What are we going to be arguing about?"

"I'm not sure yet." She chews on her bottom lip, worried wrinkles crossing her brows. "But if Edge and Valaine are speaking to their parents right now, then I know there will be a lot of planning ahead. And any plans involving you are bound to cause arguments."

"How wonderful."

After a moment of silence, she says, "Are those men currently locked up at the Lunar Court?"

"I think so. Zaeden promised that I could be the one who chooses the punishment, so..." I crinkle my brows in confusion at the abrupt change in subject.

"Do I have your permission to send someone to dole out that punishment?"

"Um. Yeah, I guess. I didn't plan on doing it anytime soon, so by all means. What do you plan on doing to them, Ryleigh? I feel a little hesitant saying yes without knowing."

"Don't worry about them, Celeste. They don't deserve your kindness, and certainly not your hesitance."

I scoff, turning away with a wrinkle of my nose. "You have always been so skilled at comforting me."

"I'm not here to comfort you," she whispers back sadly, placing a calloused hand on my shoulder. "Even if I want to."

CHAPTER 15

Celeste

"Almost there!" Ryleigh chirps cheerfully as she drags me deeper into the heart of Solar City, leaving me to trip and stumble clumsily in her wake.

"Is this the part where I get stabbed and killed?" I murmur dejectedly, shooting her a glare. "Because this looks very similar to the alley an assassin attacked me in at the Lunar Court. Sent by someone still unknown, might I add."

"Different Courts." She waves her hand dismissively, ignoring my worries.

"Different Court, same Divine."

"You think so poorly of our race, Les." I jump at Irissa's voice, whipping around with a scowl.

"Why is she here? Why does she know about this meeting? Does she even know what this is about? Who it involves?" The questions fall rapidly from my lips, worry coating each word. Irissa should be back at the castle, preparing for the long night ahead. While we've been staying with the Solars, she has been allotted a specific room—one she cannot escape from and is not easily destroyed. So far she has managed to rip a few cushions, but no major or long-lasting damage has been placed on the room. I stay with her sometimes, slipping out after she falls asleep since I know she will be safe without me there. It's been refreshing for both of us, and I think it's been a much easier transition into this life than I could have ever dreamed of.

"She wanted to know, so I told her."

"You just told her?" I gape, fuming. She never *just told me* anything, no matter how many times I pleaded and begged. "Irissa, do you know how dangerous this can be for you? What will happen if anyone finds out?"

"She can't resist me. Can you Rye?" Irissa purrs with a flirty grin.

"It's those dark eyes. I get lost in them," Ryleigh teases, laughing at my dismay.

"No, no, no. We aren't doing this. Irissa, you need to keep your paws off Divine *and* Undivine alike. You've flirted with half of the city by now, and it's quite irritating."

"I'm not doing anything." She bristles, eyes squinting menacingly. "I can't help that I'm better at making friends than you are, Les. Maybe, if you weren't such an utter fucking *bitch*, you could have some friends, too."

"How dare you—"

"How many times do I need to remind you that you aren't my mother? I'm an adult now, Celeste. I know it's hard for you to see me that way. I get it, I do. All you've ever done is take care of me, and I will forever be grateful for that. But we can't keep having this conversation. I can take care of myself. I don't need you to be the protector *or* the provider anymore. I've been on my own for months now, ever since you went off to play princess with the Divine. And I *know* you couldn't control that situation. I do. But I learned a lot about myself while you were gone. I learned that I'm capable of so much more than you give me credit for. So, please, just—just let me be my own person, okay?" Her last words are almost a shout, a desperate plea for her voice to be heard. And I do. I do hear it. I just need time to adjust, time to get myself out of that protective mindset.

"You're right," I say into the awkward silence that follows, "You don't need me anymore. I'll work on it, okay? I'll try to be better. It's just...I may have left our old life behind but, well, it hasn't left me. I do feel like a mother sometimes—it's the role I had to play. And I know I'm not, and never will be, your mom. Sometimes it's hard to see a sister when I have all of these memories of me taking care of you in a way only a mother should. When our own mother failed at the most important job in the world, so I had to take over instead. I guess what I'm trying to say is I *will* do better. And...I'm sorry."

"Thank you, Les!" Irissa swallows me into a hug, her comforting embrace settling us both down into an easy acceptance.

"I love you," I say into her hair, just as Ryleigh comes to an abrupt stop.

"Here we are!" she proclaims with a wiggle of her hands.

The broken-down building in front of us looks like it shouldn't be standing. The cracked tan walls seem close to crumbling, the building tilting at an odd angle. The roof has multiple poorly executed repairs, each spot covered in thin sheets of wood or plastic. The red door is rusted and chipped, the hinges squeaking as it is thrown open. A sign at the very top has brightly lit letters flickering in and out, the words *The Sunshine* plastered in canary yellow. I wrinkle my nose at the man gesturing for us to come in, already smelling the foul stench of a busy bar. Irissa only smiles, gliding in as though she owns the place.

"Why is it called *The Sunshine*?" I murmur discreetly to Ryleigh. Most of the buildings I've seen in the Solar Court are solidly built and clean, but this one...it's proof that the Solar Court doesn't excel in *everything*.

"Because it is anything but," she snickers back, pushing me forward.

"Oh. Great. Fantastic, actually."

The whole place is one giant room, a square-shaped bar pushed along almost the entire length of the right wall and taking up nearly half the space in the building. There are over a dozen tables and every one is full of chattering Undivine, a few Lows scattered among them. There may be a High or two, but I can't be sure. There are several groups of people standing because there is no room to sit, the distinct sounds of rambunctious laughter and the occasional crash hitting my ears. I also hear the clink of glasses and the pouring of drinks. The stench of sweat and alcohol permeates the air, burning my nostrils.

The walls are just as cracked on the inside as they are on the outside, their deep greens a stark contrast to the light color scheme outside. Paintings of suns and rays of light are splayed among them, along with a few paintings of the bar in its prime. The images are a weird contrast to the darkness in here, the dim lighting contributing highly to that observation. The atmosphere is only slightly discomforting, and I find myself squeezing closer to Ryleigh. As if noticing my subtle movements, silence swallows the room as eyes fall toward me.

I try to focus on what's in front of me as we push forward, ignoring meeting anyone's eyes. I find Ark waiting on us at the bar, gesturing to the empty seats beside him. The only empty seats in the whole place, I would guess. Irissa leaves us behind and sits beside him gingerly, smiling brightly while she does so. With that simple act, the room is alight again. Undivine cheer at our arrival, clapping us on the back as they sweep by to welcome us. Suddenly, their touches become more than the congratulations of Undivine. With a start, I realize I'm being given *power*.

The rush isn't the same as what I felt with Edge, isn't as personal, but it's a rush all the same. There are more Lows than I realized here, more powers than I expected. These Divine are giving me just a drop of their very essence, trusting me with their lives as they gather around just to touch me. They are giving me a part of themselves they can't take back willingly. *Why?* Why would they do that? How can they trust me so greatly already? They don't know me. I'm the Divine Slayer! I can take everything and will never give anything in return. Yet, somehow, I'm not a threat here. Not to these people.

Ryleigh leads me to my stool, sensing the hesitation rising. I don't want these powers, but I also don't tell them to stop. It...it feels good. I like being wanted, being praised, being revered—even if a small voice in the back of my head tells me how selfish it is to want those things. Maybe...maybe I should be selfish for once, though. Irissa doesn't need me anymore, and everything I've done my entire life has been for her. All of the decisions I've made, all of the things I've kept contained inside myself...it's all been with Irissa in mind. But I don't have to do those things anymore, don't have to punish and berate myself for wanting and needing things that aren't necessary to survival. Maybe it's time I start to live for myself—not for everyone else.

Ryleigh interrupts my thoughts as she offers me her arm, allowing me to hold it as I ascend to the tall stool. She doesn't allow me to thank her, discreetly slipping away toward the entrance to the bar instead. Very subtly, another woman does the same.

"Welcome!" Her loud voice echoes in the small room as a smile stretches across her lips. "Shall we get started?"

I can't keep my mouth closed as I stare at her. Is this the leader? The one Ryleigh works under? The one whom she answers every beck and call? I didn't realize the Undivine Army would have a Divine leader. I certainly didn't expect her to be a Royal, either, as Ryleigh told me they had none in their employ. Even now, without the usual gorgeous dress and expensive crown, she embodies the title she carries.

Queen.

"Let's do it!" Ryleigh cheers, taking a mug being offered to her. She is now across from me, standing behind the bar. She passes it to me, grinning. I sniff, fake gagging as I push it back. There is no way I'm drinking whatever *that* is: It smells like acid.

"First order of business: my son's engagement!" Cheers rise around, hoots and hollers, the banging of mugs on wooden tables. "It is wonderful news. Celeste, our Divine Slayer, is now engaged to Prince Edge. Temporarily."

"Don't say it like that," I hiss, embarrassed.

"To celebrate, we are going to invite the Royals from every other Court. So, we must prepare. All of you will have critical roles to play during this time. Everything *must* go perfectly. If we succeed in carrying out these roles, Prince Zaeden and his parents will be dead before they leave this Court." Her words are blunt and don't cause a wave of shock, as though this has been discussed many times before.

"All of these people work *in* or *for* the castle," Ryleigh whispers to me, nodding at my quiet noise of understanding.

"We plan on sending invites within the next few days. Some Courts might see it as a threat. All four Court rulers in one place? It's a recipe for disaster. Something is bound to go wrong, which is what makes this such a great plan. Some of you will be planting seeds of discord, causing little or large squabbles among the Royals. If all goes to plan, there will be no reason for anyone to suspect it was *us* that killed the Lunar Court's prince."

A voice calls out from the crowd, "Are you sure he will come?"

"Yeah, how do you know this will work?" says another.

"We don't." She shrugs, turning toward me. "What do you think, Celeste?"

I jump at the sound of my name, eyes wide as I try to form a coherent answer. "Maybe…" I pause to suck in a breath, eyes lighting up with a new idea. "Maybe we don't tell him this is Edge's engagement party. He might not want to come, considering how their departure went. Maybe we tell Zaeden and the other Courts that this is *his* engagement party."

"Yes!" cries out a new voice that is quickly drowned out with cheers.

"Get that self-centered fuck to walk right into our trap!"

"He *is* self-centered. Entitled. Narcissistic. Everything has to be about him. And he is *insanely* jealous. Silvi can convince him to come by raving on and on about how won-derful this Court is, and he will rage because she dares to even think about another Court. That she dares believe his home is inferior." I nod excitedly as I finish, encouraged by the shouts of agreement.

"Perfect! Listen, everyone. I need you all to be on your best behavior." Alvina sighs at the boos that follow. "I know, I know. Once again, we have important roles to play here. You are my eyes and ears. If any of you are compromised, we all are. I know this is the first major thing we have done as a group, and I can't tell you how excited and proud I am of you all to have made it this far.

"Group one, your main priority is to have eyes on Zaeden at all times, okay? I need someone to watch his every move, to report back to your leading officer if something seems off. We can't let this go wrong because it is our only chance. If we mess this up, it means war. And I won't risk that unless I am confident that this is going to go down how we all hope it does. That means he needs to be distracted, to be pleased. Anything he wants, he gets. Refills, new dinner options, whatever. He will have it. No act is too small. Anything to keep him from realizing what we are up to. Group two, that's your job, got it? Group three will be in charge of sowing discord between the other Courts. I don't care how you do it, so long as it's done. I want everyone on edge and ready to accuse one another of killing Royals."

"But how are we going to introduce my sister?" Irissa is the first to speak after Alvina, avoiding my eyes as she says it. "Now that we have decided to hide her, I mean."

"She won't be hidden, per se—just a momentary secret." Ryleigh is the one who answers, sending her own questioning look to the queen.

"That's a good question. Where do we go from here?" I don't recognize the voice that calls out. I certainly don't recognize any of the ones that follow.

"What if we fly her down from the roof?"

"What if we don't even make an announcement?"

"We should put her in the sexiest outfit we can find and lead her out! That'll get his attention!"

"Or maybe we should just have her walk in on Edge's arm?"

"Maybe Edge should make a speech?"

"What if he claims she is his Soul Divine?"

"Should we introduce her in front of everyone? Or should we send her to a different room where they interact privately?"

"We should make sure he is alone when he greets her!"

"Yeah, one of us could lure him off!"

I can't keep up with all of the voices, each one shouting something new and different. I try to understand, I do, but I can see Irissa is struggling, too. Is this what Ryleigh meant when she said to be prepared to argue?

"What do you think, Celeste?" Alvina once again asks for my opinion. Silence cuts through the room as they wait for my response with bated breaths.

"I think...I think everyone has great ideas. Maybe we can combine a few of them? I can wear something that'll make Zaeden jealous, sure. Something attention-catching. And maybe Valaine should be the one to make a speech after everyone arrives. She can announce then that it is also an engagement party for Edge. Then, while he is raging about that, Edge and I will walk out together after some kind of cue in her speech. Lots of eyes will need to be on Zaeden, though. I will try to keep up some shields, too, just in case he flies off the handle. Then we buy time and mingle a bit until we can get him alone. Maybe we bring out a distraction of some kind, somebody pretty and eye-catching enough to grab his attention? I don't want to put anybody in that position, but it'll be the easiest way to get him out. Once he is alone and far enough away, someone can kill him. Or several someones. But then we would need to get rid of the body. Quickly. And maybe we just...spread a rumor about him running away? Or that he was kidnapped? I'm not sure about that part." I gnaw on my bottom lip, contemplating.

"I think he needs to attack me publicly, too. If he is as enraged as I expect him to be, he'll attack first and ask questions later. At that point, anybody can be blamed for his assassination. It could be a Solar seeking retribution, an Undivine angry about what he did, or even just a silent supporter of me for all anyone could know. There would be too many theories for them to directly blame the Solar Court between the discord we will be sowing all night with the others and the attack."

The silence that follows is deafening. I can't hear anything over my own labored breaths. My eyes spin wildly from face to face but I can't read their expressions, can't understand if what I said was wrong. Was it that bad of an idea?

"Maybe you have what it takes to be a Royal after all," Alvina states with a grin, signaling cheers of agreement. "You heard the plan, everyone! Your superiors and I will begin finalizing details and assigning roles. Today was only for figuring out the basics. Now the fun begins!"

"Down with the Lunars!" comes an answering shout.

"Down with the Divine!"

"To the sky we will rise!"

"To the sky!"

"U*pon the castle we ran,*

knives and bows in our hands." One person begins to sing, a chorus of off-key voices following with the rest of the lyrics.

"Soldiers falling to the ground,
justice finally carried out.
The people cried out in waves,
done we were with being slaves.
And with no more Royals to obey,
a whole new world was made.
Though we were born as slaves,
we live to see another day.
Together we fought with thrall,
tore them down and broke their walls.
Taught them a lesson in haste,
not even Royals will be safe."

"Should I feel evil for planning his death like this?" I ask Ryleigh with a shake of my head, ignoring the sad song and the banging of mugs that follow the performance.

"No."

"Good, because I'm starting not to."

"Alright, everyone! Meeting dismissed! You know the drill! Five at a time! To you, my parting words are this: To the sky we will rise!"

"To the sky we will rise!" A chorus of echoes follows as they begin to form a line and pile out. I watch as someone begins to count heads at the door, stopping groups from exiting until the previous one is out of sight.

"What does that mean?" I can barely hear myself over the excitement.

"The Divine title was created to put us above the ordinaries. We are supposed to be descendants of the goddesses that live in the sky, but we are all equal. We all deserve to be loved by those goddesses, whether we descend from the sky dwellers or not. So we will ascend to their level, one way or another. To the sky we will rise," Alvina answers with a gentle smile. I can only nod, mystified. I try not to think about the amount of people that will suffer if this plan doesn't work. Try not to think about how I need to protect them, need to provide the change they are so desperate for. I can feel the weight of their lives bearing down on my shoulders, grounding me to this place in time. But then I think about how much better this world will be without Zaeden in it, how this new, selfish version of myself will hold no guilt over someone who has never felt guilt a day in their life.

"How did you become a leader of the Undivine army?" I ask in an attempt to distract myself, continuing to watch the place empty out. Alvina watches with me protectively, ready to interfere should something go wrong.

"I created it."

"What?" I spin toward her, eyes wide. Why would she have created it? She's a Royal!

"We aren't all bad, Celeste. Surely you can recognize that by now?"

"I'm starting to, yeah."

I feel that truth running through me in the new powers that bled into me only moments ago, in the shadows and darkness I share with only one other.

I had been wrong not only about Divine but about the Solar Royals in particular.

So, so wrong.

CHAPTER 16

Celeste

"Well, isn't this just great?" I gripe, slinging the book in my hands down into the grass as if it had morally offended me. "Another pointless read."

"Both of my books have been extremely helpful," Irissa boasts with a grin, waving her book at me playfully.

"Don't brag," I scowl back, shoving her shoulder lightly as I dig my toes into the short grass.

We sit in the Courtyard, basking in the warm light of the Solar Court. I glance at the small book pile beside me, shaking my head hopelessly. We came out here to find some peace, read, study, and learn more about ourselves. Instead, I've been greeted with a whole lot of *nothing.* I can't find anything about Absorbids in the one book that was supposed to help me, other than the basic information King Zorander had given me. How did Edge know so much about them? And the king? Is it some knowledge only Royals have access to? And if that's the case, why hasn't someone provided me with a book or something to explain this incredibly frustrating power?

"I don't mean to. I'm just excited, Les. There's so much here. I'm not sure all of it applies to me, but..." She sighs, worry flickering across her features.

"Yeah? Like what?" I encourage her to continue, to talk about her abilities to avoid my own. I don't move from my position on the ground, closing my eyes to block the blinding sun. I lay flat on my back, dress sprawled around me in a rather ungraceful manner. Even in this Court, I am being suffocated by the things.

Irissa flops onto her stomach beside me, eyes buried in her book. "Well, I've seen a lot about primary forms. Mine seems to be the beast thing I turn into. The wings and talons? I'm not sure what it is supposed to be, exactly, but other Shifters change into other things. *Lots* of other things. If I'm so powerful then what is stopping me? Why haven't I changed into something else yet? Royals even get to choose, Celeste! They can choose anything in the world they want to be, and they'll be it. Even another Royal. They can literally *mimic* other people. Yet, somehow, I'm a High Divine—possibly a Royal according to Edge—with only one form and some kind of midnight curse? No way. No way that is true!"

"Maybe your curse stops it? Maybe it inhibits your ability to change into anything else? Since you had the wings and talons at birth, maybe that's what you got stuck with?" I ponder, unsure. The familiar term of "the curse" has traveled with us across Courts. Truthfully, we aren't sure what else to call it. That makes it hard to research, because how do you research something that has no name?

"I haven't found a single droplet of information about the curse." She shakes her head glumly, looking as dejected as I feel. "Why am I like this? Why am I so different from everyone else? Why can't I be normal?"

"Why are *we* so different? Why can't *we* be normal?" I correct, attempting to make her feel less alone. "Somehow, someway, we pissed off the goddesses. And now they're laughing at the sick joke they played on our lives."

"Don't say that." My eyes pop open in surprise, Valaine's lithe figure filling my vision. "The goddesses have nothing to do with what has happened to the two of you."

"There are some Divine who actually can cast curses. I don't know of any in the Lunar Court, but..." Edge adds from behind her with a sly shrug. I roll my eyes at his typical dramatic attire: a long black cloak covering even blacker clothes. The golden buttons on his shirt ripple in the light, blinding me until I look away. "Valaine's right. The goddesses might have nothing to do with your fates."

I watch as Valaine falls next to Irissa, wrapping her arms around her with a giggle. I huff at them, closing my eyes once more. "That's a lie," I tell Edge, not bothering to look at his reaction.

"It isn't. I have two in this very Court. One a Low, one a High. Very useful on the battlefield. I once cursed someone to fall every time he drew a sword. It was quite funny." Unfortunately, the image that statement provides is truly hilarious and the corners of my lips move up on their own accord.

"You think someone may have *actually* cursed us? Really? Why would someone bother? That's insane."

"Is it, Les?" Irissa asks quietly, shifting underneath Valaine's body. "Look at me. Look at you. I'm a doomed monster. You're a doomed murderer. Would we have been either of those things without a curse? Is it all some destined fate that we can't avoid, or something we were forced into?"

"I would love to believe I would have never become the Divine Slayer without some kind of curse. I would. But that's just avoiding the truth—I *am* a murderer. I don't think it's some fate I couldn't avoid or a curse that doomed me. It's just me. It's just who I am. I have to accept that I made the decisions that led me here. I can't let myself be clouded by some false reality that doesn't exist. I killed those people. I'm going to kill more. That's all there is to it."

"If it was a curse, then your father had to have had very powerful enemies," Valaine ponders, ignoring my outburst. "Especially considering our limited knowledge of the Shadow Court's Divine. Do you want to go to the library and see if we find anything about them in the records we keep, Irissa?"

I push myself up onto my elbows, sending a glare over to Valaine. Irissa seems overjoyed at the idea, nodding vigorously. "You mean go hide in the dark corners of a secluded library and make out?" I question quietly under my breath, not wanting to know the answer. "Have her back in an hour. No later."

"Celeste! You said you would work with me on this! I'm not a child!" Irissa pouts, an embarrassed flush working its way across her face.

"Two hours," Valaine chirps pleasantly, pushing herself up to stand before reaching down to Irissa. "Don't worry about us, Celeste. All will be well."

"Don't have too much fun without me." Irissa sends a grin my way, taking Valaine's hand with a wink. Valaine's dark skin glistens beautifully in the sun, that golden undertone ever-present. Her blue streaks seem much more vibrant today, popping against the dark brown of her short hair. Looking at her now, I understand why Irissa likes her so much. Valaine is beautiful, undoubtedly so. Especially here in her home Court where she shines as bright as a beacon every time she smiles.

"What does that—"

"Bye!" she interrupts loudly, giggling gleefully as she pulls the princess into a run. I glare at their backs, forgetting about Edge until he is leaning over me. The sun I had been enjoying disappeared, drowned out by the shadows that engulfed me.

"Do you have a moment?"

"Depends." I turn my glare onto him. "Is it important?"

"The king has made a decision on the engagement issue." I sit up quickly, scrambling up with a lot of effort. Edge barely avoids our collision, stepping away just in time. He reaches out a hand, helping me find my balance so that I can face him. It should be intimidating—the height difference. He's at least two heads taller than me, but that's never been a cause of concern for me. Not when it comes to him.

I look up into his face, whispering, "What kind of decision?"

"Well, you know he has been overall acceptive of our proposal. He's been raving on about me being a genius for over a week now."

I roll my eyes, ignoring my racing heart. "Yeah? Invitations have already been sent out, so I hope he doesn't plan on canceling the party."

"Actually...he now has conditions."

"Conditions?" I raise an eyebrow, scowling.

"We have to actually be wed. Ceremony and all." He looks uncomfortable as he says it, eyes drifting away from me. My heart continues to betray me, thumping rapidly as if trying to escape. I can't *actually* marry him. He can't expect that of me. I can't do this. *I can't.*

"Why?" The one word is all I can manage to choke out. Is this why Valaine snuck off with Irissa? So we could have a serious chat about marriage?

"He doesn't want to be made a fool of. He doesn't want you to wiggle out of this deal." He shrugs simply, finally looking back down at me. "He wants assurance that you will belong to us. To me. That no other Court will be able to take you away from us. Most importantly, he wants to ensure you can't run away to their Courts without repercussions. No Court will take you after you wed me—they won't take the chance of starting a war."

"Like I had a choice in coming here!" I sputter out, eyes wide as I gaze up into his face. "Like I would choose to marry you!" I don't miss the small wince, his gaze darkening.

"You'll have to find some way to cope with the unfortunate circumstances then, won't you? We are stuck with each other for the foreseeable future. We don't have a choice."

I growl out, "You're a Royal. You always get whatever you want!"

"And what if what I want is you?" My body freezes, my breath halting at the back of my throat.

"You don't." My voice cracks and I press my lips together tightly, trying to ignore the clenching in my chest. I can't even begin to describe why I am a horrible choice for him. I don't need to. He already knows.

"Maybe. Maybe not." He shrugs nonchalantly, a forced grin appearing on his lips.

"Why don't you just...I don't know...get him out of the picture or something? Not kill him, just...I don't know. Do something!"

"You want me to kill a king for you, Little Flame?" He leans down, our noses almost touching as he whispers, "Because I will. Say the words, and it's done. You've been denied what you want for so long, but I won't deny you anything." Edge grabs my hand, thumb running across my skin gently.

It leaves a tingling sensation behind, a sensation I can't afford to look further into.

I swallow hard, whispering, "I'll have to think about it. I will let you know my decision." I don't plan on telling him to kill his stepfather, but I do want him to think I will. I want him to believe I am ruthless, that I would ask for the impossible *and* the improbable. Maybe then he will see that I am not somebody he should want.

"I'll tell my stepfather you agreed to the conditions," he says simply, ignoring the surprised noises coming out of my gaping mouth. "Honestly, I wasn't going to tell you about his decision yet. This conversation isn't why I came."

"Then why *did* you come? Other than to piss me off, anyway?"

"I wanted to show you something. A special place in the castle that I think you would like."

"Uh, why?" Why is he trying? Why does he care about me? I will *destroy* him if he continues things this way. It's inevitable.

"It's a place where we can freely share the darkness between us. A place that holds all of my secrets. A place that will allow us to safely be ourselves, to use our powers without threat of harm." He grasps my face with his empty hand, searching my eyes.

"Safe for you or safe for me?" I whisper. He doesn't answer my question, but he doesn't need to. I know the answer. *He will never be safe from me.*

"Please, Celeste." His tone is closer to a plea than I've ever heard before, his steel blue eye watching me with something I can only describe as *hope*.

It breaks me.

"Fine." My answer is reluctant, but it is the one he wanted. His hands tighten around my skin, shaking before he begins to pull me away.

I'm hesitant to follow him, to blindly trust someone who I barely know, but I do it anyway. We've known each other for a short amount of time, but the last month in particular has opened up my eyes. It has made me see what I've been denying since the moment I laid eyes upon him...and it terrifies me.

Edge seems to sense my hesitation. I feel the chill of his shadows as they wrap around me, comforting me in their cool embrace. I shudder, daring a glance into that singular steel eye as we walk side by side. I ignore the patch, not wanting to think about how it happened. He will tell me about it if and when he is ready.

"This is the one place we will be able to practice this power swap safely, Celeste. I think I can help you better understand your powers and train you how to properly use them without losing control. I promise I won't hurt you."

"I'm not worried about you hurting me." I shake my head, looking up at him with pleading eyes and shaky words. "I'm worried about my sanity."

"Just admit that you like me," he breathes back, pace unrelenting. "Despite your best efforts not to."

"I do like you," I admit into the warm air. "And I hate myself for it. The things I could do to you—" I pause, unsure how much I should admit.

Suddenly I'm being shoved into an outer castle wall, Edge's body pressed into mine as his head bends down low to whisper into my neck. I feel the familiar sweeping of his power overcome me, but it isn't because he is giving them to me. It's because he is letting them sit on the surface, trusting me with every bit of him.

"I would love to see what things you have in mind, Little Star." I can't help but think about his lips, about discarded clothes and shared breaths. "*Fuck.* I take it back. If you keep sending me thoughts like that, I won't be able to control myself."

I whimper as he pulls away abruptly, pulling me along as if nothing happened at all. "I'll try to stop."

"Good," he grounds out, pausing. "Here. Take this. I need a release." I ignore the innuendo, holding out my hand as he offers me his many rings. I clasp my hand tightly around them, watching him shake as a sphere begins to form. He struggles, pushing every bit of his power into the portal. Then I'm being tugged into darkness, our feet landing on cold and dark tiles. We stand in front of a black door, its texture and appearance stone-like. With a jerk, I realize what it is.

Obsidian.

Edge pulls my fingers apart, taking the rings back quietly. I watch how gingerly he slides each one back on, each movement precise and practiced. I don't say anything as I wait; I don't want to be the one to open this door. Even with the small amount of shadows residing within me, I feel the restriction radiating from this place. It's similar to the pull of a leash—strong and sneaky, willing to take everything I have to offer and everything I don't.

"Don't let the room overwhelm you." It's the only warning I receive before he swings the door open and pulls me into the depths of it. I suck in a breath, hands reaching up to clasp my throat in shock. I cough and sputter, struggling to force air in and out of my lungs. I stumble, falling to my knees as I gurgle on nothing. Edge is by my side in seconds, arms wrapping around my shaking form.

"Help." It's the only thing I can get out, the only plea I can speak into existence.

"It's the shadows, Celeste. It wants the shadows. Tell it no and believe you can make it stop. It will stop if you say no." His hand runs through my hair reassuringly, his drawling voice a comfort in my panic.

"No. They're *mine*," I grind out, tugging on the shadows harshly. I force them down deep inside my body, refusing to let them escape. They are a gift from Edge and I will be damned if I let them be taken so easily.

"See? It feels better now, right?"

I can only nod, feeling the restriction ebbing away. I still struggle with my breaths, but it's becoming more manageable with each passing second. Edge slowly helps me stand on my feet, my body shaking from the overwhelming pull of it all.

"What *was* that?" I question angrily, leaning on him for support.

"The obsidian."

I turn my body and take in the room, eyes wide. This is a bedroom—a bedroom made entirely out of obsidian. Every piece of furniture is carved out of the stuff. Even the bed frame is made out of the dark rock, its sleek surface shining in the sunlight streaming in from the singular stained glass window. The walls have a weird shine, too, and upon closer inspection, I notice small glittering chunks of rock embedded within the black paint. The lamp, the bookshelf, the desk. Everything is made of obsidian. The room is dark and dreary, every aspect of it making me uncomfortable and uneasy.

"This is your room," I say, realization hitting me hard as I spin to face him once more. It's a pretty little cell, designed to keep a beast in its cage. Designed to keep him weak and unstable.

I take a few steps back, swallowing hard as I realize we are alone in his *room.*

"It is. This is the only place I can sleep. Otherwise, the shadows try to take over while I'm unconscious. It's dangerous for me to be elsewhere," he says casually as if it's a nuisance and not heartbreaking.

"But you stayed in the Lunar Court? Why didn't...?" I trail off, unsure if I should ask why they didn't kill him, or take over, or whatever happens when he loses control.

"I had to come back every night. No one but my mother and stepfather knew. I couldn't speak or see anyone while I was here. Otherwise, word would spread that I can't spend a fucking night outside of my room. I don't want people to look at me like I'm some rotten child who always gets his way. It took a lot of power that I didn't always have—I suppose that's why I was so miserable at that Court."

"Hmm. That must be why you were such a whiny piece of shit all the time."

"It must be," he agrees, wincing.

"Is that why...why you did it? Why you attacked me? You never told me why...?" I play with the ends of my short hair, avoiding his gaze.

"No. I did it because...well because I could hear Zaeden's thoughts," he growls finally, fists clenching at his sides.

"What do you mean?"

"Celeste, the things he thought about you were *despicable*. Every time he thought about you he thought about pulling you by the hair, about grabbing you and pulling you down with it. Then he started having all of these awful thoughts about how he would torture you with it, pull until you bled and pleaded for mercy. He thought it was sexy and romantic, among other things. I saw it for what it was. And I wasn't going to let him do that. I wasn't going to let him hurt you." Those fists unclench as he makes a decision, as he reaches out and pulls me into his arms. I press my hands against his chest, eyes wide as I gaze up at him.

"So...you cut it. You cut it in hopes he wouldn't be interested anymore." I swallow hard, shaking my head in disbelief.

"Yes. And then fucking Kyelin was always raving about you in his mind, thinking about wrapping fistfuls of that hair around his hands. Then one day I was listening in as he left your room, and he was obsessing over this conversation the two of you had about your hair. I listened as he thought about how horrible you would look without it, how he wasn't sure he would be attracted to you anymore. That was my breaking point."

"You didn't want him to be attracted to me," I whisper, bottom lip shaking.

"No. No, I didn't. How could I? You're fucking beautiful, Celeste, and you deserve more than some asshole who won't appreciate you in every form. You deserve more than his brother who literally *dreamed* of torturing you. So, yeah, I fucking cut it. I thought, maybe, it would be enough to dissuade him from choosing you. That it would be enough to show you his true self. I guess it worked."

"Maybe I should be blaming you for how things ended, then," I whisper.

"Maybe you should."

I turn away abruptly, scrambling out of his arms. I decide to change the subject, saying, "This room will control me?"

"Yes."

"You're sure?"

"No."

"Edge, I can't do this if—"

He interrupts before I can argue, saying darkly, "I want you to learn to transport. If anything goes wrong, I want you to be able to seek safety. To take care of yourself without needing anyone to rescue you. I want you to be able to escape this castle if war breaks out within its walls."

"I would be taking too much from you." I shake my head, blinking in confusion. It takes a lot of power from Edge, and I would need to take that plus some. I won't leave him defenseless, either. "I can't—"

"You can. Your powers allow you to take and store the powers of others until you use them all. So I want you to take a little from me every day and store them for later use. I want you to build, build, and fucking *build* until you can do this. And this is the best place for you to control your intake."

"You don't get that power back, Edge," I try to convince him weakly that this is a bad idea.

"Shadows surround me all day at all times." He reaches down to cup my cheeks, shaking me lightly. "I'm overwhelmed constantly. I meant it when I said I didn't mind sharing the burden of my darkness. I gain new shadows every day, and I don't always get rid of the old ones. I never run out. I suppose that's the perks and the downfalls of being a Bender. I will never run out unless I'm trapped in a place without shadows while you suck out my essence. But here? They hide in the furniture, in the walls, in the cracks and corners of the room. There is nothing but shadows. There is nothing but you and me."

"Okay. Okay, I'll try." How can I deny him when he is touching me like this? When he is opening up and begging me to help him? When I am so desperate to share the darkness within me, too?

"Good." With a flourish his cloak drops to the floor, his fingers snapping around the golden buttons on his shirt.

I don't speak as I watch, hypnotized, my cheeks flushing as that muscled chest becomes more and more visible. I see some of the tattoos that are usually hidden beneath his clothes: a snarling beast wearing a crown, a sword, a bundle of flowers hiding a pair of cat-like eyes, and so many more I can't even begin to digest without getting closer. "Take off your shawl, Celeste."

I do as told with little hesitation, dropping the thin fabric at our feet. My dress today has no straps, leaving the entirety of my arms visible. I allow the shadows within me to dance to the surface, coating my skin in a dark haze.

"Now what?" I breathe out the question as his shirt slips to the ground beside the shawl.

"Touch me, Little Flame."

Once again, I do as I'm told. My hands reach out on their own accord, pressing into the lines of his chest. He holds his breath as they slide down his dark and scarred skin, my powers rising as they recognize his own. I watch as the shadows seep into my fingers, watch as he freely gives me the darkest parts of him. I shake with the effort it takes to control myself, feeling the draw of the monster inside of me. I listen to its whispers about taking it all. The whispers that say he doesn't want them, anyway. But once again Edge can sense my thoughts, can sense the monster rising, and he flushes it away with a single motion.

His arms encase me, hands cupping the back of my head and pressing my face into his chest. I wrap my arms around his torso, eyes flickering shut as the power drifts between us at every bare contact point. I stop shaking, forcing the beast back into a deep slumber. I won't let it overcome me—never again will I allow it to convince me to do something horrific with its hypnotizing words.

"Did you really love Kyelin?" His question jars me, his hands tangling in my hair and pressing me deeper into him.

"I'm not sure right now is the best time to talk about him—considering what happened and all," I joke, attempting to ease the tension.

"I can't stand to think about him touching you. All I can think about is how he used you and you couldn't even see it. Couldn't hear his thoughts like I could. How he played with your heart and hurt you, how he thought he could have you and anyone else he damn pleased. I can't stand to think about Zaeden threatening you, either. I remember the day I pulled you away to warn you, remember the fear for Zaeden deep inside of your mind. I was so disgusted with him. I was angry enough to send shadows his way, angry enough to barely hold in an attack. My blood boils at the thought of their hands on you, at the thought of their mouths on yours."

"Why?" I question, baffled. When we were in the Lunar Court he hardly paid me any mind. He never acted like he cared about me. Not in a romantic way, anyway. Only recently have I come to believe he might have romantic feelings for me, feelings that may have manifested upon our very first meeting. I, too, feel something deep within me reverberating for him, pulling me to him and those suffocating shadows. Had I missed out on the signs the whole time? I was drawn quickly to Kyelin, is this just another repeat of that situation? Another Royal using their powers of persuasion to make me fall in love?

"Did you really love Kyelin?" he repeats, ignoring my question. "Tell me, Celeste."

"I thought I did," I say after a long pause, pushing away enough to look into his eyes. "I've told myself over and over again that I did. That it had to be real. Because if it wasn't...then what was the point?" The shadows had stopped their consistent flow, both of us too distracted to continue their traveling. In the back of my mind, I rejoice. It feels good to have this connection, to have such a large intake of power. But I can't help worrying about taking too much, about making him too weak.

"And now?" He searches my eyes for an answer, looking for permission, or hope, or maybe even desire.

"Now I understand that what he did and said to me wasn't love. Maybe infatuation, or lust, but it wasn't *love*. You were right. He used me and I was too blind to see it. I wanted to be in love, wanted to have that connection with someone. I thought it was love because I knew what it was *supposed* to feel like. But I've never experienced that before. I didn't know. And he was enhancing everything, pushing things into me that weren't *me*.

"What he did was wrong on all levels, but...I still feel so guilty about killing him. And yet...if I hadn't killed him, I may have been trapped in a world I didn't belong in otherwise. And I would have never had the pleasure of meeting the *real* you."

"Would you take it back? After getting to know me? After having that idea of love ripped away from you?" He hesitates as he asks, clearing his throat awkwardly at the end.

"No." I shake my head furiously, chest heaving. "I wouldn't take it back. Finding a friend like you is worth it. Knowing that one day I may find that true love is worth it." The words lift a weight off my shoulders, the weight of guilt and shame and terror. It's all been building up for months, but Edge is the only one who has tried to help me through it. The only one who understands that kind of pain.

My words hang between us, my mind spinning. I'm not sure that Edge and I can have the type of love I want, despite the sudden urge to have that with him after calling him a friend. I do know something is connecting us, something more than the shadows and the darkness in our hearts. I know he feels it, too. I don't have to call it love, or even say it's romantic feelings. It just *is*. It's tension, attraction, vulnerability. And it's all utterly terrifying.

The silence is horrendous.

Edge can only stare at me, mouth closed tightly. Maybe I said something wrong. I open my mouth to speak when he finally moves, another decision made.

He takes my cheeks into his hands, jerking my face toward his. I gasp as his cool lips press into mine, moving with a ferocity I have never felt before. My hands drift down to his chest before easing back up to his shoulders and digging my nails in. A low growl escapes from under his breath, his body pushing against mine until I hit the wall. I whimper as he bites my bottom lip, hissing when it draws blood. He isn't gentle or kind like Kyelin had been, but I don't want him to be. I don't *need* him to be. We aren't meant to be gentle and slow. We are tied together with an unbelievable intensity and fierceness, and I expect nothing less from him.

Edge tastes and smells like smoke, something I hadn't expected from a man filled with shadows. Smoke and...something sweet. Like some type of chocolate that I just can't place. I don't linger on his scent, distracted as his tongue slips inside my mouth and his hands begin to roam down my body. I allow his hands to fall far below my hips, allowing him to grind me painfully against the wall. I can't form enough coherent thoughts to care about the pain, my only focus on the pure *pleasure* of it all.

But then I feel those seductive shadows sliding into me once more. I can feel myself taking from him, can feel their tug as they burrow into my skin. I jerk back with a gasp just as a large hand grazes my breast, shaking my head furiously as I try to shove him off me.

He's wrong about me.

I can't control this beast; I will never be able to control it. The last man I slept with would attest to that if he was still alive, and I feel so much more for Edge than I ever did for Kyelin. I may have found acceptance for him, may have rid myself of the overwhelming guilt, but when it comes to Edge...killing him would truly break me.

"I'm sorry," I whisper as he takes two steps back, my voice harsh. "I'm stealing from you again. I can't—I can't control myself. I have to go." I try to slip away, try to escape his touch.

"I don't care if you steal from me. Stay. Please." Edge is begging now, hastily moving forward and trapping me against the wall in desperation. "Please don't leave."

"I have to." I close my eyes, fear hardening my heart. "I'll kill you if I don't. When my emotions are high, I lose control. I can't do this. It isn't safe for either of us."

"Isn't it good that you can't control yourself around me?" he whispers breathlessly, refusing to release me. Refusing to acknowledge my fear.

"I'm sorry, Edge, but I can't kill you. I can't. Because if you die—if you die, then who will hold me accountable? Who will help me? Who will ever love me?" I whimper, my bottom lip quivering as the tears begin to fall. Edge allows me to pull out of his grip now, staggering back as he watches me in a painfully sorrowful state while I practically run to the door.

"I'm sorry," I apologize one last time, refusing to look back as I slip out the door.

I shouldn't have allowed this to happen. We can't be together—not in a real way. The pull of his power is too strong, and his death will hurt more than any of the others ever had. No, there will be no romantic future for us. We will pretend for the world but that is as far as I can take it. There is no hope that this could ever last, that lust could become love.

I'm a fool for ever letting myself believe that it could.

CHAPTER 17

The Invitation

Silvi

Prince Edge is a conniving piece of shit.

I've always known this to be true, but it must be stated. It is known that Royals cannot be trusted, a rule I have lived by while being raised in their convoluted world. But this insane idea he has concocted? It has to be the most absurd, calculated, and dangerous plan a Royal has ever created.

I wish I had thought of it first.

I sigh and tighten my hood over my head, patting a hand around my neck as I check for loose strands that may be dangling out. My silver hair, though stunning and lovely, is much too recognizable. I don't need any attention drawn to myself right now, not if I want to keep participating in these secret meetings with my true prince. Not if I want to have any time away from that stuffy castle.

I slip past an Undivine as I stride through the village, wincing as I feel his lust slam into me. Unfortunately, ignoring the lust of men and women alike is part of my daily routine. Despite the simple gown I wear, my beauty is hard to ignore. My figure is hidden completely, my dress dirtied up and torn in an attempt to fit in with the Undivine. Despite my best efforts to blend in, I still can't hide how different my body is from theirs.

I'm not as large as most Divine are, but I'm not small like the Undivine, either. I fall in the in-between range, and my curves are prominent to even the most untrained eyes. I'm tall, but not tall enough to dissuade Undivine men. Or anyone, really. Well, until they get a good look at my face, that is. Most people tend to think twice about wanting me once they see my scar, and some days I'm grateful for it.

I look up just as the man begins to reach out, but his hand falls lifelessly back to his side as his eyes widen and his lust dissipates. I scoff and brush by him, sending out waves of self-hatred as I do so. That's my favorite form of punishment for scum like him—striking them with their own emotions. It's a fast and effective method, one that ensures they forget me in their pursuit of assuaging the ambush of guilt they are struck with. I know it's not a particularly nice thing to do, but I'm not a particularly nice girl.

Growing up with the ability to feel the emotions of every other person, with the ability to manipulate anyone and everyone around me…well, it turned me into a very selfish person. My father set a good example for me, but I'm much stronger than he is and I can't always help myself. I like to punish and I like to get what I want, and it just so happens that those two things aren't mutually exclusive. When I accepted the offer to participate in the Games, it wasn't only because the Undivine Army asked me to. It was also because if I became a Royal…no one could stand in my way. No one could resist the temptations I have to offer. No one but Celeste, anyway. I sigh inwardly at the thought of her, glancing around.

The streets in this village are busy today, much busier than they usually are. I've only met Edge at this location a handful of times, but each one has been a wonderful and much-needed break from my life. They've provided me with an escape from the hell I've voluntarily placed myself in. Edge may not be great company, but anyone is better than my betrothed.

"We have the finest imported fabrics this Court has ever seen! They've traveled from the Shadow Court, a great distance, newly arrived just for you! You won't be left disappointed, I assure you. Ah, you! Young lady, step on up and feel for yourself. A lovely lady such as you can't go without the finest things in life!" I feel the tug on my arm, a vendor pulling me toward her briefly. I snarl, ripping myself away from her in a hurry. I hate the hope and desperation that she reeks of.

"I assure you, I am often left disappointed," I spit, glancing over her fabrics before loudly stating, "These fabrics hail from the Solar Court—less than ideal. I'll pass, and everyone else here should, too."

"Fucking Divine bitch!" she shouts and points as I stride away, practically foaming at the mouth in anger. I only laugh and glide away.

I actually don't mind the Undivine, despite my behavior. They aren't lesser in my eyes, and I can care less about the differences between them and my kind. I *do* mind that they failed Celeste, that they allowed her to live so poorly among them. She has been fighting valiantly in their stead, and for what reason? It should be a punishable offense, their treatment of her. They did absolutely nothing to ensure her survival.

But I will.

The crowd eventually falls behind me, the familiar dirt road leading away calling my name. I sigh in relief as I follow it, tapping my nails along the dagger strapped beneath my cloak as I approach the abandoned house. Cautiously, I look for any signs of life.

The first time I came here, a group of lunatics had decided to take up residence. I was quick to disband them, but they had managed to trash the house in their short visit. I took the time to clean things up, to place items back as they were. I don't want Celeste to return home just to discover that things aren't as she left them.

As I watch and listen I also search for any raw emotions, for any sense of lingering malcontent. There are none. So, I enter Celeste's home as though I own it. I'm surprised this place hasn't been ambushed by Undivine trying to appease her or destroyed by the Royals trying to displease her. I suppose everyone else doesn't know her the way I do. They don't recognize this hut as the only place in the entire world that holds even an inkling of meaning for her. This is the place she made her own, the place she raised her sister. This is the place she was the proudest of, despite its lack of overall beauty.

I sigh as I enter, wrinkling my nose as I lower myself into one of the beaten-up wooden chairs around the table. There's always an odd smell lingering here, as though something is rotten and hidden below the floorboards. Dust has coated most of the furniture, what little of it remains intact, that is. The walls seem as though they are caving in, the ceiling near collapse. This whole structure is a health hazard and an ugly one at that.

I'll never admit that I love it.

I like not being surrounded by finery, not having any expectations awaiting behind these walls. Even in my bedroom at home, I do not have this kind of freedom—not when servants wait around every corner. I like knowing that I don't have to pretend here, that no one will notice I don't fit in with the other Divine. That I have impure, rebellious thoughts hardly any others share. I work so hard to keep up the facade of spoiled little Divine, work so hard to make sure no one ever knows I hate myself and my kind.

It's exhausting.

I cross my arms across the dirty table and lay my head down, groaning into the cold wood. The house isn't well insulated, and the colder weather of this Court at this time of year is reflected indoors. Silverware litters across the floor, silver shining next to my foot. I kick a fork unceremoniously, shoulders hunching as I try not to think about Celeste sitting in this very seat.

"Fuck," I whisper into the still air, releasing a long breath. I'm not allowed to think about her for longer than necessary, not allowed to linger on what I've done to her. If I do, I'll fall apart and will never be able to reassemble the pieces.

"Chipper as always, Silvi," a familiar voice drawls, breaking my brief solitude.

"What's there to be chipper about, Edge? I'm engaged to a psychopath, you won't quit bothering me, and now I've been told you're marrying the girl I—" I raise my head, lips pressing together tightly as I spot the Divine beside Edge.

It can't be. She wouldn't—no. Surely, it isn't her.

My heart stops beating for only brief seconds as I take in the blond hair, the slim stature, the all-too-familiar features. It takes only a few more seconds to realize it isn't *her*. This woman is too tall, her hair too straight, her freckles too nonexistent. But she's just as beautiful, just as entrancing. She's much, much prettier than her sister if I have to be honest with myself.

I straighten my spine, painting on a neutral expression carefully. "You've brought a guest."

I twist and push myself back to my feet, dropping my hood as I send a dazzling smile her way. The stranger blushes underneath my heated gaze, a pair of white wings unfolding from her back as lust radiates off her like a blinding beacon. I typically don't like when that is someone's first reaction to me, but her lust doesn't dissipate upon seeing my face, my scar, like all others do. That lust only increases the longer she stares, and something inside of me stirs at the sentiment.

"Irissa," she introduces herself, her voice quiet but strong. An uncertainty lingers behind her words, fingers twisting around themselves as her nerves begin to show.

"Celeste's sister. Yes, I know exactly who you are." I try not to cringe when I say her name, attempting to keep that deconstructed mask from cracking even more.

"Lovely. You're both acquainted now," Edge snaps, impatient as always.

"Relax, Edge. We have plenty of time, no need to rush through this. Haven't you learned yet that the man who takes his time is always the most successful?" I purr out the innuendo, sending a sly smile to Irissa as she bursts into laughter.

"I'm not going to sit here and listen to you two flirting when we have business to attend to." Edge runs a hand down his face, flustered.

"How did you know—"

"You flirt with everyone, Irissa. Including my sister. *That's* how I know."

"I happen to like your sister, thank you very much. We have fun. It's just a bonus that it pisses you off." She sniffs, winking at me behind Edge's back as he scowls.

Irissa may look like her sister, but she certainly doesn't act like her. She seems to be much more confident, flirty, and fun compared to Celeste's strict and down-to-business attitude. Truly, she and Edge could be a well-matched pair. I watch as Irissa's wings flutter and preen, their movement creating a matching flutter in my stomach. I can't stop myself from opening my mouth and speaking to her again.

"Edge is just a hard ass." I fan myself, glancing him up and down with a carefully placed scowl. "He wouldn't know anything about having fun."

"Oh, I don't know about that," she says gleefully, the emotion slamming into me with a powerful force I am unaccustomed to. "He and my sister seem to have lots of fun together."

"Shut up, Iris." He spins to her, but I don't miss the flash of embarrassment that I can barely feel. Luckily for me, I'm much more attuned to emotions than the average Empath.

"I'll shut up when I'm wrong," she says flippantly, scowling as she begins to drift away.

Oh, how I love a girl who stands up for herself. It was my downfall when it came to Celeste; she always held her own against me. I fell for her so fast because she was the only one to see through me, and I used anger and callousness to fight against those feelings she so blatantly denied having for me. Obviously, that method didn't quite work out in the end.

"What news do you bring?" I question as I track Irissa's movements across the room, her small hands trailing across ripped wallpaper and clusters of dust.

"Have you received the invitation yet?"

"It was mentioned this morning by a servant, but I have yet to be brought in for council."

Irissa giggles abruptly, turning to me with an amused twinkle in her eyes. "Zaeden is going to be so pissed."

"Perfect. I love babysitting pissed-off princes," I sigh, rubbing my forehead absentmindedly. "What did you do?"

"Read it for yourself." I reach out to take the piece of paper in his outstretched hand, elegant lettering and glittering gold dancing across the surface. The words *Let's Celebrate* are printed boldly with a Solar Court symbol hiding behind them, along with the date and time of the event.

"You're hosting an engagement party at the Solar Court? For me? You don't even like me." I scoff, tossing the invitation to the side. It drifts lifelessly in the air for only a few precious moments, falling to the ground and sliding under the table.

"I like you," Irissa purrs, sidling next to me.

"I know. I can feel it." I whisper, reaching out to tap the side of her head.

"Stop, Irissa," Edge scowls, forcing himself between us. Irissa only frowns, tip-toeing away into the back of the house.

"They think otherwise. Besides, it's not really for you. It's just an excuse to reveal my and Celeste's engagement. This is the only way to get Zaeden to the Solar Court, and it's of dire importance that he attends."

"Ah, right. It was mentioned to me that you may kill him." I avoid approaching the topic of him and Celeste—my heart has been shattered by that woman enough times.

"We *are* going to kill him."

"Actually kill him? So soon?" I thought this plan was crazy and brilliant, sure, but I hadn't convinced myself it was real. Hadn't let myself hope that this nightmare was close to ending. Until now, I suppose.

"Yes, and I want you to take his place as leader of the Lunar Court. Celeste was supposed to do it in my original plans, but things have changed and the two of us have changed our agreement. Now it must be you."

"No. No, I can't do that, Edge. They'll never accept me as their queen. I'm from the Solar Court. They won't—"

"They will. You are his betrothed, and they believe that you have earned that spot. They believe you will have their best interests in mind simply because you are Divine. We will kill all three of the Lunar Royals and place you in their stead. I'll say you two held a private marriage before ever attending the party, that you were so in love that you couldn't wait or something. They love you, Silvi. And even if they don't, you can make them."

I huff in astonishment, allowing my anger to be unleashed. "That's all I am to you people—an enforcer. I don't want to make people feel things that don't belong to them, that change who they are as a person. I've done it my whole life, and I regret it every single time. That feeling never gets better, and it never goes away. And after what I did to Celeste, I—"

"What, exactly, did you do to Celeste?" Irissa questions as she reappears, all playfulness gone.

"It's my fault she got involved in this Divine shit. It's my fault she was almost killed." I hide another flinch as I prepare for the backlash, prepare for the speech about how horrible I am.

"Oh. Oh, yes, I forgot about all of that." The cheeriness is back, another giggle escaping her. Hot and cold, two opposites inside of one tiny body.

"You aren't mad?" I crinkle my eyebrows, feeling for the familiar emotion, but it isn't there. I can hardly feel anything from her now.

"Of course not. It's hard to survive in the world of the Divine, and Celeste and I are better off for what happened. I'm proud of you for surviving, Silvi. You did what had to be done. I can't hold that against you. Celeste was only doing what she had to do, too."

"You're...proud?" No one has ever told me that before and meant it, except the occasional moments from my dad who *has* to feel that way.

"I'm never bringing you back, Irissa," Edge hisses, fuming.

"Why not? She's making this whole ordeal a lot more tolerable."

"Yeah, Edge. Shut up and let the women talk," Irissa cackles at the dark expression that follows, dodging a stray strand of his shadows as she cries out in alarm.

"We are leaving now, Irissa. I hope you found what you came for. Silvi, make sure Zaeden accepts the invitation and that all three Royals show up. The U.A. will handle the rest. Oh, and take care of the men Ryleigh sent word about, won't you?"

"You won't be stuck here much longer. You won't have to pretend to be happy anymore." Irissa reaches out and grabs my hand, squeezing gently. I notice a new glint on her index finger as she does so, a gold band present that wasn't there before.

"I've pretended to be happy my whole life, angel. I doubt that'll change anytime soon." So often I feel that emotion from the people who surround me, but I rarely get to have it for myself.

Edge yanks Irissa into a portal before she can respond, her sad eyes watching me through the darkness. The opposite of Celeste's eyes. I shake my head and dab at my watery eyes, falling back into the chair. Upon returning to the castle I have work to do, three men who I must torture. I don't typically like such activities, but I think I will enjoy destroying the men who hurt Celeste when she was at such a tender age. Though, as much as I might find myself enjoying taking her revenge, I'm not ready to return to my life; I think I may stay here a little longer.

I'm not ready to put the mask back on yet.

CHAPTER 18

Celeste

Irissa's tiny body presses against mine in the small bed in her special room, her giggling and insistent chatter distracting me from some not-so-innocent thoughts of my husband-to-be. I know she is excited about something that happened between her and Valaine today, but I can't find the energy to be excited—or even the energy to be angry—that Valaine is courting my sister.

My mind keeps drifting back to Edge, to the feel of his hands on my body and his taste on my lips. I shudder fervently, rolling over to face Irissa.

"What's wrong, Les?" Her voice falters, red cheeks dimming. "You haven't listened to a word I've said this entire time, have you?"

"I have! You said that Valaine—well, she—um—" I stutter over my words, my own face heating now.

I have no idea what she said.

"I said that Valaine set up this really romantic picnic at lunch and kissed me at the end after asking if I would consider being something more serious! I had an entirely too cute story, Les! What are you so preoccupied with today that you don't have time for me?"

"Nothing. What did you tell her? Is she your girlfriend now? I didn't think you wanted a serious relationship right now."

Her eyes narrow into slits at my entirely too-fast answer. "Is it about your kiss with a certain Royal?"

"What? Who told you that?" I sit upright in a fury, harsh gaze on her as she laughs.

"Val." She shrugs casually, amusement dancing in her eyes. "Edge told her the other day. He was pretty upset about you running off on him."

"Still," I hiss, picking at the pink silky sheets. "He had no right."

"I just told you about Valaine, didn't I? How is that any different?"

"Well—you know—it just is!"

"It isn't." She rolls her eyes, pushing herself up next to me. I watch dejectedly as her wings rustle and shake as they stretch out, her loud groans following.

"I'll kill him, Iris." My voice is barely a whisper, my eyes clenched shut.

"You don't know that. What if you are giving up the love of your life? Your Soul Divine?" Her arms encircle me lovingly, head falling onto my shoulder.

"I thought I killed the love of my life once already, Iris. How am I supposed to go through that a second time? It almost destroyed me."

"Maybe try not to kill him?"

I stare at her, lips pursed, hardly holding in my laughter. I finally release it, the sound rising like the tide and flooding out of my mouth. Irissa laughs alongside me, our bodies shaking. "I'm serious," I say eventually, shaking my head.

"Maybe you can ask him to help you work harder on control? You're already working on your strength, I'm sure it wouldn't be hard for him to show you how to learn control; your powers are similar in intensity. Valaine says he has to wear all those rings to reel in the shadows or they overwhelm him. It sounds exhausting, but you can relate to that, can't you?"

"He's already offered to help me and has been actively helping me do so. I—well, I've been helping him manage the shadows to manage my own ability," I admit, chewing on my bottom lip. "I've been taking some of his powers."

"And how does that affect you?"

"Honestly? I think it helps. I hate my power. Truly, I do. But I don't feel this overwhelming urge to drain him dry. I haven't accidentally taken powers since we started this."

"Then maybe you can be mutually beneficial to each other. And I don't just mean with your powers." She raises her head to wiggle her eyebrows, adding a wink for emphasis.

"Irissa!" I shriek, shoving her off me.

"Celeste!" she cries back mockingly, laughing loudly. "I'm just saying. How was the kiss, anyway? Good enough for you to be sad about missing out on more, right?"

"Please, stop," I beg, covering my face with my hands.

"Come on! Just tell me!" She shakes me harshly, pouting.

"Fine! Yes! It was good enough for me to be sad about missing out on more. It was...intense, electrifying, and...and everything a girl could hope for."

"I knew it!" She releases me, giddy and proud. "You must really like him."

"I don't know." I release a sigh, flopping back down onto my back. "I think about him a lot, but I didn't think about *kissing* him until it happened. It's hard not to be attracted to him, but I'm attracted to a lot of people. And now something has changed between us, and even I can't ignore that. It was so sudden—he was kissing me and pushing me into the wall, and I just...lost control. I started draining him. I had to stop the kiss, I had to leave. The thought of killing him haunts me. A relationship with Edge is hopeless and certainly isn't sustainable. I'm a fool, Irissa. A fool for trying to be happy again, for falling into the exact trap that landed me in this Court. Maybe I just have some weirdly fatal attraction to Royals."

"Well, Royals do tend to like each other more. Valaine told me that it's probably why we are so drawn to each other.

And why Edge is so attracted to you, even when he didn't want to be. It's some kind of preservation thing."

"I didn't know that. So the attraction isn't real, then?" I frown, confused.

She giggles, flopping down next to me. "Oh, no, it's very real. I know Valaine and I are together all the time but we have been taking it slow, despite what everyone else thinks. I wish my kiss had been steamy like yours. You're much better at romance than me."

"Really? Because everyone I entrap ends up dying. Not much romance in that, Iris."

"Edge will be different. He's much more powerful than that dick Kyelin. More powerful than Zaeden can ever dream of being."

"Maybe." I shift uncomfortably, detesting this conversation.

"Plus, have you seen that body? And that ass...have you touched it yet?"

"Irissa!" I hiss again, heat flaring to my cheeks once more. "Why are you looking at his ass? Don't you have a girlfriend who's, you know, his *sister*?"

"Are you saying you don't?" The stare she fixes with me is too much, and I burst into a fit of awkward laughter. How am I supposed to respond to that? "See? I told you. You have it bad, Les, you really do."

"You always know how to make me feel better, Iris." I sigh contently, reaching out to squeeze her hand.

She shrugs, saying, "I know you, and you know me. At the end of the day, we only have each other to rely on. And we need that reminder sometimes."

It takes a few more days for me to grow the courage I need to speak to Edge again. At first, I refused to attend any more of our lessons– I didn't want to put myself in a situation where we would be alone together. Eventually, I got over the embarrassment and reminded myself I still needed to train. And, even though I came to that conclusion on my own, Edge came to it faster.

I stand in front of a counter in the kitchen, laughing with the head chef, Marlene, as I eat a delicious strawberry-flavored pastry. I wanted a snack before training, and the staff here is incredibly friendly. At least, until raging Royals barge into their workspace.

I turn upon noticing Marlene's gaping mouth, her ladle dropping to the ground. She hurriedly grabs her skirts and curtsies, breathing heavily. Edge is strutting through the doorway, furious gaze entrapping me. His shadows trail behind him like a cape, the dark clouds tumbling over each other in their hurry to keep up with his quick strides.

"Your Highness," Marlene says, voice shaking.

"Out!" he bellows, not offering her the kindness of a greeting.

"Of course." She doesn't have to be told twice, and she doesn't spare me a glance or any parting words before leaving. I sigh, placing the pastry down and dabbing my mouth with the back of my hand quickly. Well, there goes my enjoyable moment with the sweet brunette who makes the best pastries I've ever eaten.

"What's your problem?" I question lightly, attempting to hide the quiver of my hand.

"You've been missing our lessons." I don't move as he approaches, his body shoving into mine until my back is pressed to the sharp edge of the counter. His hands fall to either side of me, caging me in as his head bends forward and his gaze meets mine.

"Yes."

"Why?"

"I needed some time to think, some time to get my head on straight." I shrug, trying to push past him. Edge only lets out a grunt, arms stiffening to ensure I'm unable to flee.

"If you don't participate in lessons, someone will make sure that pretty head of yours twists at just the right angle and is never able to be straightened again. Do you want that?"

"If it's so pretty, then I guess it'll make for a good display piece. I think putting it on a stick in the library would provoke some nice conversations, but what do you think? Would the Courtyard be better?" I hiss back, swallowing hard as I avoid his gaze. "I'm sure I deserve whatever is coming to me, either way."

"I'm not doing this again, Celeste. You are coming to lessons today."

"Well, I was going to attend before you so rudely interrupted my pre-lesson snack. I had already decided to come before you came in here huffing and puffing, but I'm reconsidering my decision."

"Do you realize how serious this—"

"Do you realize how serious my powers are, Edge? What I could do to you? All it would take is a brush of my skin, of my fingers against your arm, and I could *destroy* you."

"You won't."

"Maybe. Maybe not. I don't know that. *You* don't know that. I needed time to get myself under control. Surely you can understand that?"

He spits out, "Surely."

"And in that time I've made a decision." I swallow, turning away from the venom in that steel blue.

"The decision that you are going to continue lessons? Good."

"No."

"Then what?" I avoid the spark in his eye, the hope. He thinks I've changed my mind about us, but...I haven't.

"I want you to train me in control, as we discussed and attempted once before." I'm careful to not mention how that training session ended.

"Train you in...control?"

"Yes. Mine and your powers are similar in intensity, Edge. We both have these never-ending chasms inside of us and yet you manage to keep those shadows in the palm of your hand. You never let them out, never let that control slip. *That's what I need.* I need you to show me how to do that. And if you can...*then* we can try to be more than friends. Okay?"

"First lesson," he breathes into my ear, anger releasing as he pushes himself flush against me. "Don't tease me like that, Celeste. Irissa told me that the call to use your powers is dimming now that you are actively taking in my power. I know that you aren't as off the rails as you claim to be. Don't dangle yourself in front of me like it's some game. You're going to lose."

"How do you know? I could be completely mad right now." I close my eyes and relish his touch, committing it to memory.

"You'll be completely mad about me by the time I'm through with you, but that's not what is going to happen today. Today, we train. I know you need confidence in yourself and your abilities, and I'll help you obtain that. But I *will* expect you to hold up your end of the deal, Celeste. I will train you to control your powers. In return, I want you to let yourself *live.* Do not hold back with me anymore; you never have to do that with me. We are technically engaged, Little Flame. It's time we act like it."

"I'll hold up my end of the deal," I agree, practically gasping for air as he releases me from his hold.

"I know you will."

I find myself moving with him, leaning forward as he leans back. And then he's taking a step away, his face hardening as he realizes I was unconsciously following his steps. I can't help it, can't stop myself when it comes to him. There's something about him that is magnetic, and I'm attracted to him like a moth to the flame. Or maybe he's the moth, in this scenario?

"When do my lessons begin?" I grind out, pushing my back into the counter and forcing myself to stay away.

"Right now. Take from me, Celeste. Take the shadows."

The way he watches me has every bone in my body freezing and reheating, creating a buzzing inside my skull. I suck in a deep breath as I reach out to touch him, my hand shaking. With a start, I jerk back. I can't absorb his powers—it isn't safe for him here.

"You said that we can't do this unless we are in the safety of your room. You said—"

"Forget what I said!" he bites out, grabbing me forcefully by the waist. "Touch me, Celeste."

"Your rings," I whisper, fingers dancing across the obsidian.

"They'll ground me—I don't need the room. Please, Celeste."

I can only nod, allowing my touch to dance up his arms. He wears a deep blue button-up, and I can't stop myself from watching as his thick fingers slowly undo each one. I stare at that hard chest, mesmerized, before allowing myself to place my hands over his heart. I close my eyes as I allow the monster inside of me to feed, shuddering in relief as the cool darkness enters me. It's cold and shallow like a light breeze grazing my skin. Edge stiffens at my touch, his body lurching toward mine. All too quickly I find myself wrapped in the comfort of his body once more, our arms tightly encircling one another. My cheek falls to rest against his shoulder, head nuzzling into his neck as our point of contact changes.

That overwhelming urge to take it all isn't rising, the inability to let go is nonexistent. I've been starving for so long, and I'm finally understanding what it means to be full.

Edge tilts my head back up, trailing gentle kisses down my neck. His teeth graze against sensitive skin, and I can't help but release a soft moan. I should make him stop; I don't have enough control over myself yet. But it feels so good to be in his arms, for his lips to touch my skin. I let myself enjoy it for one second, but only the one.

"Edge. I'm full." I drop my arms, voice quivering.

"Full?" he rumbles against me, unmoving. "Full as in you don't want any more?"

"As in I don't need any more." His arms slowly fall to his sides, his body retreating in a hurry. I mourn the loss of his touch, mourn the feel of those lips on my skin.

"Of course. That's great progress." He clears his throat awkwardly, fingers touching his lips absentmindedly.

"I've never felt full. Maybe...maybe you're right. Maybe I can actually learn how to control it."

"I'll make sure you can. Because the alternative..."

"I don't want to kill you, Edge. I won't. Just—please, keep your distance for now. I enjoy your powers, but I don't want your whole essence inside of me. I already have the full powers of two Divine dancing inside of me right now, one of which hates me. I don't know how much more I can take."

"How much power, or how much heartache? Because I have a feeling you could burn the world down with the amount of power you could hold."

"Maybe I could." I swallow, turning away and clamping my eyes shut tightly.

"Maybe you should."

"I don't want to be that kind of person! Why does everyone want me to be so evil?" I slam my hand into his bare chest, frustrated and angry.

"You resigned yourself to that fate when you entered my Court," he grinds out, shoving my hand away with a scoff. "Stop thinking about everyone else for once, Celeste. What do *you* want?"

"What do I want?" I whisper, flabbergasted.

What do I want? I want my sister to be safe. I want to make Zaeden pay for what he did to me. I want to hurt all of the Divine at the Lunar Court who dared to betray me. I want the world to see how brightly I can burn. I want to show them what kind of darkness and pain I can bring if they refuse to make things right.

"What do you want?" he repeats gingerly, fingers tapping against my heart.

"I want them all to pay." The words are barely a whisper, a guilty admission. "I want them to regret everything."

"Then they will," he says excitedly, frantically grasping my face in his strong hands. "We will make sure of it—starting with Zaeden."

"Starting with Zaeden," I repeat, fire burning within. For once, it doesn't shudder at the thought of me controlling it.

"You won't feel guilty over his death, Celeste. Never feel guilty about the fate the goddesses have in store for him."

"No. I will be a weapon they yield for his retribution," I breathe, hands alight in a fury with a control I've never experienced. "I will take him and the whole Lunar Court down. I will rip the Royals right off their thrones and give the Undivine the lives they deserve."

"Yes, you will, Little Flame. I wasn't so sure when I first met you, but I am now. Nothing will stand in your way."

"Nothing. No more holding back. No more caring about what everyone else wants. As long as Irissa is safe, nothing else matters. I don't care what I have to do to make it that way."

"She will always be safe in my Court," he vows in a hushed tone. "As will you."

"Don't let me regret this. I've never allowed myself a single thing in life. Kyelin was the closest thing to a choice I have ever gotten, and we both know how little of a choice that turned out to be. Don't let me regret choosing you."

"You're choosing yourself, Celeste. I'm just a bonus." His grin breaks the serious mood, a laugh bubbling out of my throat.

"I don't know that I would call you that."

"Learn to control your powers, Celeste, and you'll call me a lot of things."

CHAPTER 19

Celeste

I nervously pace around the empty bar, pausing briefly as my eyes roam over the many bottles hidden underneath the countertop. Fuck it, why shouldn't I have a drink? My hands shake as I snatch a pretty red bottle, tipping the contents into a small glass. I throw my head back as I toss the burning liquid down my throat, coughing at the unusual sensation. I glance toward the door before pouring another, my back facing the entryway. Then I take another, and another.

"A little early for shots, isn't it darling?" Edge's drawling voice meets my ears, his steps light and quiet. Urona's, however, are not.

Edge has a hand clamped around my mother's blond curls, dragging her behind him painfully. Her body flails, hands clawing at Edge as she desperately tries to escape. She screeches at the top of her lungs, curses and odd noises escaping her foul mouth. I can't hide the sick satisfaction that I get from the sight of her at his mercy, and a small part of me is relieved to see her being treated as horribly as she had treated me.

"It's never too early to drink," I say, even though I've only been truly drunk once in my entire life.

"Celeste." My mother's body stiffens, her spine straightening when my voice reaches her ears. "Oh, my darling daughter. Thank the goddesses you are here. Please, I need your help. This man is absolutely—"

"Prince, mother," I interrupt, smiling maliciously.

"Excuse me? What did you say to me?" Even now she dares to act as though she is the one in control.

"Don't refer to the crown prince as 'this man'. He is your prince, and treating him as such will do you well."

"For fucks sake!" she hisses, striking out at Edge's hands once more in hopes of being released.

Edge pays her no mind, ignoring the harsh scratching as he watches me. Once satisfied with what he sees on my face, he slings her down so that her knees slam into the hard ground. "We have a few questions for you, Urona."

"You always have questions for me. You and your persistent little friends who follow me everywhere—"

"I recommend you not insult those friends in my presence. I may forgo all niceties and rid you of your tongue." Edge's voice is coated in venom, eye hardening as he turns that gaze back to her crumbled form. Shadows rise around her, forcing her to scramble back abruptly.

"Can't you just behave for once, Mother?" I sigh, tipping the bottle into my mouth instead of the glass cup. Honestly, this stuff isn't as bad as I thought it would be…I just have to get over the burning in my throat.

"You're getting drunk before lunch, Celeste, so I don't think you have any right to be telling your mother to behave. I should be the one chastising *you* right now."

"I have to get drunk to deal with you. If I'm going to have a headache anyway, it might as well be because I went down into the bottle." My head is already beginning to lighten, and I drink faster in hopes that soon I won't have any thoughts in there at all.

"You've always been such an insolent little brat. I should have known when you came out without uttering a single cry that something was wrong with you. I mean, what baby doesn't cry? Only a monstrous one, that's for sure."

I snap my mouth shut, wincing at the harsh words. I don't have time to react, however, because Edge is taking control of the situation for me. Urona is lifted into the air by a group of angry shadows, tendrils wrapping around her wrists and ankles tightly. They tilt her upside down, dangling her above the hard earth as she screams.

"Speak to her like that again and your time in my Court is over. You will forfeit any protection previously offered to you, as well as the wealth you have accumulated in your time here. For your daughter's sake, I will leave you alive, but I won't leave you with anything worth living for. Is that enough encouragement to play nice?"

"O—of course, my p—prince." Her stuttered words and fearful gaze are enough to satisfy Edge, and he drops her unceremoniously onto the ground. Her head hits the ground with a loud "thunk" and small moans are released as the pain registers.

"Who was my father?" The liquid courage inside of me has me diving straight to the point. I no longer wish to beat around the bush: I only want answers.

"I—well, you don't really want to know, do you? You've been fine on your own, haven't you? You don't need to know about that man." She twitches on the ground as she tries to sit up, hand reaching out for a chair. I see a small puddle of blood on the ground, and I avert my gaze.

"Yes, actually. I *do* need to know." I send a trail of flames to nip at her toes, emphasizing my point. I'm beginning to understand why Edge went straight to torture the first time he got information from her.

"Okay, okay! Fine. Your father...his name was Dario High-more." Her body sags with the release of the long-kept secret, chest heaving.

"Fuck," Edge hisses, rubbing a hand across his face.

"Who is that? Who is Dario Highmore?" I watch Edge apprehensively, sucking on my upper lip. I take a singular step and stumble slightly, hands reaching out to grip the counter. I can't already be drunk, can I? I mean, sure, over half the bottle is gone, but...

"Not who I thought your father was."

"But you said that you had an idea—"

"Yes. I thought your father was his brother, Rayne. Rayne is a few years older and has been known to run off. I thought, maybe, he was managing to pull it off between his duty as heir and his duty as your father those first few years. That maybe it got to be too much and he faked his death and ran home with his tail tucked between his legs. But Dario?"

"What's wrong with Dario? I don't understand."

Urona lifts herself fully now, finding the confidence to face me. It's the first time I've seen the tears in her eyes be genuine, the first time I've seen true anguish in her features. "Dario disappeared as soon as he turned eighteen. It was thought that he had been kidnapped and that another Court was holding him for ransom. The Lunar Court seemed the most likely at the time, as they had not been on good terms in years. It's one of the many reasons trade between them has practically halted entirely. They were sure the Lunars were behind his disappearance, but they had no proof. The Light and Shadow Courts have always been close allies, so together they decided to cut ties with the Lunars. But there was never a ransom offered, never a whisper of his whereabouts. He's been presumed dead for all these years."

"I suppose that part is true," I whisper, taking another long swig of my drink. I don't bother to wipe my chin as the lukewarm liquid slides down, don't bother to hide the mostly empty bottle. Will I get alcohol poisoning from this? I hope not. "What Court did he hail from? Which Court is it that we are discussing, Shadow or Light? Both are likely enough. And why was he important enough to need a ransom?"

"Your father was the youngest prince of the Shadow Court." A small noise escapes me, my grip on the counter tightening as I stumble again. I knew this was a possibility, but it still seems unreal. My kind, easy-going father had been a prince. A Royal.

And so am I.

The vague memories I have are of him helping our neighbors, of his laughter as he tells my mother that Irissa and I were troublemakers like him. All my life I've hated Divine and have wanted to punish them. How am I supposed to allow this new reality to replace my former hatred? How can I accept that my father was one of the very people I despised the most?

"Why would he leave for you?" I snarl at Urona, laughing quietly. Who in their right mind would leave a life of royalty for an Undivine? Who would leave that life for someone like *her*?

"We were in love." Her whispered answer is plain, as though the answer could possibly be so simple.

"I don't understand. How were you able to con him into leaving with you? Into faking his death? Or kidnapping? Or—whatever." I wave my hands frantically, bottle waving with me. It doesn't make any sense—he had to have been mad.

"I worked for his family as a servant and often came into contact with him. He was always so lonely, so isolated. I hadn't intended to ensnare him, Celeste. My intentions had been much more pure. I was lonely, too, after all. I had no parents, no siblings, no friends. We were there for each other, a pair of unlikely acquaintances. I didn't mean to fall in love, but I did.

"Dario wasn't like his family, wasn't like any Divine I knew. He was kind and understanding, honest and observant. He knew that something was wrong with the world and that people like me shouldn't be treated the way we are. He knew that things needed to change, he just…didn't know how to do it. So, when he turned eighteen, we decided to run. I was only a year older, and I had nothing to return to. He told me that as long as he had me, he had nothing there, either.

"Dario wanted to live like an Undivine, to experience the harsh realities of this world for himself. We planned on going back after a few years, on telling his parents exactly what he found and how he was treated by fellow Divine. He wanted to promote change and enforce new policies. Except…I fell pregnant with you. Things weren't just about him and me anymore—they were about us. About family."

I choke a little, squeezing my eyes shut tightly. My father had always been the most loving of my parents and had doted on me and Irissa as though we made up his entire world. As though he was but a moon circling in our orbit. I never could remember much of those days surrounding his death and remembered very little before that. But if this was true, and he did give up his life as a Royal for me—for *us*—then things are so much worse than I thought. Because I killed this man, this Royal, who gave up his life as a privileged prince to take care of me. Who put a pause on changing the world because he believed I was more important. And yet, after all those sacrifices, he died at his own daughter's hands. The monster he created destroyed him before he could see his dreams come to fruition.

"The day you were born, everything changed. He didn't want to go back anymore, didn't want to bring his precious daughter into such a blood-thirsty environment. But I was so in love with him that I forgot all about his Royal status, and I allowed him to play pretend for a little longer. It was all going so well. The day he died…he was leaving to make a trip back to the Shadow Court. He told us to stay put, that he would send for us when the time was right. He didn't want to risk the family he created when the family who sired him could be so cruel.

"I wanted to go back home so badly, but he made me sacrifice my wants for your needs. I had to stay with you two because we couldn't trust your lives with anyone else, and I should have been with him on such a perilous trip. Not that it mattered in the end. You were so upset with him, so angry. Your powers manifested that day, and you sucked the life right out of him."

Rage burns inside me, hot and overpowering. *This* is why Urona always treated me so horridly, why she beat me outside and in. I was a child, confused, upset, and scared. My punishment may have been deserved—who am I to say that my guilt should be pardoned just because I didn't know any better? And yet...and yet I was still a child. *I didn't know, I didn't know, I didn't know.*

Urona continues, undeterred by the shock and anger in my features. "And because I was born powerless, I wasn't able to follow him into the unknown. I wasn't able to offer you my own life or my own gifts. *I'll never forgive you for it, Celeste.*"

Her sobbing slowly transforms into raging hiccups, her bitter anger hitting me like a whip. I stumble back at her harsh words, back slamming into the wall and the bottle slipping from my hand. It shatters upon impact, the bitter-sweet smell burning my nostrils. I shake as I try to regain my balance, my head spinning. But Edge is there, catching me before I can slip into the mess I've made. He doesn't allow me to fall, only takes me into his arms and lets me scream into his chest.

Why does everything have to be so unfair? I should have never been left to live as an Undivine—I should have been raised as a Royal. I shouldn't be marked with the brand of the Lunars, shouldn't be scarred by what those cowardly Lows had done to me. My life has been a disaster and, somehow, I have found myself right back in the Royal trap my father was desperate to keep me away from.

"I'm sorry, Celeste." Edge rarely addresses me by my true name, rarely does anything but tease, but he is more than serious now. His strong arms are the only comfort I have at this moment, his words soothing my wounded soul.

"I'm a Royal," I confirm, my brain finally beginning to become blessedly numb. Edge had suspected, had *known*, and all I had done was deny the truth.

"You are. And, quite frankly, it doesn't change anything." That's a lie, though. It changes so many things, including what we know about the Divine and inheriting powers. My blood is diluted—I shouldn't have the powers of a Royal when my mother is Undivine. And yet I do, as does my sister. I've never believed in the goddesses, but maybe I should start. How else do you explain this turn of events? Marriage, blood, inheritance: none of it matters. Maybe the goddesses truly have chosen me for this fate as the Divine Slayer.

"My whole life has been a lie. I was never Undivine. I was meant to be this strong ally because of my ties with the other half—my background. Now they'll all know I'm a fraud, and no Undivine will call me anything but."

"I don't give a fuck what anybody says, Celeste. You were Undivine, and fuck them if they don't accept you for who you are. You've fought for them every step of the way, and *fuck them* if they take that for granted."

"I don't—I have another question." I stumble over the simple words, blinking rapidly as I try to focus on a singular thought.

"Ask her, then."

"How did we come to have no powers? How did we come to be Undivine in the first place?"

"I took you two to the Followers as soon as your father died. I gave them his crown in exchange for sealing off your powers and making you forget about it all. Yours were easy, they hardly had any trouble. But my sweet, sweet Irissa...she fought them tooth and nail. I think you were so guilty about what you did to your father that you didn't have it in you to fight. You've always been so guilty, so ready to punish yourself for the wrongdoings you can't stop yourself from committing.

"They tried, they really did, but...that's how she got stuck, how she came to be cursed. I don't know, maybe it is a true curse. Maybe she hurt someone who she shouldn't have. Maybe one of those Followers realized who we were and did it on purpose. I wasn't allowed in the room when it happened, so..."

"You paid strangers to experiment on your daughters? Are you fucking serious?" Edge is raging now, fists clenched tightly behind me.

"I didn't know what to do! He made me promise not to bring them to the Royals, so how else was I supposed to hide their gifts? Celeste sucks people's souls out, for goddess's sake! What was I supposed to do? What choice did I have?"

"You ruined Irissa's life," I whisper, sobbing into Edge's chest as I picture the horrible things they must have done to her.

"*And you ruined mine!*"

Edge releases me in a fury, stalking over to my mother with thunderous steps. He grabs her by the hair once more, dragging her to the door with no gentleness. She crawls after him, screaming and begging to be released. But he doesn't stop until she's outside of the bar, doesn't stop until she is left crying in the blinding light of the sun. Then he slams the door in her face, trusting her to be smart enough not to re-enter.

"It's not your fault Celeste," he coos as he approaches, gripping my face in his large hands. "Do you understand? None of this is your fault. You were a child and an untrained one at that. Your father gave you his powers willingly, re-member? He wasn't angry or scared; he loved you and was willing to let you live with a piece of him inside of you forever. *This isn't your fault.* None of it has been."

"Then why do I feel so shitty?" The pad of his thumb swipes at a stray tear, that steel blue eye staring intently into my soul.

"Because Urona wants everyone to feel like she does. How your father fell in love with that cold-hearted bitch, I'll never know. Though that is of little consequence right now. Right now you need to focus on the fact that we have answers, Celeste. Real answers that can help Irissa."

"Right. Help for Irissa," I agree, sniffing heartily as I step around broken glass. Edge grips onto my wrists and guides me, watching me wearily. "When you do things like this it's so hard not to give in."

"Like what?" I feel him stiffen, hands tightening around my wrists subtly.

"Like not caring about my past, about what a monster I have always been. Like comforting me, and threatening to hurt those who hurt me. Like being a very attractive man whose touch lights me up inside." I don't mean to say any of it, but the words bring a smug grin to his lips.

"Anything else I should keep doing? You know, to make you cave faster?"

"There are lots of things you could do. But I won't tell you to do any of them because I'm a little inebriated right now. Is it normal to feel this drink so fast?" I can't help but lean forward and seek out his body heat, can't help but inhale his familiar sweet and smoky scent.

"You, Little Star, just drank almost an entire bottle of Divine Wine. You know—the stuff that gets you drunk after just a few shots? Time isn't a factor with this wine, it's quantity that matters. So, yes, it's very normal." He chuckles, grinning. "You were saying something about things I should keep doing?"

"Oh, yes, lots of things." I nod, pressing my cheek into his very rigid chest.

"For example?" he pushes, still grinning.

"For example kissing me like you did—" I pause, frowning. "No, I can't tell you that. I'm too upset for kissing."

"You'll be okay," he promises gently, taking my small hand in his large one and placing a kiss upon it.

Funnily enough, I believe him.

Edge was gracious enough to deposit me in my room after the scene with Urona, where I ended up sleeping half the day away. By the time I awaken it is nightfall, and the half-moon is watching me through the singular window. I awoke to find a tonic and food waiting for me, along with a note from Edge stating to meet him whenever I was up and feeling better. So, after a good bath and gaining a stomach full of food, that's what I do.

I find Edge in his room, and I hesitate to knock on the door. But, as if sensing my presence, he swings it open before I can decide to turn away and run. I ignore the pull of the obsidian, hand dropping slowly to my side. Edge is dressed in a simple black shirt and matching pants, his own hands shoved deep inside of his pockets. I focus on the tattoos on his arms, noticing a familiar one.

"That heart with the E...what does it mean?" I clear my throat as I ask the question, remembering the image from the engraving on one of his rings.

"Val did that one," he says, intense gaze dropping down to his left bicep. "It was her way of telling me to love myself."

"Oh. I thought, when I saw the same thing on one of your rings, that, well—"

"Did you think another woman gifted me that ring? That I was in love with someone else?" He chuckles as though the thought is ridiculous.

"I did." The admission has his chuckles evaporating.

"I want to show you something." The statement is abrupt, and I hardly have time to agree before I am transported away through a portal. We emerge inside the empty throne room, the large and looming chairs intimidating. The biggest one is sat to the left, its golden feet and armrests shining in the candlelight. The seat is the deepest of blacks, the cushion thick and menacing. The small one is a replica of the gorgeous throne beside it, with only a large red jewel in its head marking it as different. The walls in this room are a taupe color, and the carpet is the same deep black as the cushions. Other than that, this room is empty. No hangings on the wall, no personal touches added with paintings or pictures. This is a room meant only for receiving guests, for conducting business in a way that shows who rules over who with the simple finery only given to the people who sit in these chairs.

"Why are we…?" I trail off, unsure. Edge only goes toward the set of double doors at the end of the room, poking his head out and snapping his fingers.

"Make sure no one else comes in here," he commands, slamming the doors shut once more.

"Edge, I—"

"Sit." His commands are now aimed at me.

I only laugh, shaking my head furiously. "Absolutely not. I'm not sitting on your mother's throne."

"I don't want you to sit on my mother's throne." He stalks up to me, an evil gleam in his eye. "I want you to sit on my stepfather's throne—the throne I am meant to inherit."

"I'm not—" I screech as he lifts me in his arms, toting me to the looming throne effortlessly.

"What the fuck, Edge?" I seethe, flailing as he tosses me onto it.

"I told you to sit."

"Okay, well, I guess I've sat now, haven't I? Great, now why don't we—"

Edge interrupts me again, saying plainly, "You are a Royal, Cerina Celeste Highmore. It's high time someone treated you like one."

Then, he does the unthinkable. He gets down on his knees and bows before me.

"Edge..." I whisper, shaking. To see him bowing before me, bending the knee...it's so *exhilarating.*

"I want to worship you in a way you deserve to be worshiped. To show you that you are not a monster, that you are not evil despite the choices you *have* made and *will have* to make. We are to be married, Celeste, and you will rule my people by my side. Let me show you who will rule over me." Edge slowly begins to slip off his many rings, piling them into his hand. Then he takes my hand, slipping one onto each finger.

"I don't understand," I say, hypnotized.

"These rings keep me in control. Let them control you, now."

"They won't—they can't—" I stutter as he drops my hand onto the armrest, shaking even harder as he grips the hem of my dress skirt.

"They will," he assures me, bending down to trail kisses up my bare leg. He lifts my skirts until they are piled in my lap, hands pulling me to the edge of my seat. "It infuriates me that you have been denied simple things for so long. Denied friendship, denied love, denied pleasure. I told you once already that I will deny you nothing, and that still holds true. Allow me to show you, at least, what it means to be pleasured. Allow me to erase Kyelin's touch from your skin and replace it with my own."

I wish I had the strength to tell him no, to show him that this is a bad idea. I still don't have full control over myself, can still kill him with these simple touches. But I can't form the words. I can't deny him when he has put me on a throne and told me to rule over him, can't deny him when he is between my knees promising to give me a pleasure I have never experienced before. I gasp when those fingers curl into the waistband of my underwear, feeling cool air hit my core as he tugs them off. I grip hard onto the arms of the throne, the cool presence of his rings keeping me grounded and in control like he promised.

"Will you allow it?" he questions, his warm breath hitting *very* sensitive parts.

"Y—Yes," I stutter out, inhaling harshly as his tongue swipes out against my inner thigh. Then that mouth finds a more devious place to work, his skilled tongue working me up expertly. I almost scream at the first lick, my eyes wide and my chest heaving. Edge holds me down by my thighs, fingers digging into my skin as I cry out and beg him not to stop. And he doesn't.

He rumbles against me, licking slowly and lazily as he whispers, "You taste so *divine.*"

The complement is a double-edged sword, and I love it. I love the way he knows exactly what to say to me, love the way he knows exactly how to turn me into a weeping, begging mess. I jerk when I feel him nibble along my thigh, pausing his workings briefly. "Edge, no, please—" I will say anything, do anything, to get his mouth back over me.

"Anything?" he murmurs, and I can feel the grin on his lips. Then one of those large fingers teases my entrance, pushing inside me slowly, intimately.

"Edge," I hiss, back arching.

"Yes?" Another nibble, this time much closer than before.

"I need—I need you to—" I can barely think, much less speak.

"You need what?"

"Please—"

"You said you'd do anything, didn't you? Well, I've thought of something I want: you begging, in very plain terms, for what you want." *Stupid mind reader* I hiss as loudly as my mind can manage, moaning as he curves his fingers and hits just the right spot.

"Please, Edge. I just—I want your mouth on me. *Please,*" I manage out, moaning the entire way through.

"As you command, My Queen."

Edge's tongue moves back over me and does exactly as requested, turning me into a puddle of mush on this throne. My hands tangle into his hair, my hips thrusting as I chase after the orgasm I'm so close to having. "That's right, Celeste. Take what you want. *Take it.*" His voice is husky, the vibrations so good against me. It's all it takes to have me falling over the brink, tumbling into a blissful moment of pure ecstasy.

Edge fulfilled his promise to me, ensuring that I felt pleasure in all the right ways. I've never come so hard in my life, never experienced such euphoria after any sexual act. By the end of it all, I'm a sweaty, panting mess, and all I want is more.

My cheeks redden as Edge ducks out from underneath my skirts, his short hair sticking straight up. I watch as he pushes himself back into a standing position, leaning forward slightly as he says, "My Queen." Then he bows at the waist, striding off with an unholy smirk spread across his lips. I struggle to compose myself, to lower my skirts and think past the memory of his tongue. But the only thought that comes to mind is a devastating one.

Where do we go from here?

CHAPTER 20
Love and Repercussions

Edge

"**B**ecause if you die—if you die, then who will hold me accountable? Who will help me? Who will ever love me?"

Her voice is a painfully insistent reminder of what I have to lose, of why I need to focus on the map before me, and not the loud, clear, angelic voice haunting my mind. But then her voice brings on memories of her taste, of other sounds like her delicious moans that—no. No, I can't think of any of that right now. She is distracting me from the things I should be doing and the people I should be helping. I can't focus on her right now—despite how desperate I am to lose myself in thoughts of her.

I turn my gaze to Eleazor, staring at the map they have painstakingly put together of all four Courts as their voice snaps into existence again. "—I think the only way they would be able to attack would be from here, near the roads, but they are the ones who developed the beasts which means they may have developed a way to bypass them. If that's the case, they can cut through the woods and would be more likely to attack here." They jab a finger in two different sections of our Court, vague areas that may not even be the places we need to focus on.

"And the others?" I glance up at Amon, praying he's about to tell me something *good* for once.

"They would have to cross Brighlow Bridge, but..."

"You suspect they have a fleet?" I run a hand down my face, reading his thoughts without actually invading his mind. That's the benefit of having such close friends—you don't need powers to know them inside and out.

"Yes," he confirms, looking grave. "I do. And if they do, then we have no way to defend ourselves from the water. *We* don't have a fleet. If they cross the Dead Sea, then we won't have a chance. Your sister, of course, would be an asset if it came down to it, but I doubt they will come without an Elemental of their own to combat her."

"We don't have a fleet because we have nowhere to hide one, and if anyone knew it would be seen as an act of war immediately. Not to mention the arrogant king that rules over this Court who holds the opinion that we don't even need an *army*."

"I know. It isn't your fault, Edge," Eleazor says reassuringly, sensing my frustration.

I ignore them, questioning, "How likely do we think this is?" I don't care about the statistics, not really. I care about protecting Celeste, shielding her, and preventing her from giving herself up to save everyone else because I know she will do exactly that.

"Maybe a thirty percent chance?" Eleazor shrugs, staring down at the map again thoughtfully. "Not at all if the Shadow Court sides with us. Where the Shadow Court goes, the Light Court follows."

"We need to bring up her heritage during the party," I say, hating that I will have to use her any more than I already have—use her just as everyone else in her life has. More tricks, more lies, more games.

"Yeah, we do," Amon agrees, watching me wearily. "We don't have a choice. They will go to war for her as soon as they know she is Dario's kid. I have very little doubt about that."

"Okay. Okay, I'll talk to her about it. I don't want her to be blindsided when it happens," I murmur, thinking about those goddess-damned lips again. About that smooth expanse of skin across her legs and how it felt under my hands, my lips, my tongue—

"She won't flip out and change her mind, will she?" Amon questions with a sigh, ignoring the hiss from Eleazor warning him to shut up.

My mind empties, shadows lashing out of my hands like whips in a brief, unexpected loss of control. "Flip out?" I question, staring down at the Divine, my friend, with loosely hidden rage.

"She's volatile, Edge." He ignores Eleazor's jab to the ribs, continuing as though he's unbothered by my rage. He probably isn't. He's been my friend since we were toddlers—he knows how far to push. "She's full of guilt and pent-up aggression. Who knows what she will do with a power like that? I know you like her, and I know you want to protect her from as much of this as you can. But someone needs to bring it up, okay? If you bite my head off, so be it. She's fought tooth and nail against every suggestion, and every plan, because she is selfish and doesn't want to make sacrifices. But this is about more than her: It's about a Court. Several Courts, actually. So you need to be sure that she is going to do this, that she isn't going to back out at the last minute just so she doesn't have to deal with the repercussions afterward."

The silence is deafening, and not a single one of us dares to breathe. That is until shadows whip out from my hands and ensnare Amon around the neck, dragging him across the room and flinging him into the wall at the far end of the room. Eleazor shouts, Amon groans, and I *rage*.

"Do you know why she feels all that guilt and pent-up aggression? She killed her father when she was a child because no one taught her how to wield her powers. And then, as a punishment, her powers were taken away. Not only hers but her sisters, too. Afterward, her own mother began treating her like the monster she didn't know she was, and she could only take it. If you want to talk about the sacrifices she is and isn't willing to make, then let's talk about it.

"Celeste allowed herself to be abused and used by everyone around her until she couldn't handle it anymore. Until that innocent little girl who only wanted to be good had to be sacrificed and she could no longer play nice. Until she stood in front of a Royal who pushed her too far, and she sacrificed all that good to unleash every dark, evil part of herself into the world." I pause, yanking on the threads of darkness and ignoring Eleazor pulling on my shoulders, begging me to release our friend. Amon only stares at me, indifferent.

Eleazor always was the smarter of the two.

"She killed someone, felt horrible about it, and *still* tried to convince herself not to. Then I came in and forced her into a situation where she would have to do it again. She didn't want to be like us. She didn't want to maim and kill to get the things she wanted, the things she needed. She wasn't raised in the same world that we were. She was raised in a bubble of hardship, a kind of hardship we will never be able to understand. And instead of turning into a cold, callous creature, she blossomed into a kind, caring one. A creature I corrupted. If you want to talk about the sacrifices she's made, then we don't need to talk any further. She's made too many already.

"Yes, she feels guilty. She's allowed to. She's allowed to feel whatever the fuck she wants, even if it's an inconvenience to you and everyone else. But don't mistake her guilt for compliance or her selfishness for weakness. She's been selfless her whole life—she's allowed to finally make some decisions for herself. And the decision she has made is to stay by my side and fight. *She will not turn her back on us or our Court.*" I pant as I finish my speech, dropping my friend onto the ground unceremoniously.

"You love her," he coughs, staring at me with a glint in his eyes as Eleazor rushes to his side.

"Love isn't a factor in my opinion," I say, avoiding an answer entirely.

"Well, it is in mine," Amon argues, pushing himself up with a grimace. "And the people I love are in danger. The home I love is in danger. It's my job to protect them, protect it. You can't fault me for questioning unknown factors just because you are biased toward them."

"Yes, I can." I shrug, turning and whipping my cloak into their faces as I retreat, calling out behind me, "And if you think she's such a risk, come to a training session or two with us. Watch her, hear her, help her. You'll change your mind quickly enough."

Her words echo in my head again, reminding me exactly why I am defending her despite every reason for me not to.

"Because if you die—if you die, then who will hold me accountable? Who will help me? Who will ever love me?"

CHAPTER 21

Celeste

This is a horrible idea. Absolutely, resolutely, horrible.

I watch Eleazer approach with a deadly calm, no sign of their thoughts visible across their features. I gulp hard, closing my eyes briefly as I try to focus. I hear Amon approaching from behind, his footsteps quiet but not quiet enough—I have a feeling it's purposeful.

I force shadows into my palms, shoving the deep fear within me down into the pits of my stomach; I have to do this if I want to learn how to wield the deadly power living inside me.

"Now, Celeste!" Edge calls from the sidelines. I can picture his sly grin and mocking salute, and I try to remain focused while telling myself not to summon up the image of him on his knees before me. Flames roar up to the surface at the heart-fluttering thoughts but I suffocate them. They are becoming easier to wield and they listen to my commands more often now. I think it may have something to do with my decision to follow my own path, but I can't be sure.

"I'm trying, dammit!" I cry, teeth grinding with the effort. I hear the whistle of a blade, and I barely manage to throw up a shield in my defense. Over the past few weeks, I've managed to make those stronger, too. Now, no one can touch me physically unless I wish for them to. I will never be defenseless again. I'm in control now. *Finally.*

"Pitiful!" Amon scoffs mockingly, fists slamming down into my shield to test for weakness.

I don't dare open my eyes, too fearful of the Divine in front of me. Eleazer can seize my gaze in an instant, and their powers will severely limit my own. They can't fully take away my abilities because my powers are stronger, but I won't take the chance.

I take a deep breath, pulling shadows out in a fury. I think about the sphere Edge always starts with, think about it growing to be larger, larger. My arms shake with the effort, my head pounding. My whole body heats as the flames beg to be released, too. I don't let them out, though. When I open my eyes, a black wall of tumbling shadows stands in front of me. I think about my destination for only brief seconds, willing myself to control this portal before I jump.

"Boo," I whisper pleasantly, allowing my hands to dance across Edge's shoulders as I step out from behind him. He whirls around, a grin so wide on his face that I'm almost struck motionless. I shake off the bizarre feeling and smirk, bowing as Eleazer and Amon clap nearby. They've joined us in the past several sessions, and their instruction has improved my skills immensely.

"Bravo!" Eleazer shouts, clearly impressed. Honestly, I'm impressed, too. This is the first time I have successfully created a portal in battle. Not only that, but I was able to keep my shields up at the same time. Now that I know I *can* do it, I need to focus on speed.

My mind whirls with the possibilities that have opened up to me, but those critical thoughts are interrupted by a drawling prince. "Wonderful, Little Flame. I knew you would succeed eventually."

"Eventually?" I scoff with a raised brow before patting him dismissively, my hand lightly sliding down to brush against his ass before I move to dance past him. He grabs my arm with a low growl, shadows dancing around his large frame.

"Don't push me, Celeste. You know how I struggle."

"I know. The poor, spoiled prince isn't rewarded immediately." I pout, allowing the flames to dance behind my eyes playfully. "Whatever shall he do?"

"Maybe I'll take you to my room, and—" Edge is panting now, gaze hungry and crazed as it has often been since that night in the throne room.

Amon is the one to interrupt, clearing his throat loudly. "Let's go again, Celeste!"

I nod, pulling away from Edge with a shy smile. Every lesson has become heated and scandalous, tantalizing and sweet. Edge is becoming more and more desperate to be near me, to touch me. I'm enjoying it more and more with each passing day, finding it harder and harder to deny what we both want.

"Again," I repeat confidently. I have done it once already, after all. How hard can it be to repeat that success?

I walk back to the center of the empty field, nodding at Amon and Eleazer to signal the start of the fight. Amon is on me in seconds, leaping for an attack. I throw a shield up with my right hand, my left going backward to sling a shield at Eleazer. I don't turn to look at them—eye contact is all they need to take me down.

I shoot a line of flames behind me, laughing at the surprised cry Eleazer releases. I let a trail of flame strike out at Amon, pushing him back. They stretch around me to form a wall, rising high above me. I swallow hard, prepping myself—this is the hard part.

"Don't ever put your shields down."

I scream as I spin around, finding Edge inside of my wall. I let out a small growl, shoving him back toward the flames. He only laughs, stumbling back toward his awaiting portal. I glance down at his hand, noticing he still wears his many rings—that means he hasn't gone far. I smirk, forming a sphere of darkness in my hand.

"Want to play?" I purr, tossing my ball into the air. We watch as it grows, reaching its maximum height at a near twenty feet in the air before tumbling back down.

"What are you—"

I don't hear the rest of his sentence before we are swallowed by darkness, transported in the blink of an eye. Edge whirls toward me as we emerge, gaze roaming around our new surroundings.

"You said you wanted to take me to your bedroom, didn't you?" I grin slyly, brushing against him teasingly. The astonished look on his face tells me everything I need to know: I shouldn't have been able to do that. I definitely shouldn't be able to open another portal in this room, but I do just that.

He doesn't get a chance to grab me before I'm waving dismissively, stepping back into another portal. They're much easier than I thought they were, coming naturally now that I've discovered the secret to their creation. Maybe I was thinking too much before. That's always my problem—I think, and I think, and I *think*, but I never *do*.

"Where did you go?" Eleazer questions as I step back into the room, their eyes wide in shock.

"I took Edge on a little trip." I shrug, playing with my nails. "He wanted to go to his bedroom, so I took him there."

"You—you opened a portal in that room?" Amon questions, gaping at me.

"Um, yeah. Twice, technically. Edge seemed surprised, too. Am I not supposed to be able to do that?"

"Do you know how much obsidian is in that room? An insane amount, that's how much. It hardly controls Edge. How did you—"

"The powers I have given her were willingly given," Edge announces as he steps back into the empty field we are practicing in, interrupting Eleazer. "So she has all of the control I possess. I'm able to get into my room sometimes, but it usually takes a lot of my strength. You don't seem to be fazed."

"Well, the first portal was hard, but after that it was easy. I didn't struggle at all." I shift uncomfortably, the confidence high I was on deteriorating.

"I suspected you could hold an incomprehensible amount of power, but this just solidifies that suspicion. Celeste, you are a much more dangerous weapon than any of us will ever be able to understand."

"I guess so," I whisper, embarrassment heating my cheeks. I kick at the dead grass and dry dirt roughly, unsure of how else to respond.

"Don't be ashamed." He approaches me gingerly, pulling me to him. He grips my chin with one hand, tilting my head upward and forcing me to stare into that steel-blue eye.

"Everyone thinks that calling me a cold-blooded killer is some kind of massive compliment. I'll do what I have to, but I would much rather trade abilities with any of you."

He shakes me roughly, growling into my face, "You have never grasped the gravity of what you are, the rarity. You are so much more than a killer, Celeste. You are the *Divine Slayer*. You can make everyone who has done you wrong pay and you possess the ability to change the world as we know it. Your powers aren't some hideous monster eating you from the inside out or something shameful you need to hide away from the world. *You* aren't some hideous monster. You are a gift from the goddesses, made for this world and crafted by their very hands."

That shake has some innate part of me jumping into action, and I can't stop myself from pulling myself from his grasp and swinging a fist angrily. Edge easily blocks it with a forearm, shoving my arm back down with an enraged look in his eye. I step forward, aiming for him again with another fist. We begin to dance around each other, my fists flying and his arms blocking.

With a fury I don't recognize I scream, "But crafted to be what? What am I supposed to call myself? I'm full of darkness and I'm full of shame. Every single decision I have made has been surrounded by guilt, and I'm trying to change that." I pause after a particularly rough block, laughing mockingly as I say, "And then there's you. I was brought here to you, but what if I'm not your gift? What if I'm your doom?"

Edge scoffs, almost laughing, as he kicks out at me in his first offensive move. I screech, jumping just in time but putting distance between us I can't afford. Without fear, I jump toward him again, determined to land a singular blow on the foolhardy prince.

"We were meant to find each other, Celeste. You and I share the darkness that has isolated me my whole life, and we share this never-ending agony that tears at our very souls. And, yes, these shadows may bind us together, but they aren't the only thing. We share a common goal, a common purpose, and a common hope for the future of the Divine. The goddesses have blessed me with you and blessed my Court with the strength of the Divine within you.

"You aren't some silly, cold-blooded killer, Little Flame. You are a weapon forged for this world, a weapon no one but you can control. Never again will you have to let a Divine use or touch you without permission. You can take anyone down with just a few thoughts and a little motivation. You can punish those who deserve it."

I scoff, swinging again, again, and again. "You don't think it's a curse? Holding all this power that not one single person should be able to hold? Holding *your* power?" Edge has never seemed to care that I could steal his power, but I know how insulting that would be to other Royals. Or other Divine in general. No one in a position of power likes to *share*—especially not with a tiny Undivine incapable of controlling herself or her urges to kill.

"My power runs through your veins, but so do many others. You may believe yourself to be cursed, but I think that curse has been turned into a blessing. Use it. Use that blessing and rule the fucking *world* with it. This power may be a burden, but never a curse. Bare the weight on your shoulders, grit your teeth, and show the goddesses your middle finger, Celeste. And if you need someone to ground you to this world then I'll hold your hand while you do it."

My throat is dry by the end of the speech, rendering me unable to speak. I'm not sure what I'm supposed to say, anyway. I want to believe that everything he said is true, that I'm not meant to be this monster I make myself out to be. That we were meant to share more than shadows, that our souls are bound together in more ways than one. Yes, I am powerful. Yes, I am deadly. But between those two things, can I be anything more?

My advances slow as I debate my anger, my motions, my motivations. Edge doesn't even act as though he's worried about me trying to hit him again, his hands now shoved deep inside his pockets. That cocky little—

"He's right, Celeste." I turn to Eleazer, stunned into distraction. Are they about to start spouting off sentimental shit, too?

I manage to choke out, "Not you, too."

"I have met many soldiers in my day. I have never met one with a strength or a resolve like yours. And I don't only mean physical strength, because we both know you don't have much of that."

"That's true." I gurgle out a laugh, wiping away a stray tear.

"Your powers are beyond anything this world has seen in a very long time—if I had to approximate I'd say it's been hundreds of years. And the burdens you carry? The grief and regret? The enormous guilt and determination? Those things are what light the fire we see in you. The way you protect your sister, the way that you continue to fight for her? That is the strength we see, Divine Slayer. Do not be ashamed of the title.

"You have a heart of gold, and you will do what is right. You decided to go after what you wanted, didn't you? You want the Undivine to be free, to be able to live a life they should have always had access to. You want to change the world. *You can't do that if you let those burdens and those doubts drag you down.*"

"So you don't think I'm a horrible beast, even after seeing all of the things I can do?" The fear of myself that has weighed me down for months now slowly begins to fade away. I know these Divine—they don't suck up to people and they certainly don't *lie.* I'm no exception in their world, and they have even more motivation to not lie since we have become tentative friends.

"You aren't a monster. I have seen as much in these past few weeks. We all have. Let the shadows heal you, Celeste. You need to relish in this power, and you should be grateful for what the goddesses blessed you with. Make the Divine fear you and forget about those other things. Show them who, exactly, the Divine Slayer is."

"Stop calling me that. I don't want to be the Divine Slayer!" I hiss, wrapping my arms around myself.

Amon steps forward, brushing against Eleazer as he comes to stand by their side in a unified front. I watch the sun setting on the horizon behind them, unable to look them in the eyes as I cry. "That's what you are—own the title. You are training now to help kill Royals. You must be prepared for that title when the time comes, be prepared for that name to be chanted among the people. Don't do it for Irissa, or the Undivine, or even for us. Do it for yourself.

"Be proud, Celeste, because very few are given a title of such magnitude. Fear runs rampant among the Divine when they hear your name. Revel in that, and enjoy having power over those who treated you as though you were powerless. Make sure people continue to have a reason to fear you: It's the only way you will make it through this ordeal alive."

"Listen to your friends, Little Flame. You may not believe these things to be true, but we know they are. We see everything you are, and everything you pretend not to be."

"I killed him," I whisper eventually, tumbling onto my knees as the exhaustion hits. The ground is hard and unforgiving, pain jolting through my bones, but I ignore it. "I was so, so angry. I shoved him. That's it, that's all it took. And in the moment I had this thought...this thought that I should suck his soul right out of his body. *So I did.*

"It was agony watching him die and knowing it was my fault. He screamed at me and tried to pull me off of him, but my shields had risen around us to defend us from Zaeden's poison. There wasn't anything he could have done—I was glued to him. Then that scream froze, and he began to turn into a pile of ashes right before my eyes. That handsome, charismatic prince. *My* prince. It was torture, Edge."

"Because you thought you loved him," he says softly, watching me with not even an ounce of pity. I like that about him—he's never pitied me or made me feel like a damsel in distress. He makes me own up to all my mistakes, all while trying to convince me there's no reason to be pitied.

"I was *convinced* that I loved him, *convinced* that I killed the man I loved. And it was just as hard to realize that I didn't know what love was in the months after. Hard to understand that he used me, and would have continued to do so for the rest of my life. That I would still be there now, miserable and bitter. It left me with an even deeper fear, one I can't seem to shake. Kyelin's death was horrific, yes. But yours, Edge? It would drive me to the brink of madness. You saw how close to that edge I was after Kyelin—what do you think would happen to me if I lost you, too?

"Do you understand what I'm saying? What I've been trying to convey this whole time? Understand the enormity of the pain that I delve into every day when I imagine you as that pile of ashes and dust? I don't have full control yet so it can happen at any moment, and none of you seem to be able to grasp that concept. Yes, I am better, but that doesn't mean I'm perfect! I lived through it. And you were there, in those moments after. You thought I was out of control then? Just wait, Edge. *Wait until I kill you.*"

I can't stop the tears that slip down my face, can't stop the sobs that wrack my body. They're right: I was made to kill. I can accept that, I can get over the guilt eventually. But when it comes to Edge? There would be no coming back from that. It's why I haven't allowed either of us the things we want, why I have held him at my fingertips all this time.

"You won't kill me, Celeste," he practically screams, anger seeping out of every pore. "And even if you did, I would deserve it. You don't know half of the evil, depraved things I've done for the sake of my Court. I've killed, too. Much more

often than you, if we are being truthful. I've sent Undivine
to the noose, Celeste. I've sent them to the guillotine but I've
also been the hand wielding the blade of death. I remember
my stepfather taking my hand and forcing me to do it myself. It was my first kill, and I'll never be able to forget it. The
man...he had stolen food from the city: A whole pound of
fresh meat. His children had been without a meal for days;
he did what he thought was best.

"I remember the little boy who cried out for his father and
the wife hiding her toddler's head in her breasts. The man
prayed to the goddesses when his eyes closed and begged
them for forgiveness, begged for the safety of his family. He
didn't see when the blade came rushing down, but I did. I
saw every splatter of blood and heard every bone as they
snapped. I was ten years old, Celeste. That's when *I* became
a killer. Don't pretend like I'm some saint that needs saving.
I don't deserve that. I'm not a saint, and I won't pretend to
be one. I've made sacrifices for this Court, many that will
haunt me for the rest of my days. But at the end of those
days, I remember who I am. Will you?"

"I didn't—I don't—"

"You are no more than that blade to my father, Celeste.
Will you remember what you really are?"

"What am I?" I whisper, dejected.

"You are the hand that wields it."

I gulp down the air around us greedily, eyes shutting
painfully as he crouches down in front of me and whispers,
"Keep practicing Little Flame. Learn control. If not for yourself, then for me. I can't stand watching you destroy yourself

over it. I can't stand to be apart from you when I know I don't have to be."

"How am I supposed to do this?" I sob, shaking my head angrily as I continue to cry. "I still feel like a monster. Sure, I may be strong. I may be powerful. But what does that matter when I feel like shit all the time? I've never felt beautiful, never felt powerful. My whole life I've been used, taken advantage of, abused. How do I get past that when it's all I've known? How do I take charge over my life and the beast within?"

"It's simple: If you become the thing they fear, you become the thing that empowers you. If you tame the beast, you will never have to feel those things again."

"So simple," I say with a mocking laugh, exasperated.

"Tell yourself that, Celeste. Tell yourself right now that you will not succumb to your primal instincts."

"That's silly."

"Do it!" I jump at the growl in his voice, that deep drawl terrifying.

"I will not succumb." I swallow hard, taking a shuddering breath before continuing. "I will be powerful. I will be strong. I will be the Divine Slayer, and they will fear me."

"Keep going!" Amon urges from nearby.

"A Divine will not kill me," I whisper, lifting my head to stare into steel-blue. "I will not be afraid. I will be the very thing of their nightmares. No one will ever touch me again and I will not succumb to the beast."

Edge grins, taking me into his arms. "Good girl."

"I will have control," I breathe into his chest, my heart growing as a weight lifts from my heart. "I will not succumb."

"It's so good to have you back. I knew you were hiding somewhere in that pity party."

"Do you think we should test my control?" I whisper huskily, running my fingers across his jawline. I feel like I'm drunk on this power over myself, like I can do anything. Surely, just this once, I can have him? I can prove to myself that I can get what I want without having to fear for his safety.

Before I can urge him further, we dissolve into darkness.

His rings fall into my hands as the portal is formed and he pulls me in without saying a word of farewell to my tentative friends. I'm pressed harshly into an obsidian door, his lips slamming into mine with a passion so fiery I'm not sure how he isn't alight. I moan into his mouth, hands grasping at the back of his head as I try to press myself closer, closer, closer.

I hardly notice as Edge kicks the door open, not caring as he pushes me inside harshly. One foot slams the door shut behind us, his shadows encompassing us as we slip into the darkness of the room. I hastily pull at his shirt as we kick off shoes, my hands slipping underneath to feel scarred skin and hard muscles. We only separate for brief seconds, just long enough to rid ourselves of these encumbering shirts. Our lips gravitate back together, desperate to stay connected. As we tumble back toward his bed and I'm shoved down onto the soft mattress, my back arches up in a desperate plea for more. Heat pools within me as his agile fingers work on my pants, sliding them down and slinging them away. I'm left in just my undergarments, and I feel more exposed than ever.

Edge watches me from the end of the bed, admiring. "You're so fucking beautiful, Little Star." The words are barely out of his mouth before he climbs on top of me, kisses and gentle nibbles trailing up my leg at an excruciatingly slow pace. I hiss when he reaches my inner thighs, those angry noises changing to whimpers as he carefully marks a path around the most sensitive parts of me. When he looks up at me from under those dark lashes...I lose every bit of submissiveness that's been instilled in me.

I flip us over, forcing him to lay beneath me. Those large hands take the opportunity to roam along my body, exploring every inch of my skin. Each new touch has me glowing from the inside out, my body desperate for more. I'm sure he can feel the heat radiating from my body, those pesky flames begging to be released.

Edge's hand slips underneath my bra, the free one reaching back to undo the clasp. I gasp as those fingers find a sensitive nipple, arching toward him for more. When my bra slips free it leaves room for his other hand to reach up and grab me, and he pulls me toward him to slip his mouth around the bud. I melt into him, gasping, pleading, crying out for more.

When Edge pulls away, I duck down to kiss him. My kisses begin to descend, falling lower and lower as I crawl back at the same excruciatingly slow pace he tortured me with.

I stop when I reach his waistline, tugging in frustration at his belt. I'm desperate to be as close as possible, desperate for our skin to touch in a way I didn't think possible. When I finally manage to strip him down completely, I almost gasp in surprise. My eyes rake over his lower half, my breath leaving me as I realize how large he is.

Edge groans in satisfaction at my reaction, touching my cheeks where a blush had formed. Then he's sitting up, pulling me into his lap. My bare breasts press into his chest, his shadows and my flames slipping into the air as he rips my underwear clean off. His hands press deeply into my back, lips falling on me once more.

This feeling is unlike anything I've felt before—this lust, this want, this need. I feel alive for the first time in my entire life, and I never want it to end.

Edge shoves me onto my back, mouth dipping lower and lower until his tongue unravels me at my very core. I become a heated mess underneath him, and the noises that leave me are utterly unholy. After an eternity of me shaking and pleading for more underneath him, he finally enters me, and...it's pure bliss.

Edge isn't gentle in the way Kyelin had been, but I never had any preconceived notions that he would be the gentle type. I enjoy the roughness and the intensity that he brings. I find myself returning every bit of those frantic motions, every bit of the intensity he doesn't spare me from.

The shadows swarm us, encompassing us in a deep cocoon that I never want to leave. The flames rise along with them, unburning and leaving behind a pleasant warmth. What is this feeling? Everything about it leaves me with a sense of rightness, a sense of inevitability. How could I have ever wanted Kyelin? The thought of him makes me want to gag now. He would have never felt like this. He would have never filled this emptiness inside of me.

"Edge?" I breathe hours later when we have had our fill of one another, curling into his arms.

"Yes, Little Star?"

"Why does it feel like this?"

"I don't know." I like that he doesn't question what that feeling is, and I really like knowing that he feels it, too.

"I feel complete," I whisper eventually, leaving the words to hang in the air.

"I will never be able to have anyone else," he agrees in his own way. "You've ruined me."

"Have you had many before me?" I question with a laugh.

"Several," he admits, fingers trailing circular patterns across my arms. "But nothing ever like that. Nothing so—"

"Intense?" I finish for him.

"Yes. Among other things."

"Among other things," I say with a satisfied smile.

Luckily for us, we have plenty of time to revisit those other things.

CHAPTER 22

Celeste

I watch a servant lift a banner onto the archway above the door, pouting because its beautiful script mocks me with its faux congratulations. Everything about the decor in this room is coated with false flattery, leaving a bitter taste in my mouth. The flowers are beautiful, supposedly Silvi's favorite—not that I care. My gaze trails over the red monstrosities that climb the walls, encouraged by a Low with a green thumb. The artistry of their arrangement is breathtaking, designed to ensure the guests feel as though they are seated in a garden. The sickly sweet scent is overwhelming, yet another tool to place the viewers even farther into the fantasy. The sight of it all fills me with deep unhappiness.

I should appreciate the gorgeous archway at the door and should look upon the thousands of flowers and vines that are reaching out to touch me in awe. I should appreciate the sheer number of candles in this room and should ogle at the gold accents hidden in every arrangement and among the set tables. I should appreciate the time and coordination it took to get all of these balloons and ribbons in here and should appreciate the attention to detail when it comes to the fine lettering on the napkins and plates. Instead, I have chosen to wallow in pity—it's most likely my last chance to do so.

I stiffen when Irissa enters the room, as I have every time I've seen her in recent weeks. I haven't found the courage to tell her what our mother did, or who our father was. I know that I need to, that it's important and life-shattering news, but...the news rocked my boat *hard,* and I fear that it may sink hers altogether.

"Hello, sister," she calls, her blush pink dress brushing against petals as she approaches.

"Ho," I grumble, wincing at the reminder of Darius the simple noise brings with it. Luckily, Irissa doesn't seem to notice.

"Why so glum? Aren't you excited? This party is practically for you, after all."

I'm not excited in the least, actually. By the end of this so-called party, I will have become the Divine Slayer and will never be known as anything more. By the end of this party, I will be embracing the dark side of my nature and, despite the part of me that is thrilled at finally letting go of my hatred for myself and my powers, I know this night will change the course of my entire life. *Again*. It's a task I dread, but one that must be accomplished nonetheless.

"I don't find murder particularly thrilling," I say, sighing as I sit up straighter.

"Take a few more shots, drunkard. I'm sure it'll make you feel better." She laughs as she jabs a finger toward the shot glass next to me.

"I needed the liquid courage. If this party is to go as planned, I'll need more than a few." I don't tell her that the last time I needed liquid courage I ended up vomiting for an entire day.

"Don't stress yourself out about this, Celeste. Edge has everything under control, and the Royals here won't let things get out of hand. You're safe. We're safe. You're a fucking badass Divine and no one can take that away from you. Now, go find Ryleigh. She's been searching for you all morning."

"Yes, and I've been avoiding her this whole time quite successfully." I sigh, pushing myself up. I haven't spoken to Ryleigh much as of late as our relationship is too strained to accomplish more than a few friendly words. I suppose it's time to go spew a bit more of that asinine friendliness out.

The dress I am wearing can only be described as bridal: all white, eye-catching, and strikingly beautiful. It hugs me in all the right places, a large slit in the side showing off pale skin and allowing for plenty of movement. A dagger is strapped to that exposed thigh, just above where the scandalous slit begins. Ryleigh also placed a white headband in my hair, mimicking the beginnings of a veil. She tried to boast of her genius, but I only boasted of her dramatic tendencies.

Edge is wearing a devastating suit, according to Irissa. She claims that he looks positively regal and that there is no chance Zaeden will be able to outshine the Solar Royal tonight. I doubt Zaeden could outshine him under normal circumstances, though. The very energy Edge brings into a room is an entrapping one, and it demands all eyes follow him. There is no turning away from his presence, no avoiding his stare.

When he enters my room, my heart slows to a deadly pace. Irissa had been right—he *is* devastating. The black suit is tailored to his large form, muscles contracting under smooth fabric. A blood-red rose has been placed in his front pocket, the color matching the stain on my lips. It's a dark omen, one not likely to be missed by anyone who glances our way. It's a sign that says, "Mess with my Court, and *your* blood will be here instead."

"Celeste." The single word seems to choke him, and he has to clear his throat as his gaze lingers on my form.

"Edge," I whisper back as our bodies drift together on their own accord.

"You look phenomenal, as always." Fingers tenderly reach up to brush my cheek, the simple touch leaving a burning desire deep in my bones.

"I don't feel phenomenal." It's a scorching truth.

"Remember what we discussed; remember why we are doing this." Edge seems like a true villain at times, always convincing me to do inherently wrong things like murder. Am I the fool for listening every time? For *liking* it?

"I remember."

"Then come, my betrothed. Let us celebrate our engagement by drawing the blood of our enemies." Edge offers me an arm, a sad smile gracing his lips. It's nice to know that he, too, feels the inherent seriousness of this moment. That the weight and the pressure put upon my shoulders isn't only mine to bear.

I take Edge's arm, looping our limbs together as we turn to face our fates together. Our steps are heady, our breaths silent. We don't speak as we make our descent through the castle, and I can hardly think as we approach the future.

I love you.

The words are a shock to my system, reviving me from my numb state of mind. Edge feels me jerk, his gaze darkening as he turns to face me. The words hit my mind again, and again, and again.

I love you. I love you. I love you.

Over and over he repeats those three words, a secret only the two of us share. I can't help but leap at him, can't help but attack his lips with my own right there in the middle of the hallway. We stumble to the nearest wall, the world and the consequences to come disregarded.

"I love you, too," I murmur into his lips, a tear slipping down my cheek.

Love is terrifying. It's even scarier to know that, this time, it isn't because of some forced connection he cast upon me. It isn't because I am desperate to love and be loved. I fell in love with Edge slowly, albeit heavily. His love is similar to that of a sharp dagger, and the tip of his blade has slowly found its way into my heart. Once that dagger of love penetrated my skin, my barrier...it consumed me.

Once again, I am faced with the reality that I may lose the man I love.

"Don't die," I whimper into him, desperately trying to convey my emotions in these final moments alone.

"Don't throw yourself off a roof if I do." His words are playful, but the tightening of his fingers in my skin tells a different story.

Against his lips, I whisper out words meant only for his ears. "You were right about us finding each other, my prince. We were meant to meet and were created with one another in mind. My power may not be adjacent to yours, but it is complimentary. And because of you I see it for what it is, see myself for who I am. Before we walk into the hands of fate, I want you to know that I think our lives are tied together indefinitely. I think that the threads that bind us to this world are tied in a never-ending knot, entangled indefinitely. If one of us dies, so does the other. And as I follow you into marriage, I will follow you into death."

"The darkness I possess is yours to control. If death is where that darkness leads us, then so be it." Edge sears me with one last kiss, lips harsh and desperate as we taste each other for what could be the last time. "Let's go kill a fucking Royal."

I blush and apologize profusely as we begin to make our way back to the venue, swiping at his lips to no avail. They're stained red, the shade only a touch lighter than the shade on mine. The guards that have joined us ignore that fact entirely, focusing solely on a faraway spot down the hall.

"It's only a reminder that I am *yours*," he purrs gently, stroking his thumb across my chin. It's the last touch I get before we face the entrance to the party, the last smug smirk I see gracing those lips before I dive into the deepest part of the sea.

"Announcing Edge Zorander, prince and heir of the Solar Court," a guard bellows beside us as the familiar white doors are thrown open after a pause in Valaine's welcome speech. I can't see into the room beyond because of the wall of guards that block me from view, but I know exactly what awaits me. Only, this time, there will be Divine accompanying the floral arrangements and flickering candles. "Accompanied by his betrothed, Cerina Celeste Highmore of the Shadow Court."

The shouting begins as soon as the guards part.

Divine cower at the sight of me, their terrified screams piercing my ears. I hide my distaste and push away the roiling boil in my stomach, instead allowing my lips to tilt up into a secretive smile. I stand straight, eyes flickering across the room as though bored. I do everything Silvi's father taught me to do; his lessons, it seems, were of importance like he claimed them to be.

"What treachery is this?" The Lunar King's voice is the one rising above all others, his eyes alight with all too familiar flames. I let my own flames rise, taunting him with the power I stole from his kin.

"Seize her at once!" Zaeden demands, throwing his hands out as a sickly green poison begins to rise. Silvi had warned us of this new change, had warned that the poison was deadlier than ever before without his other half to keep it at bay. I wrinkle my nose and sigh in disappointment, allowing shadows to soak the floor and dance across the feet of our guests.

"You will do no such thing." Edge's deadly calm halts all movements, Lunar guards pausing as they await instruction.

"Oh? We won't, will we? We warned you, Zorander. We warned you what would happen if you were harboring an enemy of the Lunar Crown. You have just declared war between our two Courts!" King Mourner is red with anger, flames hardly contained beneath his tan skin. It reminds me all too much of his son—the one I killed.

"There will be no need for a war." King Zornader interrupts their standoff, no longer an amused bystander. "Weren't you listening? Celeste is engaged to my stepson and my heir."

"That changes nothing," Zaeden hisses, lashing out with his poison. Neither Edge nor I move as the green tendrils race across the floor, branches reaching out to grab me. I watch in amusement as the poison slithers across my shoe and up my leg, meeting bare skin. That simple touch allows me to absorb the poison, a new trick I have been working on in my training sessions. Gasps cry out among the crowd as that green liquid sinks into my skin, disappearing without so much as a drop left to prove it was ever there. Silvi is the only one who watches on with a bored expression, hands gripping Zaeden's arm subtly as if to appear frightened.

"You continue to disappoint me, Prince Zaeden," I say lightly, raising an eyebrow.

"They've been training her." It's hardly a whisper, but all Royals respond with equally horrified expressions.

"May I speak now, child?" King Zorander chortles, amused.

"Explain this, Horace." This voice is new, a whisper emitted by a brown-haired man clad in the gray and baby blue colors of the Shadow Court. I try not to stare at the newcomer, at the Royal I've never known but whose blood runs in my veins. I knew the Shadow Court's king would be here, knew that this moment would come, but...I hadn't dared hope it would be a happy reunion. Especially not after the introduction claiming me as one of his own. The fear that Rayne Highmore would hate me had been an afterthought, an apprehension I hid away so as not to dread this night even more. Watching him now...I can't tell if that fear has come to life.

"Let me introduce my future daughter-in-law, Celeste Highmore of the Shadow Court. Daughter of Dario Highmore of the Shadow Court." The words have their intended effect: outrage, disbelief, shock.

Arguments break out among the guests, hissed whispers and cries of outrage among the hundred or so people in the room. All know me by a different name, a name they cry out now. *Divine Slayer.*

"That's not true. It—it can't be." King Highmore is aghast, face pale and forlorn.

Revealing my name had not been an easy decision to make, but it's one we made nevertheless. Having two Courts sided together against a common enemy is better than standing alone. Convincing the Shadow Court that I need to live is essential to our plan, and the revelation was made in the hope of bringing sympathy to my side. To prove that I belong with the Divine of this Court. To gain allies in a potential war.

Prompting Zaeden to attack me had been crucial, too, and it was all too easy to convince him to do so. Seeds of distrust have been sowed and confusion has been spread among the masses. Now it will seem much more plausible that he may be attacked after he tried to kill a daughter of the Shadow

Court and a bride of the Solar's. Either Court could have ordered a hit or neither. It could be a concerned citizen, as far as the rest of the world is concerned.

"It's true, Rayne. Her mother is Urona Highmore, but you may know her as Urona Longling. I'm sure you remember her?"

"The servant girl." Rayne's fingers reach up to touch his lips in an attempt to hide his shock. When he looks at me, I can see the recognition light up in his blue eyes. Blue eyes that are nearly the exact shade of my sister's.

"I've waited so long to meet you, Uncle," I say quietly as I bow my head forward in respect, inwardly flinching at the false pleasantness in my tone.

"And—you have a sister, don't you? I have two nieces?" The man practically shakes as he lowers his hand, all while the Lunar Royals quietly rage beside him.

I finally broke down and told Irissa about our father mere hours ago, and I haven't heard a word from her since. She left my room in tears, silent and angry.

"Irissa. She is here tonight as well. I asked her to wait before joining the party because I feared for her safety. She looks much more like our father than I do, from what I've been told." I add the last part to solidify her safety, despite its truth. I've always hated how similar Urona and I are in appearance, and it's yet another burden I must bear.

"You cannot harm her. If Celeste is attacked again, it will not only be a war on the Solar Court you declare." Rayne's voice cracks, despite its harsh undertones.

"This is absolutely ridiculous—" Zaeden steps forward, practically foaming at the mouth in his outrage.

"What's ridiculous is your insubordination." King Zorander sniffs, waving at him dismissively. "Now, why don't we resume the party? Two Royal engagements! What a celebration."

And just like that, my past deeds are overlooked. The Divines no longer seem fearful, only curious. They watch me from the corner of their eyes, curious gazes following my every move as Edge sweeps me onto the dance floor. We talk to too many courtiers and dance to too many songs—my feet ache and my facial muscles throb within the hour.

I don't allow myself to be lax, despite all the best reasons to be. I watch the room wearily, on edge as I wait for a signal from one of the many Undivines here tonight. Except...it never comes. Zaeden stays within eyesight, as do his parents. I can't approach Zaeden and lead him away myself because that would be much too suspicious, and I also don't know what snag has been found in the plan. So, I continue to watch and wait. That is until fevered whispers hit my ears.

"What's going on? I swear I just heard someone whisper Irissa's name." Irissa should have arrived shortly after me, but I turn to Edge with a stunned expression when I realize she never came. I attempt to use Edge's mind-reading tricks on the crowd, but I've been unsuccessful in all previous attempts. This one doesn't go much better.

Edge's face hardens as he begins to drag me away from the crowd, pulling me toward the nearest exit and ignoring my question. "Fuck. We need to go."

I repeat, "What's going on? Why are they whispering about her? What happened?" Is she hurt? Did the Lunars attack her in retribution for the crime I have committed? Where is she now? Why did she never come to the party?

"The Lunars have her." He grits his teeth as he says it, shadows rolling off him in angry waves as we slip into the corridor.

"What do you mean they have her?" My voice is barely a whisper, my body frozen. Edge continues to drag me, but my feet refuse to move.

"From what I've seen among the minds in that room...someone intercepted her on her way into the party. There's a blood trail down the hall, and all signs point to her being taken. It has to be the Lunars, though. They must have sent someone to grab her while we were all distracted. That's all I've gathered from the people at the party, I'm not sure—"

"Edge!" Valaine is darting forward, Silvi on her heels.

"Do you know where they've taken her? What do they plan on doing with her?" Edge directs his questions at Silvi, snarling slightly in her direction.

All of our carefully laid plans, all of the built-up tension—it was all for naught. There will be no killing of Royals tonight, only the rescue of one. *If there's anything left of her to be rescued* my treacherous mind whispers.

"Oh, yes." Silvi sighs with a tight frown, as though grieved by my sister's disappearance. "They mentioned inviting you to a meeting, a meeting where they will demand that Celeste exchange her life for Irissa's. I'm not sure where they took her, I'm still a Solar and they don't trust me entirely."

"You knew?" Edge growled, shoving Silvi against the wall in a move so brutal that I took a step back. "You knew and you didn't report it to me immediately?"

"I didn't know," she snarls back at him, eyes widening as his hand slips around her throat. "I just found out! I swear!"

"Why should I believe you?"

"When have I ever lied to you, Edge?" Her voice is cracked and breathy, her greedy gulps of air audible as Edge tightens his grip.

"When you told me it wasn't so bad to lose an eye."

"A teeny, tiny lie told to make you feel better," she gurgles, face turning purple. "If you read my mind, I can—"

"I have read your mind, Silvi, and I've never liked what I found there." Despite his anger, Edge releases the pretty High. Silvi doesn't scramble away, or even grab at her throat. She only straightens, brushing wrinkles out of her dress with a scowl on her pretty pink lips.

"They told me ten minutes ago, and when I found Valaine she was already looking for me. All I know is that Zaeden was beyond giddy when he told me. He thinks that he has Celeste trapped, that she'll meet them no matter the circumstances if it means saving her sister."

A small noise escapes me at that, one of disbelief. "They think I'll agree to anything?"

That crystal gaze meets mine, stoic and honest. "They know you will."

"Well, then," I breathe out, closing my eyes and swallowing bile. I push away the panic, the fear, the guilt—that's not who I am anymore, it's not who I choose to be. Instead, I shove all those nasty things down and let the angry, vile creature inside me rise to the surface. "I suppose our plans have changed. Fuck the Lunar Royals and their privileged heir—it's high time that their family is knocked down a peg. I think eradicating their entire familial line should do the trick, don't you?"

CHAPTER 23

Celeste

The bed bursts into flames for what seems to be the thousandth time in the past hour, and Edge grumbles foul curses under his breath as he reaches for me. The flames are doused when his hand brushes across my bare stomach, my throat drying as those teasing fingers slip underneath the hem of my cropped nightshirt and rise toward my chest.

"Control, Little Flame," he mumbles into my ear, voice low and dangerous.

"I can't help it. I keep thinking about Irissa and what they may do to her. She's in her child form now and must be so scared." Haunted visions of my sister tied up and bound, covered in blood, demand my attention. I can see it plain as day, can see her broken talons and sawed-off claws. I shiver at another gory image that flashes in my mind, this vision showing one of Irissa's pretty blue eyes hanging from its socket as her childish voice begs for mercy.

"My men are out looking for her. And if they can't find her, then you *will*."

"How do we know they are actually going to ask for a meeting? How do we know what they told Silvi is real? What if they told her that because they suspected she was a spy and *wanted* her to leak information to us? What if—"

"Little Star," he whispers, the most affectionate of my nicknames.

"I'm sorry. I'm just—I'm worried. I'm *terrified*."

"Don't be sorry. If that was Valaine I would have burned my own city down just to find her. Your one desire your entire life has been to protect your sister, and that's why you brought her to my Court. I should be the one who is sorry. I promised her protection in exchange for your help and I couldn't hold my end of the bargain. I hope the goddesses punish me for it."

"Don't say that. You've held up your end of the bargain—you've kept your promise. It isn't your fault that Zaeden is an angry narcissist who is throwing a fit because he didn't get everything he wanted."

"No, I suppose it isn't." He kisses just below my ear with a chuckle, lips trailing down my jawline. "Want a distraction?"

"Another one, you mean?" I question breathlessly, my heart pounding. I've found out Edge is good at that—distracting. Every time I start thinking about Irissa I burst into flames and Edge's touch is the only thing that keeps me under control. I have just enough control not to burn him or the bed, but not enough to stop the flames altogether. Luckily for me, Edge has found a way to force my mind and my body into submission—most often with his wicked tongue. But...that also means neither one of us has slept any the entire night.

"Or two." His grin is pure evil, his eye twinkling in the dim light provided by the moon.

"How can I say no to—"

The note that slips into my room does not make a noise, but its presence has Edge jerking out of my bed as though somehow hearing it. His expression has changed from dark and lustful to one of pure, unadulterated *anger.* The fury that is written across his features as he goes to fetch the slip of paper would be terrifying to anyone who bore the brunt of it, and I find myself thankful that it will be Zaeden on the receiving end soon.

Edge stalks toward the door, his shirtless form crouching down and picking up something small. When he approaches me his lips are drawn in a tight-lipped frown, scar scrunching on his cheeks. I take the thin slip of paper from his hands, eyes roaming over the brief message scrawled across the front.

"They want me to meet them alone," I state the obvious, swallowing hard as I push my back against the plush head-board. Edge sits by my side, reaching out to trace a line across my cheek.

"You won't go alone."

"I will," I argue, tossing the note away with a scoff. "What other choice do I have? That's why they delivered the note to me and me alone."

"Which is exactly why I placed extra guards outside your room and decided to stay with you myself." He pounds a fist into the mattress, the other hand gripping my cheek firmly. "I don't know where they've been hiding her or how they think they are going to manage to slip her into this castle, but I'll be damned if I let anyone make a fool of me in my own Court. *You aren't going alone.*"

"You can't search an entire Court in one night. And we haven't had one credible witness tell us anything useful. Just a bunch of nonsense lies that got spread around. Most of the people who are loyal to you were in that room, watching the Royals themselves. There weren't any leads, and we don't want the entire Court worried about guards knocking their doors down in the middle of the night to search for a cursed Royal," I point out wearily.

"Hmph. They're lucky we can't prove it was them who stole Irissa. Otherwise, both the Solar and Shadow Courts would have declared war on them before the night was out."

"Zaeden is smarter than we realized."

"Yes, smart enough to slip a note directly into your room unnoticed by any of my staff, apparently."

"They waited until the guards switched. They had to have gotten help from someone in your employment."

"Perhaps so." He bows his head, chest heaving as he tries to dissipate the anger. "But that changes nothing right now. I will not allow you to go alone."

"You will not allow me?" I gurgle out a laugh, eyes tilting toward the back of my head as I roll them.

"You are *mine in* every sense of the word. Mine to protect, mine to control, mine to need endlessly for the rest of time. So, yes, I will not allow you."

"Control me? This is my sister we are talking about, Edge. They left a blood trail when they took her, and I have no doubts that it was not hers alone. But I still—"

"You will not walk into the arms of death willingly, Cerina Celeste Highmore. I'd rather lock you in this damn castle for the rest of your life than allow you to hand yourself over to our enemies."

"I'd like to see you try," I growl back, shoving him away from me and kicking off the blanket. I go to swing my legs over the edge of the bed, but Edge leaps over to my side and shoves them back onto the mattress. I allow furious flames to light up my eyes, fingers twitching dangerously.

"I won't try, Little Flame." He crawls over me, bending down to whisper in my ear, "*I'll succeed.*"

I shove at his hard body, slapping a hand onto his bare chest. I immediately begin to take his shadows, relentless and brutal. Edge tips his chin back and groans, not even attempting to stop me. It only makes me angrier, and I use the distraction to flip us over. I take pride in the surprise that alights in his steel blue eye, using my thighs to squeeze him tightly and trap him underneath me.

"My sister will not die because I hid like a coward in my room and waited for it all to be over. My sister will not be collateral in the war I started."

"No one said anything about Irissa dying." The golden hue underneath his dark skin glistens in the candlelight, his hands coming to rest on my hips in just the right way. And, damn, if it doesn't turn me on.

"Oh? Then what's your solution?"

"We storm the room, we don't give them a chance to fight back, and we eradicate them quickly while you wait here." He tugs my pelvis into his, grinding me against his body. I grit my teeth to stop myself from releasing any noises of pleasure, attempting to keep a straight face.

"No. That opens up all kinds of possibilities, most of which end with a dead sister. I will show up alone, and I will suck the life out of anyone who tries to keep her away from me." I rock my hips lightly, deciding to play this position to my advantage. Edge lets his head fall back, eye patch sliding up with the movement. I reach down and pull it free, staring down into his bare face for the first, and what could be the last, time.

His eyelids cover most of the space, a deep red left where an eye should be. That 'x' shaped scar stretches across his lids, puckered and prominent. I can see him waiting for my reaction but I give him none. Instead, I bend down and gently kiss the crossing point of his scar to reassure him that he doesn't have to hide any part of himself from *me*.

"I'll figure out an alternative. Just let me think." The words are coarse, his throat seemingly constricting.

"I'll go alone." I swallow, heart pounding. "But we both know there is no stopping you from chasing me beyond my death. Maybe...maybe we can let them think I didn't tell anyone. That I was too scared and weak to tell any of you. I'll stay here, hidden in my room, and you can make it seem as though I have been ordered to do so for my safety. Just shout angrily at a few people—I'm sure your grumpiness will get the point across to anyone in the nearby vicinity. No one will mention a ransom or a note—we will let them believe they succeeded in scaring me into coming alone. Then I'll put a cloak on and slip out the window so that whatever Lunar spies around believe I disobeyed your order and left to go meet them anyway. After enough time has passed you can come in with reinforcements. I'll need to be alone long enough to convince them to release Irissa and get her to safety. Amon and Eleazer can be sent to watch the two main entry and exit points so we can ensure the Royals don't escape, and extra guards will need to be placed around the castle perimeters, too."

"That's not a bad plan." His lips turn up in obvious relief, fingers loosening. "Aren't you becoming quite the devious little princess?"

"Devious, monstrous, *wicked*," I murmur, rolling my hips once more.

"If the goddesses have determined that this is our last night together, then I plan on making it the most pleasurable night of your life." Edge flips us once more, straddling me as he begins to strip me of my clothes. I blush under his heavy gaze, arching into his caress.

"The most pleasurable, hmm?" I tease, gasping as his hands cup my breasts. Hot kisses trail up my stomach, teeth skimming against my skin.

"You'll have forgotten all about our impending doom by the time I'm done with you." I moan as his lips close around a nipple, hands clawing at his back. I know his words to be true—he's proven that over and over and *over* in the early hours of the night.

"Then make me forget," I whisper as those lips begin to delve even lower.

Edge delivers on his promise, distracting me with each tantalizing touch. His fingers expertly circle me, his tongue dancing inside of me. By the time he's done with me, I'm a shaking mess, and I haven't even had his dick inside of me yet. I whimper as he lines up to my entrance, thrusting up before he can thrust down. In one fluid motion, we join together, our heavy breaths and loud moans echoing in the darkness. I manage to flip back onto him after only a few strong strokes, and we both groan as my hips begin to move. I lean back and close my eyes, riding him until I do exactly as he said I would: *forget.*

"I told you I don't try," he whispers, lifting my hips up and down when I can no longer move. "I succeed."

I love the sounds he makes when he has finally come, love the relaxation I so rarely get to glimpse. In these moments he isn't Prince Edge of the Solar Court—he's only a man.

I tip over onto my side, panting. "So you did." Then I begin to trail my hands across his chest, gripping a very sensitive part with a bubbling laugh. "Can you do it again?"

"I think I have new, better words to describe you," he breathes out as he hardens underneath my touch.

"Do you?" I lean over to trail kisses across his muscled chest, lips brushing over tattoos and scars.

"Insatiable, demanding, *cruel.*"

I cackle, climbing over him and lowering myself. "If cruel is what it takes to be satisfied, then cruel I will be."

The decision made in haste late last night has led me to a street far from the castle, alone and vulnerable. I went to the room on the second floor of the castle as instructed, but there was only another note left to greet me. A note that led me here.

I don't knock before entering the Divine household I have found myself on the doorstep of, ignoring the all-too-bright yellow paint on the outside walls. Though, I must say, the inside is just as much of an eyesore. The walls here are a puke green, the furniture all an odd shade of gray. Swirling patterns of pink dance across the tiled floors, and a strange stone stairway sits on my right. Upon the first glance at my surroundings, my eyes found the one person I had come here for.

Tears sting at the corner of my eyes as my gaze falls to Irissa, and I force them to stay where they are. The Lunars are here watching my every move, as well as two guards who are holding Irissa down. They have her hands and feet bound in iron cuffs, blood staining her beautiful blush dress that never got to greet the party. I almost choke at the sight of that blood, but I clear my throat quickly in an attempt to hide the noise. I maintain my bored expression despite the nerves and the relief that runs through me, raising an unamused eyebrow at her as if to say *Really? You got yourself kidnapped?*

"I came alone, as requested," I say lightly to appear nervous, glancing between the Lunars expectantly. "Let my sister go."

"I don't think I will yet. Seize the Absorbid." Prince Zaeden snaps his fingers and two more guards approach from a hidden doorway. I almost laugh at the absurdity—two Lows are being sent to contain *me*? Once upon a time, the thought of even one Low would have been a terrifying one, but things are different now. I know who I am and what I am capable of.

"You agreed, Zae," I whisper with a hint of desperation, forcing myself to send pleading eyes his way. Once, I would have broken down in tears and been unable to even speak to this man. I would have hidden away like a coward, and I expect that is exactly what the devious prince believes I will do. Unfortunately for him, the Divine Slayer doesn't cower.

Arms wrap around my waist and pull me back, and I can almost taste their power already. I'm shoved to my knees, a foot pressed against my back as I am forced to bow. I stay limp, pressing my lips into a hard line. Why do I keep finding myself in this position, being forced to bow before men who do not rule over me?

"Beg for her life, Celeste, and I will *consider* releasing your sister." The boot in my back digs in a little deeper, but I manage to tilt my chin up defiantly with a wicked grin.

"*I don't beg.*"

The hands that hold me are bare, their fingers encircling my wrists. Clearly, these men have not been warned about what I can do with bare skin. I throw a shield up between us and the Lunars, focusing on the simple touches. The Low on my left has exceptional flexibility and the one to my right can track down lost objects. I'm not sure how I know, but the moment their power enters my body, I do. Both are interesting powers, powers I may come to enjoy owning. Wouldn't it be nice to never lose another sock, or to never worry about being unable to touch my toes?

The beast inside of me snarls its teeth as I allow it to break out of its cage, greedily snapping at the powers I am offering. I've never taken two at once before and I've never felt a surge of energy so strongly. I feel entirely too full too fast, but I don't allow myself to stop. I gorge on the power of the Lows, avoiding the decaying hands and the radiating screams coming from Queen Mourner and her two remaining guards. Instead, I focus on my sister. Her gentle blue eyes meet my brown ones, her unassuming gaze reassuring.

"Who's next?" I rasp whenever I no longer feel pressure on my wrists, whenever I feel full from all of the raw power I had consumed. I'm not sure I can take any more power without dispelling a lot more, but I'm willing to try if that's what it takes.

"Y—you can't." Queen Mourner stumbles back, eyes wide in fear.

"I think she can." The familiar, drawling voice chuckles as the body it belongs to transports in behind me. "After all, it does seem to me that she was provoked into attacking." Edge is gone before anyone can lift a hand to attack, appearing next with a guest.

"Yes, I quite agree," Alvina says as she pops up beside her son, her disdain on display. "How terrible that the Lunars attacked us in such a dishonorable way."

"Yes, their Court will be very disappointed to learn of their untimely demise. A stray rebel, perhaps? Maybe a concerned Shadow Court citizen loyal to their king?" The Solar King chuckles, tapping his chin thoughtfully after Edge makes another trip. They must have been waiting for him somewhere nearby, otherwise this dramatic entrance would be draining him far too greatly.

"This is a coup," King Mourner whispers, eyes flicking between us all in shock. Shouldn't he have expected this? Shouldn't he have known that it was always going to come down to this?

My powers alone are enough to cause a war, as he has implied many times. Once I revealed my heritage and my betrothal, he should have stepped away. Wouldn't that have been the smarter option? To step away and form a new, better plan? He and his son are narcissists, though, and they just couldn't help themselves. They couldn't leave after having been jilted so fantastically by a former Undivine like me—the scum they have the displeasure of ruling over. So, they decided the only thing to be done was to take my sister: the last mistake they would *ever* make. Kidnapping and harming Irissa was enough for *me* to declare war, enough to have me forgetting all of the guilt and self-hatred that comes along with being an Absorbid.

"Congratulations!" Valaine laughs mockingly as Edge appears with her hand in his, and it's a strange sound coming from her kind, easy-going self. "You aren't an idiot after all."

Everything happens so fast.

The two guards holding my sister release her, shoving her toward the ground and making their way toward me. Edge steps in front of me, unleashing a dagger from his belt. The two Lows quickly find themselves surrounded by a cloud of darkness, a cloud Edge waltzes into with ease. We all hear the grunts, the cries, and the shouts that follow. No one moves in those slow minutes, all unsure of what is to come. When Edge walks back out, dagger and hands coated in blood, reality hits.

Not mine he whispers into my mind reassuringly.

The blood-coated prince is the final straw for the Lunars.

I jump into action and throw up a shield around the Solar Royals, narrowly saving them from a blast of fire aimed at me. The heat wave pushes against the barrier, and sweat is already beginning to form on my brow. I struggle to hold my shield in place, pushing hard against the raging flames. The heat pauses abruptly as King Mourner sags, turning to the only son he has left during my moment of restoration. Their conversation doesn't last long.

Poison is now making its way to my shield, prodding at its edges as it searches for holes to sink into. I glance over at Edge, throwing my head toward the Lunars. As always, he knows exactly what to do.

Edge opens a portal, grabbing his mother and dragging her through. The pair appear behind Queen Mourner, Edge's shadows coating King Mourner and Prince Zaeden in one overpowering move. Alvina grabs Queen Mourner's head, squeezing tightly. Her fingers dig into the Royal's temples and the sides of her head, holding her in place. The Lunar Queen seizes and screams in agony, a noise I have become far too accustomed to. I watch in shock as Alvina fries the woman, her electric shocks stopping the Royal's heart entirely. I never thought to question Edge's mother's abilities before, but...wow.

"May the goddesses receive your soul and carry it with them to the afterlife," Alvina whispers gently, removing her hands from the now-dead queen. The body drops like a sack of potatoes, limbs limp and skin emitting a burnt flesh scent. It's entirely disgusting, and I know I can't be the only one who gags when it hits their nostrils.

"You fucking bitch!" Zaeden roars, the cry barely escaping his lips before he leaps out of the shadows and tackles Alvina head-on.

I scream, shields dropping as I race forward. Flames roar to life beside me, but I hear them sizzle out as they are met with the force of Valaine's water. I continue to race to the Solar Queen, slamming a shield around her just as Zaeden begins to pour poison into her skin. Edge leaps on top of Zaeden, prying him off his mother with a growl of fury.

The sound of skin-on-skin ensues, fists flying and powers rising. I throw a shield around Edge, willing it to stay strong in my desperation to keep him from being poisoned. I slide down to my knees when I reach the Solar Queen, examining her shaking body for injuries. I cover my mouth to try and hide the panicked noise that escapes me when I see the deep cut that slices down her side, blood leaking uncontrollably. Fuck, did Zaeden have a dagger? Has she been poisoned already? If he still holds that dagger, will Edge be given the same infliction?

"You'll be okay," I swear to her, bottom lip quivering as I gulp down the sweet lie. There's too much blood, and too high of a chance that the poison has already entered her system. Can these new tracking powers I possess find poison? Can I even control those long enough to find out? My hands shake as I press down on the wound in an attempt to slow down the bleeding, her warm blood seeping through my fingers in a red wave.

"Valaine," she whispers all too quietly, shaky finger pointing across the room.

Valaine has been backed into a corner, the Lunar King pressing in. It's a battle of the elements, and the structure around us shakes as the flames slowly eat away at the wood and the water slowly deteriorates it. I can see those blasts of water becoming weaker, can see how her body is already beginning to wilt.

King Zorander appears beside me, eyes wide as he, too, falls to his knees beside his wife. He reaches out to stroke her hair, fingers shakily touching her wound. When his hand comes back wet, he bows his head and weeps. I've never pictured him as more than an angry, diabolical king. Never thought to wonder why the rebel leader may have married him in the first place. But it's obvious that he loves her in the tender way he pulls her into his arms, in the gentleness as he cradles her to his chest. King Zorander ignores the battle his step-children are facing, ignoring their impending dooms as he bends down to kiss her for what may be the last time. I might cry, too, if I wasn't so goddess-damned worried about the others.

I stumble up to my feet, pushing off of the couch next to me and leaving the rebellion leader with her husband as I head toward Valaine. I throw a shield her way, briefly blocking the cascading wall of flames. Out of the corner of my eye, I see Irissa crawling forward, tears streaking down her cheeks and one wing bent at an awkward angle. I don't have time to help her, don't have time to choose which sister to protect. King Mourner's attention is already on me, my shield attracting his gaze. At least his attention means I don't have to choose between my sisters.

I meet the Royal's flames with my own, using his own dead heir's power against him. I can sense the fury that this action brings whenever the pressure increases, can sense his unending rage for what I've done to his son in that blazing gaze alone.

I can't push past the strength of that rage, can't get close enough to touch his skin. Can I absorb his powers when I already own a matching one inside? Can I own a set of the same power, or does it equal out to only one? I'm not sure what will happen or what the consequences may be, but I'm close to finding out.

Valaine stumbles to my side, holding her chest as she heaves. Fighting a fellow Royal is something they have never had to experience, and it is taking a toll on the princess. I'm almost certain she's never had to use this amount of power all at once before, never had to expend so much energy into one person. Royal powers seem endless until they are turned on each other, and then that strength seems abysmal.

"Celeste!" I hear the panic in Edge's voice, his shadows swallowing us whole. Then he is by our side, dragging Valaine into his arms as he watches me. He transports her to what appears to be the kitchen, and I can barely see his form from here. He seems to be helping her to the ground, depositing her safely away. I see Zaeden fleeing from behind me, the coward bailing before he, too, is murdered.

"I need some help here!" I call someone, anyone. My call was answered by the last person I wanted to be involved.

"I would say it's been a pleasure, Mr. Mourner, but, well…it wasn't." Irissa's soft voice is the one that answers my call, her words clear across the roar of the flames. I scream in horror as she appears from behind the Lunar King, that bent wing glaringly obvious in the light of the flames. And in that light, I see the Royal turn, dagger in his hand as he stabs in a panic at the face that barely reaches his chest. With one fell swoop the dagger embeds in her left eye, blood gushing from the wound in a crimson waterfall. The dagger doesn't embed farther than the tip, but it's enough to pierce straight through the piercing blue orb.

Irissa's outcry of anger, of pain, reverberates around the entire room and into my ears. I can't move as her arm reaches up and through his flame-covered chest, the glint of a talon winking at me from across the room. Those sharp talons slice into pliable skin, the cut quick and brutal across his neck. The action rips a guttural scream from her throat, her arms and hands aflame as she stumbles back.

A second Lunar Royal has met their death by a Highmore sister's hands.

CHAPTER 24

The Death of a Monarchy

Silvi

The knock on my door resembles more of a panicked pounding, and fear flutters through my heart at its implications. Has someone been hurt? The wrong someone, I mean. Have our plans failed? Has Celeste been injured, or worse, found dead?

"Open the fucking door, Silvi. We have to get out of here, now!"

"Zae? My love?" I'm unsure how I manage the calm response; I can only blame the intense training I've endured since the tender age of birth. I scurry to the door as fast as my feet can, opening it hurriedly.

"Come on." Zaeden grabs me by the hand and pulls me from my bedroom the second the door is open, tugging me down the hall in a matter of precious seconds.

"What's going on? What's happened?" How had he escaped? I can feel the panic radiating from him in harsh waves, the fear rising with each rapid beat of his heart. It's clear that the plan had been followed, and even more clear that it hadn't worked out entirely the way we had hoped.

"The fucking Solars tried to kill me. Mother is dead, and Father is not far behind. We need to get out of here before they kill us, too. They were too distracted by my father to chase after me, and I will honor his sacrifice by surviving." I almost laugh at the seriousness in his gaze, at how gullible his admission is.

I've played such a good role in this scheme that not even he knows I am a traitor.

"My own Court," I whisper fearfully, hand reaching up to cup my throat. I push bravery and confidence into his system, watching in amusement as he puffs out his chest meaningfully. If I can get him somewhere confined, I'll kill him myself.

"Don't worry, my love. I'll get us home safely." Never mind that this *is* my home. Never mind that that little nickname he uses for me holds no true meaning—he seems to forget that I can tell the difference. That I am one of the only people in the world who was able to catch onto his bullshit within the first five minutes of knowing him. Poor, innocent Celeste never had a chance against his charms.

Zaeden's quick strides turn into a full-on sprint, and I force myself to memorize this moment. It's all too fitting to watch the cowardly prince flee my home. I leap at the chance to steer him astray, tugging on his arm harshly to capture his attention.

"Let me guide you, my love. I know this castle like the back of my hand, know every exit. I know what secret doors the servants slither in and out of—we'll escape the very same way Celeste herself did." It's a sick kind of justice I plan on serving to the prince in leading him to his death, a death that will be the mirror of Celeste's journey to freedom from *him.*

"Of course. You're right." I'm not sure I've ever heard those words leave the prince's mouth before, and, oh, are they sweet to digest. They're fueled by his fear, fueled by his rage that seems to swarm his entire being.

I take a sharp left, leading him into a small alcove that was hidden by a large hanging tapestry. A singular door awaits us, its tiny knob branded with the Solar logo—the sign of a servant's entrance. I am quick to pull the door open, ushering the walking-dead man inside. Upon shutting the door we are swallowed by the darkness, and it is only I who remains calm and unbothered. I only have to allow a hand to drift along the wall as I run, my heart racing with adrenaline alone. The small dagger strapped to my thigh seems too heavy now, its presence a thrilling one.

"Fuck, I hope you know what you're doing," Zaeden whispers, and I can taste the delicious fear that soaks that statement. Most days, I hate what I can do. I hate how emotions feel and taste and sound. But today? Today I am grateful to know how the prince will feel in his final moments, and I am goddess blessed to be the cause of those feelings.

"Of course I know what I'm doing." I scowl in the dark, freely glaring for the first time in months. Oh, how freeing it will be to not be with this man any longer.

I lead Zaeden toward the left once more, fingers digging into the crack of the small door I had been searching for. I slip my hand down to the knob, twisting it silently and allowing it to swing open. I stumble to a halt as he slams the door behind him, panting. "What now?"

"Switch places with me, I'm going to peek out and ensure we haven't been followed before we go any further." I know we haven't; I would have felt another emotional presence long before they got close enough to attack.

"Yeah, okay. Good idea. You do that." Zaeden sighs heartily, leaning back against the wall as he watches me in the dim lighting. I ease the door open, popping my head out and making a good show of searching for signs of life.

"We need to stay here for a moment, I hear footsteps," I lie easily, gently locking the door after closing it behind me. This room is a safe place for the Undivine should the castle be under attack. I suppose for a Divine in these circumstances, it can't be considered as such.

"The Solars will pay for this," he remarks, green poison dripping onto the floor like oil.

"I'll make sure of it," I promise slyly, glancing at the singular candle lit on the wall.

"I hoped marrying you last night would provide us with an extra layer of protection," he admits after a long pause, and I see doubt flickering in his eyes as I approach. The poison slowly slinks back to its master, disappearing under soft and unmarred skin. "That when the time came you would be able to hold your own against a Royal."

He had hoped that my allegiance would stay with him, that he would have an extra soldier in this war. My poor, hopeful little prince. So naive, so sure.

"Oh, yes. I can hold my own now," I purr, placing my hand on his shoulder and trailing fingertips down his arm. My hand continues to travel lower, and Zaeden groans with each purposeful touch. He jerks when I brush my hand against his cock, cursing.

"Silvi, we can't right now. Goddesses above, you're ravenous." He pants as I squeeze lightly, my lips brushing against the shell of his ear. My free hand slips down to my thigh, fingers dancing across the handle of my weapon.

"Mmm, yes. *Ravenous*. Lustful, I've been told. But isn't this all so exciting? Isn't your heart just *pounding*?" The words roll off my tongue, dagger sliding up and out as my light squeeze turns harsher. I grip his balls as tightly as I can, laughing quietly when he hunches forward and cries out in pain. The dagger in my palm is light, and I don't hesitate as I plunge it into the depths of his black heart.

"Silvi? My love?" Zaeden's shocked eyes turn angry, his poison struggling to rise as that pounding heart begins to fail him.

"My love." I sigh quietly as though disappointed, jerking the dagger back out in one swift move before wiping it along my dress and placing it back on my thigh. Then I begin to push fear into him without holding anything back, forcing his body to shake as he clutches his all too vital organ.

"Y—Y—You b—bitch." His words barely manage to escape the coffin that is his mouth, his body falling hard to the ground. He pants as the air becomes too hard to breathe, eyes wide as his powers fail him in his dying moments. The fear is washing over him, and I wonder what will do him in first—the heart *injury* or the heart *attack?*

"What a fitting end for the prince who was never going to be king. Powerless in your last moments, just like your twin. A shame your essence won't have the opportunity to live on in another like his does," I murmur with a pout, crouching down to face him one last time. "May the goddesses damn you, my dearly departed husband."

I place my hands against the stab wound, allowing the warm blood to soak through the cracks between my fingers. Zaeden watches on with wide eyes, so overcome by the fear that he isn't able to bring even a drop of poison to the surface.

"W—Why?" he whispers, most likely his final words.

I gave him my most vicious smile, saying only, "Why not?"

I watch as his final breath escapes him, waiting until his heart has stopped completely. I stay crouched until his Royal blood has soaked into my dress and his eyes are hollow, and I wait until there is no possible chance of revival. Only then do I fall to my knees and pull his body to me, clutching onto him as though truly in despair. I crinkle my nose at the overpowering smell, knowing there is only one last thing left on my list to complete. I allow myself one final glance at Zaeden, one final moment to memorize this feeling before committing my last act as a prince's wife.

I open my mouth and I begin to scream.

CHAPTER 25

Celeste

Edge watches me with a weary gaze, sagging shoulders lifting up and back as a servant enters the room. Whispered words are shared with his stepfather, and off the Undivine scurries. We wait for King Zorander to speak to us as we sit in the blindingly white healing room, watching him stroke his wife's hand. She lays on a white cot, hardly breathing and entirely unconscious.

"Silvi has been found," he says at last, nodding toward his son.

"Unharmed?" I question, rising from the uncomfortable wooden chair. My back aches, a deep throbbing present in my lower back that probably has just as much to do with the seating arrangement as it does with the fact that I had to help drag dead bodies around all afternoon.

"As far as we are aware."

"And Zaeden? Was he found with her?"

"Oh, yes. He most certainly was." The grin that alights the Cruel King's face is terrifying, and I am quick to step toward the door.

"We will go investigate the situation. Let us know if we are needed here." Edge clears his throat, raw emotions hidden rather poorly in his words; we can all hear the sadness and the worry.

"I'll be here." His whisper barely meets our ears, but it's a clear enough dismissal.

Edge and I leave the sterile room, nodding to Romanus on our way out. I managed not to kill him during my last visit, but only barely. My last memory from this room is with me in Alivina's place, and I'm not entirely sure I enjoy this role reversal. My actions have given her consequences, and I feel immensely guilty despite knowing she chose to be there to-day. Maybe a little less guilty knowing she's been ruling over the entire Undivine Army right under her vicious husband's nose and these circumstances are better than what would have happened if he found out.

"Do you think Silvi killed him?" I question Edge, scurry-ing behind him in my fresh change of clothes. No leftover blood, no cuts or scrapes along the fabric, no scorch marks, and no evidence there was a fight at all.

After Irissa killed King Mourner the entire room had erupted into chaos. I rushed to my sister's side, pleading to all the stars in the sky that she would get to fly again. That she would still be able to see. I had to wait for Edge to transport his mother before getting help for Irissa, but she and I both agreed that was for the best. While Irissa had been in pain, she knew she wasn't on the verge of death. She was brave and didn't shed a single tear, only told me of her kidnapping and how the Lunars kept her in that house tied up and silenced with tape. She said she couldn't remember what happened in those hours while she was transformed, but she woke up with a bent wing and a damaged talon or two. She suspects she did it to herself.

King Zorander left to be with his wife, of course, so that left me, Edge, and Valaine to clean up the mess left behind in that house. Edge was running out of fuel, and so were we. Needless to say, we couldn't transport the dead bodies anywhere. Our solution? Drag the Royals out into a back alley where Eleazer and Amon could meet us and burn the house down to the ground. All it took was a little encouragement of my weak but eager flames, and no one suspected a thing. Eleazer and Amon took over the dragging of the bodies, hiding them until Edge could regain some strength and set the stage in the room the Royals were staying in. As far as I understand it, their bodies were found in their bed covered in blood. The rumor I heard from a maid in the hall was that they died while asleep last night, murdered by an assassin from the Moon Killer organization.

"I've never underestimated her skills," Edge grumbles bitterly, distracting me from images of dead bodies and houses set aflame.

"Mmm. I can't say the same." We fall into an uncomfortable silence as we head toward her quarters on the second floor, my heart racing all too fast. I shouldn't be worried about her or her safety, but I am. Had Zaeden poisoned her? Had he hurt her in any way?

Edge doesn't knock when we reach her room, only pushes the door open and strides in without a care. I follow behind rather reluctantly, head bowed down just in case she is indecent. What I find on the ground is a trail of blood, and it has my head snapping up in a flash, decency or not.

"What happened?" I breathe as my eyes fall on her bloody form. Her simple baby blue dress is coated in a dark liquid, the bottom half practically dipped in the stuff. Her face has been splattered with tiny little droplets, her dark hands covered in the dried substance. Silvi doesn't seem alarmed in the slightest to see us there, and she only smiles grimly at my horrified expression.

"I cleaned up your mess," she says simply.

"You killed him," I declare, eyes wide.

"Of course I killed him, you idiot. What else was I supposed to do?" She sighs, flipping red-tinted hair out of her face. I glance at the servant in the room only to realize it is Ryleigh, and I almost sigh in relief. "If this blood dyes my beautiful hair red, I swear I'm going to bring Zaeden back from the dead and kill him all over again," she murmurs under her breath, glowering at the long strands.

"You did exactly what you were supposed to, dear, and you are lucky to have come out unharmed." Ryleigh pats her cheek gently and ignores her comment about Zaeden, trying to lead her into the washroom.

"I seem to always be cleaning up your messes, Celeste."

"And you always seem to be creating mine," I say softly, relieved that she is fine. How I can still care for this woman, I do not know. I can at least be assured that this time, it is myself deciding to care and not her freaky powers.

"Oh, how we have ruined one another." She looks at me as though I am the only person in the room, and I shift uncomfortably. How can she possibly still have romantic feelings for me? How can she possibly want me anymore after the things we have done to one another, the things we have said?

"I'm sorry for the part I have played in your ruination," I say finally, clearing my throat. "I fear I have judged you too harshly, and I can see my error." My words are formal, almost forced. But I mean them.

"I'm sorry, too. For everything." She bows her head in respect, taking in a shaky breath before turning crystal eyes to Edge. "Zaeden and I were married last night underneath the full moon's light."

"You were *what?*" I screech, covering my mouth in surprise.

"So you're a widow now." Edge chuckles, running his knuckles down the back of my neck reassuringly.

"I am."

"And did you…consummate the marriage?" Ryleigh is the one to ask the awkward question, one that will no doubt be asked by other Divine.

"Several times," she purrs, but I can see the pain hiding behind her phony smile. "I'm quite certain the guards knew exactly what was happening."

"Then it's official. You are the Lunar Queen," Ryleigh pronounces, clapping her hands happily.

"I am the Lunar Queen," she agrees, but she seems to be far less happy about the circumstances.

"You don't want to be queen?" I question, frowning. She and I participated in the same battle to win that crown, a battle in which she was determined to be the victor. She's continued to play out her part in the Lunar Court and has stayed by Zaeden's side even though I have no doubts it was difficult to do so. She sacrificed so much for a crown…a crown she apparently doesn't want.

"Truthfully? No, no I do not. But I have never had a choice in the matter and I still don't. I will do as my Royals command me and I will listen to whatever orders I am given. I am a loyal subject. I will do the bidding of my master." She bows lowly to Edge, waiting there.

"I do not want to force you into that position, but…"

"But her position as Lunar Queen is essential to any plans we may devise in the future," Ryleigh fills in, turning to Edge. "We can't plausibly replace her without a fight from the other Courts. She is the rightful heir to the Lunar Court and is now considered a Royal. She already had a high enough surge in power to defeat Zaeden. Her powers will only increase in time as she lives in her own territory and feels the full moon's awakening. If you want the advice of the U.A., then I will speak on behalf of the group and vote that she stays."

"All good points," Silvi states plainly, still waiting in her bowed position.

Edge stays silent for a full minute before making his decision. "You will return to the Lunar Court within a week's time, Silvi Merkelly, and be indoctrinated as their queen. Once there you will await orders from me."

"As you wish, my prince." Silvi raises, sending me one last scorching look before Ryleigh drags her into the washroom to rid herself of her husband's blood.

"Was that the right decision?" I ask quietly, watching the doorway she had disappeared into.

"It was the only decision."

Edge and I were called back to the infirmary only hours after meeting with Silvi, and we found Valaine and Irissa had beaten us there. Ryleigh decided to join us, choosing to allow Silvi to rest. Irissa's broken wing is wrapped tightly in a handful of bandages, her hands and arms in a similar state. Her burn marks could be worse, but Romanus isn't sure how well they will heal. He did as much as he could, but he used a large majority of his powers to help Alvina. A shallow cut to Irissa's thigh was the one that left a trail of blood during the party, and it was thin enough to be healed by Valaine herself. Her eye, though...it wasn't able to be healed. A large bandage covers it now, and the sight of it has my knees weak. Edge, Silvi, Irissa...is this what being a Royal means? Losing eyes and taking lives? Is this the sacrifice for ruling, and is it worth it?

"Mother," Edge whispers, pushing his way to her side as we enter the room and distracting me from my near-hysteric thoughts. Alvina blinks up at him, smiling softly.

"My time has come, son. You've been summoned to speak your goodbyes."

"No. No, this isn't goodbye," he argues, wrapping his strong hands around her frail ones. His stepfather stands to the side and watches, arms crossed over his chest.

"The Army," she whispers to him frantically, conspiratorially. "You must continue to fight for them. You understand what I'm saying, don't you?"

"I won't take your place." He shakes his head, grinding his teeth.

"No, Valaine will." Valaine nodded her head solemnly as though this had already been discussed. Ryleigh is close enough to hear, and she, too, nods.

"What is she speaking of?" King Zorander questions, brows furrowed.

"Nothing, Stepfather," Valaine chirps, sending him a soft smile.

"The Undivine are counting on us. We can't let our world continue in the way that it has for so long. The Undivine—" She stops abruptly, clawing at her chest.

"What about the Undivine? What does she mean they are counting on you?"

"Oh, fuck," Irissa whispers, backing away fearfully as King Zorander begins to stomp toward us.

"Horace, no—" Alvina gurgles, struggling to breathe.

"You're fucking working with Undivine? You? A Royal?"

"She's not the only one," Valaine comes to her defense, and it is her betrayal that hits him the hardest. His face contorts with the shock of the truth, eyes wide and mouth gaping like a fish.

"You, my daughter? You would betray me in this way? Betray all Divine?"

"I am only doing what is right. Celeste knows exactly why we must work with the Undivine, exactly why we must demolish this ridiculous syst—"

The king is guided forward by rage, hands reaching for me. Ryleigh jumps in between us suddenly, cursing loudly, and his hands grab her instead. A gurgling scream rises from the most terrifying woman I know, those screams lasting only seconds before being cut off abruptly. With an eery silence her body falls, bones and organs on display.

I cry out in shock, readying myself to rush forward, but the movement only serves to draw his attention back to me. He leaps and grabs me by the neck as his powers rise, an acid that instantly burns through my clothes to my skin. The pain is all too familiar, reminding me of the power of the beast I fought on the road here. He has never revealed his powers in my presence before, and, fuck, if they aren't strong. Fear, pain, and unbridled rage fill me as I gasp for air, my vision already beginning to fade. "You are the reason that all of this happened. You have destroyed my family and will continue to do so unless I do something about it. The Lunars were right about you, *Divine Slayer.*"

I can't speak from how tightly he is gripping me, and I can already feel my face turning red. Tears burn my eyes as I claw at his strong hands, attempting to suck his powers through the touch. But I am wearing training gear from working out my worries with Amon and Eleazer, my gloves are still on, and my jacket collar is too high. No bare skin is touching, and I can't grip onto his powers other than to take away what he has already expelled. I don't go without air for long, though.

Blood splatters against my cheeks and into my eyes, and I know the Royal's shocked face will forever be burned into my memory. Not a word leaves his lips, only strangled noises as he releases me and stumbles back. I shake as he falls to his knees, our hands reaching up simultaneously to caress our necks. Edge grips a bloody dagger in his hand, fury radiating from every pore. Then he kicks outward, knocking his stepfather on his side. The man's eyes are left wide open and empty, life absent from the once furious gaze.

"You killed him," I whisper, more surprised than upset. I can't bear to stare at Ryleigh, at her horrendously disfigured body. My first friend—gone in only seconds. If only I had made amends with her—if only I had known she wouldn't have the time to earn my forgiveness.

With a dread so painful that my heart clenches, I turn to stare at my best friend. The liar, the loudmouth, the rebel. She looks up at me with sad eyes, regret staining those tear-filled cheeks and following her into the afterlife. I crouch down, refusing to stare below her neck, and gently close her lids with two fingers. I choke on a sob, hastily turning away and back to Edge.

With a gentle fury, he says, "Don't you remember me telling you I would if it's what you wished for?"

"How did you know I wished for it?"

"Because I know my cruel little Divine, and death knows her, too."

My gaze trails from the king to the queen, and I notice that she is no longer awake. Her eyes are shut tightly, her chest unmoving as she lays unnaturally still. I hear Valaine falling into my sister's arms, sobbing uncontrollably as she screams for her mother. I stumble into Edge in utter shock, unsure of who is comforting who.

Two Royals lay dead here, along with an Undivine—three more casualties in this game for the throne.

EPILOGUE

Edge

She asked me to kill a king for her, so I did: I didn't even make her beg. She didn't need to, because I wanted to kill Horace Zorander, King of the Solar Court. I've wanted to kill him from the moment I met him, from the second he opened his mouth and introduced himself as the new ruler and not as my new father. And, fuck, had it felt good to have his blood on my hands. It felt good to finally, *finally* get what I wanted. To know that I will no longer have to do foul, horrific things in his name. That I won't have to be controlled by my master, no longer a dog on a leash.

I am free. Celeste *freed* me.

She doesn't know that, but I will tell her every day for the rest of my life just so she knows what she means to me. I'll get down on my knees and bow before her morning, afternoon, and night. Every hour, every minute, every second I will devote to worshiping her. She may not want it, may not like it, but I want her to feel every bit of my gratitude. To feel every ounce of my love.

I didn't think about the consequences when Horace Zorander's hands slid around Celeste's throat. I didn't think about my mother watching me kill her husband in her last dying moments, didn't think about the consequences of killing a king. I just acted. I lashed out, desperate to protect her. To keep her, selfishly, in this world with me. I don't regret it. How can I when she's here with me, safe and in my arms?

I stare down at the beautiful blond in my arms, her lids closed and her breaths light. She's so relieved. She knows it, I know it, and how can I regret giving her peace? How can I regret making her feel like this Court can officially become her home? To put it quite simply: I can't.

I'm scared—no, terrified of being a king. I've been raised my whole life to take over this responsibility, but it still doesn't feel real. I didn't think I would become a king until much later in my life—until my forties, at the least. I thought my duty as the Cruel Prince would overtake everything else about me until there was no repairing the damage. Maybe it can't be repaired now. I'm going to try, though. I'm going to try and show the world, show *Celeste*, who I am. Who I can be. Who I want to become.

I stroke a hand over her wild curls, breathing in her sweet and intoxicating scent. If I could press her any closer, I would. *Safe, safe, she is safe* my mind shouts constantly. My Little Star is ferocious and brave, strong and capable. Yet...I was petrified. I was mourning her the second she walked into that house alone—when she fought against two Royals as though it was nothing. When she absorbed powers inside of herself and killed two men even though she swore she would never do that again in her first conversations with me at this Court. I was worried that it wouldn't be Celeste who returned from that place, but a shell of her.

My fears were unfounded.

Celeste has changed. I have changed. We changed each other and will continue to do so in the years to come.

I've never thought she was weak, or fragile. I've always pushed her to be more, to be stronger, to be less conscious of herself. Sometimes I worried I was pushing too hard. Now, holding her in my arms, I know that isn't true. My sweet star is here, safe and uncaring. She hasn't once mentioned killing those men, other than to tell me that her new powers are fun to use and not terrifying like the flames. It was wonderful and all too exhilarating to know that she just...doesn't care. Or that, if she does, she isn't letting it control her like it did before.

I don't want to be king, but I want her to be my queen. I want her to stay by my side forever, to never hold back, to always love me. It's a want, a hope, a wish. I pray to my new goddess, the woman I love, that she grants it.

Tomorrow I will be crowned King of the Solar Court and will belong to them, but tonight, and every other night of my life, I will only belong to Celeste.

Celeste

"The past few days have been some of our saddest," Edge bellows on the balcony high above the crowd, a gilded crown placed carefully upon his brow. They cheer him on, crying out our names from far below. Edge has officially been crowned king, and soon I will be declared his queen. Though, now that his stepfather is dead, we are no longer on a timeline—we will be allowed to choose *where* and *when* we get married.

"Through that sadness, we prevail!" I cry out, smiling bravely. Alvina is dead, Ryleigh is dead, and so are many others. Lives and eyes were lost, and I can't say it was all worth it because who am I to say what the price of a life can buy? Who am I to determine that a mother's life was worth mine? I'm getting a happy ending, but I'm also inheriting a mess. I may be horrible for saying this, but...I would pay the cost time and time again if it meant a true *change* for our society, and I think both Alvina and Ryleigh would agree.

"The band of assassins that struck out at the Lunar and Solar Courts have been caught and are awaiting punishment. So far we have gathered enough information to know that they were intent on starting a war between our two Courts, an intent that they were unsuccessful in accomplishing. They thought the war would create jobs by effectively building up new clientele, but they were wrong. Instead, we have found ourselves unified and stronger than ever before. We have found ourselves new allies within the Shadow Court, and we plan on forging alliances with the Light Court as well. And now one of our own holds the Lunar crown, which means our relationship with our oldest allies is stronger than ever. Rejoice in the knowledge that good things are to come! Rejoice in the knowledge that our lands are well on their way to healing. We have high hopes that this unification will please the goddesses and that our barren lands will once again be fruitful. We hope our sacrifices are enough, and we pray to them for guidance in this new age of rulers."

The crowd erupts at the end of his speech, crying out for their new king. Some may expect him to be the same as his stepfather, cruel and strict, but they have no idea of what is to come or of his true plans. The Divine may not have let him be crowned if they had.

We have decided to blame the murders on the group of assassins that attempted to kill me all those months ago—the
Moon Killers. Silvi has ordered all members to be tracked
down, a precaution for anyone willing to say otherwise; it's
been rather easy to find people who proudly brandish a
tatted sword with the name of their group on their necks.
I'm not sure if Edge plans on killing them, and I refuse to
ask. I never found out why those men wanted to hurt me or
who hired them to do so, and I don't want to find out now. I
just want them to be punished.

Edge and I retreat into our fortress, hidden away from the
world once more. Not everyone is happy about this change
of events, especially the Lunars. There is an outrage in their
Court over a Solar citizen being queen, but Zaeden had been
set to marry her long before he actually did. There isn't any
legality to the claims of illegitimacy, and there is no way to
overthrow her without the use of force. Now that her week
at home is over, she will be sent back to her new kingdom.

It is she who greets us upon our entry, her head bowed low
in reverence. "My King."

"Silvi. To what do we owe the pleasure?"

"I have a favor to ask of you."

"Ask and I shall grant it."

"I wish to bring a Solar citizen back to the Lunar Court
with me." Silvi clears her throat quickly at the end, hiding
her fumble behind a pink-nailed hand.

"Oh? Who will you be taking with you?" My eyebrows
crinkle at the strange request. Silvi doesn't have any friends
that I know of—at least, not beyond this room.

"Me." I can't stop a gasp from escaping my lips as my sister steps out from behind her. Her wing is still bent at an odd angle, but it is no longer bandaged. A thin cut trails across it, feathers missing from the damaged area. Her hands and arms are still wrapped tightly, despite the many healing sessions she has endured. And her left eye...the lids are puckering tightly, black stitches visible.

"You...you want to leave?" My throat threatens to close in and my heart nearly collapses as I watch her with pity. I had been sick with worry for my sister those few months I spent in a castle without her...can I do it again?

"I do." Irissa bows to Edge, avoiding my burning eyes. They've come here as citizens wishing to gain permission from their king, not as friends or family. "Silvi and I have discussed my curse at length, and she—and I— believe that the first step in reversing it is returning to the Lunar Court."

"Oh." I swallow, forcing myself to breathe. Edge's hand on my elbow grounds me, reminding me where I am as my world spins impossibly out of control just as I had righted it for the first time in so long.

"Don't be angry, Celeste. Or sad—I think that would be worse."

"Do you?" I choke on the words, sucking on my upper lip to hide the shaking of the bottom. How long have she and Silvi been speaking? What makes her believe that Silvi is the one who can help her solve this problem? Or that she can even be trusted?

"I know you worry about me, and I understand why. But do you remember the discussion we had about me being an adult? Part of growing up is making hard decisions such as this, and I can't follow you around everywhere like some kind of pet for the rest of my life."

"Yes, you can! I'll make you a lady in waiting or something. That's a thing, right? I can do that. I can make sure you belong here, with me."

"I only came here because I had no choice—*you* gave me none. And I do not blame you for what happened, just as you do not blame me for my affliction. But I'm tired of this exhausting existence. I don't want to be the cursed Shifter anymore. I want to be in control of my body and my mind. I can't live this way for the rest of my life. I want to seek out the Followers to learn more about the mysterious goddesses we all pray to and the powers they are blessed with because of their worshiping. I think they are the only ones who will be able to tell me what to do and how to fix this." She gestures wildly to her wings, a desperation in her eye.

I wanted to be the one to help her break the curse, wanted to be the one who helped her gain that control. And I know the true reason she no longer wants my help: I have two kingdoms to rule. So, she sought out company from someone just as vulnerable as her. I can't call Silvi my enemy any longer, but I'm not entirely sure I can call her a friend, either.

"What about Valaine?" Something must have changed between them, as they always seemed so close.

"Since her mother died we have discussed our relationship and have decided it is no more than a fun fling. She doesn't want anything serious right now because of everything that has happened, and I don't want to stay here and make her feel guilty over that decision. I liked her, I really did. I still do. But we both want different things in life, and the things I want can't be found here." She shrugs, and her nonchalance sobers me.

She truly isn't a child anymore.

"Alright. If this is what you want, then I won't stop you," I whisper, shutting my eyes tightly to not face her glee.

"I permit your request, Silvi Merkelly, on behalf of the Solar Court. Is there anything else you require for your journey?"

"Just transportation."

"A carriage is already waiting for your presence."

Irissa races to me suddenly, throwing her arms around my neck. "Goodbye, sister. I love you."

"I love you more." A single tear slips onto her shoulder. Then the two women depart, leaving us alone.

"I can't believe she's leaving," I say once they are fully out of earshot.

"Can't you?" He raises a brow, pulling me into his chest. "She's right, you know. She can't live like that forever. And we have our hands full right now with the transition of power happening between our two Courts, as well as with making plans to get rid of the Divine system. We don't have time to help her in the way she needs us to."

"Silvi is going to have her hands full, too, you know. Not all Lunars are going to be accepting of a Solar queen."

"Silvi has the natural ability to walk in a room and make everyone in it love her without using a drop of her power. Her charm holds much more weight than you give her credit for."

"Her charm is what got me into this mess in the first place," I scowl, tracing a finger along his bicep.

"Oh? Is that what you call our relationship? A mess?" I can't help but let out a low moan as his hands begin to move over my backside, lips brushing against my neck.

"Maybe not our relationship," I amend, glancing back toward the door from which Irissa had left. "But the situation we have found ourselves in? Yeah, that's messy. We killed our way to the top." And others died for us on that journey.

I bow my head in shame, but Edge tilts my head up with a carefully placed hand under my chin. "We did those things to ensure no one else will have to."

Becoming a Divine was a challenge I hadn't been prepared to face, but it was one in which I succeeded. I fought against what it meant to be a Divine for so long, fought against the stigma of the horrifying creatures I had always cowered away from. And yet...I still became the exact thing I had tried so hard not to be: a killer. I killed Dove, then Kyelin, then those two guards. Those were the deaths by my hand, but what about those I had indirectly been responsible for? Will anyone else have to suffer by my hands? I must ensure I work hard in the future to make sure the answer to that question is *no*. To ensure Ryleigh and Alvina didn't lose their lives in vain.

For now, none of that matters. I swore that I would bring change to this world, and I plan on standing by that promise even if the goddesses don't hold me to it. It's time to step into the role that fate has guided me into, time to become the wicked creature I was born to be.

It's time to demolish the Divine.

A NEW LIFE

Silvi

I watch Irissa from under my eyelashes, our bodies jostling as the carriage begins to move. The carriage is larger than most, and we both quite easily fit into the space. Yet, I inch my body closer as though it's unavoidable. Maybe it is. Irissa is an enchanting woman, and she looks so similar to her sister—it's entirely pleasant that she doesn't act like her.

"What do I need to do first?" Her question awakens me from the haze I had found myself in while watching her.

"Find the Followers," I state the obvious, smirking.

"Yes, I know that. We've discussed those plans already. I am speaking of the events after that. What should I ask them when I get there? Where should I search for answers?"

"You search with the goddesses," I answer simply.

"I don't understand."

"You and I are very similar. Especially now that we share this physical trait." I tap her left eyebrow with a small smile, avoiding the fresh, puckering wound below it. "We were born with powers no others can understand. Only the goddesses can tell us why and to what end. Our world has long forgotten them and their good deeds, but the Followers have not. Though their knowledge is secret, it is worth seeking. I fear only they can lead us on the right path."

"Why have they been forgotten, do you think?"

"Because Divine view themselves as all-powerful," I say, staring out the single circular window as my home fades away. "Why worship a power they know nothing of when they can get the powerless to worship them instead? Why worship when you can be worshiped? That is the question Divines have faced for centuries. They don't care that this narcissism is the most likely cause of our land and animals dying. It's all about control and who holds it."

"Then why still pray? Why still uphold promises sworn if they don't think the goddesses exist to punish them?"

"Fear. Fear is a powerful motivator, and these weak prayers and tiny offerings are the only things that may be keeping the goddesses in line. And goddesses help us all if they decide that isn't enough one day."

Irissa falls silent, the clapping of hooves the sole interruption of said silence. Our journey will be a long one, and I do so hate travel between Courts. But alas, this journey leads me to a new life, a new kingdom, and a new friend.

If only I had the capability of enjoying them.

Acknowledgements

A big thank you to my wonderful husband for helping me in this journey and showing me the kind of love I am honored to write about. Thank you to my amazing beta readers, who entirely changed this book for the better. Thank you to my street and arc teams who continue to support me through the end of this series. And as always thank YOU, my readers, for supporting a small indie author. Without you, none of this would be worth it.

ABOUT THE AUTHOR

M.N. Lash, despite having a bachelors degree in biology and minors in chemistry/psychology, is a stay-at-home mom from Alabama. When she isn't reading or writing you can find her crocheting or attending to her many pets. Cruelly Divine is her third book, and she is readying to publish her fourth novel, an installment in the Draxmere Academy of Conjuring Series. You can also find her on Instagram for updates on future works @m.n._lash

Also By

The Divine Providence Series
Royally Divine
Cruelly Divine

The Draxmere Academy of Conjuring Series
Conjuring A Grim
Book Two Releasing 2025